Babycakes

A Novel By

Katrina Thompson

The characters, events, and circumstances in this story are entirely fictional. Any resemblances to any person who is living or dead, place, or event are merely coincidental.

For more information visit www.KatrinaThompson.net or send an e-mail to Imaginarium@KatrinaThompson.net

Copyright © 2014 by Katrina Thompson
All rights Reserved

ISBN-10: 1500260797

ISBN-13: 978-1500260798

Without limiting the rights under copyright reserved above, no part of this book may be reproduced in any form whatsoever without the prior consent from the publisher of this book.

Typeset by Rukyyah and cover designed by Erotic Ink Designs

Printed in United States of America
10 9 8 7 6 5 4 3 2 1

Special Thanks

CHEESY EDDIE'S

602 South Ave, Rochester, NY 14620

www.CheesyEddies.com

Acknowledgements

    I would first like to thank God because without him, none of this would've been possible. I would also like to thank my family and friends for their continued support. You have always been there for me and I will forever remember what you have done for me. Lastly I would like to give special thanks to those I have never met however you took the time to read my work. I may never be able to meet you but you have my gratitude. I hope that you will continue enjoying my work and maybe take the time out to release your own imagination.

Thanks Paul for your continued support and friendship!

Katrine

Also by
Katrina Thompson

The Starfire Ever Moore Series

Starfire

The Last Starfire

Starfire: The Awakening

Starfire Evermore

Scarred

Contents

Mix	1
Pour	63
Bake	173
Frost	268

Mix

Chapter 1

"I hope Mad gets here soon," Ana said to Fran while they sat at the round tables of Torrid looking over her black curls. "Coming to this club was all her idea anyway. Why can't we just go out to dinner instead of clubs like normal people?"

"No one's normal anymore Ana," Fran replied waving her hands to the music.

They became startled when they felt a strong arm wrap around each of them. "Luke," yelled Ana. "You scared me."

"Sorry," he grinned with his crooked smile and kissed her on her cheek. His drink made a clanking sound in her ear, chilling her shoulder into a pinch. He sat down at the table next to Fran asking, "How long have you guys been here?"

"Ah almost half an hour," replied Fran looking down at her cell phone.

"I'm not surprised. I wish I learned how to work on Mad's time instead of on time," joked Ana.

"Then you wouldn't be your punctual self." Luke shook the ice in his glass and sipped the amber liquid with a slight grin still on his face. Ana always loved his smile. The first time she caught sight of his warm expression she was ten years-old. Madison and her family had moved next door to her four years prior. Ana always found herself left out because her three brothers were at least five years older than her and thought her company to be a bit childish. Her parents had only wanted a boy and a girl but since her mother kept having sons, they decided to just give up. However when they did, Ana came along. Her father, a lawyer hardly found the time to really be there with them anyway. His clients took up a lot of his moments with the family and her mother, Hannah, indulged herself with the excitements of being a stay at home mom. Taking the boys to practice, cooking, cleaning, all of which Ana watched eagerly waiting to partake in. She sat over in her corner letting her imagination run away with her, anticipating for the day that she might be able to hang with her brothers. They told her that once she reached the double digits in age, she would be able to join in on their escapades but when Madison came along the loneliness and her desire to be with them faded. Almost as if she had been adopted by her family, they took turns spending the night at each other's house and were still able to get up in the morning and run off to school on time. They even travelled together. It worked for both families. Neither girl found themselves alone.

      The year that Luke came to visit Ana welcomed him but quickly became upset with him for taking her spot on Madison's floor. Which in time she learned was the false story her father coerced Mad's parent's into telling them to avoid sleepovers. Only the more time she spent with him, she saw Luke as a friend instead of foe. When they first met it was only for a brief moment but as the years went on, he grew too old to want to spend a portion of his summers with his aunt and uncle in upstate NY. The school breaks not attended in an all-boy's camp were spent away to his family home in the Hampton's but for the aging Luke, he wanted the busy life. He was two years older than Ana and Madison and with him growing up in New York City, there were so many other things he could do. Or as Ana thought, it was a way for him to keep his mind off of missing his mother. She had always known that he lost her shortly before he started visiting. They tried not to bring up her absence but since Madison's mom was her identical twin they knew her appearance bothered him. She had been the victim of a horrible car accident. A taxi drove through a red light hitting another vehicle but she wasn't in either of them. She was walking across the street with the young Luke at her side. Trying to protect him, she pushed Luke out of the cars path and was hit. His father, Leif thought it best for him to spend some time away from home. Even with his repeated dismissal from both the city and himself, Luke always came back. He loved them. The busy lifestyle and his father's companionship were what kept him going. That was whenever he could pull him away from his work.

    Not until Ana and Madison attended college did they realize how much they loved the city as well. Ana enjoyed her time at Berkley studying fashion but Madison reveled in the nightlife. She and Luke always went out to all of the "happening places" as Madison called them and return to the apartment they shared in Manhattan so early in the morning that she never heard them come home. Luke's father bought the building and gave him one of the units when he started college as a gift. However after he left, he let Madison and Ana stay rent free. When Madison moved to Connecticut with her husband, Peter, Ana felt left in the wake. She refused to live at Luke's place without paying so she and Luke worked out an arrangement. He didn't want to get rid of the apartment and the location was perfect to spend the night if he left a party and didn't feel like going home or hung out too long with Ana. They grew closer after Madison moved away. Though they both had other friends, they had a bond. They were like brother and sister. Everyone noticed, even the girls who wished to cling by his side.

    Luke was definitely a playboy. Ana couldn't believe that one person could go through so many women. She almost felt sorry for the hopefuls who thought they had a crack at the Stokes fortune. His father was an activist shareholder who in the recent economy had made more money than most deemed possible. He moved in like a shark with a necktie devouring everything in sight. When Luke described him to Ana she always got a chill down her back. It was when she met him that the frigidness of his glare froze her feet in place. He held a stern demeanor and never smiled. That was until she gave him one of her cupcakes. Ana was famous for them. She used to make the treats for Luke and Madison all of the time. Her grandmother often whipped up the confections from scratch with her mother and she followed in suit, teaching Ana the skill. They always made him happy. She was surprised Luke didn't have a muffin top spilling over the waistline of his pants from all of the cupcakes he devoured. But then again with his frequent pelvic exercises, she knew exactly why. Luke was very fit, making sure he kept his masculine physique with daily workouts, which years ago he convinced Ana to embark on as well. His brown eyes and clean cut appearance was enough to make any woman swoon. She guessed that he had to stay in shape with his plan for a philandering lifestyle.

She sipped on her Coke and Grenadine as the refreshing drink popped tiny bubbles on her nose and she watched in the distance how he tried to push an undesirable woman he slept with a week ago away. Once he began walking over to the table Ana figured he was going to need some help.

"I would like for you to meet my girlfriend, Tasia." Ana, using the other half of her name Anastasia, waved as she always did covering for him as the mystery woman he made her out to be whenever he needed an excuse. She wondered if that was why he often brought her out with him or to his parties. Unlike his friend Maximus, Ana seemed a better back story when he found himself trying to get rid of other girls.

Another set of arms flew around Ana but she was certain who they belonged to when she saw the large ring on her finger. "Madison!" she shouted, hopping off of her chair wrapping her own about her.

"Wow, I thought that you were going to freak out on me for being so late."

"I guess I threw you a free pass because I never get to see you anymore but don't make it a habit. Wait, you're always late," she laughed.

Katrina Thompson

"She may have forgiven you. I however, haven't," Luke said walking over to her after finally getting rid of the nameless girl.

"Oh come on Luke, cut me some slack." Luke gave her a grimacing glare. "Okay, I owe you one but for now, you can get me a drink."

"As always, the lush has returned," he joked wrapping his arm around her waist. She slapped him in the chest pushing him backward. "Do you want a refill?" he asked Ana who was almost finished with her drink.

"No thank you."

Madison studied him as he walked away sure of his previous actions. Leaning in she asked, "Is he still using his Tasia line?"

"Of course," Fran shouted over the music.

"And I can see that you are still alcohol free."

"That I am."

"Oh come on Ana, you must break out of your chains someday. You're thirty-two years old. You have to live a little before you have no life to do so."

Fran threw up her hands saying, "That's what I keep telling her."

She eyed them both but shot her defense at Madison. "That's pretty nice to hear from a woman who comes here to get away from hers."

"Hey when you have two kids and a husband, you'll want some freedom too. I haven't been able to use the bathroom in peace for over eight years."

"But I would love that, to have a husband to run home to and a family."

"You might be able to if you'd put yourself out there," Madison replied flopping her leg over the other as it bopped to the beat of the music.

"Put myself out there, out where? I'm here and the only guy that tried to hit on me looks like he just got out of high school."

"That's because you look like you just got out of high school," said Luke handing Madison her drink.

Madison laughed saying, "You can't really talk Lucas Stokes. You look like you magically stepped out from the pages of your senior yearbook."

"Yeah Luke and let's face it. The difference between us is if I pounced on the opportunity I'm labeled a cougar while he's seen as a pimp."

"Well come on cat woman, it's time to stretch your legs." He reached over her shoulder grabbing her hand so that he could twist her around and out to the dance floor. She watched the lights bounce over her brown skin when he raised her arm and pulled her closer. Hiking her skirt up as she curled her arms about his neck Luke leaned in. Cradling his head towards hers he took in her floral scent and said, "You still have some moves old lady."

"And you still have eyes on you." She peered over his shoulder, looking at the girl he had turned down a few moments before.

He spun her around to see the girl whose name had escaped him and smiled. "Well maybe we should give her something to be jealous of."

"Oh stop it Luke. I let you continue to use Tasia as your excuse to get rid of them, not to make them jealous. Besides, it's not right."

"What's not right?"

"I don't know Luke. These girls are swooning over you and instead of turning them down; you love um and leave um in less than 24 hrs. Sooner or later what you've been doing is going to come back to bite you."

"Are you talking about karma," he said in a spooky voice that she descried over the blaring music. "Don't worry your pretty little head about superstitions. I don't plan on ever falling in love or getting married for that matter so karma won't affect me."

Ana laughed pushing him away before she yanked him back in by his collar. "Sometimes love catches you before you fall."

***

Katrina Thompson

Ana picked up her phone to stop the annoyance of the beeping alarm she set to wake her. She always set it using the irritating sound instead of music to avoid being lulled back to sleep. She turned to the window to allow the early morning sun pry her eyes open from her almost sleepless night. Madison had stayed the whole weekend which meant reliving their college years by staying up extremely late and eating enough junk food to cover her quota of one desert a day for the next two weeks. She loved her cupcakes just as much as Luke did and insisted she make a batch. Like always, Ana had to fight Luke to stop him from eating the last two cupcakes she set aside for the kids at her job. That also meant where they were, there he would be.

It was like old times having them both around in the apartment they once shared. The environment had never been the same after Luke left but then again he returned. Movie nights became the norm for her and Luke. They made the event a "must have" at least once a week. As the years passed, curling up on the couch with old and new flicks had become their annual Wednesday night. But before Madison had left out Sunday afternoon to return home, Ana had to speak to her about something that had plagued her for several months. Only she wanted to do discuss the situation with her friend face to face.

Ana plopped down on the couch beside her coyly stating, "So I've thought long and hard about a choice I made."

Madison turned to her licking frosting off of the cupcake wrapper. "What is it?"

"I wanted to tell you that I'm going to have a baby."

"A baby? You're pregnant? I thought having children out of wedlock is kind of against your religion."

"It is. I'm not, not yet. I mean... that's what I was raised to believe but I'm getting older Mad. I won't have much longer before time takes the decision away from me."

"I get what you're saying but you never wanted to raise a baby alone. Are you sure about this?"

"I...," she took in a deep breath, "I had to change my plans. Believe me," she admitted standing up. "If I had my choice I would be living the life of my boss. I would be running my own fashion company like Korina with my husband right beside me. I would employ a nanny but I'd spend as much time with the children as I possibly could. That's the life I wanted."

"I know but technically it's not too late for you. I mean so what if you aren't a fashion designer. Find another profession. There are other options out there for you."

Ana cocked her head, glaring at her friend. "Why are you so against this?"

Madison wiped her mouth and stood up saying, "I know you Ana. You are a very patient and loving person but this decision seems like you're jumping into a life which doesn't only affect you but everything you dreamed of."

"This is what I've dreamt of, minus a husband but it's also what I want. So much so that I've been saving up money for over a year to make sure I can support us while on maternity leave and I've already talked to my boss about allowing me to bring the baby along, if need be, while I'm with the girls. Even Donna upstairs offered to babysit for me if I wanted the extra help."

"Wow, I guess you have been thinking about this for some time. Did you already go to the clinic?"

"No, I haven't worked that part out yet but I plan on getting pregnant by October. That way I'll bypass most of the hot weather which means I can still wear my coat in the winter and large sweaters to cover my belly in the early spring. Not only that, but, Fashion Week in New York will be over so Korina won't need me as much for the girls."

"Seriously, how long have you been thinking about doing this?"

Ana laughed, "Since the last time I had a date hit its five year anniversary."

"Ana," she sighed. "I thought you had a date last week."

Katrina Thompson

"Yeah, a dinner date with Fran. We hardly get to hang out with Korina having me running around town with Korey and Kailey or with Diana constantly calling for my help."

"Okay, I'm not going to fight you on this since your mind is settled on the matter. But did you tell your parents about this?"

"Oh no! I'm just going to return home for their anniversary in March and show up pregnant. I figure in my vulnerable state they won't want to upset me so neither of them will badger me about the choice I made."

"Good call!"

***

Ana quickly grabbed her messenger bag and the two cupcakes she rescued from Luke. She raced downstairs certain that Torrance, Korina's driver, sat patiently waiting for her. She initially had a town car for her and Korey but after Kailey came along she got an SUV. When Ana opened the main door to her apartment building Torrance met her stare as he leaned against the passenger door. Like her, he was punctual. She would come down early but he always seemed to be at her doorstep, waiting. His nibbled lips turned to a bright smile when she walked over to him.

"Good morning Ana," he said opening the door. The sun gleamed across his shiny brushed cut hair and ebony skin.

"Good morning. Thanks," she stated as she always did, sliding into the truck. He walked around the front and hopped in, driving to the Upper East Side where Korina lived with her husband Steve and two daughters. Almost six days out of the week Ana had to be to their house to get the girls ready for school or practice. Korey was a pianist, studying several times a week and Kailey had dance classes just about every Saturday morning until the summer when it turned into play dates. Today's event was a birthday celebration but before the party, she had to get them dressed, fix their breakfast and pick up coffee for Korina and Steve.

She always ran errands for the couple even though they had an assistant. Her employment was almost pointless. Diana hardly ever got through a day without needing Ana's help. If her question wasn't about where one of Korina's designs was located, she required assistance with picking up things she neglected to get or providing her with the name of a constituent or place Korina referred to that she didn't know and felt too embarrassed to inquire further. They never kept up with the names of things unless they were important people. The girls gave their own titles and it was everyone else's duty to figure out what they mentioned. Not even their parents understood, but Ana did.

  Torrance opened the door for Ana, allowing her to slide out carrying their coffee and the kid's cupcakes. He closed the rear door and stood at the truck to wait for Steve and Korina. If it were up to her, she would probably work every day. Her family was her first priority but her business was knowingly her first love.

  Ana let herself into their Park Ave home with her key and walked to the kitchen. Even with the six floors she could tell that Korey was awake. She often turned on her music in the morning. The rhythmic sounds glided down the banister and twirled mimicking the floral air that welcomed her. She was addicted to the piano like her mother to fashion. Kailey was more of a free spirit. She was six years younger than Korey so they often clashed, albeit the four year old loved her sister's music. Ana loved it too. She enjoyed seeing their passion for what they did.

  Working for them wasn't the profession she had planned on doing in life but being around their family was as close as she was probably going to get. She had gone to NY to become a fashion designer but no one was biting. Luke's father had a friend who had an acquaintance with a designer in need of a nanny. After all of her experience with a few side jobs babysitting during college for extra money, Luke mentioned her and she got the position. Her duties on the other hand had changed from caretaker to periodic housekeeper, shopper, back up assistant and sometimes chef. She didn't mind. The time she spent with the girls felt like being with her nieces and helping Korina was her link into the fashion world. She never visited Milan or Paris but quite often she was able to attend parties just to bring her something that Diana had forgotten. She also stopped by her office from time to time and on the rare but pleasurable occasion, Ana provided feedback at Korina's will.

"Ms. Ana!" Kailey shouted from the top of the stairwell in a pair of shorts and knee high socks, flapping her arms against her fairy wings.

"Hello silly bird," she greeted her. "What are you wearing?" she asked walking up the stairs towards her.

"They're my wings," she replied turning so that Ana could see them. "Korey gave it to me. I'm a fairy now."

"Oh a fairy huh?" She peered over her shoulder's remembering how she used to play with the growing girl when she was not much older than Kailey. "Well do you know what the best part about being a fairy is?"

"No what's that?"

"You can fly." Finally reaching the little girl she picked her up, spinning Kailey around the corridor as she giggled until she landed on her hip. She walked down the hall with her when she noticed Steve in the library. "Good morning Steve. Your coffee's on the counter."

"Okay thanks," he replied approaching the door. "If you catch a glimpse of my wife can you tell her that I'm downstairs? I seem to have lost her in the closet again."

"Sure thing," she answered with a grin, carrying Kailey over to Korey's room. She put Kailey down. "Good morning Korey."

"Hey Ms. Ana I'm glad you're here. I need your advice. Should I wear my hair up or down?"

"Hum," she said as she sat down on her bed. "I think you should wear it down." Ana watched her posing with different flowers against her elongated curls while her sister danced behind her. "You've always liked playing in the mirror but something's different about you." She leaned over with a curious smirk asking, "Are boys attending this party?"

"Ms. Ana," she laughed.

"There is! Oh how cute."

"I don't want to be cute, I want to be gorgeous," she replied pouting.

"We can make you both but first I have to make you two breakfast."

"Ms. Ana wait." Korey walked over and sat down on her lap. "What does it mean when someone says you're hot?"

"Did one of the boys at school say that to you?"

"Yeah Alec said that I was hot but I wasn't. He laughed but I was too embarrassed to ask what he was talking about."

Ana didn't feel she was the best one to talk about guys with her track record but being a little naive about the opposite sex was something she could relate to. "When a guy says that to you it's just like saying you're gorgeous. Do me and you're parents a favor. If Alec or any other boy says that to you, say thank you and walk away. You're too young to take things further."

"Got it!" she smiled.

Ana fixed her bang and smirked, even a ten year-old got more play than her. *How embarrassing.* "Where running short on time so what would you ladies like for breakfast?"

"I want Fruit O's," Korey answered scooting from her lap.

"No I want boot toast," whined Kailey. Ana grinned listening to the names they created for food. Like most other things they didn't call by their actual name. Though extremely shocking coming from children whose parents go to France at least once a year.

"Come with me ladies. I want to show you something."

"Can I fly there?" asked Kailey with her rosy cheeks.

Katrina Thompson

"Yes you can," she said scooping her in her arms. She led them over to the library which had books lined against the wall shaped in an oval. Amongst the lounging furniture in the room a vintage brass world globe stood in the corner. The Bryce's had traveled around the world but for some reason teaching the girls about their travels was left up to Ana. She place Kailey down in front of it saying, "Can you find the boot?"

Kailey looked down at her shoes answering, "But I'm wearing sneakers."

"She meant on the map Kailey," grumbled Korey annoyed.

"Oh so you do know."

"Of course I do Ms. Ana. It's right here," she announced pointing her finger.

"Good girl. Now what is that to the left?"

"France. I know that because mommy went there last year when you came to stay with us the whole week."

"Well did you know French toast or boot toast as you like to call it," she said tickling Kailey, "is also known as German toast or 'pain perdu' by the French. No one is really sure where it came from but it could've actually started with the Romans."

"Where did Fruit O's come from?" asked Korey with a scrunch in her nose.

"I think Kellogg's," laughed Ana. "Let's compromise, Fruit O's and regular toast today, Monday French toast. Deal?"

"Deal," shouted Korey happy that she got her request but Kailey wasn't too pleased.

Ana crouched down giving her a light grin. "Oh come on. I'll let you eat your cupcake after breakfast. It'll be our little secret," she whispered.

"Okay," she smiled.

Ana turned to leave when she noticed Korina at the door. "Good morning Korina. I didn't hear you come in."

"Good morning."

"Steve's downstairs and I brought you some coffee."

"Thank you. After you've finished fixing them breakfast will you call Diana and tell her to pick up the dry cleaning. I need my jacket for dinner this evening."

"Will do," she replied with a bit of inner laughter. She was always able to get away with speaking to her that way but Diana would've had to say, "Yes Ms. Bryce" or "when would you like that Mrs. Bryce."

After feeding the girls, getting them dressed and calling Diana, Ana rode with Torrance to drop them off. During their lessons she went shopping at the grocery store for the family and then right back to get the girls for the party. Luckily she didn't have to go with Torrance to collect them up but her job wasn't quite over. Diana was unable to stop by the cleaners because she had forgotten to pick up the fabric samples.

"Why are you constantly saving her?" asked Torrance looking in the rearview mirror which was how most of their conversations transpired.

"Because helping her helps Korina which in turns helps our boss make money." She leaned forward saying, "The professor makes a decent living but between her family fortune and the business, I'm pretty sure she's the one who pays us."

"Good one," he laughed with his bright smile. "Well I don't think whoever pays the bills pay you enough."

"Thank you Torrance."

Chapter 2

Weeks had gone by and the courage to make her dreams come true had dwindled though they were constantly on her mind. They almost shouted their plea the moment Luke stopped by for their midweek dinner and a movie. He had been doing so since he moved into his own place 14 minutes away in the Art District. Tonight was his choice and as he did every other month, he popped in one of the Star Wars films. They were the one thing she knew for a fact he and his father had in common, aside from them both loving her cupcakes. Ana nibbled on the crust of her pizza looking at the television as the light sabers dashed across the screen however Luke was watching at her.

"What gives?" he asked flipping back her dark curls noticing her barely eat.

"Oh ah nothing. I just had some things on my mind."

He leaned over picking up the remote from the coffee table and paused the movie. "So what's up?"

She squirmed in her seat. "Eh I don't want to get into it."

"You know that you can talk to me about anything."

"This is just one of those things…" she said tossing her crust on her plate. She collected his and walked to the kitchen. "I've wanted to share this with you for a while now but it's really important and I'm not sure of how you're going to take my request."

"Do you need some money? Tell me how much. You know I can never say no to you so just ask."

Ana ran her fingers through her raven hair and clung to the edge of the island. "No," she laughed. "I think this would be easier if what I wanted was money." She walked around the counter grabbing his hand and brought him over to the couch. Turning to him she took in a deep breath and confessed. "Okay, what I wanted to talk about is having a baby. I want to make one with you."

"Come again?"

"I know that this is out of the blue and there's probably a million questions rattling in your brain but that's been on my mind all day, all week, well actually longer. I've gone through many dateless nights and I think it's time to just jump," she said enthused yet exasperated, "jump into being and create my own family."

He leaned over whispering, "Are you gay?"

"No and why are you whispering?" she laughed.

"I, I don't know." He sat back. "I'm just in shock I guess."

She mirrored him, in a sense becoming smaller to Luke, as she slunk in the chair making a thump sound. "So you know that I've been dreading getting older but I don't think that I've really explained why. I'm almost thirty three years-old and I have nothing to show for it."

"Oh I see. You have gerascophobia, a fear of getting old. I've been there and what's a better cure than getting away from all of this." He slid closer to her saying, "I think it's time for us to take a trip. I was planning on going to Hawaii for my birthday. You can come with me. I'll rent-"

"Luke no, it's not the blues," blurted Ana, cutting him off. "I'm running out of time."

"There's more than enough time. I mean what, are you saying…are you dying?" he laughed. Ana dropped her head in dismay. Thinking the worst Luke grabbed her arms for her to look at him. His eyes went wild with a thunderous rumble. "Is it true, are you dying?"

"Oh God Luke, no, I'm not dying. Just let me finish. I'm getting older and I, at times I feel like I can literally hear the dials ticking away. Soon I won't be able to have any children."

"You're not that old Ana," he replied releasing her arms. "How about you get a cat or a cute little dog? I told you before. You can have a pet."

"Really Luke, this isn't about having something to curl at my feet or depend on me. I don't want to grow old but aging is inevitable. I love cats but I gave up buying one year's ago because I'm afraid of becoming the old cat lady. The common factor here is no matter what I do, time will continue to pass by. It's different for you." She stood up saying, "You don't want any and you still can if you changed your mind at eighty. I'm at the point in my life where if I get pregnant they might consider me high risk just because of my age." She turned towards the window. "I always thought that I would find Mr. Right and I would finally move out of your apartment. We'd get married and then start a family. Maybe even start my own business but I can't even get a date. I'm like a walking repellent for men. They should really use me for testing purposes." She turned at the sound of Luke clearing his throat. "So again my question is would father a child for me?"

Luke began coughing.

"Are you okay?" she asked walking over to see if he needed some water.

"You really want me to… to do this?"

"Yes." She smiled. "I know that creating a life with me is a lot to ask but you're my best friend. I always felt that babies should be created from love. You're the only guy that's technically not family, I love. Well there is Max but I mean you are like one of my brothers so I thought who better."

"I'm flattered but I just think you're rushing into this decision."

"Did Mad talk to you?"

"You told Mad about this?"

"Well," she paused, "I've told her everything that I planned but she doesn't know about my request to you. She thinks that it's going to be with a donor." She sat down beside him, collecting his hand in hers. "I don't want anything from you. Your lawyer can draw up the papers taking away your parental rights so you don't ever have to worry about their paternity coming up in the future unless you want it to."

"Ana," he whispered, "There's something that I need to tell you."

"What is it Luke?"

"You being single," he started with a stalled voice pulling away his hand. "It's not entirely your fault."

"What do you mean?"

"Um there were a couple of guys that wanted to go out with you but they didn't amount to anyone you'd be interested in."

"Luke what are saying?"

"You're a good girl Ana and the guy's…well I know that they were just looking for a quicky."

Ana stood from her seat. "How long Luke?"

"Ah don't be mad with me okay."

She blew off and crossed her arms with anger and frustration.

"Since college," he replied mimicking her restless sigh.

"College!" She shook her head. "I was with Greg in college."

He swallowed. "After Greg of course. I figured you would be thankful that I was looking out for you."

"It's one thing to look out for me Luke but do you realize I haven't been on a date in over ten years. Here I thought I was the reason. I felt like I wasn't pretty enough or smart enough or or…"

Luke could see how what he had been doing to her only hurt her. "Ana," he said wrapping his arms around her, "I never meant to hurt you."

"I'm tired Luke. I think you should go."

"Ana please, I want to do this for you."

Ana laughed. "Do you really think I would want to have a baby with you now? I'll just go with one of my back-ups."

"Back-ups, but I thought you said-"

"Goodnight Luke."

He grabbed his jacket from the coatrack and walked out to the hallway. He didn't want to leave, especially when he overheard her crying from the other side of the door but he realized that he had said too much.

***

Unable to sleep, Ana's morning wasn't any better than the night before. She realized Torrance took notice to her quiet yet sorrowful demeanor. To calm his concerns she straightened in her seat and curled her tight lips into a grin, hoping that he didn't want to exchange pleasantries. She didn't want to talk about anything. Luke on the other hand called her cell almost every hour and sent unanswered texts. She couldn't talk to him or see him for that matter. How could he do such a thing? It was the same way her brothers treated her all throughout high school. She didn't even have a date for prom. She went stag with Madison who brought Luke as her plus-one.

When she got home, she tossed her things on the counter and began kicking off her shoes when someone rang her bell. "Delivery for Ana," announced the voice on the intercom.

She hit the buzzer allowing him to come up. In his hand he held a single daisy with a card. The look on his face was that of embarrassment but Ana understood. "Thank you," she grinned pulling out the $2.00 she had shoved in her pocket after buying takeout. "I'm sorry, that's all I have." She closed the door behind the puzzled deliverer and set the flower down. Unraveling the envelope she slid the tiny card out which read:

I understand why you wouldn't want to hear from me but I can't go on with my favorite girl hating me. I truly didn't mean to hurt you. I only tried to protect you. Please find it in your heart to forgive me.
Luke

  Ana placed the card down and filled her empty hand with the lonely flower to smell it. He knew that she loved daisies but he gave her just one because he used the same gesture when they were children. He left the back door open and her kitten ran away. She forgave him then and was certain that she would have to forgive him now.

***

  She had a busy day even after dropping off the girls so she couldn't stop by Luke's office to talk to him. Thankfully after his plea the night before he didn't barrage her cell phone with e-mails or text messages. She thought that she would've been able to speak with him after work but unfortunately Korina had everyone working late on her new fashion line and though Steve was home, he hadn't prepared anything for dinner. A full day's work. Ana grinned snacking on her hot dog. She hadn't made a meal for herself in almost a week but she didn't mind being there for the girls. She repositioned her bag over her shoulder and decided to walk to Luke's house instead of taking a cab until Torrance pulled up honking the horn.

  "Hey," she waved walking over. "What are you still doing out here?"

  "Steve called me over to give you a ride home. He didn't tell you?" Ana cocked her head to the side. Torrence grinned. "Of course not. Hop in."

  Ana scooted in but she got in the front instead of her normal seat behind him. "I thought I'd ride up here tonight."

  He drove off glancing over at her. "Did you already get something to eat?"

"Yeah I did," she smiled. "I stopped and got a hot dog. I was on the way to Luke's house."

"Oh I can take you there."

"You remember his address?" she asked.

"Um hum."

Ana eyes wandered out the window trying to put her lines together. She never really remembered a moment where she had to apologize for anything to Luke. He usually made the blunders. She rummaged through her hair and propped her arm on the door.

"You sure you don't want to go home?"

"No I'm fine I just have to do something and it's plaguing me a bit."

"Do you want to talk about it?" he asked making a turn.

She smirked and shook her head. There was no way she wanted to discuss her dateless life.

It wasn't long before he pulled up to Luke's apartment. "Thanks for the ride," said Ana turning to him.

"You don't have to thank me," he chuckled. "It's my job."

"Right."

"See you tomorrow morning at 9," he yelled out the door as she closed it. She gave him a quick wave and threw her bag across her shoulder.

Should I use my key or knock? She stood in the entryway to his apartment taking in a deep breath. Without thinking she rang the bell waiting for a response. Normally he would be working out that time of day. *Maybe I should've let myself in.* She moved closer and overheard the TV through the door. Her eyes dropped to the floor, refusing to look at the peep hole which would darken when he approached. She feared that if she saw him, she might walk away, ashamed over being so rude.

Seeing that the unannounced person was Ana, Luke quickly opened the door. "Ana, I didn't know you were stopping by," he said tousling his brunette quaffed hair.

"Come on in. I was just watching a movie. Do you want something to eat?"

"Oh no," she squeaked with a nervous grin. "I wanted to stop by and apologize to you."

"Apologize?"

"Yes I-"

"But I was the one-"

"Luke please let me just do this." She pulled her bag over her shoulder and set it on the couch. His condo seemed so much bigger than her two bedroom unit. The first level was the size of her whole apartment. Along the walls he had beautiful art pieces but never any photographs. The absence of photos was something he got from his father. Luke told her that he didn't like pictures because all they did was remind him of the past. After the death of his mother, Luke said that all of their captured moments were taken off of the walls. Being with Madison and her family didn't really help. They loved taking photos. Ana had even hired Madison's mother, who refused to be paid, to be the photographer for their anniversary party. She took her attention from the artwork finally able to compile her words. Ana turned to Luke saying, "I shouldn't have gotten so upset with you for doing what you did. My brothers treated me the same way and I guess your actions brought me back to the years of being stuck under the Bloom thumb. Where my parents weren't, there they were."

"You had a right to be upset Ana. I overstepped my bounds."

Ana smiled and wrapped her arms around his waist. She looked up at him and said, "I knew you would understand. I don't get why I was so afraid to say it."

He placed his finger beneath her chin replying, "You should never be afraid to tell me anything."

"I know. I just didn't want things to be weird between us after what I asked of you. You're like a brother to me and as much as I wanted to kill you," she smiled, "I would totally regret it."

He kissed her on her forehead and she unraveled her arms reaching for her bag.

"Wait, where are you going?"

"Home. I haven't been there all day and I feel like I've been neglecting my bed."

"Ah so you were up all night thinking about me," he cooed walking to the door.

"Yes, I wondered which would be more devastating, killing you in your sleep or to push you out of your office window."

"Ha...ha, very funny." He held the door open and watched her step beside him.

"I know." She kissed him on the cheek and walked away.

Luke clung to the door for a moment before he let the barrier sway closed. He brushed his hands over his face and ran to his room grabbing his shoes and jacket.

***

"Beautiful night isn't it?" asked Luke walking behind her.

"Yes, I thought so," she grinned flashing her hazel cat-like eyes over her shoulder. "What are you doing out here?"

"I didn't have any plans for the rest of the night so I figured I'd walk you home. Also, there is something else."

"What's that?"

"You mentioned back-ups. Who are they?"

Ana licked her lips and shied in sudden embarrassment. "Promise me you won't laugh." Luke held one hand over his heart and the other over his mouth. She gave in replying, "Okay my second pick was Max."

"Max, are you serious!"

"Yes," she replied astonished by his reaction.

"Max is a dog. Technically we both are, which is another reason why I'm shocked that you asked me."

"You're not dogs Luke. The way I see things, you guys get away with what those girls allow you to. So if you are in fact dogs then they're just…"

"Say it, say it…"

"No Luke I'm not going to say the B-word."

"You're so cute," he laughed. "The B-word." She shoved him in his side and continued walking until he wrapped his arm around her neck. "So who else did you list as a candidate?"

"You might not know him. He's Donna's brother, Javier."

"Donna who lives upstairs from you?"

"Yeah, he heard us talking about my plans. She's willing to babysit for me when I'm unable to bring the baby to work."

He walked by her side silent for an awkward moment until he said, "So how many people know?"

"Well there's my boss, Mad, Fran, Donna, her brother and you," she replied counting with her fingers. "I didn't want this to get out, especially not about the father. I wasn't even going to tell my family until my second or third trimester. It was a stupid idea. I should wait now that you've come clean about cock blocking me."

"Did you just say cock?"

"Oh stop Luke. I've said it before."

"Sure you have," he chuckled.

When they got to her building she was shocked that he came up. She threw her bag on the counter and pulled off her jacket. She glanced over her shoulder and noticed Luke removing his as well. "I didn't know you were going to stay. Do you want to make this a movie night?" she offered with a joyful grin.

"No I was kind of in the mood for something else," he answered with a quiet voice.

"You're right," she said grabbing his chin. "I have a sweet tooth also. Do you think we should do chocolate or vanilla cakes?" she asked releasing him and walked over to the kitchen. She turned on the water to wash her hands when she felt Luke's hand around her waist and the other turning off the faucet. She swiveled towards him with a curious glare.

"I was thinking that maybe we can make something else."

"Luke," she replied with her heart suddenly leaping from her chest. He brushed the hair from her face and leaned over to kiss her when she protested. She unhooked his arm with her wet hands saying, "Luke, wait, I think we should talk about this first."

"We've already discussed your plan and since it sounds like I'm the best candidate, why not try now."

"Because I was thinking more along the lines of a turkey baster or something, and we don't even have a contract."

"What fun would a baster be?" He looked down at Ana brushing her hair behind her ear. He stood at least a foot taller than her and standing this close to him, she never felt so small. "We don't need a contract. I trust you." A grin curled in her quivering lips but she wasn't quite sure why. Luke brushed her face with the back of his hand asking, "Are you nervous?"

Finally having a definition for what she was feeling she answered, "Yes, yes I am. We should use the baster to get pregnant. I saw it on TV. I would be-"

Luke placed his fingers over her mouth. "That wouldn't be traditional and if not for nothing, you are traditional."

"I think that my request would suggest otherwise," she countered.

"You know, you're right but..." before he finished he planted his lips upon hers. She never thought what kissing Luke would really be like. She gasped at his abrasive touch. His embrace was so unexpected but so was Luke, impulsive for things which excited him. But the more he pressed his lips against hers she couldn't resist allowing him in. They were so soft and when his tongue wove around hers, it danced around just as good as his nimble feet on the club floor. Unlike their normal trysts, she didn't feel as though he was using her and she didn't want to run to the nearest seat. Being in his arms was somewhere she had been but now she imagined as if she belonged. When Luke released her, her eyes remained closed, locked in the moment until she perceived his hand in hers. She unlocked her hazel irises and gazed down as if hypnotized, following the motion of his feet which led them to her bedroom.

He turned on the light but breaking her silence she said, "Can we keep the lights off? I don't want you to see me naked."

"I've already seen you in the nude." He smiled.

"When?" she asked Luke with her breath once again abandoning her.

"After prom." He grinned with his cool demeanor shaken. "You ah left your curtain open."

"I can't believe you were peeping at me."

"No I looked outside and your window just so happened to be there, opened with a hot girl standing in my view." Luke kissed her again pulling down her sweater. Quickly, he tossed it over to the chair in her room and returned to the solemn Ana. He could tell how her nerves plagued her but like when they were children, he coerced her. He curled his back, bending over to capture her once again with his lips, kissing across Ana's neck. He sensed the tension in her veins beneath her skin ease as her head tilted back and his tongue tasted her collarbone. He brushed his fingers along the nape of her neck until he cradled her head in his hand. With a grin on his lips he whispered in her ear saying, "You see? This is a lot easier when you just let yourself go."

Ana's eyes unfolded, staring at her best friend whose lips had sent her into ecstasy and whose voice became the only thing capable enough to bring her back. She felt no more need to protest. She wanted her first time to be special and at the moment he was the most important man in her life. He was kind and she realized now with his lips overtaking hers, that he was very passionate. He was also right. Just like the first time he made her dance at prom. She did have more fun when she let herself go. Stepping back, she smiled as she pulled her shirt over her head and tossed it on the floor. To avoid Ana changing her mind, he removed his own clothing, copying her. He unbuttoned and unraveled the layers from his body. He watched as the smile in her eyes once again turned into a nervous glare when she unfastened her pants. They represented the shield between them both. For her, a veil which she decided he had the rights to and for him, it was the final step towards something he wanted for years.

Luke peeled away the last layer, his boxer briefs which fell to the floor around his ankles. His eyes were locked on Ana when he stepped from them, over to her still wearing her underwear. "Are you sure this is what you want?"

Ana nodded.

"Are you afraid?" he asked raising her chin with his finger.

"A little," she answered, swallowing deeply after her confession.

Luke smiled. "You can touch it if you want.

"Luke, don't treat me like some virgin. I've seen a penis before."

His brow creased in confusion. "I, I thought that you were."

Ana licked her lips, taking a few steps back. Luke was confused and afraid at the possibility of turning her off. He covered himself. "Ana, I didn't mean to-"

"I am Luke. I, this is…this is just…" She looked up at Luke. "This is not how I imagined," she confessed, "but I hope you know how happy I am to share it with you. I can't believe," she smiled, "that you would do this for me." She stepped closer saying with a whispering voice, "You are making my dreams come true."

Luke's heart began to beat uncontrollably. He took her into his arms and pressed his lips so hard against hers that he thought to stop in fear of hurting her, but only for a second. Lost in his touch, Ana was swooped off of her feet and laid on the bed. He climbed on top of her and pulled her hair back strand by strand. "I hope you realize that you are still a very beautiful girl."

"Luke… if this doesn't work," she shook her head and plopped back down with the heavy thought. "Thank you anyway."

"I'm sure this will be my pleasure," he returned with a smile, running his hand along the curve of her hip, toying with the strap of her panty. "Just promise me one thing."

"What's that?"

He smirked. "Don't refer to me as being like a brother anymore."

***

"So much for the nice weather," said Lucas looking out the window as he propped his chin on Ana's shoulder. She twiddled her fingers along his knuckles, watching the rain slither down the darkened pane. "Are you alright?"

"Yeah, I am." She answered turning towards him though she was still a little sore. "I just never envisioned my first time that way. I mean, was I okay?"

"You were amazing."

"Don't lie to me Luke. I want the truth."

"I am telling you the truth." She sat up giving him a look but his grin didn't falter.

She lied down on his chest asking, "What were you going to say in the kitchen before you kissed me?"

"I was going to say that I can easily persuade you."

"No you can't."

"Oh yeah, I got you to move in with me years ago and I'm the one that gets you to go out with us almost every weekend. Which by the way I want you to come out tomorrow with Max and I."

Katrina Thompson

"No I have too much to do. Korina's gotten into the bridal biz and has everyone on their toes. I've never seen so much lace and tulle in my life. She's dedicated a whole room in the house to the project. Kailey almost lost a hand trying to play in it. I feel like I'm on security duty now."

"Well I guess you're going to need a bit more persuasion." He rolled over Ana, begging her please as he kissed her neck.

"No," she laughed.

"Oh come on. You don't want to go to Hawaii for my birthday so do this for me."

"I would love to run off with you but Korina needs me. I will go with you guys but don't think that you can use kisses to coerce me to do stuff. It didn't work before and it won't work now."

"Before? I never kissed you before."

"Yes you did. I mean the first time was a mistake but the second time you wanted me to ask my brother to borrow his car. When I wouldn't you tried to kiss me so I begged him to do it."

"I vaguely remember."

"Mad didn't take a picture of that but I do have one of the other." She scooted from beneath him and reached down to the drawer of her nightstand. She pushed aside her recipe book which she filled with her different cupcake ideas and pulled out a scrapbook, placing the binder on her lap. She flipped through the pages until she stopped at a much younger photo of herself and Luke. They were captured in a quick glance at one another. Their lips hovered close enough to have kissed but on each of their faces a smile was perched. "We're not actually kissing but it was taken right after. You were upset about being left there yet again by your father. Mad and I was in the house making cupcakes with my mom and saw you sitting in the backyard, all alone, sulking. After Mad applied the sprinkles, we ran outside to give it to you. Your back was to me so I almost startled you but Mad surprised us both when she said cheese. I guess you were turning to kiss me on my cheek but instead your lips landed on mine."

"Wow, you have an amazing memory."

"I probably only remembered because of this," she confessed rubbing the photo with her thumb, "and because I experienced my first kiss with you as well." When she moved her hand he noticed one of the photos on the other page. It was an earlier photograph of his mother with his aunt Lana, Ana and Madison. She tried closing the book but he held his fingers in place to stop her. "I'm sorry I forgot that was there."

"It's okay. When was that taken?"

"I think a year or two before the accident."

He ran his hand across the keepsake of his mother and closed the book. "Is it okay if I ah stay here for the night?"

Ana took the binder and set it down on the nightstand replying, "This is your place."

"I meant here with you."

"Of course you can." She sunk down on the bed cradling him in her arms.

***

Keeping up her promise to meet the guys out for the night Ana rushed off after leaving Korina's dress shop in the fashion district. Luckily she had ordered food in for them so she didn't have to find something to eat. Torrance dropped her off at home with an hour to spare before Luke's car was coming to get her. Feeling a little different after being with him she couldn't help not ignoring the old facade of becoming a woman. She tried on several dresses but as usual her first choice was the best. The sequenced, silver dress was backless and draped the ruffled like satin material in the curve of her back. She paired it with diamond earrings that Luke had gotten her and pinned her hair in a Mohawk to cover her back ever so slightly. She may feel bolder but she hadn't become that brave.

Katrina Thompson

She scurried down the steps to Lucas' car. The driver had just pulled up. Luke stepped out wearing a black shirt and pants, looking his usual handsome self. Ana walked over nervously clutching her strap praying that it didn't slip. Max also jumped out running over to her with a gray shirt and black pant combo. They both echoed an ad from a Maxim Magazine.

"Helloooo my amazing Anastasia!" Max greeted her as he did quite often, mimicking his best Russian accent. He spun her around and kissed her on her cheek. "It looks like you'll be my date this evening since we match."

"We're all single my friends," interjected Luke yanking Max from Ana. His quick movement caused her strap to fall but she caught the wavering strip right before the garment dropped from her breast. Luke notice but played off the near mishap saying, "Let's go party before all the good ones are gone," he suggested flashing her a wink.

At the club Ana decided to continue her new air of adulthood mingling. She caught a glare of Luke and Max leaving them both behind. Max looked on curiously noticing how she had come out of her shell. Normally she only went out on the floor to help Luke.

"What's going on with Ana, she's different?" Luke took a sip of his drink, giving Max his back as he tried to find her in the crowd. Max eyed Luke turning towards him. "There's something going on and I want to know what it is."

"There's nothing going on, Ana just wanted to have some fun tonight. I thought you did too?" He studied his silent friend and blew off. "How about I get you another drink?"

"You can after you tell me what's going on."

"Okay," he said tossing back the last of his Scotch. "We made, ah, we had sex."

"You did what!" he shouted flailing his arms about. "I knew it man. It was going to be you or me. I never thought she would've had it in her to finally get it in."

"She's not that type of girl, woman so don't talk about her that way," said Luke in her defense. "She wants to have a baby so she asked me to help her."

"Come again? You're telling me that my chocolate fantasy has been holding out all of this time because she likes chicks?"

"What? No she's not into girls." Luke grinned in embarrassment over thinking the exact same thing. "She's getting older and she hasn't had much luck with dating so she thought to ask me."

"It's because of you that she couldn't."

"I need another drink." He stormed off, bypassing Max and over to the bar. Slamming his glass down he shouted out to the bartender, "I need a shot. Make that two."

"No make that three," instructed Max. He squeezed in beside him leaning over the bar asking, "Does she know?"

"Yes, I told her."

"Did you also tell her about Greg?"

Luke cracked his neck and replied, "Greg was so long ago."

"Dude you single handedly ruined their relationship."

"No I didn't. He never wanted to get married. He told us so and what he wanted from her, Ana would never give. He would've taken her all the way to Boston and for what? Their relationship was going to end sooner or later. Besides you know her and I told you how she was raised. She was never going to go against her parents request so I was just helping her."

"Telling a guy that his girlfriend plans on being a virgin bride would send any dude with a boner sailing. Besides, it looks like she did, with you."

"You know what Max, I shouldn't have said anything. She told me not to tell anyone anyway." He took one of the shots tossing it back but before he could swallow the other, Max grabbed the glass from him and quickly swallowed the contents. Perturbed, Luke grumbled, "I got the second one for me."

"Well I needed it. I can't believe she didn't ask me. You two have been skating around each other for years but I put all the moves on her and she didn't consider me."

"Yeah well you were her second choice."

"Really! Do you think that if your stuff doesn't work she'll give my boys a try?"

"You're my boy but you're not going to touch her."

"Wow and there – it – is."

"There what is?" questioned Luke with a crease in his brow.

"You are in love with her."

"No I'm not." He lowered his head thinking about their night together with Ana's legs coiled around his hips while he laid on top of her. He didn't want to leave her embrace. With a sigh he continued. "I must admit it was a little weird but that's because she's like a, like a…"

"You can't even say it anymore. She's like a sister to you. At least that's what she used to be. Thanks a lot."

"Thanks for what?"

"I was going to dream about her tonight. I got to graze those mountains but you actually got to climb them. I envy you."

"I'm only saying this once Max. Don't talk about her like that."

Max waved the bartender down again. "Two more shots my man." Luke watched as he poured them out and Max handed one to him. "Cheers man."

"What are we celebrating?"

"No, not celebrating, we are saying goodbye to you being a free man."

"No! Nothing's changed. It's an arrangement just to give her the baby that she wanted. I don't want a family or a wife and I am definitely not in love."

"Okay then what are we doing here talking. Since you're in denial and you've made it perfectly clear that I can't even have some fun with Ana, we have to find you someone else."

"He doesn't need to," announced a cool voice over his shoulder hearing the end of their conversation.

Max walked away saying, "That's my queue."

The woman was tall and had legs that seemed to never end. She spun around him pressing her body against his. Her perfume curled within his nostrils. "So from the sound of your conversation you are looking for someone. Am I good enough?"

Luke peered into her eyes, turning off his previous thoughts to search out Ana saying, "I don't know. How about you show me?"

She grabbed his hand and led him to the swamped dance floor. As packed as it was she still found a way to bend over and gyrate against him. Her silk dress slithered through his fingers when she turned to him kissing his ear with her breath. "I'm kind of a sure thing and I can feel that I'm just the right girl for you. Do you come here often?"

"Oh yeah I do."

She turned again moving out of his line of sight when he noticed Ana across the way. Her strap had fallen from her shoulder and he followed her fingers as they ever so delicately pulled her garment into place without skipping a beat. It was as though she stood still, illuminated by the colorful, wavering lights before but Luke was the one who remained fixed, frozen in place. The girl popped back up saying," Are you ready to get out of here?"

"No," he answered, snapping out of his frigid state. "I came with some friends and they look like their having fun."

"Oh come on. We can have our own fun. Why don't we go back to your place?"

He took another glance at the mingling Ana replying, "Okay." Grabbing her hand he led her over to Ana, suddenly aware that he didn't even get her name. "I'm sorry," he said pulling her to his side, "what's your name?"

"Candace."

Luke walked over to Ana and grabbed her at her waist, stealing her from her dancing partner. "Hey Ana this is Candace." Ana waved as usual to his new friend. "We're going to head out but you can have the car. Max is somewhere around here so just let him know when you want to go home. That is unless you want to leave now."

"No I think I'll stay."

"Are you sure?" He asked pleading with his brown eyes for her to go home. The sight of the other man's hand on her back was more than enough cause to get her out of there. She never wanted to dance and to see her with a complete stranger made his blood rush through his veins. He could feel his temperature rising from the reaction. He let go of her hand hoping that she didn't notice the change in his composure. "I thought that-"

"Luke it's okay. Go and have fun."

He hung his head, twirling his neck towards Candace. "Are you ready?"

"Definitely."

***

"I must be honest with you. I knew who you were when I approached you Luke," Candace cooed hooking her bra before she stood up and slipped into her dress. "I recognized you from one of the shareholder's meetings last week for Lux and Morgan."

"You're the receptionist."

"You remembered." She grinned over her shoulder. "I saw you and I thought you realized it was me but obviously I was wrong. It seems as though you have something, or should I say someone else on your mind. So I can understand how you could forget."

"No my mind is clear now thanks to you. Do you want me to call you a cab?"

"No I got a friend that lives nearby. I'm just going to bunk with her."

Babycakes

Luke got up to walk her downstairs when she turned to him saying, "Thanks for a fun night. Maybe we'll get together again sometime."

"Who knows, crazier things have happened," he smirked.

He closed the door behind her but he couldn't escape how he truly felt. He went upstairs to his room and turned on the shower. *All Ana had to do was say that she wanted to leave,* he thought to himself looking in the mirror. He would've left Candace behind in a heartbeat. Why did she plague him so? So what they slept together. She was one in thirty, possibly even forty. *Was it really that many? Why did I add another?* The bathroom filled with steam, blinding him of his reflection. His mind on the other hand was clouded with doubt.

***

After leaving the club Ana hadn't heard from Luke in days. When he didn't show up for movie night she had planned on stopping by his place but he said he wasn't feeling well. Perplexed, she decided to wait until Thursday to visit him at work. She finished running one of the errands on her list from Diana and went to his office. Stokes Holdings, written in gold, shined just as bold as the man who founded the company.

"Is that Ana I see," Lucas' father, Leif called out to her.

"Hello Mr. Stokes."

He grabbed her in a hug, wrapping his large arm around her. Luke resembled him almost as if he were Leif's younger self. He looked pretty good for his age but he managed to keep up his youthful image by staying productive. "How have you been?"

"Alright. Korina's got me running crazy lately with her new line."

"So she's finally ridden herself of Diana?"

"No," laughed Ana. "I wish I could stay longer and talk but I stopped by to visit Luke. Have you seen him around today?"

"I did but he went out for lunch after our meeting. If I see him again I'll tell him you dropped in."

Only after picking up a sandwich for lunch, Luke found himself wandering around a jewelry store. He tapped on the counter, peeking at the earrings and certified rings, sparkling with his every move.

"Is there an item you would like to have a closer look at sir?" asked the eager salesman.

"Um no I was just looking."

"Well surely something brought you into the store today. Maybe there's a certain question you'd like to ask a young lady perhaps?"

"No I ah, yes I am looking for something. I'm going to Hawaii and I would like to purchase a waterproof watch."

"Ah! Follow Winston right over here sir." The man waved his fingers with his keys jingling over his elbow.

Luke raised a brow to the overzealous clerk, quickly choosing one of the time pieces. He pulled out the tattered wallet that his mother had given him and noticed how the clerk eyed its beaten state but he didn't care. He made his purchase and left the store with his tiny bag.

There were so many people out that day. The weather was still holding up beautifully and it seemed as though everyone wanted to get out for lunch. He walked through the mob, taking in the cool fall breeze when he heard a voice from behind.

"What did you buy me?" asked Ana creeping up beside him.

"Ana!" he shouted. "How did you find me?"

"I didn't get a call from anyone saying you were lost. Wait I take that back. You've been distant lately and I think I know why."

"Oh," he said stopping in front of everyone, not caring how annoyed they had become.

"I get that you got weirded out by what we did but don't be. Who knows, it may not have even worked."

"Are you going to Max if it doesn't?" he asked folding his arms over his chest.

"No," she grinned almost shocked by his comment. She placed her hand on his arm saying, "I only want things to go back to the way they were before." She took his face in her hand. "We should have no regrets with what we did. I don't, so why do you?"

"I don't. I had a lot on my plate. I'm working out a deal at work and planning a trip to Hawaii all by myself. It would've been so much easier if you were going with me."

"Luke that's not fair. You know that I have to save my vacation. Korina only gives me two weeks of personal time a year. I'm down to three days. If you told me earlier I could've saved some time or-"

Without thinking he hushed her with a kiss. Ana jerked at his sudden spring of emotion but didn't push him away. Luke was quick with his approach and stepped back smiling. The look in her eyes was unreadable. He was too afraid to find out what she might have thought of his onslaught of fondness so he immediately blurted out, "I'm just busting your chops."

"Fine." She blinked furiously and shook her head. "You said that you were sick and now it's because you've been busy. How is it that you find time to shop?"

"Yes time, that's exactly what I bought. I got a watch to complete my look on the beach."

"Now I know what not to get you for your birthday."

"You don't have to get me anything."

"Yes I do."

"No you don't. I'm going to throw a party before I leave town at my place. In three weeks' time I want to see you in that little green dress I love at nine."

"Oh no! Not a house party. I always have to be on second floor duty."

Katrina Thompson

"That's because you're so good at keeping everyone in check. When you tell them to stay downstairs they listen to you and knowing Max he'll be too busy talking to the ladies."

"Speaking of Max, did you ask him to go with you on vacation?"

"Yes but he already used all of his vacation and I'll be gone for almost two weeks. No point in going to paradise for just five days."

"Will you be back for Thanksgiving?"

"Oh of course. You should know that my appetite wouldn't allow me to miss it."

Chapter 3

Being drained of energy seemed a common occurrence for Ana but when the nausea began, she had a feeling her night with Luke may have actually worked. Her visit to the doctor's office proved it. In disbelief, Ana sat in Korina's kitchen after she received the phone call about her blood work. Even though she planned having the baby, the idea of finally becoming a mother was unreal. She placed her hand on her stomach with her thoughts in an uproar. *Who should I tell? Should I even tell anyone?* Luke scheduled his party for the following evening but she didn't want to overshadow their fun. Besides that, she never wanted to make her decision an issue for him. The pregnancy from that point on was going to be her experience and no one else's. Fran knew and so did Madison. Maybe she could ask her to visit and tell them both. Then she realized the holidays were soon to approach. Madison would be busy with Tyler and Brooklyn. She and Peter planned on going upstate to be with her parents. No, telling anyone now would be too early. *I should wait until the second trimester to tell anyone.* "That's what I will do."

***

"It's a celebration!" Luke shouted opening the door to Ana who showed up almost an hour after the party started. He grabbed her inside, kissing her cheek. "You're late."

"I'm sorry, I know."

"It's okay, several of my guest recently arrived." He took off her jacket seeing the green dress he asked her to wear. She donned long teardrop earrings which held a purple stone that brushed against her shoulders. "You granted my wish."

"This was the least I could do for your birthday."

"Well you look amazing."

"Hey that was my line," said Max walking over to them. He had been talking to a couple of girls who were possibly models. Ana scanned the living room noticing how almost the whole first floor was covered with tall beautiful woman. "At least it used to be," he mumbled looking at Luke.

Ana projected her statement to Luke as she continued canvasing the area and commented. "I see that you weren't thinking about me when you planned this party."

"The guest list was my idea," admitted Max. "There are some guys coming but for now, the caterers are still here."

"Oh gee thanks Max."

Luke kissed her on her cheek asking, "Aren't we enough for you anyway?"

"Luke, why would you-,"

Max pulled her away saying, "Before the party really gets started why don't we have a little fun." He took Ana by the hand dancing to the house music. She had given Luke an evil glare but with Max pressuring her to dance, the comment was forgotten. They moved with the beat of the rhythmic sounds as the girls began to surround them, dancing in a circle until Max deleted himself from the equation. He stepped back joining Luke at the counter. He leaned over to pick up a bacon wrapped scallop and grinned at Luke. "A sea of beautiful woman and still you can only see her."

"Stop Max."

"I will. Once you stop denying yourself of what you really want."

"I know what I want."

"And what's that?"

"To have some fun."

Luke excused himself and went outside for some fresh air however, just as Max had promised, there were other party guest that arrived. Not a lot of them were men but it didn't make a difference for Ana. She was too preoccupied with watching the stairwell and the clock tick away with her tired eyes. She had been out all day running errands and only got one hour or so of rest before she had to get ready. She had eaten a sandwich in hopes that smelling the other food wouldn't affect her. She feared morning sickness but the uncontrollable vomiting barely came. Luckily her stomach was settled however she wished the party would end soon. Luke had to take a flight out in a matter of hours but today signified his actual thirty-fifth birthday. There was no calling it quits.

"You don't appear to be enjoying yourself," Luke said plopping down on the chair which had just become unoccupied. She found the only empty spot to relax in the house and was sitting on the arm, staring at the stairwell. "You know, when I put you on second floor duty I didn't want to ruin your time here."

"You didn't. I mean you're not. I'm having a good time but I think I'm going to get going soon."

"Leaving," he grinned pulling her into his lap. "I can't let you go. I'll be gone for almost two weeks and I'm going to need help cleaning up the place before I do."

"What are you talking about? Zelda's coming in the morning to clean."

"Yes but who's going to eat all of the leftover food? I don't want it to go to waste. You have to stay and scarf it down with me."

"Luke I don't think that I can this time."

"You know I'm tired too. I should get some rest if I'm going to fly out in a couple of hours." He kissed Ana on her cheek, scooting from beneath her to usher out his guest.

Ana got up protesting. "Luke, you don't have to end your celebration."

"It's alright Ana. I was going to soon anyway. It's already after 1am."

Luke cleared out all of his guest, including Max, and went to the kitchen to find a snack. Ana joined him, hopping on an empty spot of the counter. It wasn't the first time they stayed up late eating the leftovers from his party but it was for closing one out early.

She looked at him while he bit off a shrimp, leaving its tail behind. "Why did you end your party Luke?"

He picked up another shrimp biting it. He finished chewing and put the tail in the trash. "I told you, I'm tired and I wanted to spend some time with you before I leave." He leaned towards her and Ana immediately shot back. "What was that about?" he asked amused.

Confronted with her memory of his sudden kiss outside of the jewelry store, she felt sheepish. It was a friendly kiss but could she, did she want more. "I thought," she said embarrassed, "you were going to kiss me."

"Would that be so horrible?"

"Um no but after what happened, I just don't want to blur the lines," Ana replied, fumbling her words. The truth was that her feelings for him were in an uproar. However, her emotions were much easier to blame on hormones than love.

Laughing, Luke reached for another shrimp and handed it to her. "I think we've past that point."

She smiled and took a bite out of it. She swallowed the little sea creature and said, "Sorry I don't know, it just seems like we've been spending a lot of time apart lately and with you being gone for so long…"

"You're going to miss me," he grinned.

"Get over yourself," she replied laughing along. She flung the tail of the shrimp on a napkin nearby and quickly hopped off of the counter. She wasn't sure if her abrupt actions or the late snack caused her current status but what she did know was that the baby didn't like it. A familiar sensation arose. Her jaws began to water and she felt the chunkiness collecting in her throat. Ana ran over to the sink unable to control herself.

Luke leaned over and held Ana's hair waiting for her to finish before he said anything. After the assault on her stomach was done, she turned on the water to rinse out the sink and her mouth from the acidic aftermath. Luke handed her a towel to wipe her face. She was so humiliated that she was unable to even look at him. She slid down the cabinet and sat on the floor with her head sunk in to her chest. He propped her hair behind her ear asking, "Are you sick? If I knew that you weren't feeling well I wouldn't have asked you to come."

"I'm not sick," she answered covering her mouth with the towel. "I'm pregnant."

Luke fell against the cabinet as though the wind had been knocked out of him. "I can't believe it! I thought it would take more than once. Well technically twice but..."

"Tell me about it. Now do you understand why I don't want to ruin things?"

"Kissing me won't ruin things. I see it as sweetening the deal."

"Even with vomit breath?"

He laughed, "Even with vomit breath. Why didn't you tell me?"

"It's bad luck to tell anyone so soon. *Aside from the father.* Besides I never wanted you to have to deal with any of this. You did your part," she grinned. "Luke," she said touching her stomach, "thank you."

"I only did what you would've done for me." She smiled and rolled her legs beneath her to get up. He helped her and watched as she fixed her dress before she went to the closet to retrieve her coat. "Where are you going?" he asked following her.

"I'm going home. You need your rest. It's a long flight to Hawaii."

"I've been there already. You don't have to warn me. You need your rest too." He plucked the jacket from her grasp and took her hand in his. "We're not blurring the lines if we just sleep, are we?"

Ana shook her head replying, "No we're not I guess."

He turned off the lights and guided her up the stairs to his room. She had been there before but she never slept in his room. His bed was so large and at the moment she was so tired that being put off with the amount of woman which may have curled in his sheets didn't matter. He walked over to his closet removing his shoes while she removed her earrings. She slipped off her heels and went to his bathroom for a toothbrush. He always kept spare ones. No doubt for one of his dates but yet again, she tried not to think about it. After she was done, she stepped out to find Luke standing with a T-shirt in hand.

"I thought you might not want to wrinkle your dress."

"Good thinking." He tossed the top over to her and she sheepishly curled into the bathroom to take off her clothes. Ana placed her inexpensive gift to Luke on the hook sticking out from the door and walked out twisting her hair around her fingers. She returned his smile as she crawled on his bed, lying down next to him. She fluffed the pillow beneath her head and flung out her arm, catching the blankets between them. "Did you set your clock?" she asked, making sure he didn't miss his flight.

"Yes it's set for five o'clock."

Ana yawned, moving to the right side of the bed. "Good I'll get up when you do. Goodnight Luke."

He crept over to her side, taking her in his arms. "Goodnight Ana."

She felt his lips brush against her spine at her neck and his hand rose up her thigh resting along her waist. She turned towards him and he rolled on top of her. "I thought we were going to sleep."

"We are but since I'll be gone for so long I thought we should use our time wisely. And besides, I'm only holding you."

"Right now," she giggled, "you're on top of me."

"I'm not hurting you, am I?"

Ana took in a deep breath. "No, you're not," she answered but she wasn't sure if she meant it.

Hearing the hesitation in her voice, Luke rolled off of her and curled his arm around her. As she lay on her side, pressed against him, he fought to keep his hand away from her stomach. She was right about one thing, the relationship between them was changing but he still felt the same way about being a father.

***

Luke's alarm seemed to chime just after he drifted off to sleep. He slid from beside Ana to take his shower pack some final pieces but when he was finished he didn't wake her. He peeked over at her peacefully sleeping in his bed. He remembered her years ago swearing never to sleep there. He sat down next to her to pull the blankets up but the thought of the little being growing inside her swept through his mind. He pulled them back, finding the courage to touch her and ran his hand over her stomach whispering, "Hey in there. I know that I shouldn't be talking to you but I didn't want to leave without saying something. You couldn't have a better mom than Ana but you deserve to be raised by a good father. It's not me." He dropped his head and sighed. "I didn't think you could ever exist but now that you do, I guess I can't wait to meet you." He leaned in kissing Ana where the child they created slept. "Goodbye."

His decision to allow her to sleep was unselfish but unpredicted by Ana. Hours later she turned towards the light that shined in through the crack in Luke's curtain. She could hear the sound of a vacuum roaring beneath her which meant Zelda had to be there. That also meant she was going to be late for work. She hopped from the bed in a rush, although her speedy exit turned out not to be such a good idea. "My phone, where is my phone?" she asked the silent walls, trying to brush off the unwelcoming waive of nausea. She surveyed the room but realized her cell lied tucked away in her purse downstairs. She ran to the bathroom flinging off Luke's T-shirt, brushed her teeth and threw on her dress. She spun around towards the clock. It was already after 9 so she knew that Torrance would arrive to her apartment at any moment. Who was she kidding, he was probably already there. She ran down the stairs almost startling Zelda.

"Ana, I didn't know you were here."

"Yeah I got tired and slept over."

"So you and Mr. Stokes-"

"No," she shouted, "just sleep. Um have you seen a tiny gold purse lying around anywhere?"

Zelda leaned over to the coffee table handing her the handbag. "I thought I would be visited by a guest this morning, ringing the bell for it. I'm sorry if I woke you."

"Oh no I'm glad that you did." She smiled with glee reaching into her purse for her phone. She noticed a missed call from Diana but she would have to read the text she sent her later. No doubt it was probably something she needed her to do. First she had to get a hold of, "Torrance thank God you answered. I'm at Luke's house. Can you pick me up here?"

"Yeah, I'll be there in about ten minutes."

After hanging up, Ana read Diana's text which as she guessed, held another request. Korina wanted the sketch book left by her assistant in her work room. She had to go to the house anyway so picking it up wouldn't be that difficult but she needed her designs ASAP. So now she would have to get the girls, stop by the office, then retrieve the girls again and make them lunch. Hopefully their father would be home so that she could do the grocery shopping. "Another busy day," she said plopping on the couch.

"You look tired. Maybe you should go back to bed," suggested Zelda.

Ana smirked looking down at her ending call but glanced at her stomach. "I wish, except resting doesn't exist in my world." She shoved her cell in her purse and noticed that Zelda had perfectly placed her jacket over the back of one of the kitchen chairs. "I better get downstairs. I'm so sorry I can't stay and help."

"Don't worry, this is my job." She watched her walk to the door looking at her feet. "I didn't see shoes anywhere around here but I'm pretty sure you'll need them."

"Shoes," she giggled tapping her head. "I think I left my brain up there too. Wait that didn't come out the right way but you know what I mean, ugh!" Zelda laughed as she ran upstairs to retrieve her shoes and embarrassingly escaped.

When she got downstairs Torrance was just pulling up. She yanked the rear door open climbing in. Torrance peeped over his shoulder at her but quickly turned back once she noticed him looking. "I'm sorry I'm late. Luke had a party last night and clunked out," she said summarizing her tale.

"You don't have to apologize." Ana settled in her seat dismayed at his brash tongue. "So are we still stopping by the deli?"

"Yes definitely. There's no way I could make the girls breakfast now."

***

With Kailey on her hip Ana ran around the block to get her to her dance lesson on time. The heavy traffic seemed worse that day compared to others but it didn't help leaving the house almost fifteen minutes late. She put Kailey down on the steps allowing her to walk up to the entrance. They stepped inside and scurried to the ballet room right as the teacher began their floor stretches. She removed her bag placing it on the side with the other girl's belongings while Kailey pulled off her coat. After the assurance that all was well with the teachers light smile, she slipped out the door and closed it behind her, catching her breath. When she went outside Torrance still hadn't gotten to the studio. She walked back in his direction looking out into the traffic for the black truck. Her phone began to buzz in her purse with a message from Diana asking her of her location. *Working*. Ana wanted to reply, but with the view of her ride nearby, she quickly typed that she was on the way and wove through traffic to get in.

"Where to now?"

"To Korina's office," she breathed.

"I have to say," said Torrance looking in the mirror, "I've never seen you this disheveled before." She ran her fingers through her hair and pulled out her lipstick. "I didn't mean in that way. You are very beautiful, look nice, I mean nice, as always. I only meant that I ah, I never saw you in such a rush."

"Yeah it's definitely not my normal forte. Trust me I won't let it happen again."

Ana slid out of the truck again and walked into Korina's studio. Like the Stokes office, her name greeted you at the entrance. KB Fashion House, The Core of Fashion, was painted on the wall in exquisite letters. The gray paint and silver additions made the emblem appear so elegant. She often wondered how she might have decorated her fashion house. Her favorite color was blue but Tiffany's owned the shade she loved. She would've found some way to incorporate the soothing hue. Ana strolled back to reality with a bit of reluctance, once again aware of being on a time crunch. She went up to the second floor where Korina's office was held. The area was covered with swatches just like the one at home but these were of vivid colors and prints.

"Thank you Ana," said Diana startling her. She grabbed the book and placed it on her desk. "See you later," she blurted out over her shoulder without acknowledging her.

"You're welcome."

"Ah Ana," Korina's serene voice called out to her. "I didn't know you were stopping by today."

At least she was pleasant about me stopping by. "Yes I-"

"She noticed that I left my notebook and was nice enough to drop it off," Diana rudely interrupted her to cover her own tracks.

"Oh well that was considerate of you. Diana did you ever locate my sketchbook? I specifically remember giving it to you this morning to place in my bag."

"Yes," she answered retrieving her work as though the binder had been there all day.

Korina turned her focus on a dress form positioned nearby saying, "Ana dear, look at the ruching on this design. Do you think it's too much?" Her eyes were focused on her along with Diana and one of Korina's designers. The woman with her short haircut and heavily made-up face grinned as she looked at Ana as though her dress were stuck in her stockings. She pulled on the tail of her frock to check just in case and became frozen in place. "Come now Ana I want to know what you think. Your style has always been rather put together if I should say so. I mean look at you. Where are you headed off to after work?"

She nibbled on her lip as Korina tapped her finger against her cheek waiting for a reply. To admit she had been wearing the same clothes she had worn out the night before was more than she was willing to admit. Torrance already knew and he was one too many. Even with just sleeping in Luke's bed she felt guilty. After he asked her if he was hurting her, she wanted to say something different. Although she decided to answer what she felt would make things okay between them. It wasn't okay when deep down, she realized at that moment, maybe she wanted more. "Brunch, I mean lunch with a friend," she quickly mumbled lying.

"Ah well we shouldn't keep them waiting."

Ana walked forward looking at the gown on the headless statue. She envisioned herself in its place. If she wore the ensemble, where would she like the ruching to hit? Would it be at the curve of her breast or at the indentation of her hips? She ran her fingers along the fine fabric saying, "I don't think it's enough." She took out several of the pins straightening out the area and re-gathered the material. She pinned it in place with what she had and turned to Korina. "I thought the bodice needed something else."

"Hmm," she replied tapping her finger on her chin. "Justin," she said turning to the other designer, "What do you think?"

"The alteration does extenuate the waist and brings more attention to the bust. This will flow better with the line."

"I agree. Good job," she acknowledged the bedazzled Ana with the wave of her hand. "I'll see you on Monday."

With her queue to leave Ana smiled happy that she was actually able to lend an idea to Korina with witnesses. No one would believe it. Not even she did. She bypassed Diana's glare giving the receptionist a quick wave before she walked out of the office to the truck. She wanted to call Luke but he was probably still on the plane. She picked up the phone to call Fran when Torrance caught how happy she appeared.

"What's got you all excited?" he questioned her turning from traffic.

"Korina," she giggled, "she asked for my advice on something and she's going with the design."

"That's wonderful. I knew you were able to perform Diana's job but it sounds to me like you should be working directly under her."

She dropped her cowardly gaze with a smile. "I went to school to become a fashion designer but I guess I didn't quite cut it. I figure God has something else in store for me." She rubbed her stomach returning her view outside. "Let's get the girls."

"Don't you have to go to the market?"

"I do but I won't have enough time before we pick up the girls. I think we should drop them off with Steve before heading to the store."

"Sounds like a plan."

"I'm sorry Diana really threw us off with stopping by here. You didn't have anything planned for the afternoon did you?"

"No just spending time with you," he smirked looking in the mirror.

***

Although traffic didn't ease after picking up the girls, Ana was able to get the grocery shopping done and went back to the Bryce's house to unload them. Thankfully Steve was home and made lunch for him and the girls. She put away the last of the bags happy that the day was finally over. Steve walked into the kitchen to pour a cup of coffee. She never understood why people drank the bitter addiction. In her book the best part of waking up was just to see another day. She probably got that from going to church. You shouldn't become addicted to anything but Steve had at least three cups from sun up to sun down.

"Is there anything else you guys need before I leave?" she asked.

"Yes I do." He took a sip from his mug and said, "Korey keeps asking me if we're having tomato balls for dinner but I have no idea what she's talking about."

Ana laughed reaching over to the book shelf in the kitchen. "She means stuffed tomatoes," she answered pointing to the picture. "Sorry I'm trying to convince them to call things by their real names to make life easier on everyone but they have concocted their own language."

"Yes well thankfully you can decipher it."

Ana pulled on her jacket and walked over to the stairwell. "I'm leaving girls."

Though Korey's music was playing they both heard her. Kailey came running down the stairs. "Are you coming back tomorrow?" she asked.

"No Kailey, tomorrows Sunday."

"But who's going to help me fly?"

"Fly," she said bending down to her, "but you're not wearing your wings."

"I can go and get them," she beamed.

"Let's allow Ms. Ana to go home Kailey. She'll play with you on Monday."

Kailey leaned over giving her a hug. "Goodbye Ms. Ana."

"Goodbye and be a good girl for daddy okay. Korey I don't think I have to worry about you albeit the same thing applies." She grinned and wrapped her arms around with a tight squeeze before she went out to the truck. Torrance was parked a little bit away but when he saw her come out he drove to the door. She got inside as usual and let out a sigh.

"You're not tired are you?" She glanced up at his amused appearance in the mirror confused. "I was thinking. Since I have to pick up Korina in an hour I should get something to eat. Do you want to join me?"

Ana didn't really want to. She hadn't taken a shower all day or hardly ate anything but she was running around town on empty. "Come to think of it, getting a bite to eat would be a good idea. Sure, why not? What do you have in mind?"

"I was going to let you decide."

"Right now even cardboard seems appealing," she giggled.

"Cardboard, I think I'll pass on that but maybe pizza will do. I know of a place that makes one of the best slices in Manhattan."

"Well what are we waiting for?" she said climbing into the front seat.

***

Standing at the window of Mom & Pops with their piping hot lunch in hand, Torrance cupped his to take a bite but paused awaiting Ana's first bite. However, she, too, clung to her food with a weird look upon her face. "What is it?" he asked.

"We spend what, at least two to three hours together almost every day and I know nothing about you."

He put his pizza down replying, "You only have to ask."

"Okay, where are you from?"

"I'm from Michigan but I came here thinking that I could make it on Broadway."

"Broadway," she crooned, "I never pegged you for the theatre type."

"Yeah, neither did my parent's which is why I took any job thrown my way to afford living in the area. As time went on and I hardly got any gigs that were worth mentioning I lucked out and was hired by the Bryce's," he said holding out his hands. "I never thought my endless escapades, running around New York would pay off but what I do now has in ways unimaginable. I drive an amazing vehicle for an amazing boss who employs amazing people."

Ana picked up her pizza laughing.

"What is it?"

"It's funny. My friend calls me Amazing Ana."

"You ah mean Luke?"

"No my friend Max. Technically he's Luke's friend but I adopted him as my own as well after college."

"So how long have you known him, Luke?"

"Since I was ten years-old. He's my best friend's cousin. My family adopted him first." She smiled. "He lived here and when we graduated from high school we both moved from upstate to go to college. He's been in my life every day since."

"As a friend?"

"Yeah like a brother," she answered with the word scratching her throat as it left. "Do you have any brothers or sisters?"

"No just me. How about you?"

"I have three older brothers," she replied after swallowing the last bite of her pizza.

"Oh wow."

"Yeah my parents kept trying for a girl until they got one. My father," she grinned, "called me his little orphan Annie. My mother on the other hand didn't like it and decided to name me Anastasia."

"I think your name is beautiful too."

Ana swallowed deeply noticing the tone of Torrance's voice. *Is he coming onto me?*

He caught the astonished yet puzzled pose that washed over her and reached for her empty plate. "We better go before I'm late."

She nodded and followed behind him. He tossed the plates away and turned towards her when he observed another patron as they scooted out their chair. Ana quickly moved to avoid the hit and clutched her stomach like she was protecting something. The man apologized and she walked by tossing her hair behind her ear. "Ready?"

Torrance held the door open and ushered her to the truck. Ana latched her seat belt and peered over at him. "Thanks again for lunch. You were right."

"Right about what?"

"Right about it being one of the best slices ever."

"You're welcome."

Ana stared out the window noticing that they almost reached her house and their informational lunch had gone cold. Was she wrong in thinking that he was hitting on her? Even so, how would she respond? She never saw him that way, not that he was bad looking. He had a smile that would light up even the darkest of stages. She could only imagine the bright lights bouncing off of his ebony skin. The sun alone brought out the beauty in it. She turned to him saying, "Is something wrong?"

"Wrong, no nothing's wrong."

"I just thought we had a nice lunch together, getting to know each other and now you're so quiet."

"I'm sorry I didn't mean to be rude. I was just…"

"Just what?" she asked with a curious grin.

"I didn't want to pry but I just realized that you're pregnant."

"I'm not."

"It's okay you don't have to hide it from me. Girls only look at food the way you did if they are purposely trying not to eat or if they're turned off by what they're eating. I know you eat pizza so that wasn't an issue. However, when I saw how afraid you became when that guy almost bumped into you, I was certain."

She curled towards the window, upset over his discovery. "You're right again, but can you keep this between us. Only one other person knows and I don't want the news to get out just yet."

"I ah didn't even know you were dating. You always seem so busy," he chuckled, unconvincingly trying to hide his disappointment.

With her head still hung low she replied, "I'm not. I'm having this baby on my own." She cleared her voice and said, "Between you and me."

"Yeah Ana, whatever you want. I won't say anything."

***

So tired from her week Ana stayed home Sunday to get some rest. She was shocked that Torrance had figured out that she was pregnant. She decided to tell everyone she was artificially inseminated but at the time, the words didn't form in her mind. She hadn't thought of how to answer anyone questioning her situation. What would she even say to the baby? Pulling back the covers she walked over to her mirror to take a peek at her not so changed stomach. She stroked her accomplishment with grin. "I know you're in there. I can't wait to hear your little heartbeat to prove it. I can't wait to see your fingers wind around mine or marvel at your bright eyes looking back at me. I wonder if you'll have mine or… Well it ah won't matter who's you have or what the color. You will be my little girl or boy."

Katrina Thompson

Her attention wavered with the sound of her buzzing phone on the nightstand. She ran over and immediately swiped her finger across the screen to answer when she saw Luke calling.

"Luke how are you?"

"I'm missing my favorite girl."

"I miss you too. What are you doing?"

"I am lying out on the beach taking in the sun. I know that its hurricane season but I don't regret coming here one bit."

"I was kind of surprised you wanted to leave but I understand, you had your heart set on going."

"Everyone needs a vacation Ana and I don't mean staying at home in bed, working for Korina while they're on vacation, visiting your parents, or my cousin."

"Hey I went to Vegas."

"Two years ago."

"Luke I don't want to talk about it anymore. I get it. Tell me more about your trip."

Chapter 4

The autumn air flew in like the wings of a dove in the opened sky, gently blowing the rust colored leaves from their set places. Shops were preparing for the holiday season ahead and thankfully for Ana, Korina decided to have food catered so they didn't require much grocery shopping but she had to run some of Diana's errands. She went out of town for Thanksgiving, leaving Ana behind to pick up the slack. But no matter how much Korina wanted her to do, she had to stop by Mr. Stokes office.

Ana always did around the holidays and she hadn't stopped by since she went looking for Luke. She made a special batch of cupcakes for him. He loved her strawberry shortcake recipe with strawberry filling, vanilla cake and strawberry infused frosting. She placed them in a pink bakery box as an added touch to present her treats to Leif after she was done with her last stop. She had to pick up swatches that were at the office and drop them off at Korina's house before she headed home.

With everything she had to do, she was afraid that by the time she reached his office he would no longer be there. However she was in luck. His assistant escorted her to his office made of glass, as she called the open room. The only walls were those attached to Luke's. The window of his corner office went from the ceiling to the floor. He liked to watch his employees to ensure their productivity. All he had to do was look up from his seat to scan all those under his employment. He could also see anyone approaching the reception desk, only no one had the ability to take a gander in. The tinted glass was perfect for his domineering personality. He must have noticed her come in because she detected the smile on his face before the receptionist told him of her arrival.

"My Ana," he wailed with his arms outstretched, "is that what I think it is?"

"Yes they are," she smiled walking over to give him a hug. "Happy Thanksgiving!"

"Same to you," he said taking the box. He led her to his office and set the treats down on his desk. He opened the lid and pulled one out, devouring half the cake with a single bite. "Oh honey you just made my day," Leif mumbled with a bit of the filling coating his front teeth.

"I would say," she laughed taking a seat. "I would've tried to come over last week if I had known you wanted them so badly."

"You can stop by every week if you'd like. I'd I love for you to visit and bringing a couple of these won't hurt." He winked. "My son was right. You need to get into the baking business."

"He talked to you about that?"

"Sure he did and you're other little project."

Ana's eyes popped open. "He told you?"

"Yeah, your parents are going to love the Paradise Halls for their anniversary party."

"Oh that, yeah," she replied relieved that he wasn't referring to the baby. "I never could've planned it without him."

He walked over to the other side of his desk and anchored his right leg on the side. "I want to talk to you seriously about this Ana," he said looking at her giving Ana the Stokes stare. It froze her just like the Bloom gloom her father used to give. "I really think you have a gift. There are a lot of good bakeries nearby. Despite my appearance I can't get enough of them but none of them compare to what you can do."

"Thank you Mr. Stokes. That means a lot coming from you."

"Well when you're ready I would love to work with you on getting a place. I'll loan you the startup fees and you can pay me with your intake."

"That's very generous of you but I-"

"Will need some time to think about it," he said leaning forward.

"Yes," she smiled knowing that no one told him no.

He walked over to Ana giving her another hug. "That's my girl." He pulled her away asking, "Doesn't Lucas get in tomorrow?"

"Yes he does," she replied.

"Well tell him I said hello when you see him."

"We were planning on having dinner at my apartment. You're invited too if you want to come."

"That's very nice of you but I'm heading off to Chicago in a few hours on business and California by Friday evening for a little fun. Everyone needs a vacation from time to time you know."

"Yeah, that's what I hear."

***

Looking out the window Ana glanced over at her phone as it buzzed with a message from Luke. Even on his trip with land and water parting them he found a way to make her laugh.

Torrance peered over his shoulder asking, "What do you have planned for the holiday?"

"Luke and I were just having dinner at my place. How about you?"

"I'm heading out on a flight to Michigan in the morning. That way I can miss the prep work and get there right in time for the food."

"You sound just like my brothers," she laughed. "When I go home for the holidays I don't hear from them until it's dinner time."

Katrina Thompson

He pulled up to Korina's house to let Ana out and parked. She ran up the stairs letting herself in when she began to feel a little light headed. She slowed down and clung to the rail for balance. She shook off the dizzying sensation and went up to the fourth floor which was set up for Korina's bridal designs.

"Ana you are a life saver," she said reaching out for the book. "Come," she directed Ana, grabbing her hand. She brought her over to a mannequin wearing a simple wedding gown. It looked perfect. The spaghetti strapped dress flowed like a dream around the bodice of the figure. The corset wasn't visible but you could tell how the form framed the body of the dress.

"It's beautiful Korina."

"I thought so too, but I think it needs a little something."

Ana's hazel eyes scanned the gown analyzing what she considered to be perfect. She cocked her head to the side noticing a pink spool of ribbon lying in the chair. She leaned over pulling the satin from the spool and wrapped it around the waist. She tied a perfect bow just above the navel and snipped off the extra to settle aligned with the matching end. "What do you think?"

Korina took the scissors from her and placed them down on her desk. She hung back, tapping her chin like she always did when she processed a new idea and said, "You are a wonderful nanny Ana but sometimes I think you've missed your calling."

Ana felt as though her breath had escaped her. This was the second time within two weeks that she asked for her help and liked it.

Korina picked up her book of swatches flipping through them. "I was thinking that we could do this design in another color. With the addition of the ribbon I can leave the dress as crisp and white as designed but give the bride the option to change the color of..." She turned and saw that her words had fallen on deaf ears. Ana was lying on the floor. She knelt down beside her, tapping her face but Ana didn't wake. Korina ran over to her desk scrambling for her phone. She tried to arouse her one last time however she still wouldn't open her eyelids. "Ana don't worry. I'll get you some help."

Pour

Chapter 5

When Ana woke, the strange faces startled her but they didn't faze her as much as the doctor who informed her that the baby was gone. She sensed her body ball into numbness. She entered the day with the idea of her healthy baby inside of her. She never considered the possibility of it no longer existing. She didn't get to hear its heartbeat or feel the flutter of their kick. She didn't even get to see a photo of it. Her first appointment was going to be on Monday. 'It's just something that happens with pregnancies', the doctor told her. They said that she was dehydrated. Ana believed them. She neglected her own hunger and thirst to ensure Korina and her family had been situated. She was running herself ragged but she had to work. She curled on the bed frozen in disbelief until they released her. She got dressed, collected her things and quietly found her way out of the emergency area. She bypassed several people in the halls, unwilling to meet their gaze. The metal doors opened, letting her leave just as she entered them, empty. She didn't know how she was going to get home but she figured that eventually her legs would stop, then she would worry about it.

"Ana," whispered the familiar voice.

She looked up at him saying, "Torrance, what are you doing here?"

"Korina asked me to make sure you were okay. Are you, okay?"

She swallowed her neck with her chin, unable to hold back her tears she cried, "I lost the baby."

He wrapped his arms around her stroking her hair while she shook in grief. "Is there someone I can call for you?"

Again she shook her head no.

"I'll take you home okay."

Ana walked where he led her. She remembered getting into the truck but the night collected the buildings and trees into one big blur.

Torrance opened the passenger door to lead her to the entryway of her apartment. "Do you want me to come up with you?" he asked.

She shook her head no.

"Are you sure there's no one I can call? How about Luke do you want me to call him?"

"No," she said flashing her hazel eyes. She turned walking up the steps and searched her bag for her key. She was unable to see the hole from her tired eyes. She allowed the key to slide into the lock as her hand trembled. She overheard his footsteps drawing near so she wiped her cheek saying, "Thank you Torrance for everything."

He stopped mid-step seeing the light smirk on her face before she closed the door. Even with her heart shattered into dust she tried to put on a happy face.

***

Luke climbed up the steps with a bag full of goodies he had gotten Ana from Hawaii. He knew that no matter what she would've told him not to get her anything but he spotted so many things that reminded him of her. He knocked on her door however Ana didn't answer. Just like his phone call the night before or any of his texts that morning. Concerned he pulled out his key to let himself in. He envisioned walking into her turkey scented kitchen with cornbread dressing on the side and candied yams. Only all that sat on the counter was her bag and jacket. He closed the door and dropped his sack of gifts next to her belongings. He quietly moved to her room and unlike the rest of the apartment which tried to catch the light of the afternoon sun, her room was dark. The curtains were drawn and she lied on the bed curled in a ball. He took off his jacket and scooted behind her.

He brushed her forehead saying, "You don't have a fever. Are you sick?"

"I'm not sick," she replied with a still voice.

"Well something's wrong," he whispered wrapping his arm around her stomach. He could hear her begin to sniffle and the trimmer in her spine. "Ana is it the baby?"

"There is no baby."

"Ana why didn't you call me?"

"It was my baby Luke. I never wanted you to feel like you had to deal with it."

"Deal with it." He turned her over brushing the hair from her face. "Ana no matter what the situation I'm here for you. Why would you think otherwise?"

"Luke I asked you to do this not only because I love you but because I knew that you would let me handle things myself. You would never say that I was raising the baby wrong or feeding him or her bad food. You would never take it away." He saw tears well in her eyes and she curled back into her ball.

"I feel the same way about you too, Ana, which means that I will always be here for you. I know for a fact that you would be a wonderful mother. We can even try again whenever you're ready."

"No," she cried. "This was a sign. I shouldn't be a mom and I was wrong to try and make something happen that shouldn't."

"Ana you shouldn't-"

"Luke," she sighed, "I know that you came over for dinner but I didn't get a chance to make anything. Maybe you should go."

He looked at her for a still moment. He had never seen her so crushed. Luke brushed her cheek but she only drove her face further into her pillow. Unable to leave her wallowing in pity, he slid from her side and grabbed his jacket. He was gone for less than half an hour but when he returned Ana kept to her same motionless spot. He dropped his bags on the counter and hung up his jacket along with hers on the hanger by the door. He went back to Ana's room and walked around the bed to face her. She was awake, looking at the closed curtains. Upset he cracked the curtain and crouched back to her side. Her eyelids were so swollen that he could hardly see her hazel eyes which were covered with red lines drowning them out.

"Ana when did you lose the baby?"

With eyes still gazing at the unmoving creak of sunlight she replied, "Yesterday."

"When is the last time you got some sleep?"

"Yesterday morning."

"Ana," he sighed and kissed her forehead. He rubbed her shoulder looking in her eyes. They were blank just like the emotion in her tone. The loss of the baby took the life out of her. He stood up and closed the curtain completely before he began taking off his clothes.

"I don't want to make another baby Luke," her voice squeaked so innocently.

Luke bit his lip, a bit amused that he could draw out some emotion though almost hurt. "You don't have to but I think you need some sleep." He pulled the covers back seeing her in the clothes she probably had on yesterday. He plucked her from her sweater by drawing the garment over her head and she unbuttoned her pants easing them off. Sliding beneath the covers he curled her against his chest looking down at her. "Since the curtains are keeping you awake, you can't stare at them anymore."

"I can't close my eyes Luke," she whispered with her lashes blinking away the tears. "Whenever I do all I think about is the baby." She began crying again. Her eyes begged for sleep. She held out on what would seem like bliss to only find nightmares just as the images she fought with her thoughts.

Katrina Thompson

"Ana it will all be okay. It just wasn't the right time for you to be a mom but you will get pregnant again and when you do, you'll look back at this moment and love them even more for it."

"Them?"

"I know you Ana, you won't stop with one."

"You're okay with that?"

"I'm okay with whatever makes you happy." He smiled and kissed her although this time on her lips. He tightened his arms around her and could already tell that she was calming down.

"Luke."

"Yes," he answered.

"Thanks for coming back."

***

With Ana's gentle snores Luke eased from beside her and went into the kitchen. He didn't want the food to go bad so he placed it in the fridge and closed the door. He leaned against the counter rubbing his face with his hands. He didn't think that when he told the baby goodbye they would never get to meet. Upset he went to the sink turning on the cold water to cool down. He took a hand full brushing it against his neck, blowing his anger into the air. It seemed like a lot of things didn't work out for her but she had finally gotten what she wanted and he was able to give it to her. He slapped the faucet off and reached for a towel when he noticed the calendar on the wall. A bright red circle encased the appointment she scheduled on Monday. He ripped it from the wall and tossed it in the trash. She may be asleep at the moment but he was going to help her get over the loss. However how was he going to get over disappointing her?

Ana slept for only a couple of hours though she had missed a night's rest. When she woke, Luke flocked to Ana's side and kissed her on her forehead. "Did you get enough sleep?"

"I think so," she said sitting up. "Were you sitting there the whole time?"

"Not the whole time." He smirked. "I know that you are still upset but we still possess so many things to be thankful for."

We.

He pulled the covers back saying, "Why don't you take a shower and I'll get dinner ready."

"You cooked?" she asked surprised although her bewilderment was also from his words of encouragement.

"No I didn't. I got Two Wong Fu's."

His confession pulled her from the questions which began forming in her mind to create a clever statement. "Oh, the traditional Thanksgiving Day meal."

"Yes but I'm sorry it's going to be reheated so it won't taste as good."

"That's okay," she replied hanging her head. She turned stepping out of the bed to leave the room.

Luke held his concerned state while he listened to the water pour and tumble around Ana. She seemed to be perking up albeit not out of character. *Always hiding.* His lips thinned at the thought. He waited for the right moment to heat up the cartons of food. He set them perfectly in place on the counter in front of the chairs. Normally she had holiday themed napkins, plates and flatware arranged on the dining room table but he had no idea where she kept those. Still waiting for her to come out he decided that maybe he had enough time to try and find them. He opened the cabinets in the kitchen finding empty space and baking pans. With the clang of the metal he hadn't noticed that she was standing next to him.

"What are you looking for?"

"I was trying to find your platter with the turkey in the center?"

She cocked her head to the side with a smile to ease his tension. "I get what you're trying to do but you don't have to. I'm okay. So much so I realized that I have been taking advantage of you."

"Ana you could never take advantage of me."

"No Luke I have. You gave me one of the most unbelievable gifts. Even for the smallest amount of time I was a mom. I will never be able to repay you for such a gift but there is something I owe you."

"You don't owe me anything," he replied crossing his arms.

"Yes I do. If memory serves me right, I owe you a movie night." She collected two of the containers from the counter with chopsticks and plopped on the couch. Luke walked over as she put them down on the table before she loaded the movie.

"So what are we watching?"

"I figured we could finish watching Star Wars."

"Really, you don't mind?"

"No I don't," she answered starting the movie.

They slunk down on the couch propping their legs up as they slurped their noodles and stole each other's chicken. Often, he poked his sticks inside Ana's container pulling out pieces and replaced them with his much hated broccoli. After a few bites, Ana set her food down on the table and focused on the film. Luke watched the movie but he still kept an eye on Ana. She was acting just like Ana. It seemed odd from the girl he had walked in on hours before. She took phone calls from the girls who were told not to call her. They brought a smile to her face that even he couldn't. Maybe those were her children. She had been taking care of them since Korey was a toddler.

After the movie ended Ana got up to put in another leaving her vibrating phone on the couch. Luke picked up the annoyance and caught sight of her quick text. "Who's Torrance?" he asked.

Ana looked back and reached for her cell. "He's Korina's driver. You don't remember him?"

Luke shook his head not paying attention to her question, only thinking of his own. "He knew about the baby?" he asked sitting forward.

She read the text and sat down next to him, sending a reply to Torrance. He was checking up on her. She finished and placed her phone on the table saying, "He figured it out a couple of weeks ago. I hadn't even told Korina but I guess he did when I ah, lost it. He waited for me at the hospital to take me home."

He moved closer but she grabbed his leg and gave him a light smile. She peered over his shoulder with a tired grin, "I have something for you." She leaped from her seat, stepping over him and went into the kitchen, pulling a box from the top of the fridge. She placed the container on his lap and sat down beside him. "I made these in advance. They're something new but I thought it would be a little refreshing after dinner." He opened the box seeing the chocolate clouds with green shavings sprinkled on top. "They have a mint filling inside of them," she said hanging over his shoulder.

"Well if they taste half as good as they look I know that I won't be able to stop eating them." She reached in retrieving one for herself and settled back. "Hey I thought you said they were for me?"

"You can't possibly eat them all." His lips curled into a smile. "Can't I have at least one?"

He closed the lid replying, "I guess." He placed the box on the table and walked over to the door.

"Where are you going?"

"Nowhere, I wanted to give you something." He picked up the brightly colored bag and hopped over the couch just missing Ana. She laughed as he settled down and said, "Here, I got you some stuff I saw while I was on vacation."

She smirked peeling her gift open. On the top of everything a vibrant colored material greeted her. She removed the garment from the lot to find a dress that wrapped around her neck. She placed it over her head to measure against her frame. "It's beautiful Luke."

"I thought you would like it. Keep looking there's more."

She removed her dress and reached in pulling out a box which held a tri-colored ring, a bracelet made of tiny stones and something wrapped in tissue paper. She unraveled the teal packaging when Luke remembered purchasing a tiny stuffed fish for the baby. Ana squeezed the animal between her fingers with her brow creased. "How cute," she whispered unintentionally, sitting back.

"I'm sorry Ana I forgot about that."

"It's okay." She placed the toy in the bag along with her other gifts and leaned over giving him a hug. "Thank you Luke. I loved everything. All of it," she said after kissing him on the cheek. "I'm going to put them in my room."

"No I'll do it," he urged tugging the bag from her grasp. He quickly moved down the hall and through the door to escape her view. He plucked the tiny fish out of the bag and tossed the plush in the trash. Knowing that Ana would notice what he had done, he swallowed the ill-fated gift in the wrapping paper. When he went back to her, he found Ana cleaning up the take out containers. He hoped that the forgotten gesture didn't affect her and judging by her silence he felt it was diverted. Well at least she wasn't crying. He helped her clean up, watching her silently move throughout the kitchen. He knew that silence. It was the same way he acted when he lost his mother. He remained numbingly quiet and then cried behind doors. He waited again for her to shed some tears but nothing came. She didn't even talk to him. When she was finished, she went back to the couch. He sat down beside her and shockingly she curled into his arms. To hold her in his arms wasn't awkward. She always seemed comfortable there but usually because he pulled her in them. They watched another movie and just as promised, Luke ate two of the cakes and set two aside for Ana but she hadn't finished the first one. She only licked away some of the frosting. Since the day he met her, he had never seen Ana eat the petite desert without a fork. He retrieved a utensil from the kitchen but still she didn't eat.

Ana had gotten up thinking that Luke was leaving so she headed for the door. He looked down at her taking her hand in his. "I hope you didn't think that I was going to leave you here all alone. I was just putting my keys in my jacket pocket."

"Luke I'm okay really. I don't want you to worry about me."

"It's not your choice. Besides tomorrow is the biggest shopping day of the year. I know you're not going to miss out on the occasion. You'll need me to carry bags."

"I think I'll pass this time." She croaked, still trying to show a brave face she smiled.

"I figured you would but at least I got you to smile." He returned her grin saying, "I'll sleep in the extra room if you want but I'm not going home."

"Okay, okay but if I hear you snoring you're out."

"I don't snore." Ana walked away looking over her shoulder. "Do I?"

***

Luke twirled in his blankets until he made out something that sounded like screeching through the walls. He opened his eyes scratching his chest quizzing the noise until he realized that the high-pitched noise was Ana crying. He tossed back his covers leaning on the bed, wondering if he should give her the space she kept asking for. Even if she wanted it, he couldn't do that to her. He crept from his bed and walked to her room slowly pushing the door open to find her curled on the bed. Once again her body trembled as she cried. He stepped over, lifted her blankets and climbed in behind her. He glanced over her shoulder and saw that she found the tiny fish he had thrown away.

"I'm so sorry Luke," she sobbed. "I didn't mean to wake you."

"You didn't," he replied pulling her over to him. "I had a feeling you would find that."

"Why did you throw it away?"

"I didn't want it to upset you any further."

"It, it doesn't. I just never knew that I could miss someone I never met." They were both silent with their thoughts. Luke listened to her sniffling but he couldn't take his mind off of what now plagued him.

***

Surely as the trees lost their leaves the calm air gained its chill. The holiday season didn't start out the way Ana had hoped for but Christmas was a day she couldn't spend lying in bed weeping. She had always tried to make the event a special occasion with Luke because he lost his mother two days before the celebrated day. Each year when the holiday approached, she could still tell that he wasn't completely over her absence. Every other year they spent it with Madison but not this one. Ana decided she would throw a Christmas Eve party.

She invited Fran, Max and Luke. Each of them was able to bring a guest. Ana's was going to be Torrance. She found him to be such a comfort to her since she lost the baby. Korina showed signs of sympathy as well, easing up on the errands she had her running. With so much free time she found herself thinking about who she lost. Before she smiled at the people she saw walking around happily as a family but now the sight of them only made her angry of what she could've had. Maybe a man wouldn't have been by her side but at least she would've held a baby in her arms.

Putting her thoughts aside, Ana walked out to the truck noticing that Torrance wasn't the cheerful chauffer as he normally was. She leaned forward looking at his glossy eyes and dry nose. "Oh no you're sick."

He peered over his shoulder at her with a remorseful glare. "Yes I am."

"Oh Torrance why are you here then. I could've gotten a cab. You should be in bed."

"I had to come since I wouldn't be able to attend your gathering tonight. I figured my gesture would go to waste if I didn't give these to you."

He reached over handing her a bouquet of flowers. She hadn't noticed them sitting in the passenger seat, wrapped in brown paper with a twisted rope tied in a bow around the arrangement. "Torrance they're beautiful, thank you."

"I thought they would look great as a centerpiece."

"They will." She took in a whiff of the white roses and lilies. "It's just horrible that you're sick." She placed them beside her saying, "I know for a fact that Korina is working at home today and it is Christmas Eve. I think that after you drop me off you should go home. There's no point in you coming back out again."

"No it's alright. Just sit back."

Ana eased back but she immediately pulled out her phone to text Korina. It didn't take long before they arrived or before she got word back from her. Torrance stopped in front of the house and unlocked the door. Ana leaned over saying, "I spoke to Korina and she says that you're done for the day."

"Ana I still need to take you home."

"No I will get a cab. You go home and get better. I'll need a ride on Wednesday." She gave him a light smile and opened the door scooting out. Settled, she held on saying, "Merry Christmas Torrance."

"Merry Christmas Ana."

***

The flowers Torrance had given her really did fit perfectly in the center of her table. She decorated the dining area with white linens and her tiny tree with blue and silver decorations. The windows nearby where covered in lights and crystal ornaments in the shape of snowflakes which hung from the curtain. She was expecting the rest of her guest at any time. She still wanted Torrance to see how much she appreciated the floral arrangement so she sent him a text with a photo of his gift. He quickly replied, in which she sent another hoping for his good health.

Not too long after Fran arrived early with a guy she met two months before. Rolland was a stockbroker who had seen her out for lunch one day and couldn't resist stopping. Like Ana she wasn't lucky in love but so far Rolland seemed like a good guy. He was tall and with Fran being equally towering they looked really nice together. Ana handed Fran the food to place on the table noticing how playful they were with each other. It reminded her of Madison and Peter when they first started dating. She walked over with the wine glasses setting them down right before the doorbell rang.

"Max," she jeered with her large smile. "Merry Christmas."

"Merry Christmas to you too," he replied kissing her on her cheek. Turning towards the young lady beside him he reached his arm around her shoulder and said," This is Nelly. Nelly this is the Amazing Ana."

"Nice to meet you Nelly," she greeted her, opening the door to let them inside.

"You too Ana. We brought this for you." She handed her a large bottle of wine in which Ana inspected with a smirk on her face.

Max noticed and said, "Technically it's for the guest. She doesn't drink."

"Hey you never know," she countered.

He turned shaking his head.

"Hey, um have you heard from Luke? I texted him hours ago and I still haven't gotten anything."

"No but I'm sure he'll be here soon."

***

Babycakes

The stores were closing early for the holiday but Luke still hadn't gotten a present for Ana. He had been trying to figure out the perfect gift for months even though she told him not to get her anything. Unable to make a decision, he found himself back at the jewelry store hovering over the same counter. Ever since they spent the night together he noticed that his thoughts were never clear when it came to her. He loved her but he couldn't be in love with her. He promised himself never to feel that way for anyone.

"So why are you here?"

Luke felt as though he was talking to himself but it was the same store clerk that assisted him before. He glanced over at him with his crooked smile. "Hello Winston, I was just looking for a gift."

"Ah the perfect Christmas gift for a perfect young lady."

"Yes well," he answered shaking his head, "I wasn't referring to rings. I was thinking…" his voice trailed off as he scanned the cases to find the right item. The clerk walked behind the counter following him until Luke stopped. "That's it," he said pointing to the keepsake.

"A charm?" he asked.

Luke looked down at the cupcake charm and the others surrounding it. "I'll get her a bracelet."

"For now," grinned the clerk.

"I'm not shopping for a ring because I'm not in a relationship."

"That's good to hear," Candace said tapping her nails on the counter.

"Candace what are you doing here?"

"I am picking up a Christmas gift for myself. What are you doing here?"

"I'm picking up a gift as well." Luke turned to Winston who gave him a weird glare. He shook his head slightly to make sure the clerk didn't say anything and began selecting charms.

"A gift for a girl. Do you have a daughter?"

"No I don't have any kids."

"Huh," she smiled. "So you're single, you don't have kids and you're a successful businessman. How is it that you're still single?"

"I'm single because I choose to be. That's it," he clarified for the now so annoying clerk as well.

"Are you sure?" he asked. "You don't want to add a heart. We have a wonderful selection-"

"No, that's it," he barked with a not so polite tone, handing him his card. "Will you wrap it as well?"

"Certainly sir."

He turned from the counter giving Candace his attention. "So you're buying a gift for yourself. No family to go to either?"

"No I plan on curling up on my couch with takeout if I'm able to find anything open."

"That's not a way to spend Christmas Eve."

"Really well what are your plans?"

"I'm going to a friend's house for dinner."

"Your receipt sir," said Winston sliding the slip on the glass towards Luke with one hand and handing him a pen with the other. He held out his purchase asking, "Are you sure you don't want to browse our collection of rings today Mr. Stokes? I can give you a really good deal."

"No, this will do. Have a Merry Christmas," he belted out annoyed. The clerk smiled nodding his head and walked away. Luke watched him leave when a thought came to mind. "Hey Constance."

"Candace."

"Yes Candace that's what I said isn't it?" She shook her head. "No well I'm sorry. Why don't you come with me to my friend's house? I have to stop by my place first and get changed but my driver can take you home later."

"That sounds wonderful." She wrapped her arm around his and he walked her out to his car.

When they got to his condo Candace came up with him to freshen up. Luke went upstairs and threw his keys on his dresser along with the bag he had gotten from the jewelry store. He walked into his closet to find something to wear however the longer he spent in the diming room he was beginning to regret inviting his guest. The evening ran from the crawling pace it seemed to take on earlier. Ana called him but he didn't answer out of guilt on their way there. He could've. *Why didn't I?* Nothing romantic was going on with him and Candace, still the regret lingered. He only made the suggestion to prove the clerk wrong. He unbuttoned his shirt and flipped off his shoes when he heard a tap on the door.

"I thought we could have a little fun before the party."

He turned and saw Candace standing behind him in her bra and panties. "We can't Candace. We're going to be late."

"Is this friend a good friend of yours?" she asked walking over to him. She pressed her lips against his and wrapped her arms around his neck.

He pulled away her ruby clutches answering, "She's my best friend."

"Then she'll understand."

***

Ana looked out the window almost wishing that the hanging crystal snowflakes were real. The thought of her unborn baby and its first Christmas crept into her mind giving her chills. It wouldn't have been until next year but being pregnant was the only gift she wanted, more than snowflakes.

She loved that season the most. Watching the snow fall on the trees and the lights twinkle along the houses were her favorite pastime upstate. But when Luke came into her life all she thought of was his loss and how he was handling it. She hardly ever visited her family for the holiday to make sure he had someone there for him. She didn't know where he could be but she was shocked that he still hadn't shown up. She took a sip of water and set the glass down when she felt a hand on top of hers.

Mr. Stokes had joined them for dinner which was something he almost never did. He, too, didn't like that time of year but over the last couple of years he had been changing. "Don't worry about him." He smirked rubbing his thumb against her skin. "You know Luke. He doesn't like this time of the year."

She placed her hand on top of his with a sigh. "I'm not worried. I was just wishing for snow."

"Are you crazy?" asked Max. "Dry sidewalks are a blessing, dry glasses on the other hand is a different story. Something else needs your attention Ana," Max said holding up his glass. "My glass has gone empty." She picked up the bottle of wine to pour more but he stood up from his seat picking up one of the empty goblets and served a glass of wine to Ana. "I know that you don't drink but this is your party and you're bringing your guest down. Here." He shoved the filled glass in her face.

"You're not bringing me down," said Leif with his deep brown eyes looking over at her. "The food was delicious and don't think I didn't see that red velvet cake in the kitchen. Wherever Luke is, he's missing a treat. Let's make a toast to Ana!" They all picked up their glasses and raised them towards her. "Ana you are a wonderful cook and hostess. I'm glad my son has you in his life. I never thought that when I sent him to be with his aunt, he would meet someone like you. You brought joy back into his life but I don't think you realize how much joy you bring to all of ours. Thank you Ana for being you."

"To the Amazing Ana!" Max shouted.

Ana shrieked in embarrassment but raised her glass clinging it with everyone else's. She sipped her wine and reached over hugging Luke's father. "Thank you Mr. Stokes."

"Enough with this Mr. Stokes. You're not twelve anymore. Call me Leif."

"Okay," she grinned.

Babycakes

"And be a dear. Cut me a slice of that cake."

Ana got up to serve the cake but Max grabbed her hand. "Ah ah ahh, you have to finish it." Ana laughed but Fran cosigned.

"Do it Ana, it's our gift to you. Break out of your shell and do different things," she urged her with the speed of her Latin tongue.

"Different things like succumbing to peer pressure?"

"Sure if you want to put my suggestion that way, now drink."

Tired of fighting it Ana guzzled the wine and held up the empty glass as her accomplishment. They all cheered, even Leif which shocked her. She was having fun and they were able to take her mind off of her worrisome thoughts but only for a moment. *Where was Luke?* She went to the kitchen to cut the cake when the doorbell rang. She eyed the door wanting to run to the wooden barrier. She was beginning to serve desert so Fran got the door.

"It's Luke," she shouted with cheer until she pulled on the doorknob for her tardy friend and saw not only him but his guest, Candace. It wasn't like him to be that late but she now understood why. She looked over her shoulder and moved to the side to let them in.

"Hello everyone. I'm sorry we're late." He scanned the room for Ana but she had already turned away. When he surveyed the space again he realized that his father was sitting at the head of the table.

Leif stood and closed his suit jacket as he walked over. "Hello son."

"Dad, I didn't know you were going to be here."

"Yes, Ana invited me but I was just about to head out." He leaned over the counter saying, "Ana can you wrap that up for me?"

"It's still early dad. Do you really have to go?"

"It's already Christmas Luke."

Luke glanced down at his watch and over to Candace. "Oh I'm sorry I guess we lost track of time."

Katrina Thompson

"I'm confused," whispered Nelly. "Isn't he with Ana?"

Max laughed. "No he's not."

"But the way his father talked-"

"Shhh, I want to hear this," he said quieting her.

Ana handed Leif the plate of cake and walked around the counter. "Thank you so much for coming."

"Thank you for inviting me," he replied throwing her a wink. He eyed Luke, quickly wiping his smile away. "I'll see you in the office tomorrow son."

Luke nodded his head and stepped aside for Leif to leave. He cleared his throat and closed the door behind him. "I really am sorry for missing dinner but I ran into a friend. This is Candace."

Fran studied Ana and then turned to Rolland who had a puzzled appearance on his face. The air in the room had turned stuffy. She could feel the tension and questions floating around them with no one brave enough to calm them. She stepped up to the plate and over to Luke's companion. She smiled saying, "Come on Candace there's still a lot of food left over. You'll just have to heat it up."

Luke followed Ana around the corner while she continued to cut slices of cake. He leaned against the counter and coiled his neck to turn from her sight. "Ana I didn't mean to be so late, honest."

"Luke," she sighed placing the knife in the sink. "It's okay alright. It's not that big of a deal."

"Then why is everyone making it out to be?"

"Luke your dad came to dinner and he never comes. It would've been nice if you were here to finally spend a holiday with him, with all of us."

"My father is fine. You guys are the ones that look like you lost your puppy or something."

"Are you trying to find some reason to not deal with today or something?"

"No honestly Ana…"

She placed her hand on his cheek looking into his eyes. "I know how hard this holiday can be for you but we can't let yet another be marred by loss." She, too, coiled away from him and closed the cake dish. He watched her shoulders collapse and her head sink. She faced him with a tired smile saying, "You have to be hungry. Why don't you go and get something to eat."

Luke felt like he had been punched in the stomach. He only thought to rid his mind of his own thoughts. However when he finally did, he had forgotten to think about her. He walked over to Ana, collecting her in his arms.

She hugged him back and noticed around his arm the curious Candace. "You should join your guest. I don't want her to get jealous."

He pulled away quickly confessing, "We're not serious."

"Really," she grinned. "You never date one girl more than once and you brought her here so she better mean something to you."

***

"We're going to head on out," Max told Ana placing his glass on the counter.

"Let me get your coats," she replied leaving the couch. She and Fran had been enjoying getting to know Nelly and Candace. They both seemed like very nice people.

Max held out his hand in protest. "It's okay. I'll get them."

He walked to the room and Luke followed. He closed the door behind him whispering, "Now that we're finally alone you have to tell me what happened before I got here?"

"Nothing happened. Your father looked like he was enjoying himself. When you came he decided to leave."

He took in a deep breath crossing his arms. "I guess I'll speak with him later but I smelled alcohol on Ana. Was she drinking?"

Max chuckled. "Yeah we got her to drink."

"Why would you make her do something she didn't want to do?"

"What? Are you serious? You always make her do stuff."

"No I don't."

"Really. This is coming from the guy who makes her act like his girlfriend or when you make her come out to the club knowing that it's not her scene."

"Max I ask her, I don't make her."

"What's the end game Luke? Let's be truthful here. You brought Candace, why? You know that Ana wants to be with you just as much as you want to be with her. Didn't you see her face when you walked in?"

"No I didn't and she doesn't want to be with me."

"Who asks their best friend to father their kids?"

"She only did that because I've ruined all other chances that she had," he replied turning from him.

"Well obviously she's not pregnant and she hasn't come to ask me for help which means that you two are still hooking up. It's not about a baby anymore."

"We're not sleeping together and she was pregnant." He unfolded his arms and walked over to him. "She lost the baby."

"Who lost a baby?" asked Fran walking into the room.

Max's eyes widened and Luke pulled her around the door. "Ana didn't tell you?"

"She knows too!" Max shouted pointing at her.

"Yes." He turned to him mouthing, "But not about me."

"You're telling me that Ana got pregnant and she didn't tell me, why?"

Luke let go of her arm and whispered, "Because she was only a couple of weeks along. We shouldn't be talking about this anyway. She doesn't want to have a baby anymore so this discussion is over."

"Wow I knew that you had the hot's for her but after bringing another girl to her house you don't have the right to boss us around," said Fran twirling her neck as she pointed at him.

Max threw his arms over his head, flailing his fingers as he shouted, "So you see it too, thank you."

"Listen we are all adults here and right now I feel like I'm in high school. Ana and I will always have a connection. We appreciate what we possess, you guys just don't understand." He reached over grabbing his and Candace's coats. "Oh and by the way this is my apartment so I can bring anyone that I want here. Excuse me."

Fran stepped aside allowing him to walk out of the room. He couldn't even look at Ana after what he said. She hadn't told Fran about the baby and she was apprised of her plan before him. He walked over to the door and was met by Candace. He held out her coat for her and could sense Ana walking over. His eyes slowly rolled up to hers which were just as bright and cheerful as always.

"I have something I wanted to give you before you left." She brought a tiny box from behind her back announcing her present with a twinkling voice, "Merry Christmas." Candace stood awkwardly by watching as he ripped off the wrapping paper and opened the lid to reveal a new black leather wallet. "I know that you're attached to the one your mom gave you but I thought it was time for a fresh start."

Ana was probably the only other person besides his father that knew why he still carried the battered money holder. It was the last gift he had gotten from his mother. It became very sentimental to him but at over 20 years-old the leather appeared ashen, the edges were frayed and the pockets worn out. He tucked her in his arms saying, "Thank you." When he turned, Max and Fran were right behind him with their guest eyeing them both. A crease formed in his brow that he tried to straighten but he was sure Ana had seen when he pulled away. Trying to play it off, he grabbed Candace's hand. "We should go."

Katrina Thompson

"Thanks for the lovely evening," Fran said wrapping her arm around Ana's neck.

"An amazing evening," Max shouted.

Ana laughed covering his mouth to quiet him. "The neighbors will hear you."

He hugged her and walked out of her apartment passing Luke on his way outside. He held the wallet in his hand and looked at Candace. She stepped over to him with a smile on her face and with something obviously on her mind. "It's late," she cooed stroking his chin with her finger. "Why don't I crash at your place?"

He took her hand and led her outside to his car that just pulled up. He opened the door before the driver got out and leaned inside. "Ana's going to need my help cleaning up. Richard will take you home."

"Wait," she said grabbing his arm. "Will I see you again?"

"Yeah sure I'll call you."

"Give me your phone."

"What?" he asked curiously.

"Give me your phone," she ordered holding out her hand. He handed her his cell and she began typing in information. "When you get a chance call me. I would love to see you again." She leaned over kissing him and slid inside to allow him to close the door.

He waited until the car drove away and pulled out his key to the apartment. *What was he going to say? What could he say?* He walked up the stairs and put in the second key to her door. Ana turned startled, bumping into the corner of the counter. She fell to the ground grabbing her knee.

"Ana are you okay?" he asked dropping everything on the floor.

"Yeah are you," she replied holding her leg. "Owe."

"I'm sorry I just felt so bad about leaving you to clean up so I came back to help."

"I don't need any help Luke. Go home."

"This is my apartment," he grinned.

"You know what I mean," she countered still rubbing her leg. "All I was going to do was load the washer anyway."

"Well now I will load since you can't walk."

"I can walk," she said standing up. "Really go home."

"I can't, my driver already left."

Ana shook her head and started collecting the dishes. "Was Candace okay with you coming back?"

"Yeah, Ana I told you we're not serious." He walked over rolling up his sleeves and turned on the water to rinse off the glasses. "Are you jealous?" he asked looking over his shoulder.

"No." She laughed. "I happen to know how women think," Ana admitted the obvious, blinking her eyes. "I wouldn't be too happy if my date put me in a car on Christmas when he should be with me."

He picked up the glasses from the counter and placed it on the rack replying, "I'm where I should be."

***

It was almost three o'clock in the morning before they finished cleaning. Since they started, Ana figured they should just complete the task. She went to the bathroom to get ready for bed and Luke settled in the spare room to pull out some pants to wear. He still hadn't talk to Ana about the real reason he had stayed behind. He took a seat on the bed and accidently sat on his coat. The box holding her bracelet poked his leg, reminding him that he hadn't even given her his gift. He stood up and began removing his clothes overhearing the sound of her moving about in the shower so he waited. He wore out the floor boards, waiting not so patiently but stayed in his room until she left the bathroom and climb into bed. Finally giving the wooden planks a rest, he wandered to her room and gently knocked on her door before he pushed it open.

"Are you still up Ana?" he whispered.

She turned on the dim light on the nightstand replying, "Not up, but I'm awake. Why?"

"I ah forgot to give you your gift."

She sat up protesting. "I told you not to get me anything."

"I told you the same and you did anyway."

"Touché."

He climbed on her bed handing her the box. She ripped through the paper and opened the lid, revealing the charm bracelet. She ran her fingers across the tiny trinkets smiling. "I love it!"

"I knew you would the moment I saw them." He pulled her hand down saying, "I got the snowflake to remind you that it was a Christmas present."

Ana grinned remembering her wish for them not so long ago.

"The cupcake, well I think you can figure that out. The daisy is for you of course."

"What's the angel for?" she asked curiously.

"That's for the baby. I thought that even though it's no longer with us, you should still have something to remember him or her by."

Tears welled in her eyes as she wrapped her arms around him. "Thank you Luke. I couldn't have ever imagined..."

"Imagined what?"

"You've changed Luke. You were always sweet, something that a lot of people don't get to see behind the starched business suits and your iron clad wit but this was very thoughtful."

She let him go and sat back on the bed, closing the box. She placed her gift on the nightstand and wiped her cheeks. "Are you sleeping in here tonight?" she asked.

"Sure," he answered pulling the covers beneath him.

Ana reached over to turn off the light before she slid down beside him. Settling into her blanket, she nestled her head on the pillow and flashed him a smile.

"Ana," he called out her name just as her eyes closed. "There's something I must confess." She opened them as he spoke though he was hard to see. "I never wanted a baby and sometimes... Losing the baby may have been my fault."

"Why would you think something like that Luke?" She sat up looking at him. "It wasn't your doing."

"I feel like because I didn't want a baby, it was taken from us."

"Us?" replied Ana clutching her chest.

"You, I ah meant you. I never really got over losing my mother or my father leaving me behind. Don't get me wrong. I loved the summers I spent upstate and the trips we went on but ever since my mom passed away I cringe at the thought of... Every time my father said goodbye I wondered if it was for the last time and when I left for Hawaii I told the baby goodbye."

"We all have to say goodbye at some point Luke. Some never get a chance to." She lied down on his chest saying, "You can't blame yourself for this or your father for sending you away. You both were trying to cope. Maybe he went about it the wrong way but you should've talk to him. You should confront him?"

"No."

"Why not?"

He studied the ceiling in silence.

She could sense his contempt of the idea. She sat up saying, "I get it now."

"Get what?"

"You hide behind work and all of those girls but deep down you don't want to get attached to anyone because you're afraid of losing them."

"No I'm not."

She leaned over stroking his hair. Even in the ill-lighting she admired the thick tendrils. The touch of her hands running against his scalp sent chills down his spin, with his eyes adjusting to the bare lighting in the room he was captured by her stare. "We don't keep secrets from each other, remember?"

"It's not a secret because it's not true."

"Whatever you say Luke." She continued to tousle his locks. "You don't have to feel like everyone is going to push you away or leave. Your father loves you. You have to realize that beneath his cover up, is the man you once knew. Promise me that you will at least talk to him about it. No matter what you're keeping from me, you and your dad need to discuss what's going on between you two." In the darkness he was silent. Ana stopped mid stroke, grabbing at the strands and tugged. "Promise me," she ordered.

"Okay, okay I promise," he chuckled. "That's called coercion you know?"

Ana ignored him, releasing the bundle. "Have I ever told you how much I like your hair?"

"No." He reached for her hand and pulled it down to his chest asking, "Is that why you asked me to have a baby with you and not Max?"

"How'd you guess?" she replied laughing.

He threw her back on the bed holding her arms above her head. She giggled until she heard Luke's voice. "Ana I want to ask you something and I need the absolute truth." He let go of her wrists though he stayed on top of her. "Have you ever had feelings for me?"

She smiled flashing her teeth which made him happy. "Yes," she answered. "But it was a while ago."

"When?"

"Why Luke?"

"Indulge me."

Ana blew off. "It was a little after you moved out of here. Mad said you were into me but you wouldn't admit it. She was so sure about your feelings that she bet her room on it. I don't know I guess with the thought of us being together I started looking at you as more than just a friend." Embarrassed she was happy that the lights were off. She sighed and continued saying, "Mad asked you one day when you didn't know that I was listening and long story short she really missed this room."

He lay down beside her remembering the conversation he had with Madison about Ana. He told her that she was crazy to think he liked her. Not someone quiet like Ana. He knew then that he didn't mean it. He wanted her to leave him alone about the issue but it all made sense. Madison was reluctant to release the larger room to Ana as her trophy. However now he understood the reason he thought she relished over her winnings. Locked away for days without joining them to do anything, she was upset.

Ana turned to her side looking at him. She propped her head on the pillow and asked, "What's wrong?"

"I remember."

"It's in the past," she said shrugging her shoulder as though she weren't hurt. "The good thing is that we didn't let a relationship ruin our friendship."

"You think that's a good thing?"

"Yeah, how many girls are able to be friends with guys for as long as we've been? That's why I was afraid to blur the lines but I could never think of anyone else to be the father of my baby. That is at this point in my life of course. Since I'm not married, I figured you would have to do." She laughed. "Goodnight Luke," she quickly wished him, leaning over to give him a kiss. She gave him a peck on his solemn grin and lied back down but Luke eased over returning the gesture. He ran his hand beneath her, holding her shoulder as he caressed his lips against hers. Shocked, Ana placed her hand on his chest. "Luke, stop," she said taking a deep swallow. "What are you doing?"

Void of an answer he began kissing her again. She started to protest once more but he took her hand in his intertwining their fingers and thrust his hips against hers. Everything inside of her wanted to stop yet her legs widened and her heals held him in place. She realized then that there was one thing holding her back, her heart.

Katrina Thompson

***

Waking up with Ana in his arms was not how he had planned his morning but he wouldn't change anything. All he wanted was some time alone with her, even if it was just to sleep by her side. He brushed the hair from her face gently scraping his fingertips across her cheekbone. She actually had feelings for him all of those years ago and he unknowingly broke her heart. Maybe Max was right and there could be something between them. He drifted back to sleep until his filled arms felt empty. He opened his eyes and realized that Ana was nowhere around but the smell of food permeated the room. He sat up wiping his face and ran his fingers through his hair before he hopped from bed and headed for the kitchen.

He found Ana standing at the stove scraping eggs on a plate. At the sound of his feet slapping against the floor she grinned. "Good afternoon Lucas, nice of you to join me when everything's done."

He looked around at the spread she set on the counter and sat down on one of the stools. The pancakes were piled on a single plate with butter which began to melt and trickle down the sides. The curled bacon appeared crisp and lean. And when she brought over the eggs, he noticed how light and fluffy they were, just as he liked them. "Wow it's a good thing I stayed over here last night."

Ana sat down beside Luke handing him a glass of orange juice. Nervously she pulled her hair around her ear. "About last night Luke," she sighed, "we can't do that again."

Dismayed he raked his attention from the food and stared at Ana. "I thought that we had a good time."

"I did, don't get me wrong. Last night was unbelievable but even if you don't want to be honest with yourself, I do. We're two different people who want two different things in life. I don't want to jeopardize our friendship with sex."

"I never wanted last night to be like that for you."

"Wait! Luke don't think I... I enjoyed our time together. It wasn't just sex for me."

"Then what was it?"

"Luke don't make me say it."

He turned his whole body towards her with his eyes wide and his heart thumping inside of his chest. "No I want you to say it."

"I know you don't want to admit it but Luke, you're not the only one afraid of losing someone. If we keep doing this that is exactly what will happen."

"It doesn't have to be that way Ana."

"You may be right but I can see how this," she emphasize with the wagging of her finger between them, "can cause us harm, even if you can't. And I for one don't want to take the risk. Luke," she said shaking her head, "I shouldn't have asked you to make a baby with me. I was lonely and to be honest envious of other peoples lives. I was wrong to try and get something before I was blessed with it. I wasn't raised that way." She shook her head. "Instead, I almost jeopardized one of the best things that ever happened to me. I should've been happy with the things I do have and don't want to lose." She placed her hand on his cheek and kissed his lips. "That means you."

***

Luke stayed with Ana the rest of the day but without an excuse to stay another night he went home. He finally gained the courage to tell Ana about his affections for her but she obviously didn't feel the same way. He decided to walk, though the cold wind whipped around him. As much as the chill should've numbed him, he didn't react to it. He felt frozen before he left her place. He wanted to be with her but what she said was the same way he thought of her. He didn't want to lose Ana and she didn't want to lose him. It really was what was for the best.

Katrina Thompson

***

With the kids being out of school Ana had to spend the most of her time at Korina's house with the girls. She was almost happy that they were out because she needed something to keep her mind off of what happened with Luke. Her love life had never been an eventful one. Her only real boyfriend was Greg. She started dating him in her sophomore year and thought that they would spend forever together. That was until her senior year. Greg had gotten a job offer in Boston and they began looking for places to stay but she noticed his swaying tendencies around finals. By the time she walked the stage their relationship had dwindled to only fond memories and failed dreams. He told her that he changed and without much detail, the decision to start a new life without her.

Ana was heartbroken but when Madison confessed how she thought Luke wanted to be more than friends, she figured Greg was taken out of the picture so that someone else could enter. That was almost twelve years-ago.

Without a steady date and trapped in the house with the kids, she didn't have to deal with Diana and her constant needs. She was stuck in the office with Korina. She had almost a whole floor dedicated to her designs but she still wanted to work from the office, keeping her eyes on everyone. No wonder her and Leif were such good friends. She loved her girls but being in the office also kept her focused on her work. Ana fought to keep Kailey away from the rooms of silk and tulle wishing that she might have a moment inside the enchanting space herself.

For the moment however, she would have to live in their world of make believe. They had their own play room on the second floor. The furniture was child size but she found the windowsills and walls of plush animal's great places for her to sit. She sketched several dress designs while watching Kailey and Korey find entertainment in playing their video games. It wasn't a hard job but sometimes she felt like she wasted her talent away. Unable to get her mind off of her pity party, she closed her book and went downstairs to make lunch for the girls when she got a text. It was from Luke. She hadn't heard from him since Christmas but New Years was on the way and he always threw a party. Just as she thought, he was sending her an invitation. Her bracelet clinked against the counter as she leaned over responding that she had to work. The Bryce's were attending a gathering that evening and she didn't know when she would be able to leave. She put the phone down and went to the fridge when she made out the sound of her cell buzzing.

"Hello," she answered.

"Ana what do you mean you can't come?"

"I have no choice. I'm watching the girls."

"Don't they realize it's New Year's Eve? No one works on New Year's Eve."

"I am and if I weren't you know where I would be." Ana usually went to church on New Year's Eve and would join his party shortly thereafter.

"I know but that doesn't make me stop asking you."

Ana reached down pulling out the zucchini from the fridge. She placed it on the counter replying, "Maybe I'll stop by for a little while after I leave the Bryce's? How does that sound?"

"That will work with me."

"I'll talk to you later Luke," she giggled shaking her head.

"Ana wait, what are you doing tonight?"

"I'm working. The Bryce's have a dinner date so they asked me to stay late."

"Okay well I'll see you at the party."

***

Breaking away from the honking horns and blaring street lights Torrance looked in the mirror at Ana. She seemed to be stuck watching them also. To break the ice he asked with enthusiasm, "What do you have planned for New Years?"

She flashed her hazel eyes planting them on his reflection in the mirror replying, "Unfortunately I have to work."

"Oh," he replied. "A buddy of mines was having a party and I was going to invite you to make up for what happened last week."

"That was nice of you but it's okay I understand." She grinned. "It's not your fault you got sick."

Ana returned her view to the lights of the cars that drove by. It wasn't long before she had gotten home. "See you on Monday," she said to him, thankful she had Saturday off. He turned in his seat to watch her leave so she gave him a final wave and hopped out of the truck. She had worked a twelve hour shift and was ready to wind down on her couch beneath her blankets. Being at home with the girls was fun but when video games didn't conquer Kailey's attention, she turned to Ana. She felt like her arms were going to collapse from so much flying. Then again it was good exercise. With trying to fit in her dress for her parent's anniversary party and Fashion Week looming, she was going to need her energy.

Korina hardly had anytime with the family between January and March. She kept Diana on her toes which meant that Ana had to be also. She enjoyed her job. It brought her even closer to the one thing she loved more than cooking. The colors, the fabrics, the flashes of the cameras, she craved it all. She almost loved Diana's incompetence because that meant she became a part of the life she so desired.

She unlocked her door noticing the sound of the TV and as she walked inside her nostrils perked at the smell of Chinese takeout. Luke must be here. She removed her shoes and took her things to her bedroom when she heard him in the bathroom. She dropped the items on the floor and rushed down the hall realizing that the sounds he made were because he was sick. She gently knocked saying, "Can I come in?" But Luke didn't answer. "Luke," she called.

"Yeah."

"Is it okay if I come in?" She peered down seeing the doorknob turn and stepped back to let him out however he sat down on the tiles. "Ah honey," she almost whispered looking at Luke's pale face and watery eyes. She pulled a cloth from the cabinet and rinsed it in the water. But before she could attend to him, he leaned over the toilet spewing out whatever he had eaten. Ana knelt down beside him and ran her fingers through his hair. When he finished he turned towards her with a bit of the retched food on the side of his mouth. She grinned in remorse wiping his face. "Are you okay?"

He shook his head. "I think it was the takeout."

"Where did you get it from?"

"Two Wong Fu's," he cringed.

She stood up dampening the cloth in the water. Luke flushed the toilet and sat on the lid. His face was still clammy so Ana wiped it again. "Do you think you're alright now?"

He hugged her around her waist and planted his cheeked against her stomach. "I hope the worst has passed me but my stomach is still upset."

She tossed the cloth in the sink and held on to him for a moment. "You'll probably feel better if you lie down." She grabbed his hand and led him to the guest room. He took off his shoes, shirt and pants while Ana pulled back the covers and put the garbage can near the bed. Luke lied down and Ana placed the blankets over him. "I'll be right back," she said before she escaped the room. She turned off the TV and collected the containers from the table to toss them away. She inspected the fridge for a bottle of water and noticed the other containers of takeout inside. He brought her something to eat as well but there was no way she was going to. She tossed those in the trash and went back to Luke. Placing the bottle of water on the nightstand she looked at him coiled on the bed and reached over putting her hand on his forehead to make sure he wasn't running a temperature. He took her hand in his as she sat down saying, "Do you want to go to the hospital?"

"No I'm okay but will you stay with me?"

"Of course. I wasn't going to leave."

With a grin on his face he closed his eyes and Ana stroked his hair. After she thought he had fallen asleep she reached over turning off the light and was about to stand when he held on to her hand. "Ana," he croaked with his scratchy voice.

She smiled and retrieved the bottle of water for him. "Here sit up and drink some of this." He let go of her hand and sat up to drink. "How do you feel?"

"I think I…" His face grew pale and eerie. She made out the rumbling sound coming from his stomach, churning the undesirable food. He threw the covers from his legs and raced to the bathroom.

Ana knew there was nothing she could do to help him but she still felt awful that he was going through it. She sat on the bed waiting for him to finish thinking that maybe she should call a cab to take him in. She pulled her phone from her pocket and began toiling through her numbers for cab companies when he returned. She shot up from her seat and bent down to pick up his clothes. "You should get dressed. I'm calling a cab to take us to the hospital."

"No Ana I'm okay. It will pass."

"You don't know that."

"No I don't," he said climbing in the bed. "But I do know that I'm not going to the hospital. Besides, I have a wonderful nurse right here." He reached out his hand and lightly yanked her down beside him. "I'm sorry that you got stuck taking care of me. You had a long day and this is probably the last thing you wanted to do."

"It's okay Luke. What are best friends for if they can't hold your hair when you're puking or tuck you into bed?" she crooned. Ana kissed him on his forehead and again reached over to turn off the light.

"Ana," he said in the darkness of the room, "Do you love me still?"

"Of course I do."

"Even with vomit breath?"

She laughed and leaned over kissing him again. "Even with vomit breath."

***

The next morning Luke woke to the sound of chirping birds and sunlight. He was able to sleep through the rest of the night without any more vomiting or diarrhea. He turned in the sheets thinking that Ana was beside him but when he sat up he noticed her sitting in the chair next to the window. She had to be tired because even though the shades were closed the sun streaked its morning light across her face and it wasn't fazing her. He got off of the bed and slid his arms beneath her carrying Ana to her room so that she could get some proper sleep.

Ana woke to her buzzing phone on the nightstand. "I'm late for work." She shrieked shooting up with her mind racing. She threw back her covers and grabbed her robe to go to the bathroom when the phone buzzed again and again alerting her of a phone call. She raced to the seemingly impatient caller answering, "Hello."

"Ana I've been trying to get a hold of you," said Korina. "The girls wanted round cakes with a side of peeps for breakfast but I have no idea what they are talking about. When you didn't answer I resorted to giving them cereal. Now they want fry sandwiches for lunch. Ana please tell me what on earth these children are talking about. I swear I don't know how you handle them without walking around with a book of their meanings."

Laughing Ana replied, "They wanted waffles with eggs for breakfast. And for lunch they were asking for cheeseburgers with fries on them. Korey likes to put her fries on her burger so she came up with the name. I'm so sorry. I really am trying to break them out of that. They possess such a wild imagination."

"Well when it comes to food they better stick to the common names or they're going to be eating cereal whenever you're not around. I'll let you go but in the future make sure you answer your phone."

"Yes Korina. I'm sorry." Ana allowed her to hang up as always, in case she had something else to add, and plopped down on her bed. She had just made headway with Korina in the fashion world and she took a step back for a few extra Z's. But luckily it wasn't a work day and she wasn't late. "Luke," she said slapping her hand against her mouth. She pushed her robe hanging on the back of the door to the side and pulled it open. Relief settled in her chest when she walked down the hall and saw him sitting on the couch with his feet propped up on the table watching TV. He was obviously okay so she went to the bathroom to take a shower. *I'm so tired.* She just remembered that she hadn't fallen asleep in her own bed so he must have put her in there. She finished with one last look in the mirror riddled with disappointment and went to the living room to Luke. He gave her a smile and patted the seat next to him to sit down. She scooted in next to him wrapping her arm around his stomach and rested her head on his chest. "Do you feel better?"

"That I do," he answered happy that she once again curled up beside him without him placing her there. "Here, I went and got you lunch. I figured you would be hungry."

"You left?"

"Yeah I thought it was the least I owed you for last night." She opened the bag laughing when she caught a glimpse of a burger and fries. Totally against her diet but since he had done her the favor she had to eat it. She only had about two more months to maintain her weight loss to look fabulous in her dress for the anniversary party. He squeezed at her waist asking, "What are you laughing at?"

"Oh nothing." She took a quick glance at him. "Did you eat?"

"No, I'm kind of afraid to at the moment but you go ahead."

"You need to also. I can make you something."

"No," he grinned. "You're off duty. I have my water and I'm doing fine."

"Nurses are always on duty when they see someone in need."

"Okay well then you're fired."

Ana shot up in shock. "You would fire me?"

"Yes you freak," he said pulling Ana back to her spot, "but I'll take care of you. I'll always take care of you."

Katrina Thompson

Chapter 6

Being in New York during New Years was always an exciting time. Everyone seemed happy to bring in the New Year however most took at least a moment to remember what happened in the past. With all of the good things going on in Ana's life she couldn't help but think of the baby who once was. She would've been about twelve weeks along now. Even though Luke had thrown away her calendar, she still kept track. She knew that counting the days for the baby to arrive was pointless but she found the time hard losing something else she wanted so badly. She looked down at her arm holding the bracelet Luke gave her as the charms twinkled along her wrist. It was wrapped around Korey and Kailey who had both fallen asleep even though they begged to stay up and watch the ball drop. Ana knew they wouldn't be able to last so she chose Korey's bed to cuddle up on and watch TV until the time came.

At the stroke of midnight Ana felt her phone buzzing on her leg. She didn't want to disturb the girls but when her cell buzzed again she thought it was a call. She reached down and saw a text from Torrance wishing her a Happy New Year. She slid her arm from beneath Kailey and quickly texted him back. Luke was always the first to send her wishes. It was such a surprise to have him text her to even say anything. She felt her phone vibrate again seeing a text from Fran and another from Mad but first she had to read the second text. It was Luke.

Happy New Year! He inscribed. *Hope to see you soon.*

Happy New Years to you too! I will try, Ana quickly replied. She had brought extra clothes just in case the

Bryce's got back early enough for her to attend. She finished texting her other friends and turned off the TV before she took Kailey off to bed.

She took a shower and got comfortable on the bed in the guest room she always used whenever she had to do an overnight stay at the house. She was looking forward to seeing her friends but if the Bryce's hadn't come home by 2 o'clock she wasn't going. However, as luck would have it they came home shortly before 1a.m. Ana was surprised but more so happy. With the girls asleep they had no problem with her leaving. She ran to the closet where her red dress and coat hung. She hadn't worn the ensemble since her thirtieth birthday. The dress was vibrant and sleek. She spent so much on them that she didn't want to ruin its appeal by wearing it so often. The tightly fit form curled along her body and fanned out at her thighs. The scarlet coat was made to compliment with a high collar and skirt which matched the dress. She paired it with her red bottom shoes, pleased that the snow had held up and was off.

When she got to his apartment she was excited to hear the party still raging on, though she was sad about Max's departure. Before she was even able to knock on the door he opened it with a red head clutched at his side.

"My Amazing Ana what took you so long?" he asked wrapping his free arm around her.

"I told you, I had to work," she reminded him, kissing Max on his cheek.

"Oh yeah I forgot. Well there's still a lot of people here as you can see and Fran's somewhere with Ronald."

"It's Rolland."

"Yeah, that's what I meant."

It was a good thing that his apartment was right around the corner otherwise she wouldn't let him go with his date. Who on the other hand also appeared to be a little out of it. Ana turned his face toward her asking, "Are you sure you can get home?"

"Oh Ana, you always worry. You have only one life to live. Seize the day."

"Okay," she said letting go but he pulled her back in.

"No Ana really." His eyes turned serious. He stood so closely that she could feel his alcohol induced breath against her skin. "Seize the day. You know what you want so go after him. Tell Luke I'll see him on Friday."

She smirked and kissed him again. "Get home safe okay?"

"Will do," he replied releasing her and turned to his date. "Our night is just beginning."

Ana watched them walk down the hall to the elevator before she went inside. The apartment was still pretty packed. Her eyes sifted through the crowd surveying the strands of moving hair and pumping fist in search of Fran or Luke.

"Over here Ana," shouted Fran dancing with Rolland. She walked over taking off her jacket. Fran's bluntly cut bob swayed to the beat of the music until she turned to give her a hug. "Happy New Year girly. Did you just get here?"

"Yeah and it looks like the party just started."

"Nah it started at ten and it's been poppin' ever since."

"Looks like it." She scanned the room again and asked, "Do you know where Luke is?"

"Um I haven't seen him for a while but will you be a doll and get me a drink?"

"No problem. Rolland do you want one too?"

"No thanks I'm done for the night."

Ana smiled and twirled on the floor heading for the drinks. She tossed her jacket on her arm and picked up a glass of wine for Fran still keeping her eyes open for Luke. She brought the drink over to Fran and decided to hang out with them until he popped up. Eventually he would find her, he always did. Only several songs later and mingling with the crowd he hadn't caught up with her. One of the other guests mentioned to her that she had seen him go upstairs. It wasn't like him to leave the first floor with all of those people at his place. Concerned she headed to his bedroom. After what he had been through over the weekend she was afraid that the queasiness hadn't gone away. She placed her coat on the rail and pushed his door open. She stepped one foot inside with the other paused by her findings. The man that she thought might be curled on the bathroom floor vomiting or lying down was doing so but with the enjoyment of a woman cradled on top of him. Ana stared, shocked and justified in not wanting to sleep in his bed. She stumbled out of the room so quickly that she almost forgot her belongings. Turning back, she grabbed for it making the bright bundle fall on the floor. So distraught she tumbled with the skirt of her dress flowing like a blooming wave. She held her leg, cringing from the scrape on her knee. The blood dripped down to her ankle as the pain radiated beneath her skin but the wound didn't stop her from getting up and running down the stairs. The crowd was still enjoying the party but she had had enough. Ana wove through Luke's bouncing guest and slipped out the door.

Why care? She wasn't the first and she wouldn't be the last. She wrapped her coat around her waist, neglecting the buttons as she walked in the cold wishing she hadn't seen what she saw. She not only witnessed his actions but quite often became a part of his shenanigans so she shouldn't be surprised. She wiped her nose and begged her feet to keep moving. The discomfort in her knee still plagued her. However, she would rather suffer an injury ten times worse to not have seen it. She picked up her pace sprinkling the ground with her silent tears. She had no reason to be upset. He didn't belong to her and he did nothing wrong. Maybe she was the one that had the problem. Maybe she was wrong. Maybe her feelings weren't something she could ignore.

***

Katrina Thompson

Weaving through the crowd Luke searched for Max. He tried to get Ana to come out for the evening but once again she had to work. He found him eyeing people in the crowd against the wall already sipping on a drink. When he spotted Luke he relinquished his spectator point to join him.

"Hey Lucas old boy," he poked his head over his shoulder, "where's Ana? I thought you two would be inseparable now."

"She had to work," he replied. He placed his glass to his lips to drink but Max's question made him curious. "Why would we be inseparable now?" With Max's silence he shouted, "Max!" He turned towards him. "Why would we be inseparable?"

"Oh come on you two are still playing this game. I swear I'm going to make a move soon." Luke's brow creased so harshly that he took the comment back. "It was a joke," he chuckled. "I just thought that after the New Year's party you guys finally worked things out."

"There's nothing to work out and besides she never came."

"Yes she did and she looked unbelievably…well I think you would know better than me. She had on this-"

"Max," he said grabbing his collar. "When, when was she there?"

"Luke man calm down. What's the problem?"

Luke swallowed his drink and shook his head. "It all makes since now. She'll reply to my texts but she won't answer the phone. She said she had to work but whenever Korina makes her work overnight she told me ahead of time. She must have seen me man."

"Seen you what?"

"You remember that girl that was hanging on me all night?" Max's eyes wandered, searching his thoughts until he recalled her and nodded. "Well after I went upstairs she followed me."

"Really Luke! Even in my drunken haze I think I finally got through to her. She was going to admit her feelings for you and you screwed it up."

"I didn't screw up anything. She already made her feelings perfectly clear."

"What did she say?"

"She doesn't want to ruin our friendship so it doesn't matter what either of us feel." He blew off and said, "If she saw me with that girl then perhaps it was for the best. This was her decision."

***

Luke knew that his suspicions where correct when Ana wanted to cancel movie night two weeks in a row. Frustrated and unwilling to give in, he went to her apartment anyway. He let himself in through the locked main door but when he got to hers he knocked. With no answer he rang the doorbell so that he didn't walk in on her. She might be upset and using his key probably wouldn't be the best idea. Just as the chime went silent the door cracked open.

"Luke," she whispered and licked her lips. "What are you doing here?"

"I came to see you." She opened the door and tucked her hand back beneath her blanket. Her face was flushed and her eyes appeared very tired. "You're sick."

"How perceptive," she grinned and plopped on the couch. "I told you that."

He ran his fingers through his hair and sat down beside her. "Yeah, you did." She wasn't lying. *Maybe she didn't catch me.*

She eyed Luke, waiting for him to say something but he only stared at the TV screen. "Well."

"Well what?"

Exhausted by her sleepless night and the lack of Luke's empty conversation she slid down on the chair.

Luke finally peeled his eyes away from the TV saying, "I think you're the only person I know that's totally into the Titanic but you don't like sailing."

She kept her eyes on the screen, trying to stay awake as she replied, "I like sailing, however I don't like getting sick."

"I remember when we were younger Mad had to beg you to turn the channel. You were the only kid I know that would rather watch the Discovery Channel than hang out with your friends."

She repositioned herself to look directly at him with conviction in her voice. "And I remember you telling me that it would all be a pile of metal at the bottom of the ocean by now."

He grinned sitting back. "You were right."

"So," she sighed clearing her throat.

"So what?"

She closed her eyes and laid her head down. Popping back up she said with annoyance, "Luke I'm sure that you didn't come over to watch the movie because you never want to even though you know it's my favorite so what do you want?"

"I just wanted to make sure you were okay."

"I'm tired and I-"

"Well you took care of me when I was sick so I'll take care of you."

"Luke you don't have to. I don't want you to catch whatever I have."

"Then we'll have to get you better. Did you eat already?"

"Yes," she replied almost afraid to eat but did. "Torrance brought me some chicken noodle soup."

Torrance. Fixing his face he looked at the bottle on coffee table saying, "I see that you're drinking water. Did you take some vitamin C or drink juice for-"

"Luke," she laughed. "I'm okay really. Technically I was on my way to bed anyway."

"Okay well then to bed we go." He picked up the remote turning off the TV and curled towards Ana with a large grin. He reached beneath her scooping her in his arms to carry to her room. When he turned on the lights he sucked his teeth in dismay. "Oh Ana you must be sick not to have made the bed this morning."

She chuckled covering her mouth with her blanket. "What, did you think that I was lying?"

"No," he lied. "I didn't think you were." He set her down on the bed. Ana pulled away her blanket and set it beside her before she lied down. Luke covered her with the comforter and gently tucked her in. "I'll go and get your water."

When Luke walked back into the room he noticed Ana fiddling with her phone to wake her in the morning. He took her cell. "Oh no, what are you doing?"

"I'm setting my alarm for work," she said licking her dry lips.

"You're not going to work."

"Yes I am. I have to get the girls off to school."

Luke climbed over her and slid the phone on her nightstand. He lied down next to her and tucked her into his chest. "Get some rest Ana."

Tired of fighting with him she tucked her face into her blankets and went to sleep. She was only asleep for a short time before being awakened by a wave of nausea. Luke was at her side, holding back the strands of hair which had fallen from her ponytail holder. As she tried to disregard the contents of the toilet she found her cowardliness as a way to cover the joy she held inside for having him there. She was even happier when she woke, still nestled against him.

He gazed down at her smiling. Her straight hair curled against her temple from their body heat or her temperature. He wasn't sure. Luke swept his finger across her brow. "Did you get enough sleep?"

She sat up wiping her face and asked, "What time is it?"

He glanced at his watch before he replied, "It's 7:22."

"You let me sleep too long." Groggy she tossed back the covers and attempted to rise only her limbs hung over the bed.

Luke laughed and pulled her back by her shoulders. "Lie down Ana or you might fall over."

She just might. Ana felt a little dizzy but didn't want to admit it. "Where's my phone? I have to call Korina."

"I already took care of it. She knows you're not coming and the girls are set for school. You need more rest."

"But what about you? Don't you have to go to work?"

"Don't worry about me Ana." He kissed her on her cheek and pulled the blankets over her. "Ana," he said ready to discuss the party but as her name left his mouth, he coward away.

"Yeah," she replied still waiting for his response.

"Nothing."

***

Just as soon as the holiday season was over, New York City geared up for fashion week. Ana prepared herself for the hustle and bustle of the catwalk but because of the new line, Korina had hired more employees. Ana's services in the fashion world were no longer needed. She was so excited about walking through the mist of the hairspray and watching every detail of the makeup applied to the models faces. She wanted to hear the squeak of the wheels on the racks filled with the beautiful garments they brought in to be shown. And even the click of the camera flashes as the photographers captured every moment. They never wanted one of her but she always imagined that one day she would be at the end of the runway opening her arms for applause and her work displayed on women almost two feet taller than herself. There was no need to complain. To work in the world of fashion may have been her dream but it wasn't her reality. Besides, at least she was able to come as close as she did. She wasn't there with Korina when her career began, though seeing how her bridal line came to life, Ana could never forget. For now she would have to sit deeper in the shadows of the Bryce's home to provide assistance whenever someone left something behind or needed to pick up some of the gowns. Before that was her job.

Reality forced her mind to once again go back to what she was actually hired for, taking care of the girls. Ana had gone to stay with the Bryce's just before fashion week began. The girl's schools were letting out for spring break the following week and then Korina was off to Milan and Paris. She had hoped that one day they would all get to go but with school and the girl's weekend classes they were stuck in the states.

Ana didn't mind being there with them especially because they managed to keep her thoughts off of other things. Though her leg had healed, she couldn't forget what she had seen. She knew the kind of man Luke was so she shouldn't be surprised that he slept with someone else but to witness their rendezvous confirmed it. She was almost happy to be sick the last time she saw him. At least with her blanket she was able to hide her face. Now because of her job she hardly ever did. She missed him but the time apart was greatly appreciated. As much as the separation hurt, she realized that a relationship between them would never work. There would always be some girl in his past that could come back to annoy them and she couldn't forget the fact that she would never fit in with his family. They were like Stepford wives, blond and perfect. She would question whether or not Luke was a part of the family if it wasn't for his father's dark features and him being perfect.

Unfortunately with everything she tried to block out of her mind and his exclusion from her own personal life, he still found a way back in. Her birthday had come around again and with the sound of the Bryce's doorbell, she knew who it was. She left Kailey in her room and went down to the foyer. Luke's smile froze her steps when she pealed the door open. The light seemed to change around him. The sun crawled from the sky, yet the purple and pink hues collected behind him like a portrait of a Greek god. She had to escape her thoughts and replace them with the one thing that would recoil her. Trying to play off her infatuation she masked her face with a fictitious smile. "Luke, what are you doing here?" she asked.

"I know that you're getting older but even you couldn't have forgotten your birthday."

"I'm trying and failing to forget a lot of things," she replied bashfully. As much as she didn't like the memory of him with the other girl the image was helping. "What's all of this?" she asked looking at the bags in his hand and the large box displayed on the other.

"This is your birthday dinner celebration. It's a little low key for my taste but since you're stuck on kid duty I thought pizza would be a good choice."

"Cheesy bread!" shouted Kailey running into the foyer hugging Ana's leg.

Ana laughed picking her up. "I guess it was a good idea." She looked at her saying, "It's pizza remember Kailey?" She nodded and Ana flashed her eyes at Luke. She noticed a weird expression on his face but she was trying to ignore direct eye contact with him as well. "Um Kailey, you remember Luke right?"

"Yes," she replied wrapping her arms around Ana's neck. "Can we eat now?"

"Wow I didn't know you were hungry."

She placed her hands on Ana's cheek keeping her face locked on hers saying, "You didn't ask."

"Good one," she said plucking her from her hip. "Go wash your hands and tell Korey to come down and eat okay."

Kailey nodded and went running back upstairs.

Ana turned to Luke taking the pizza from him. "You really didn't have to do this."

"Yes I did. One of these days you're going to have to stop protesting every little thing I do for you."

Babycakes

She glanced over at him with a crooked smile. "I only say it because you do too much. I could never repay you for everything you've done for me over the years."

"And here I thought this wasn't enough. Remind me when I finally buy our house together that a ranch will do."

"A ranch, are you insane. Can't you tell that I've grown accustom to at least five levels," she said throwing her hand in the air, "and I won't take anything less."

"I'll keep that in mind."

***

Bringing pizza was definitely a good choice. Korey had eaten three slices alone but she managed to keep enough room for desert. Luke had brought cupcakes and movies to help wind them down before bed. He passed one out to each of them but before the girls tore into theirs he cautioned them to stop. "It's Ms. Ana's birthday. We have to sing Happy Birthday to her." Ana cocked her head to the side smiling. He reached into his pocket pulling out a single candle. "I hope you didn't think you were going to get away with not making a wish?"

Ana grinned, tousling her hair. "I guess I did."

He placed the tiny white candle in the center of her cake and reached back into his pocket retrieving a lighter. "Are you ready girls? I don't want to light it too early and let wax melt all over."

"We're ready," answered Korey.

He leaned over lighting her candle and the girls began singing. Ana looked down at Kailey who sat beside her with pizza sauce on the corner of her mouth. Across the table Korey was wailing the ballad next to Luke. It was nice having them all there for her birthday even though she didn't want to celebrate after her thirtieth. The idea of getting older was not something she enjoyed but Luke always made sure she did. Last year she had to work however Luke convinced the Bryce's to give Ana the night off so that he could throw a dinner party at his house for her. He didn't stop there. For her gift he got her a pair of diamond earrings.

When they finished singing, Ana took her queue in the festivities blowing out the candle. Kailey wrapped her arms around her and she leaned over kissing her forehead. "Hurry and eat your cupcake so that you guys can start the movie." She pulled the candle from her desert looking over at Luke. "Thanks for everything."

"It was my pleasure." He picked up the half eaten desert dissecting the pastry with his eyes. "I wish these were yours. They're so much better."

Ana grinned and got up to get a fork to taste her birthday treat. It wasn't bad but she had better. Before she could finish, Korey devoured her treat and reached over for the movies. "You'll only have enough time to watch one so make sure it's something you really want to see."

"But what about what I want to watch Ms. Ana?" asked Kailey with frosting overtaking the sauce around her mouth.

Ana retrieved a napkin and wiped her face. "I'm sure Luke will let us keep it until you watch the other ones, right Luke?"

"Oh yes," he replied popping in the last of his cupcake.

"See. Now go upstairs and we'll join you in a minute." Ana followed Kailey with her admiration of her hopping off of the chair and ran after Korey. She reminded her so much of herself, running after her brothers. Luke stood up and began collecting there trash but Ana protested. "I can do that."

"No it's your birthday, I'll clean up," he replied taking the plate from her hand. She let him but she still had to wipe off the table so she went to the sink pulling the cloth from the cabinet underneath. She rinsed the cloth and wiped off the table when she heard Luke from behind asking, "So what did you wish for?"

"If I told you," she said walking back over to the sink, "it wouldn't come true."

"So they say."

She put the cloth beneath the sink and felt his hands reach around her hip twisting her. He sat her on the counter with a big grin. "Luke, what are you doing?"

"I am giving you your gift."

"My gift? I thought all of this was my gift," she laughed throwing her hand towards the table.

"Nope that was dinner. This," he said holding up a tiny box," is part one of your gift." He placed it in her hand saying, "Open it."

She pursed her lips and tugged the ribbon from the box. She set the tie aside and pulled off the lid revealing a fabric pouch which held a charm in the shape of the Eiffel Tower. "It's pretty," she cooed holding the trinket between her fingers.

He took the charm from her and clasped it on her bracelet. "Part two is a vacation." Knowing that she was going to say something in protest, he placed his hand over her mouth and dropped his grin. "Before you turn me down I'd like to start off by saying you owe me. My best friend stood me up on my birthday but here I am on hers eating cheesy bread and not so tasty cupcakes." Ana's lips trembled with laughter behind his fingers. "Not to mention I will end my evening watching a child's movie. Need I say more?" He began moving his hand when her head nodded to still deny his gift. Earlier that day he had gone back to the jewelry store hovering over the same counter when the sales clerk came over.

"Do you ever have a day off?" he asked Winston.

"No I don't because I'm waiting for the day where you finally purchase one of these," he replied stretching out his arms over the glass case which held engagement rings. "That is unless you have changed your mind and you've decided to run off with the blond."

"Do you talk to all of your customer's this way?"

"No just you. I sense that there's something you want but you can't decide. Since you're still looking, I'll be over here if you need me," he pointed as he walked away.

"Wait I do know what I want. I want this," he said pointing to the charm.

"So you say. Would you like this one wrapped as well?"

"A bow will be fine for this one. Nice and simple."

"Yes she probably is a nice, simple type of girl."

He pulled out his wallet replying, "She is."

With words forming upon her lips, he placed his fingers back over her mouth saying, "I see that you're going to need more convincing so I will tell you why I got the Eiffel Tower. I want to take you there. I want to take you to the stores just like you ogle on TV. I want to buy you clothes like you wish you could've designed." When he perceived the questionable look in her eyes he took in a deep breath and stopped. The words were forming in his thoughts. *I love you Ana. I always have.* If he even uttered the words she might turn him down and that he couldn't bear. He licked his lips and with a nervous grin he continued. "As much as I would like to do for you, you won't let me. This is one of those things that is not negotiable."

When he moved his hand away this time he was greeted with a smile. She wrapped her arms around his neck whispering in his ear, "I don't deserve you."

He stepped back. Her face was no more than inch from his. He wanted to kiss her but he knew that she wouldn't want him to. He fought the urge and held her cheek in his hand saying, "You're right." You deserve more.

Chapter 7

Fresh from her stay at the Bryce's house for almost five weeks, Luke and Max insisted that Ana come out with them. She wanted to go home after hardly spending any time there but of course they convinced her to go. The bright lights and loud music brought her back to the moments she desired to experience at the fashion shows, the clothes on the other hand were not to be desired. She moved on from her misfortune and followed in between Max and Luke. Fran was invited as well but she and Rolland had other plans. However Ana was used to being the only girl. She clung to their side for a portion of the night hearing the stories about the things she missed until she went into the crowd heading for the restroom.

She filtered through the dark yet florescent lit club, stepping back and twirling to bypass the wavering patrons. It wasn't a long walk there but going back, sifting through the colorful stream of moving bodies she wondered if she should just stop and dance. Before she could decide, she felt an arm reach around her waist, turning her.

"Torrance!"

"Hey Ana."

She hugged his neck shouting over the music. "I thought you were one of my friends. How are you?"

"I'm good. I didn't know you came out to places like this."

"Yeah my friends make me but I still have a pretty good time."

"It looks like it." He took her hand, twirling her and began dancing.

Katrina Thompson

Max raised his arm holding up his drink while he sifted through the crowd to find Luke. Out of the corner of his eye he caught a glimpse of Ana's pink dress and her new dancing partner. He grinned and shook his head advancing toward Luke. He lowered his arm and stood beside him, looking at the energized people.

Gazing through the hopping bodies Luke leaned over asking, "Have you seen Ana?"

Max peered over to him replying, "Funny you should say that."

"Why is that funny?"

"Because I did just see her dancing with some dude. He looked familiar."

Luke arched his head trying to see over the bobbing heads but it was useless. "Ah well good for her." He took a sip of his drink and then another, guzzling down the remaining contents of his glass. "It's kind of lame in here tonight. Maybe we should call it quits."

"You're right, there aren't any good catches out there but we should let Ana have some fun. She's been cooped up for weeks. Unless you don't like who she's having fun with."

"I don't know what you're getting at."

Almost as if she had heard her name, Ana came over holding the hand of someone who looked very familiar to Luke.

"Hey guys, this is Torrance. Torrance, this is my friend Maximus, but we call him Max and you remember Luke right?"

"Torrance," said Luke shooting out his palm to shake so that he could release it from Ana's. "Nice to see you."

"You too my man." He shook his hand and Max's as well.

"You're Korina's driver right?" asked Luke.

"Yeah, she finally gave us both some time off I guess," he laughed looking down at Ana and took her hand back. He whispered something in her ear with the envious glare of Luke and shockingly Max before he walked away.

"Where's he going?" asked Max over the blaring music.

"To get a drink," answered Ana.

Luke relaxed his upset composure and wrapped his arm around her neck. "Max and I were thinking about heading out. Are you ready?"

"So soon," she replied curious. She stepped away, eyeing them both. "Are you okay? I mean usually you don't like leaving this early."

"Yeah I'm, we're fine. I just don't see a lot of potential tonight."

Ana turned as though she was looking for Torrance but he came back on her other side and touched her arm. "I got you a drink."

"Oh Ana doesn't drink," announced Luke as if someone was asking.

"I know," laughed Torrance. "It's Sprite."

Ana smiled shaking her head and swallowed some of it before she felt his hand around hers. "Are you ready to go back out?"

She set her glass down and let him lead the way without taking another glance towards the guys. Max noticed and awaited Luke's response, although his eyes hadn't wavered from the spot that she disappeared into the crowd.

"I don't understand why you torture yourself this way."

"What did you say?"

"Why are you doing this to yourself? You're obviously in love with her otherwise you wouldn't be plotting Torrance's demise."

"You don't know what you're talking about and I'm not mad."

"I didn't say you were mad. I'm saying you're looking at him like you could kill him for messing with your girl. Just face it Luke. Ana's hot and if you're not going to be with her, someone else will."

"Is that what you think, that he has her? I can have her back at any moment."

"Oh yeah," he laughed. "Prove it." Luke took Max's drink swirling the contents around the glass with his eyes sifting throughout the room. "Um I was drinking that."

"I know you were and now, I am."

"What are you doing?"

"I'm waiting for the right moment and looking for someone."

"Who?"

"A girl I would hook up with."

"I think we've already established that there's only one of those here."

Luke swallowed Max's drink and turned to him. "I've already told you that she doesn't belong with me. I'm just proving a point."

Max threw up his hands and Luke was off. He followed behind him to see where he was going when he spotted a blond girl dancing with a rather buffed individual. He was ready to go though he wasn't prepared to be thrown out if they got in a fight. The last thing he wanted was to get into one. But instead of Luke going to the girl, he took a left turn towards Ana. They weren't dancing anymore but they still appeared to be having a good time. Max beamed with amusement. Unable to look away he stumbled on the packed floor until he found a spot against a wall to watch Luke's plan play out.

"Tasia," he said in her ear. "I need your help."

Ana arched her neck to catch Luke's request. "Now?" she questioned Luke.

"Yes. I can't shake this girl that's been bothering me all night."

"That's why you wanted to leave?"

"Yeah but I see that you want to hang out with your co-worker so…" he purposely called Torrance because he wasn't going to let him be titled anything else.

"Will you excuse me for a moment?" asked Ana turning to Torrance.

He nodded and Luke pulled her over to the dancing blond. Ana moved with the beat of the music, following his lead but between her sway she leaned back saying, "You know if you stop messing with these young minded, jealous girls we wouldn't have a problem."

"Well I can't have what I want so I'll make use of what's given."

"What are you talking about?"

"Nothing, come closer."

Before Ana could respond he took her head in his hand pulling her face next to his and began grinding his hips against hers. "Luke what are you doing?"

"Making her jealous." He kept his eyes on the blond girl and finally found a moment when she looked in their direction. Ana saw and wrapped her arm around his neck. Pleased that his plan had worked he had to get rid of one last annoyance. He whispered in her ear saying, "Kiss me."

Ana pulled away just enough to see him. "I can't."

"Why not? It's not like you haven't done it before."

"That's right I haven't. Not to make anyone jealous." She looked over where she left Torrance but couldn't find him. "Luke was this about making her jealous or Torrance?"

"Why would you think I would want to make him jealous? I didn't even know you guys were dating."

"That's because we're not."

"Okay then, so what's the problem?"

Ana hung her head embarrassed that she implied he was being cruel. "I'm sorry. I didn't mean to insinuate you being so malicious."

"It's okay I just thought it would help. This chick doesn't believe me when I say that I settled down."

Because you haven't and you probably never will. Ana turned, which he wished she hadn't but the girl bent over and began dancing more provocatively than before. Seeing this she whipped her hair around and landed her hazel stare on Luke. "I'll do it. Just let me know when."

Katrina Thompson

He kept his face pressed against the side of hers not caring when the blond was looking. His plan had worked and he'd hoped that Max was watching because he proved him wrong. He prematurely salivated in his victory, feeling his heart beat faster and his lips tremble. He placed them against her ear saying, "Kiss me Ana."

She ran her fingers through his hair and locked her lips on his. She had done the deed to help him but she almost felt guilty for displaying such an act of intimacy with Torrance nearby. They weren't dating however something about him was different from before. Yet, the touch of Luke's lips against hers couldn't be denied. He ran his hand down her back pressing her hips to his and coiled his fingers in her hair. Her fingers slipped beneath his jacket and held onto his belt unable to let go. The tone of the music changed but the slow melody didn't stop them. The rhythmic tune only enticed Ana and Luke.

Trying to catch her breath, Ana pulled away. *What am I doing?* She rolled her head to the side and turned to see if the girl was still looking. To her amazement their scheme worked. She was gone. Ana exhaled, releasing his belt buckle which she didn't realize she still clutched with a firm grip. Sheepishly she shied from looking at him saying, "I think it worked."

"Yeah," replied Luke. "I think it did."

***

Max stepped aside hanging on the door to let Ana out as she waved goodbye to Luke. She leaned over giving Max a kiss on the cheek and left. He watched her walk inside and looked in the car waiting for Luke. He held out his arm to guide his way but he didn't come. Annoyed he got back in the car and plopped in his seat. "Are you serious right now?"

"What is it now Max?" asked Luke focusing on nothing in particular out the window.

"Wait Richard," he said to the driver, "don't leave yet." He sat up looking over at Luke. "You two literally were one step away from filming an unforgettable porno out on the dance floor and you're asking me what is my problem. Kudos you proved it. She loves you and you love her. Stop with the façade and go up there and make as many babies she wants."

"You can drive Richard." He dropped his gaze from the window turning to his outraged friend with a twinge of guilt. "I may have proved my point but I tricked her into doing it."

"Oh you didn't see what I saw. Ana was feeling it."

"Well it didn't work, not on her or him."

"It didn't work on him because he didn't witness it. He slipped off into the bathroom shortly after you took her away. But I'm telling you man-"

"Max you don't have to say it alright. Yes, Ana is everything I could want or ever possibly need in a woman. I admit it but I can't be with her so let's end the discussion."

"If that's what you want I will. I will let my two best friends miss out on an unbelievable opportunity but only if you tell me why?"

"Why, Max? She deserves more. She wants more than what I can give her. She was right. I don't want to lose her and if I have to sit on the sidelines and watch her move on with her life then that's what I'll have to do."

"It's never worked for you before so I guess we'll see how it goes."

Luke sat back in his seat replying, "It will work this time."

***

Another busy week loomed on Ana but the more than likely restless period promised a joyful weekend. She purchased tickets to travel back home for her parents anniversary celebration. She planned to leave out Thursday right after work in order to handle the final preparations for the party. Luke was going as well, but he wasn't coming in until Friday evening. Happy to finally get away even though she returned to a place she had spent most of her life, she grabbed her bag and raced out of the building for her ride. As always, Torrance was outside waiting for her. He pulled up to the door and she hopped in.

"Good morning Torrance," she said cheerfully.

"Good morning. You're very bubbly today. I never pegged you for a morning person. What has you so happy?"

The truth was she never really liked getting up early but she found the mornings, the best time to work out since she often left work late. However, this morning was special. "Oh I was just thinking about this weekend," she answered.

"What's happening this weekend?"

"I'm going upstate for my parent's fiftieth wedding anniversary."

"Their fiftieth, wait how old are you?"

"Torrance don't you know never to ask a woman that?" she laughed crossing her legs.

"Yes," he said looking in his mirror, "I understand, but I'm curious."

She brushed her hair behind ear replying, "I recently turned thirty-three."

Torrance slammed on the break to stop from hitting someone in shock. Ana's bag fell on the floor tipping out its contents. "I'm so sorry."

Ana picked up the items in her purse replying, "It's okay." She peered upwards giving him a smile and made out the annoyance of the other drivers with their honking horns. She looked over her shoulder as if she would be able to see the traffic. He quickly focused back on the road driving.

"I ah, thought you were younger."

"Thanks, I get that a lot but it's a good thing I guess," she grinned.

"Yeah, really good." He glanced up to the mirror again moving his eyes back and forth as so not to hit anyone saying, "This past weekend was fun. I had no idea you could dance like that."

Babycakes

"Yeah my friends make sure I get a lot of practice. I didn't know you liked places like that, albeit I didn't picture you as someone who liked Broadway either."

"Let's just say my friends dragged me down there too, but I still had fun thanks to you," he chuckled.

"Have you ever gone to any of the shows?"

"I went to see Cats," she replied with a bit of embarrassment, aware of how long ago the show ended its run.

"Do you not like them or you just didn't have the time?"

"Time and companionship." She smirked. "I convinced my friend Mad to go with me but we never got around to seeing anything else and now that she's off living in Connecticut…you get the picture."

"What about Luke? You guys seem close."

"Ah we are but I know he doesn't like that stuff so I don't want to bother him with it."

"Well sounds to me like you need new friends."

"New friends?"

"I mean more friends. It can't hurt to have another."

"No I guess it doesn't," she replied looking at his reflection with a grin mimicking his.

***

Ana hadn't been home in over a year but everything seemed to be the same as when she left. The March air felt cool against her skin and the people, well she was still in New York. It didn't compare to visiting her relatives in the south. Her mother, Hannah and father, Gerald picked her up from the airport but she had to get right down to business to make sure everything was set up perfectly for the party on Saturday. Hannah, on the other hand had another idea. She forced her to go shopping for a dress before they went to buy groceries for the dinner Friday night. However her mother's inability to shop for herself was almost a good thing. Ana and her brothers planned the gathering so her parents were completely blind to their actions. The dresses chosen by her mother from her closet wouldn't have worked. They hired a minister to renew their parent's vows and the reception hall was decorated in the same pale yellow that they used for their first wedding. The event was going to be spectacular and more importantly the whole family finally had the chance to be together. Her three brother's Nathaniel, Jameson and Roman were going to be there with their wives and kids. Madison and Peter were coming with their children and Ana had invited Luke. There was no sense in him not being there when he was like family. Even Madison's parents were attending.

  The following evening Ana assisted her mother with cooking and as always, her brother's came just as Hannah made the finishing touches to their family dinner. Her eldest brother, Nathaniel was the first to arrive with his wife Jackie and their two kids. Roman the youngest of the brother's showed up next with his wife Latika and their four kids. The house, though rather large, seemed pack with all of them there. Her other brother Jameson wasn't coming until later with his wife Shakira and their three kids. They rearranged the furniture to make room for everyone but there were still more to come. Ana had to pick up Luke while Madison and her family were driving in late that evening. They decided to stay at a hotel but Luke took the opportunity to recapture his youth by staying with his aunt and uncle.

  Being with them brought back so many memories of her life at home. Her eldest brother with his tall stature always clung her to his hip beneath his arm. His other arm wasn't empty with Jackie at his side but he said there would forever be a place for Ana. He was so concerned about her and when their father wasn't being over protective he would be. For years he had asked her to come back home and work for the family business. Ana never wanted to study law. Two of her brother's did and one of their wives worked at the office before they got married. Her brother Jameson was a successful musician and they didn't force him to change careers but she could tell they weren't happy with her choices. Her father never stopped telling her.

After dinner Ana threw on her coat to head outside but her father stopped her before she went out the door.

"Where are you off to Annie?"

"I told you dad, I have to pick up Luke from the airport."

"Luke, did he come with your date?"

Blowing off Ana replied, "Okay so I don't have a date, thanks for reminding me. I don't want to be late dad."

He grabbed the door and ushered her outside. "I didn't inquire about your date," he eyed her, "or lack thereof, to be rude honey. I just thought you had finally found someone."

"It's okay dad. Hey you never know, maybe I'll find my one true love tomorrow before I leave."

"Or at the airport," he chuckled opening the door to her mother's Prius.

"See dad that's what I like, optimism."

He closed the door and she put the key in the ignition, revved up the engine and drove away. If it were only that easy to find a husband at the airport. She rode along the dark expressway with her empty finger perched in her eyesight as a constant reminder of her parent's disappointment. She needed something to make her take her mind off of the conversation. The radio didn't help with its unfamiliar songs. She felt as though she lost touch with everyone and everything, once again watching the world go by. At least Luke would join her soon. He was often the source of her joy. Her foot pressed on the gas to reach him sooner. The last time she saw him was on their awkward movie night. He wasn't his normal clingy self and she was almost happy that he kept his distance. If he held on a minute too long she wasn't sure if she would be able to let go. The kiss at the club may have been for show but his touch, his thievery felt so real. He didn't just steal her from

Katrina Thompson

Torrance, he stole her heart and Ana found reclaiming her stability difficult. She could no longer tell the difference.

She pulled into the airport, driving around the loop and met him at the curb with his bag in hand. She smiled at him but she failed to hold her glance in fear that she would never turn away. Was it desperation or loneliness plaguing her? Either way she had to let her depressing thoughts pass. Ana stepped out of the car meeting him at the trunk where he grabbed her in a hug.

"Welcome to Rochester," she said into his shoulder.

"Thanks."

"How was your flight?"

He let her go replying, "Boring but I'm certain the ride home will be much better."

"No doubt. I still can't believe I let you talk me into paying for a first class ticket."

"It's the only way to fly."

She grinned and walked around the car. "Come on, I'm sure you're probably hungry."

"Did you cook?"

"I helped," she answered getting in.

"Good enough."

***

Arriving to the house Ana wasn't shocked to find that almost everyone had left. The time was well after twelve o'clock and they had a busy day ahead. The lights painted the Morrison's windows also. They knew Luke was coming in late but Ana didn't want them to drive all the way to the airport. She unlocked her door turning to him. "So do you want me to wait for you to drop off your things or are you going in after you get something to eat?"

"I'll meet you over there. The last thing I want to do is keep them up after they allowed me stay as their guest." He leaned over kissing her. He wished his lips could rest in their place and run his hand through her hair but he let go. "I'll see you inside."

Ana brushed her lips coolly dropping her fingers so that he didn't notice her delight in his touch and nodded. She watched him get out before she cut off the engine and went inside. She was putting her key in the lock when Roman pulled the door open.

"Hey Ana, we were just heading out."

"Oh, okay. I'll see you guys tomorrow."

He peeked behind her at their mother's car and back to Ana. "I thought you were picking up Luke?"

"I did but he wanted to speak with his family before they went to bed."

"Got yah, well I guess we'll see him tomorrow as well." He kissed her on her cheek and let her inside. She waited until they left, waving goodbye and turned to close the door but Luke was right behind her.

"I thought you invited me over for dinner?' he joked.

"I did, I just... I didn't-," she laughed, shaking her head in embarrassment.

"Is that Speed Racer I hear?" a voice shouted from the dining room. Ana's brother Jameson had finally joined the gathering.

"That would be me," replied Luke walking over to the lengthy man who came out to greet him.

Ana looked on curiously as the two of them greeted. "Why is it you call him that again?"

Jameson wrapped his arms around her shoulders resting his chin on her head answering, "Because your friend here had gotten not one but two tickets driving my car."

Ana gasped, "Is that why you had me ask him to borrow his car?"

"Of course it is," answered Luke with a large grin on his face.

"Ah Ana you're so gullible. I don't know how you survive in New York."

"That would be because she doesn't do anything other than work or hang out with me."

"Thanks for backing me up there Luke," she said pushing her brother away. She looked down when she felt her phone buzzing in her coat pocket. She plucked the cell out to view the caller. "I have to take this but you remember where everything is Luke?"

He nodded and craned his neck to allow his eyes to follow as she walked upstairs, wondering who she was speaking with. Like a prickling notion he realized Jameson caught wind of his concerns so he quickly averted his focus on the kitchen. "The foods this way?" he asked pointing in its direction.

"Yes," belted out a stern voice. "But I know you're not going in there without saying hello first."

"No sir. Hello Mr. Bloom." He put out his hand to shake Ana's fathers when he pulled him in for a hug.

"How are you doing son?"

"I'm fine thank you." Mrs. Bloom came out behind him throwing her arms around Luke. "And Mrs. Bloom you're looking as beautiful as ever." She really was. Ana's grin appeared like her mother's whenever he complemented her. Both Bloom women were simple yet very complex by their amazing personalities.

"Oh hold on now Luke. You already have one of my girls. I will fight you to the death before you take the other."

Shocked he immediately denied his remark. "I don't…I mean I'm not with Ana. I just- We're just-"

"Calm down son, I only meant with you in New York. Speaking of which, I wanted to discuss something with you." He threw his arm off his shoulder and led him away from his wife.

Luke was used to being in a conference room battling out major business deals but holding his stance, having a one on one conversation with Ana's father always made him nervous. He was a lot like Leif. He was also a business man, owning his own lucrative law firm and yet, he made time out to be a father.

In a hushed tone he leaned in towards Luke with a question. "How's my girl doing down there?"

With unlike Luke behavior he shrugged his shoulders replying, "She's fine."

"Huh," grunted the man who's usually full of rebuttals.

This was beginning to be an awkward encounter. Luke's senses peaked. He straightened his back realizing he already stood as tall as possible. With his "boardroom stance" in play he noticed how a drop of sweat fell from his brow in retreat from his nerves and he started to feel uneasy. Against her father, none of the tools Leif taught him might work. He had to say something and quick. "Ana has a job she enjoys and she seems happy," he mentioned to lighten the discussion and possibly calm his stomach which coiled in anxiety.

"Happy, yes but this is my Annie we're talking about. I know my little girl is grown but she hasn't changed. Her happy face is the same as the unhappy one." He took a step back crossing his arms saying, "I'm grateful for your involvement in her life and for taking care of her, just as I asked but I know she's not. Her mother and I worry. I've raised three boys who have done well in their lives but they are boys. Ana's not getting any younger and I fear that the path she's taking is only going to leave her with a lonely life as someone's 'fetch it girl.'"

Luke was thrown off and appalled by her father's disregard for Ana's work. She was wonderful with the girls and her non-contractual duties for Diana certainly meant a lot to Korina, even if she never mentioned how much. He found himself blinking several times over to remove the distasteful glare from his eyes. "Mr. Bloom I understand how you might think she's not happy in New York but she is. She has other career goals," he responded, pleased with the words which left his lips verses what really lied within his thoughts.

"What other career goals?"

"It's not too late for her to be a designer or even a pastry chef," he blurted out to sell her father on her life choices.

"She's been up there for over ten years Luke. She's not going to become a designer and this is the first I'm hearing about being a chef. I think that the best place for her would be here at the firm and I need you to help convince her."

Luke's heart froze in his chest and his eyes filled with rage. She couldn't leave him. He lowered his chin to mask his fear, though he had to face him. Mr. Bloom wasn't someone you said no to but this was something he couldn't let happen and that he didn't agree with. He raised his head ready to brace himself for the inevitable showdown between him and Ana's father when she walked over.

"What are you two over here talking about?"

"We were talking about you of course," answered Luke amused by her timing.

"Oh?"

"Yes, I was wondering what happened to you. You don't want your guest to starve. Go and get him something to eat," ordered her father.

Ana grabbed Luke's hand and led him in the kitchen. An array of foods littered the countertops. Luke smelled the delightful scents at the door even though they had gone cold. The macaroni and cheese was crisp around the edges the way he liked it. The collard greens were sprinkled with pieces of smoked turkey and the yams were covered with marshmallows and walnuts exactly how Ana always made them. When he finally took his eyes off of the food, he saw her standing in front of him holding a plate.

"It looks as good as it tastes but you won't get to eat anything if you just stand there looking at it."

"Oh yeah I was just surprised at how much stuff is here."

"Then you don't remember our Sunday dinners."

He did. They came roaring back at the sound of her family's laughter but he had suppressed the memories. He always wished that his parents had joined them. He understood with remorse that his mother could never join them but it would've been nice if his father had. He took the plate from her and began fixing his food. He skipped dinner knowing they would have a feast prepared. Ana detailed her work and plans for the morning while his food warmed up in the microwave. Once heated she sat by his side, keeping him company while he devoured everything on his plate since she had already eaten. He wiped his mouth and stuck his fork into the piece of peach cobbler she scooped out for him. He watched the vanilla ice cream melt into the cracks of the crummy crust as he asked, "Are you happy being with me?"

"Being with you?" she asked bashful.

"I meant living in New York?"

"Of course, I love living in New York," she replied almost disappointed. "Why?"

"I don't know. I was just asking." He took a bite of his desert crunching on the sweet pastry and fruit. "This is delicious."

"I thought you would like it."

"You made this?" he inquired with enthusiasm, pointing his fork at the fruity desert. She smiled nodding her head. "You never cease to amaze me Ana."

She reached over running her fingers through his hair asking, "Why would you ask me about living in New York?"

Luke stopped mid-chew thinking that when he answered her earlier she believed him. He slowly finished chewing his food trying to conjure up a better one before replying, "Your family is so nice. It's going to be hard leaving on Sunday."

"Yeah they are, but having you there with me makes up for it."

***

Jumping out of bed Ana raced to the bathroom to take a shower. She had stayed up all night watching TV with

Katrina Thompson

Luke and her father until he left them alone. Ana thought it funny how he fell asleep before her. He never clunked out first. His hair, after being tousled by Ana, had fallen on his brow. She quietly giggled with the memory of watching him as he gently snored in front of the light from the television. Ana now she regretted her late night movie binge. She woke up late and quite tired. She still had to wash, blow dry and straighten her hair as well as stop by the florist before she went to the banquet hall. The party house did a portion of the decorating but the rest was left up to her and her sister-in-laws.

After she was done she packed up her clothes and swept her tendrils in a ponytail when she raced out of her house. After her father put the box of decorations in the car, he threw her mother's spare key inside her purse but she couldn't find them. She was searching for them on her way to the car when she noticed the one in the Morrison's yard. The black Cadillac roared at her with steam coming from the engine. She thought that maybe Madison and Peter left the kids at home and came on their own but when the window rolled down she stopped in her tracks.

"Need a lift," Luke wailed out from the driver's seat. He brandished a crocked smile and got out of the car to help Ana who began walking over with her hands full. "I figured it would be nice for your parents to show up in style." Her father's Navigator was going to transport them to the party but he wouldn't let Luke drive it after his track record and he was in charge of getting them to the celebration since Jameson got in late. He and his wife had enough on their plate so they asked Luke to be their chauffer.

He took the bundle out of her hands and walked over to the trunk, putting her things inside but Ana stood still, watching him at the door. "What are you doing?"

"Well I had nothing to do so I figured I'd go and help you set up. Don't worry I'll make sure I'm back here in time to pick up your parents."

She searched once more, finally finding the key. "There are some boxes I have to get out of the car. I'll be right back."

"They've already been taken care of. Your dad and I loaded them a little while ago."

"Oh," replied Ana tossing the key in her purse. Luke ogled Ana as she walked around his rental chariot with her ponytail flopping behind her. "This car is amazing."

"Not as amazing as you are."

"Max wouldn't like you using his line," Ana pointed out with a twinkle in her voice.

"It's not his anymore."

***

After they picked up the flowers from the florist Ana and Luke headed out to the party hall. It was built like a European castle with pointed roof tops and stoned walls. The high ceilings and artistry was perfect for their mother who had focused on her painting after the kids grew up. Roman and his wife picked the spot after they held their wedding there over fifteen years before and thought of the location. However it was Luke who was able to book the room at such short notice. He carried in the yellow lilies and foliage while Ana almost struggled with her things, refusing help. Her sister-in-laws weren't there yet so it would be up to her and Luke to get started. They walked through the long corridor into the banquet hall and were greeted by two large doors that opened inward. The ornate barriers welcomed guest to view the elaborate chandelier on the ceiling that lit the beautiful Persian rug. The tables were methodically placed around the room which had a wooden floor set in the center for dancing. As they walked in they both realize that with each step, they headed towards the makeshift altar on the far wall. The party house employees assisted them by decorating the stage with a podium on either side of a wall of fabric streaming down from the banner which read, *Happy 50th Wedding Anniversary.*

Ana turned to Luke with her eyes fluttering and her feet paused. Escaping their walk down the aisle she skidded over to one of the tables laying her dress across the back of a chair and her kit down, careful to avoid the place settings. The flatware gleamed beneath the lights and the linens were meticulously folded in the water glasses. All her family needed to do was to add the party favors, dueled framed photos of the couple on their wedding day with a recent photo in the same position.

"Um you can put those on the altar. Jackie's going to arrange them when she gets here." She turned trying to deny his glare and took her queue for an escape by traveling outside to retrieve some of the party supplies from the trunk. *So awkward.* She went back to the car pulling out one of the boxes when her phone began vibrating. Diana sent her a text about several of Korina's designs. She got to spend more time in the office than Ana but still she needed assistance. She quickly texted her back and saw Luke pulling away the box she had put down.

"Even on vacation I can't get from work," she joked.

Luke peered down at her asking, "Have you ever thought of doing something else other than being Korina's nanny, like possibly talking to her about bringing you on as one of her designers?"

"I thought about that. She's asked my opinion on several occasions which blew my mind every time. There was someone else in the room, someone who could've given her advice but she asked me." She paused in reverie. "I don't want to push the issue because I love the girls but, maybe, in time she'll see my potential and ask me."

"Why are you bringing it up?"

"I don't know it just seems like your talents can be used in other areas."

She smiled picking up another box. "Well for now I'll have to use them on decorating the room in there. Thanks for helping me."

"Anytime."

***

With the candles lit and flowers all in place Ana focused on getting ready for the party. Her family finally showed up to help her and Luke finish. Latika had called to inform her of their youngest daughter, Joy's upset stomach. Since she was going to pick up Shakira they were both running behind but they still managed to complete everything except she didn't get a chance to change before guest started to appear. While Luke had gone to get dressed and pick up the Blooms, Ana raced to grab her things and scurry to the restroom. She found a tan, floor length gown that curved her figure. All of her dieting had paid off. The glitter in the fabric twinkled and accented her chocolate skin displayed through the barely-there back with jewel-lined pockets, perfect for her phone. She wore her silken locks parted down the center and straight. She threw on some make-up and dashed out to Latika's car where she planned to store her things since Luke hadn't arrived but by the time she got outside he was pulling up. She tossed them in her trunk anyway and fixed her hair.

Latika looked at her with her lips curled and her arms folded. "Why are you so fidgety?"

"I'm not being fidgety." Ana shook from the cold and felt sick to her stomach but her nerves always got the best of her in stressful situations. She turned towards her grinning. "I just want everything to be perfect."

"It will be," she proclaimed hugging Ana at her shoulders.

Ana felt her cell buzzing away again and retrieved it from her side. Latika waited for her to finish and plucked the phone from her. She placed it back in Ana's pocket and glanced over at the car waiting for their parents to get out to scoled her. "Try and focus on having fun and worry about work on Monday."

Katrina Thompson

Her father exited first wearing his tuxedo and leaned over to help Hannah. She wore a long cream gown and the off-white coat Ana gifted to her when they were out on their shopping trip. Ana and Latika waved at them with glee marveling their appearance.

Ana leaned over saying, "I'm going to wait out here for Luke. Make sure they don't go inside." Latika nodded and went after them as they walked up to the door while Ana watched Luke park the car. She blew into her hands hoping he would hurry, wishing she brought along a jacket. The weather had been nice earlier in the day and with her track suit on she had totally forgotten about what she needed to wear later. Feeling a buzz at her hip she reached into her pocket and quickly replied to Korey's text.

Luke parked the car and turned to lock the door when he spotted Ana standing in the parking lot. He had seen her in dresses before but nothing like that. She was a vision of beauty as her hair swayed with the breeze and the fabric hit every curve of her body. "Down boy," he said to himself turning away as he was also demanded to his unwilling nether regions. *She's not for you or me.* "You can do this." He took in a deep breath and walked towards Ana with her aura drawing him closer. She had a certain radiance about her that he couldn't deny. Her beauty drew him to her ever since the first day they met. He had gone outside, unable to deal with being left behind at his family's house by his father. He sat at the curb sulking, wishing that his mother could come back even if it were only for one day. He wished that his father would also return but he didn't. He took him there and left the same day. Ana had been outside playing near the pond and saw Luke. She sat down beside him, a complete stranger and nudged his shoulder. He looked over ready to scold her but she was so pretty. Her hair was up in ponytails and her cheeks were just as chubby as they were now.

"It will all be better soon," she said to him with a squeaky voice.

"How can you say that when you don't know me?"

"But I do," she smiled. "Your Madison's cousin, Lucas, right? I'm really sorry about what happened to your mom."

"My mom," he said wiping his nose, "You knew her?"

"Yeah, she was really nice."

They both turned towards her house at the sound of her brother calling her inside. She got up brushing off her shorts. "I better go before I get into trouble. It was nice meeting you Lucas."

"Wait Anastasia, you can call me Luke," he shouted over his shoulder.

"Luke!" Ana called out to get his attention. With a large grin she hugged one arm at her stomach and waved with the other. "Come on Luke it's freezing out here."

He snapped out of his hypnotic state and unbuttoned his jacket to wrap around her. "What are you doing out here?"

"Waiting for you," she answered with her teeth chattering.

"Are you okay?"

"Yeah why do you ask?"

"Because you look like you were in a trance or something."

"I was marveling the gorgeous woman shaking in the middle of the parking lot."

"Thank you," she replied glancing over at him. "You don't look bad yourself."

"Ana!" shouted Nathaniel from the door.

Luke tightened his arm about her saying, "Seems like old times."

"What do you mean?" asked Ana.

"It reminds me of the first day we met."

Ana smiled hugging his jacket around her trying to recall the event. Unable to grasp the memory she just shook her head and walked inside. Her brothers were waiting for her along with her parents who appeared to be in complete shock of it all. They had already told them that they had planned a renewal of their vows. Her mother was still wiping the tears from her face.

Ana removed Luke's jacket from her shoulder and handed it to him. "You should take your seat now so that we can get started. Peter and Madison are sitting at the table on the right in the front."

He shrugged on his jacket and kissed her cheek. "See you inside."

Ana smirked and went over to her mother and sister-in-laws. Her father's law partner and best friend, Raymond also stood in the hall waiting to go inside. "So are you ready to take the big leap again mom?"

She hugged her arms around Ana replying, "Oh Ana I feel like I've leaped into heaven. I can't believe what you all have done for us."

"No big deal," she said hugging her once more. She felt her phone buzz and buzz however the messenger would have to wait. She could hear the reverend beginning the ceremony and her father followed by Raymond walked inside the room. "We're starting," she whispered with glee to her mother, grabbing her hand to lead her over to Shakira who held their flowers. Her brothers lined up with their wives and the music began. Ana's heart stuttered as though it was her getting married. She gave her mother's hand one last tight squeeze and stood behind Roman and Latika. She took in a deep breath and walked through the large doors. There were about sixty guests in attendance with all eyes on her. She tried to retain her composure though she was very nervous. She was comforted by the grin on her father's face but the fact still remained that she was alone. His friend probably wouldn't have even been in the wedding if she had someone to walk with.

Trying to forget her possible future of becoming a lonely spinster she stood in front of Jackie and looked towards the door. Her mother was standing with a bouquet of white lilies bunched together before her. Her smile was so big that Ana thought her rouged lips would become a permanent fixture. She walked forward as the guest stood. Like Ana, she couldn't take her eyes off of Gerald. While everyone watched, Hannah turned to face her husband. Ana focused on them as well however she noticed someone else in the distance. Luke was looking of course, making her feel awkward in her own skin. Startled by another buzz on her hip she returned her attention to her parent's ceremony.

***

After the wedding vowels which neither Hannah or Gerald had time to prepare were spoken for all to hear, the couple was saluted and the fabric which hung from the ceiling was pulled back behind the pedestals, revealing the head table set for two. Dinner was served shortly after with either a choice of salmon or stuffed chicken breast. The celebration was going just as they planned. The delicious food permeated the room like the Blooms home the night before and the music melted into a cornucopia of sounds from the last fifty years throughout the night. Everyone was enjoying themselves but poor Joy still wasn't feeling well and Ana could relate. She hadn't felt right all evening. She held Joy in her arms until Latika relieved her while the others talked or took advantage of the dance floor. They kept each other company until her father pulled her from the table, forcing her to dance.

"Were you trying to deny me the father daughter dance?" he asked swaying her across the linoleum.

"No I was just keeping Latika company. Besides dad, the father daughter dance is for the father and bride."

"Father of the bride. Now that's a nice title." He peered down at Ana saying, "I never should've asked Luke to look out for you. He's done too good a job."

"Dad," Ana replied with her voice escaping her. She had been so upset with Luke for what he did when her father told him to keep potential suitors away.

Katrina Thompson

"I never thought that I would be getting remarried today but I'm glad you were able to come. I missed my girl, my Annie. Have I ever told you how much we miss having you around? Seeing you on a computer is not the same as twirling you on the floor," he laughed. "Now that you're here it's had your mother and I thinking. Maybe you should move back home." Ana opened her mouth to protest but he continued. "You can stay in your old room while you work at the firm. If you want to go back to school we can help. Oh Annie," he said tucking her head under his chin, "you would love being here. I even have a young lawyer in mind that would be perfect for you. His name is Tryton Brinks. He's been with us for six years now and I think you two would be a good match. He planned on attending but he had a family emergency."

"Dad," she whispered as her tears began to sprinkle his arm.

"Yes Annie."

"May I be excused?"

He slowly released her but she couldn't face him. She wiped her eyes and funneled through the dancing guest. Luke was talking to Jameson but he perceived from her posture that she was upset. He too, excused himself and followed after her. When he got out to the hallway she was nowhere to be found so he went outside. He didn't see her there either. He figured that she had probably gone to the bathroom so he stood along the wall waiting for her. When she opened the door he could tell that she had been crying but she tried to hide it with one of her smiles.

Luke walked over taking her hand in his and pulled her around the corner. He planted her against the wall and leaned over coming eye to eye with Ana. "You don't have to put on a show with me. What got you so upset?"

"I really don't want to talk about it," she answered trying to hold back another rain storm.

"You can tell me anything, you know that."

She walked around him wiping her face. Her phone began buzzing again. She reached into her pocket and pulled out her cell to read the text from Korina. Luke took the annoyance from her. "You have been on that thing all night." He shoved it in his pocket saying, "Don't they know that you are on vacation?"

"You assume its work. How do you know it's not a friend or a boyfriend? Oh wait, I know, because my father made you keep them all away. My whole life," she cried, "he's controlled. I thought moving out of town would finally give me some independence but even now he's trying to tell me what to do."

Luke was stunned. Her father told him to watch out for her safety but keeping the guys away was his ploy. He pulled his hands from his pockets to come clean. "Ana I-"

"Luke no!" she shouted, cutting him off. He did the same thing to you that he did to my brothers. I was so upset with you because of what he did and now my mother is cosigning his plans. I can't take this anymore. Will you drive me home?"

"Ana no you can't leave." He grabbed her into his arms holding her tight. "We're celebrating your parents wedding anniversary despite what he said to you."

"I'm tired of being the screw up Luke. No matter how much money Korina pays me I will never be successful in his eyes. I'm the daughter that they tried repeatedly to have and not only am I not married but I have no children. I watch someone else's, work as their assistant and sometimes cook their meals, yet my career means nothing to him. I thought that if I stayed in Manhattan their opinion of me would change. Eventually I could come home and say to my father, I did it! Korina hired me on as a designer but still nothing."

He dodged a bullet with her father getting the heat on keeping potential suitors from her. However Ana was talented and her boss may be a family friend but she was blind not to see her abilities. Her lack of being more successful was not her fault. He made a sound in his throat almost like a grunt. "It's Korina's failure not to notice what a gem she has right in front of her."

Ana looked up at him with her eyes trembling in their sockets. "That's what all of the questions were about earlier. He got to you again." She snatched herself from his embrace but he grabbed her hand spinning her into his chest swaying. "Luke please let me go."

"No."

"Luke!"

"Ana dance with me. You haven't danced with me all night. If you want to go when we're done, then we'll consider this your last dance and I'll take you home."

Tired of fighting she gave in. His hand held her back steady and he clutched her hand in his. He hadn't realized it earlier but she was wearing a ring. She never wore rings. He tucked his chin in her shoulder asking, "Where did you get the ring?"

She turned her head avoiding his lips and leaned back. "I was in my mom's room while she decided what jewelry to wear with her dress. This was the ring that my father gave to her when they were dating and she felt I should have it."

"I was shocked. I thought you never liked wearing them."

"It's not that. I just took something literal my mom told me when I was a little girl." She grinned. "She said that fingers are like heads in which men lay crowns. But only one can rest upon this finger," she said wiggling the digit. "It's some superstitious thing about not wearing a ring on your wedding finger."

"Crown huh," he laughed. Ana smiled and lowered her head. Luke dropped his, resting his forehead against hers saying, "Is that why she named you after a Russian princess?"

"You know," she paused. "I don't know."

Luke licked his lips, rubbing his thumb along her bare back. He noticed the warm sensation overwhelming him as he held her in his arms. No matter what job she had, he was sure her place wasn't there. She took in a deep breath, allowing her anger to escape from her nostrils against Luke's. He noticed his palms go clammy but he couldn't release their position. *Do you feel the same way?* He wondered. But just as he built the courage to inquire, she rested her head on his shoulder.

"Thank you Luke for coming with me. I couldn't have ever done this without you."

He drew in her hand placing it on his other shoulder and kissed her neck. "You're welcome Anya."

***

The car ride home was spent in silence. Ana sat in the passenger seat while her parents were chauffeured in the rear. She hadn't said a word to her father since their dance. She had the eerie feeling that he eyed her the whole way.

Luke pulled up to the Bloom's door to let them out. Gerald escorted Hannah to the entrance and let her in before he returned to Ana saying, "Would you like some help bringing in your things?"

Still not wanting to speak with her father she turned barely looking at him and replied, "No thank you."

Luke reached over taking her hand. "Are you sure you're okay?"

She nodded and handed him his jacket before she grabbed her items from the trunk. She leaned in kissing him on the cheek. "We got an early flight and it's late. I'll see you in the morning." She turned and walked inside without looking back.

Since he was driving them to the airport and returning the car at the office located onsite, he parked the town car in their driveway and traveled to his aunt and uncle's house. They had already left and gone to bed before he got home but they gave him a spare key. He went upstairs into Madison's old room and threw his jacket on the desk chair. He scanned the room which no longer held the fluffy

Katrina Thompson

pink blankets and stuffed animals from Madison's childhood. Her parents turned her room into a guest room but her desk was still there. He remembered sitting in the seat, a different one from now, with a handwritten note to Ana. He decided to tell her how he felt after prom. He dodged Madison's many questions about what he had been writing while she lie with her legs up in the air on her bed, flipping through the channels. Luke fiddled with the note the remainder of the weekend until his uncle called him down to take him to the airport. He could hear Ana's voice mingled with Madison's at the bottom of the stairs to say goodbye. *What if she says no?* He couldn't face her ever again if she didn't want to be in a relationship. He refused to lose her so he immediately tore the note into shreds. As Luke walked down the stairs he spotted her chubby cheeks, bouncing with laughter over something, to him, it didn't matter. He wished his skin didn't blush from his emotions but he couldn't hide the joy he felt from seeing her.

    His fingers brushed along the wood thinking of how different things might have been. He never factored in the possibility of her saying, yes. He also never thought that the celebration would've turned out the way it did. Luke recalled Ana's excitement about the trip although now, all he pictured was her long, sad face. Both he and Ana eventually returned to the party but Ana just hid behind Joy, holding her for the rest of the night.

    He lay on the bed for some time until he grew restless. Curious he got up and went to the window to find Ana's light still on in her room. He considered going to check on her but Gerald never allowed any boys without the last name of Bloom upstairs. Seeing how she wanted to be alone, he dropped his gaze and noticed the kitchen light blaring through the shades. Ana had hardly eaten so she was probably grabbing a late night snack. He quickly turned off the lamp in his room and ran out the back of the house hoping he would catch her before she went to bed. He gently knocked and was shocked when Gerald came peeping out the window.

He unlocked the door with a smirk on his face. "I thought we told you goodnight," he questioned Luke, letting him in.

Luke closed the door behind him embarrassed. "I thought you were Ana."

"Well that's one person I've never been mistaken for. What brings you by at this might I say early hour?"

"I wanted to make sure she was okay."

"After I upset her or because she knows that I'm right?"

Luke walked over, putting his uneasy hands in his pockets. His temperature rose again, however this time in anger. "I understand that you don't feel she's made the best decisions in life but I assure you that she is happy."

"Okay," he replied topping his sandwich with a slice of bread. He cut it in half and pierced the cutting board with the knife. "Happy but not secure. My daughter is talented just like Jameson. Even as children I worried about them the most. Jameson was always the wild one but his energy turned him into a wonderful musician. Ana was all over the place though I tried to keep her grounded."

"By using her brothers to shield her from the world."

"Yes." He pulled the blade from the board and placed it in the dishwasher. "She's my only daughter. Excuse me for being a little protective but I see that you are too. Isn't that why you pay her bills?"

"You know about that?"

"Of course I do. She never borrows money from us yet she lives in an amazing apartment by herself and she's a nanny. She gave me access to her account when she was younger. I'm not sure if she forgot or maybe she doesn't care but I've kept an eye on her since. I've checked her bank records and see that she pays you only five hundred dollars for rent yet your father owns the building. Who else would pay for her utilities and let her stay there for so little."

"She's my friend. I would do anything for her."

Katrina Thompson

"Including coming all the way here to take her to prom."

"I only joined them because she and Mad were going stag. I went with her and Ana." Gerald took a bite out of his sandwich slowly chewing the mound as he eyed him. "Sir I hope you know that I would never do anything I thought would hurt her." He held out his hand pleading, "You and I both know that she would do anything to please you. Please, don't ask her to stay."

Gerald grabbed another bite and put his sandwich down. "That's my Annie. She's always trying to calm everyone's concerns or make everyone happy. I remember staying up late at night with her and Hannah. It was our little thing. The boys were sent to bed but if she wasn't sleepy, we would let her curl up on the couch with us. Often times we fell asleep before Annie and she'd tug on my ear saying, 'daddy you should go to bed.' Even when we took her out on Raymond's boat and she got sick, she was worried about my shoes she had ruined."

Luke laughed. "What is the deal with her and boats anyway?"

"No not boats, sunken ships. She's always had a thing for deep sea wrecks. I thought her fondness was due to her quest for hidden treasures or some childhood fantasy about mermaids. She used to be really into those too. I believe it's just about beautiful things which never reach their full potential." He kept his eyes on Luke as he walked around the counter. "After seeing you two together I can see that you also have an eye for beautiful things. Maybe you should check on her and make sure she's okay."

Luke ogled the doorway and spun to Gerald. "Upstairs?"

"Always following the rules. You're one of the good ones Luke." He took another bite and sat down turning his back to him. "Second door on the right."

Luke walked out of the room but he kept looking towards the kitchen to make sure Gerald's permission wasn't a hoax. When he was in the clear he went up the stairs that he had been forbidden to step foot upon since he was a child. The wooden steps creaked as he climbed one after the other towards her room. He softly knocked on the door so that her mother didn't hear.

Ana answered surprised. "Luke what are you doing here?"

"I wanted to make sure you were okay."

"I told you before that I was okay."

"And you were lying." He scanned the area with his brow creased. "What's with the bins?"

She had two large containers sitting in the center of the room with things already packed. She walked over placing the contents she held inside answering, "You've never been up here before. How did you get in?"

"Your father let me in. Now answer the question."

"My father," she laughed sitting down on the bed in disbelief. She shook her head saying, "Nathaniel's room was turned into a guest room and the other is used by my mother for painting. My room," she said looking around, "is just as I left it. They left everything the same, certain of my return." She picked up a teddy bear and walked over to the box placing the plush inside. "I couldn't sleep so I went up to the attic and got these down. I thought there's no way I'm staying or even coming back. This is no longer my home but the more I pack I feel like I'm just making room for my things. My dad offered me a whole new life in what seemed like minutes, a place to stay, a job, even a husband. Everything planned out when I've taken over ten years to figure it out. Look at me, I'm the same girl that was standing here as an eighteen year-old with her life ahead of her. I look in the mirror and even though the reflection hasn't really changed, I'm not that girl anymore. I'm losing time in New York Luke. I'm wasting my life away."

"No you're not. You have a career. You have people that love you and can see your potential."

"I've worked for Korina for years. It's now wishful thinking." Suddenly she realized that the phone that had been nagging her all night was nowhere in sight. She ran to her closet unzipping her bag to search.

"What are you doing?" he asked stepping over to the opened door.

"My phone, I need to find it."

He reached into his pocket and held out the device. "It's right here."

Ana blew off with sigh of relief. She thought for a moment that she left her cell at the banquet hall. Her thumb scrolled through the texts which weren't bad but when she checked the voicemail she became frazzled. "OMG," she said tossing the phone on her dresser.

"What is it?"

She dropped her head between her shoulders and tucked her hair behind her ear. "Korina's upset with me for not having my phone. I can't believe this happened again."

"It can't be that bad."

"You didn't hear her voice."

Luke ran his fingers through his hair and shook his head. "Then quit."

"What?"

"You feel like this job is going nowhere, quit. You feel that your father is right in thinking you need a change in your life, then change it but don't leave New York. You think you're so old that you can't even have the family that you've always wanted, then start now."

"Luke why are you-"

"Ana you know what you want so why let others dictate what you should do. What, to make them happy?" He stepped closer saying, "What will make you happy Ana?"

"I'm afraid that I don't know anymore," she whispered unable to project her voice.

He took another step pressing her body between him and the dresser. "Yes you do." He leaned over kissing her until she pushed him away.

"Luke," she said turning from him, clutching on to her furniture. "I can't...I can't take losing another baby or you."

"You could never lose me."

She looked at his reflection in the mirror and turned to further her argument but his lips stole her thoughts away. He clutched Ana by her waist and set her down on the empty dresser. Her legs wrapped around his body pulling him in for more. Willing to oblige, he took her over to the bed. He placed her down, unbuttoned his shirt and pulled off his tank returning to her embrace. He couldn't control himself. All he wanted was to be with her, to taste her, to make her happy. He pulled off her shorts with her panties, hearing something tear as she yanked her top over her head. She pressed her chest against his as he embraced her for another kiss. He felt her heart racing as quickly as his own, unaware of the person listening outside.

Hannah overheard the shifting furniture and woke. She went to Ana's door but Gerald hopped up the stairs and stopped her.

"What are you doing honey?"

"I heard noise coming from Ana's room so I wanted to check on her. She seemed upset earlier."

"Ana's fine. She had a guest stop by, that's all."

A guest. She placed her hand on the knob to enter when Gerald protested.

"Honey no, let her be. I think that we've intruded in her life long enough."

Chapter 8

Is this real? Ana was beside herself. She reveled in the touch of his breath caressing her skin. His body pressed against hers straightening out all of her unpleasant thoughts. Although somehow this time felt different. She kept her eyes closed in fear that if she looked at Luke all of her emotions would come flowing back and over take her.

He sensed something amiss with her. He kissed her ear and asked, "Do you want me to stop?"

"No, don't stop." She opened her eyes pleading with him. "Don't stop."

Luke smiled, kissing her so passionately that she couldn't deny her feelings any longer. Her fingers raked his back and her legs coiled around his urging him for more. Unable to control himself, Luke thrust his hips against hers until he could move no further. It was now Luke who fought with his feelings. He held the wooden headboard afraid to touch her. He thought that if he did, he would never let her go. His knuckles turned white from clinging on so tightly until he felt Ana's hand brush against his arm reaching for his hand. She laced her fingers in his and climbed on top.

If only. Ana released his hand, placing it on her breast as her body moved to the song she made with her retreating breath. Being with him was like living in a world they had created all on their own. A secret love that only they could possess but she knew that it was only so that her dreams could finally come true. He was doing it all for her. It wasn't just a small favor between friends. They were creating a life together. *Another life.* Fear rose in her chest at the thought of it not working. Losing her angel as she called the first baby was devastating. She couldn't bear losing another one of his children but Luke was right, creating a family was the only thing she really wanted. That is because her designing career was going nowhere and she could never have a real relationship with Luke.

He pulled her down, kissing her until he rolled over whispering in her ear, "Ana." He breathed so heavily that her hair blew against her pillow. "Ana," he said wanting to say what he really felt but he was speechless. How could he tell her how much he loved her? How could he tell her that he denied his feelings because deep down he didn't want to lose her either? What they were doing blurred the lines but they had taken things far beyond obscuring the meaning of their relationship. At the sign of his release, he rested on top of her, tucking his face into the pillow unable to see her.

He moved and his head nestled on her chest, Ana stroked his back until she couldn't bare the absence of his voice. She ran her fingers along his neck, coxing him to turn to her. When he did, she looked at him and kissed his nose with a timid smile. "Luke," she whispered and took in a deep breath. "I know that maybe you shouldn't but, will you stay with me tonight?"

Luke pecked her lips and smiled. He got up to turn off the lights before he rejoined her on the bed. She scooted over and curled at his side, resting her head on his chest. "I guess this means you will be coming back to New York?"

She stared up at him replying, "I don't know what I was thinking."

"You were hurt. You're parents want what they think is best for you." He placed his finger under her chin grabbing it between his thumb saying, "Just like I do."

Ana sat up, running her fingers through his hair. She leaned over to kiss him goodnight but he held her head in place. He rolled back on top of her and ran his palm down her neck. Resting his forehead on hers he whispered, "Ana you know that there's nothing I wouldn't do for you."

"I do," she replied placing her hand on his.

"I want you to be happy and...and-"

Katrina Thompson

She massaged his cheek with the soft skin of her knuckles to ease him. "Luke you're shaking." He kissed her again, claiming her as he buried the unspoken words in his mind. *If only*, she thought closing her eyes as she surrendered to him. For that moment he was.

***

The next morning neither of them had set the alarm clock, though somewhat unfortunate for Ana, who found it hard to sleep. She never saw Luke in such a raw form. When he spoke to her, she always listened but last night as they flowed from his lips, she almost felt them. Maybe his affections towards her did exist. Able to sense but unable to say the words, words like I love you. They said them before, although their confessions were on a more friendly level. She looked back at him sleeping peacefully and gently brushed the hair from his brow. Even with his eyes closed she hid her smile. Ana glanced over at the clock and noticed the late hour so she left him behind and went into the bathroom to take a shower. She combed her hair wrapping it around her fingers into a bun on the top of her head, pinning it in place. She reached behind the curtain, turned on the shower and put on her cap before stepping in. The water welcomingly caressed her skin, warming her after pulling off her blankets and walking on the wood floor. She ran the sponge along her body allowing the suds to trickle down when she endured the chill of cold air on her back.

"Luke!" she said, startled by his entry. "What are you doing in here?" she asked shying away.

"I figure we could kill two birds with one stone."

"Two?"

"Yeah, we can work on having the baby and take a shower." He plucked the sponge from her hands and lifted her hips before pressing her against the wall. Swallowing her lips with his, he pulled the curtain closed behind him.

***

Babycakes

Refreshed from their shower, Luke helped Ana take her boxes up to the attic and hurried next door to get ready for their flight. Ana finished packing and went downstairs trying to hide the enthusiasm in her face over what had happened. Her parents were still upstairs but she knew that her father was aware of Luke stopping by. Hopefully he wasn't aware of him staying last night. She yanked on the handle of the fridge and pulled out a container of juice when her phone went off. After the neglected messages, there was no way she was going to miss another text or call. She picked up her phone and read that Torrance wished her a safe trip home. *How sweet.* She texted him back and continued making her breakfast when Gerald entered the kitchen. She hadn't forgotten their discussion from the previous night however he did let Luke come upstairs. She reached in the cabinet she pulled out two glasses and poured grape juice in each of them. He walked over to her and graciously scooped the drink from Ana.

"Cheers," she said hitting his glass and took a sip.

"What are we cheering to?"

"A truce. We won't discuss last night and you'll be satisfied with my decisions."

He set his glass down without drinking. She knew that her temporary respite would be short-lived but she had to try. He took her glass from her and wrapped his long arms around her. "I think that we should discuss our conversation whether you like it or not. Annie," he sighed. "You know that I only said those things because I'm concerned about you. I have to confess something to you." He let her go and picked up his glass. "Have a seat with me." They walked over to the table and sat down. "Hannah and I never had to hide the fact that we gave your brother's more Leigh Ways in life. They were boys and in our family that's the way we brought up our household. For girls on the other hand, well they were kept as sacred as an extinct flower. 'A spoiled woman didn't make a good wife,' is what my father told me.

Katrina Thompson

Your mother and I thought since we were both raised that way, you should be also. When you turned eighteen we figured you would go off to school and make something of yourself. We thought the move to Boston with Greg could open endless possibilities. Everything seemed fine but then you let him go and got this babysitting job. It just caused us concern. That was so long ago honey."

"Dad I think first I should tell you that he dumped me and I didn't really want to go to Boston anyway. Most importantly I'm not a babysitter dad. I do a whole lot more. Who knows maybe I won't even be working for her in two, three years from now. There are so many possibilities in New York but the key words here are New York. I'm not moving back here. I already packed up the room so you guys can use the space for whatever you want."

"So that's what you were doing last night. Your mom heard furniture being moved about. The noise made us wonder."

Ana's eyes went wild and she dropped her stare knowing that definitely wasn't what caused the ruckus. She took a sip of her juice hoping that her father didn't see the look on her face.

"And this morning."

Ana choked and grabbed a napkin from the holder in the center of the table. She wiped her mouth ready to plead her case. "Dad what-"

"I'm referring to the attic honey," he pushed through his teeth but noticed his daughter still trying to compose herself. "Are you okay?"

"Yes, yes I'm fine," she answered sitting back in her chair.

"So I saw you and Luke last night."

Ana's heart began to race. How could she explain the situation to her father?

"After you hadn't returned to the party I went after you and found the two of you in the hall. Is there something I should know?"

Babycakes

Ana stood from her seat and took her glass over to the sink. "No dad. We're just friends."

"Very good friends."

"Dad, what are you trying to get at?"

"I'm just trying to figure out his intensions."

"There are none dad. We're just friends. He gets me and I, him." She leaned against the counter looking at her father. "I understand that you and mom don't agree with the decisions I make in life but I'm still trying to figure it out. Please give me time to do so?"

He walked over kissing her on her forehead. "All good treasures need to be hunted. I only hope that he won't wait too long before another sailor discovers it."

***

On the ride to the airport, Ana's often timid behavior around men appeared before Luke. He however, portrayed his normal self, making up conversation while she nervously gazed out the window. She was so happy that her parents were unaware of what transpired in her room last night but why would he think they were more than just friends. She turned from the blending trees when she felt Luke's hand land upon hers.

He brought it to his lips kissing the back of her hand. "Why are you so quiet?"

She smiled resting her head on the seat looking at him. "I spoke with my father about last night. He thought that the moving furniture was because I was packing up my room," she laughed. "Could you imagine if they found out what we did?"

Luke swallowed deeply. "Yes and on that note I think that I should update my will," he chuckled.

Ana rubbed his hand looking over at him. How silly their conversation. They were both adults yet both she and Luke feared her parents. Thinking of their previous conversation she asked, "Did you ever speak with your father?"

He quickly glanced over to her and back to the road. "No I haven't but I don't need to."

"Luke you promised."

"I know," he blew into the air. "Don't worry, I will, okay."

She may not worry about their relationship at the moment but the topic wasn't far from her thoughts. Nor was the idea of returning to the real world. Ana didn't want to say goodbye to "her Luke" but she knew that once they did, their secret world no longer existed.

***

The work week was looming and though she was able to smooth things over with Korina, she was still in the hot seat. Monday morning rolled around and no matter her exhaustion, Ana got up for work. Torrance was waiting outside for her as usual but today he held the door open for her.

"Good morning," she said with a curious glare.

"Good morning Ana." He clutched her hand and helped her inside.

She waited for him to settle in before she leaned forward asking, "What gives?"

"Oh I just got here early and thought that I would get the door for you."

"Huh," she said sitting back.

"So how was your trip?"

"It was definitely memorable," she grinned thinking about Luke even though their relationship hadn't been defined. They did however, act unlike their normal selves on the plane. She noticed how his stare seemed to last longer or when she came close, he stole tiny kisses. "How was everything here?" She asked to think about something else in hopes that her cheeks didn't blossom like roses from cheer. "I heard from Korey that Diana had to take over for me."

"Yes she did. There's more than one reason why I got here early. We definitely missed having you."

"I missed the girls too. Even though they text me non-stop."

"Not just the girls." He looked in the mirror capturing her eyes in his reflection. "Ana I was thinking about our last conversation and was wondering if you wanted to hang out some time?"

"Hang out?" she asked pulling back her hair.

"Yeah, I have tickets to the Phantom of the Opera this Saturday. Since you mentioned how you like Broadway, I figured why not ask."

"That's so nice of you to think of me. I don't have any plans so sure, why not?"

He smirked in the mirror and continued driving. When they got to the house he turned to her saying, "Good luck."

"Why would I need luck?" she questioned him, afraid that she was going to be penalized for her ignored texts.

"You'll see," he grinned.

She got out of the truck and went inside. Torrance frightened her beyond comparison but when she caught sight of Kailey, she understood his early arrival. Her long, golden hair was chopped in different layers. She walked over to her dropping her bag and the Bryce's coffee on the floor. She hugged the little girl in her arms asking, "What happened to your hair?"

"Korey gave me a haircut."

"Korey did this, why?"

Korina came down the stairs replying, "Diana was supposed to be watching them which included getting them ready for their lessons. Korey tried to do her hair per Diana's request and when the comb got stuck, she cut it out." She walked over running her hands through the uneven layers. "My salon is booked until next week and your hair always looks nice. I hoped that maybe you could fix it."

Katrina Thompson

Ana looked up surprised but ready for the challenge. "Yes I can try and make her look presentable. Do you have scissors?"

"There's some in my bathroom. Steve is in the kitchen already so you can groom Kail up there."

She picked up Kailey to take her upstairs when the eggshell colored walls twirled around her. She put her down and took hold of her hand while she clutched the railing with the other. She gave her a slight smile with the hopes that she didn't notice what had happened. "Let's see what we can do about this head of yours."

"Oh and Ana," Korina shouted up the stairwell. "Welcome back."

Ana wasn't experiencing the morning she envisioned although she was happy to return. She still had to feed the girls and get them off to school but Ana managed to layer Kailey's hair into a nice haircut. Her remaining locks fit to her face and luckily it was long enough on the top so she didn't have to cut her golden tendrils much shorter. After she got them off to school she had to do the grocery shopping which hadn't been done last week and pick up the Bryce's dry cleaning.

Even with her busy day, she stole quick glances at her phone wishing that Luke would text her or call. She had spoken to him briefly Sunday evening but after their time upstate she was curious if whether or not he considered the same thing she did. Perhaps they should be more than friends. Tuesday had gone by and they barely spoke, diminishing Ana's thoughts on a possible union. Wednesday rolled around and she couldn't wait for his visit that evening but he called and cancelled saying that he had to work late. She thought to go to his place to confront him but she was too tired. When Thursday came she decided to visit him for lunch. There was no way he was getting out of seeing her. He may not have felt the same way but they always said that what they did wouldn't ruin their relationship. She was headed up to his office when she spotted him sitting at a table outside of a soup and sandwich shop. She slid down in the seat in front of him as a smile grew upon his face. Ana however was a bit shocked since he seemed to be avoiding her.

"Hello Luke," she greeted, crossing her arms in front of her.

"Ana," he said leaning in, "what are you doing here?"

"I would love to say on this beautiful day that I ventured here to eat but I have other motives. I came here looking for you. I feel like you've been avoiding me."

"Avoiding you, no I've just been busy with a new acquisition," he lied in his defense though he was working on a big project. He smiled because he was overjoyed to see her but most of all he was happy to have so many other people around. He couldn't be alone with her without wanting to be with her. They had obliterated the lines that she didn't want blurred and he feared that he could never return. He pulled himself back to the conversation saying, "Speaking of which, I have to go out of town to complete the deal. I was hoping that we can all get together before I do. I've already told Max and Fran about my plans. I didn't get around to it but I was going to ask you as well."

"Okay when?"

"Saturday."

"This Saturday?" She unfolded her arms and sat back. "I don't know if I can make it Saturday."

"Why, what do you have planned?"

"Torrance invited me to a play Saturday night. I think it will get out in time but he was nice enough to ask me to join him. I'm not sure if he'll want to hang out afterward."

Luke sat back drawing more distance between them. Ana could feel her heart stutter. "So are you and Torrance together now?" he asked with a bitter taste in his mouth.

"No Luke, he asked me out as a friend. He likes Broadway shows just like I do and thought to invite me."

"I could've taken you."

"You don't even like musicals," she grinned.

"That doesn't mean that I wouldn't take you if you asked."

"Luke this is pointless." She stood from her seat and stepped over to him. "I'll be there but remember you're not my only friend." Leaning down she kissed him on his cheek and walked away.

***

Just as Ana promised, she went to the show with Torrance and out to the club with her friends after the performance. The Phantom of the Opera was as animate, yet depressing as she had imagined. The swinging chandelier and beautiful voices amazed her. The Phantom however, broke her heart. It wasn't his fault that he was disfigured. All he wanted was to be loved. No matter his appearance, didn't he deserve at least that much? Torrance had enjoyed the show as well though he had seen the production before. Ana promised that the next time they went it would be her treat. But maybe next time she wouldn't wear heals when she was going out afterward.

The Matrix wasn't far away so she decided to walk instead of taking a cab. She had been feeling fatigued though she hadn't worked out in days. She figured the exercise would be fitting. As she approached, the rhythmic sounds blared down the street before she reached the door. Certain that everyone was already inside, she carried her weary legs pass the waiting line on sheer momentum. She looked back to the eager patrons, suddenly appreciative of her best friend's clout. The beat of the music was intoxicating. She wandered throughout the first floor of the room looking around for a familiar face until she looked up and saw Max. She smiled and walked over to the steps to find them blocked by Luke.

"I thought you would never get here."

"I made you a promise," she replied starting to go up the stairs.

"Yeah after your date."

Ana turned to him stepping back. "It wasn't a date Luke."

He leaned over kissing her. Short and sweet but to Luke, a stolen moment he wished he could hold on to. "So it wasn't. Come on. I got us a table."

"Great because I need to sit down."

He took Ana's hand, stepping around her and led her upstairs. She instantly spotted Max who sat at the table with a girl she didn't recognize. When he saw Ana, he got up and lifted her in his arms, planting a kiss on her cheek. "Ana!" he said putting her down. "How was the play?"

"It was great. You should go."

"Musicals aren't really my thing but from what I've heard they are your new friends. I thought he was coming with you."

"No not tonight." The truth was that she didn't even invite him. After her run in with Luke she wasn't sure if it was a good idea to bring him around.

Luke pulled out a chair for Ana and she humbly obliged. He sat down next to her and Max escorted his date away.

"Where's Fran?"

"What?"

"Where's Fran? I didn't see her downstairs."

"I'm right here!"

Ana stood up hugging her and Rolland who clung to her side.

"Hey girl, how was your date?"

"It wasn't a date," replied Ana exasperated. "He just had an extra ticket and no one to go with."

"Ana I get that you don't go out much but believe me when I say he's looking for more than just companionship."

Luke got up, wrapping his arm around Ana's shoulder. "She doesn't need companionship because she has me."

Fran grabbed his cheek between her finger and thumb saying, "You're a playboy. Anyone could have you.

Ana needs to settle down. We're not getting any younger you know." She placed her hand on her chest with a smirk on her face. On her finger was a diamond ring sparkling in the colored lights.

"Are you serious?" she asked rhetorically. She looked at Rolland and back to Fran. "Congratulations!" She hugged her and pulled her hand in for a better view. "Good choice Rolland."

"Thank you. I thought so myself."

Luke gawked in embarrassment. They had only been dating for a couple of months and he was content on making her his wife. *How was it so easy for him?* "Yeah congrats, I'm really happy for you guys."

Fran took Ana's hand and dragged her from the boys. "Now that I have you away from Luke tell me the truth. What's the story with Torrance?"

"I told you Fran," she laughed. "I can't say there's nothing there. I caught him looking at me during the play." Her cheeks were so plumped that her dimple poked through. "I ignored him. I felt so awful."

"Listen it's okay to take baby steps but you know this guy. He's hot and obviously he thinks you are. Why won't you give him a chance?"

"He hasn't really said anything to me Fran."

"Oh I get it." She cocked her neck to the side and stood directly in front of Ana. "You're holding out for Luke. Aren't you?"

"What, no I'm not. Our relationship is unconventional but this is Luke, he'll never admit his feelings and I'm done fighting with mine. Not to mention the awkward situation we would be in if things didn't work out. But that's beside the point Fran. I haven't stop trying to get pregnant. If I do, it's not right to Torrance."

"You are. I thought after you lost your first you were going to stop."

"What did you say?"

Fran realized that Ana never spoke to her about the baby. Technically neither did Luke, she just overheard the conversation. Unable to back track she answered, "Luke was concerned about you so he told me."

"He told you. How could…"

"Ana don't be mad at him. Your relationship is unconventional like you said, but there are two things I'm certain of. One is that he loves you. And two, you need more than companionship."

***

Ana hung out with Fran until her feet began to beg for mercy so she went up to the table Luke had reserved. He was looking down at the crowd, twiddling his glass between his fingers. Ana sat down in front of him asking, "Why are you up here? Normally I'm the one watching the table."

"Oh I was thinking about work that's all."

She propped her arm on the table, resting her chin in her hand. "Where are you going anyway?"

He took a sip of his drink saying, "I am traveling to China. Do you want to come with me?"

"I would need vacation time and I don't see Korina giving me anymore of that. That is unless you can wait until the girls are out of school. They're going out of town and won't need me."

Luke grinned. "Unfortunately I can't wait. This is one of those major deals that I can't screw up. I would say quit but I know there's no way to convince you of that."

She smirked, watching him reach over and brush the hair from her cheek. "Are you okay? You look tired and kind of pinkish."

"That's because I am," she grinned.

"Then why did you come?"

"Because I promised you I would."

"Right, I don't even know why I asked. You should go home."

"No you're going to be gone for a week."

"Ah I knew you would miss me."

Katrina Thompson

"Yeah just make sure you don't stay long ok."
"I promise."

***

Sleeping almost the whole day away Ana enjoyed her time off. She didn't remember a day that she was able to spend all to herself. She had fixed a large breakfast and attempted to stick to her diet but she was so hungry and sleeping so much didn't help. When Ana woke, she pulled out her mixing bowl and heated up the oven. Shortly thereafter the smell of freshly baked cupcakes permeated her apartment. She climbed back into bed to curl up with her second cupcake and turned on her TV when she felt her phone ringing. She picked up her cell and saw Luke's photo displayed on the screen. She updated the picture after he sent her a selfie from his vacation. Her finger hovered over the screen to answer but he hung up. It wasn't the first time. He always butt dialed her. She was going to call him back but decided not to. She put her phone on the nightstand and sunk beneath her sheets, dipping her fork in her cake.

Her mind wandered into sleep, thinking about her time with Luke at her parent's house. She wanted to run her fingers through the strands of his hair and indulge in the beat of his heart against her chest. But she couldn't forget what Fran had said. She was right. Luke's heart could never be hers. She almost felt guilty now for asking him to be the father of her baby. Their relationship wasn't marred by her request but her heart was definitely impacted.

"Ana, Ana wake up," Luke whispered in her ear.

She turned towards him rubbing her eyes. "Luke what are you doing here?"

"I couldn't sleep."

"You couldn't sleep so you came all the way over here to wake me," she replied sarcastically rolling the rest of her body to face him. "You are weird," she said wiping her eyes again.

"Can I ask you something?"

"I'm awake now." She sighed.

"Why won't you take me up on my offer?"

"What offer?"

"The pastry shop. Your cupcakes are so good."

She tucked the pillow under her head and closed her eyes replying, "Luke I have to work in the morning."

"Ana." He lied down beside her alerting his tired friend of his presence.

She opened her eyes and said, "I can't because you and your father have done enough for me. He gave you this apartment and even though you don't live here anymore he doesn't make me pay what I really should. You don't even charge me the amount of everyone else. You bring me food every week and you get me gifts even when I ask you not to. That's only the tip of the iceberg if you think about the fact that I asked you to be the father of my baby. What more can you give than life?"

"I can give you whatever you want."

She smiled replying, "Sleep would've been nice but since you're depriving me of that I would say lay off the idea of me borrowing money from you. I have another project that I'm working on anyway. So can I get some sleep now?"

"That depends. Can I stay?"

"Luke," she whined wanting him to stay but hoped that he would change his mind.

"Oh come on its late."

"That didn't stop you from coming." He pouted his lips pleading with her. "Fine," she replied rolling over.

Luke got up to remove his clothes. Wearing only his boxers he slid in the bed next to Ana. He wrapped one arm around her, tucking Ana into his chest and curled his other arm under his head. He closed his eyes trying to sleep but with her now in his arms he couldn't resist being with her. Thinking about her is what kept him up anyway. He called her earlier but he couldn't say what he wanted to. He licked his lips tasting the sweet taste of lemon upon them from his recent raid of her kitchen. He opened his eyes to look at her. He might lay off of the cupcake business for now but he would bring up the proposal again.

Ana's breathing began to change and he was sure she had fallen back to sleep. He leaned over her and kissed her neck. "Ana," he whispered hoping that she didn't answer. When she remained silent he built up the courage to at least utter the words. Luke licked his lips again, saying, "Ana I've wanted to tell you something for years but I have to admit I'm just afraid. I feel like once I say…once I say that I love you, things between us will never be the same."

When Ana stirred he was frightened that she caught his confession. He moved his arm waking her. She turned towards him and he couldn't resist placing his lips on hers. She was like a magnet drawing his metallic skin closer to her. Her eyes fluttered open and he rolled on top of her. He began kissing her neck and reached up her long shirt, pulling down her panties.

"Luke what are you doing?" she questioned him, surprised by his touch.

He kissed her again, ignoring her question as he pulled down his boxers and pressed his body between her legs. He couldn't stop. He had to make her feel what he wouldn't allow her to hear.

***

Luke had abandoned his spot beside Ana by the time she woke in the morning. She texted him and he replied that he was on his way to the airport. She couldn't be upset with him for leaving without saying goodbye because it wouldn't be the first time. He never really liked goodbyes. She also couldn't stop thinking about his visit. Maybe he finally realized that they should be together. The suspense was killing her but she couldn't discuss it with him. It was her idea for their relationship not to change. But perhaps she was wrong. Sure he was with other woman after her, but she pushed him away. However their time together upstate changed things. She would have to wait to find out how, when he got back. Until then, her mind was complete jelly. So jiggly that she didn't hear Torrance talking to her.

"So what are you going to do tonight?" he repeated.

"Oh sorry my mind was somewhere else. Normally Luke and I had movie night but he's out of town so I guess now I'll be curling up on the couch by myself." Ana smirked, shrugging her shoulders.

"You don't have to be alone because he's away. Would you like to do something with me? We can still have movie night if you want." He grinned.

Ana shied away once again thinking about Luke. That was something they did together. But why would it be so wrong if they were just friends. She craned her neck to look in the mirror at his reflection. "You're place or mine?"
"We can do it at your place since it's closer. I'll bring dinner and you pick the movie."

Ana found picking a movie Luke might like so much easier than with Torrance. She didn't know if she should go with an action flick or a musical. She selected two movies to let him choose from and made cupcakes for desert. She had taken the others that she made on Sunday to Leif, Monday. He was pleased of course and offered her the same deal he had done before. She didn't quite detail her reasons out for him as she did with Luke but he understood and let her go with gratitude. When she heard the buzzer, she went to the intercom, allowing Torrance to enter the building. She unlocked the door and caught sight of him as he took the final step. He changed his clothes, to her surprise, but his smile was the same as his reflection.

"Welcome to my home," she announced stepping aside to allow him in.

He leaned over kissing her on the cheek and scanned the space. "You have a nice place." He turned saying, "I hope you like Chinese food."

"That's fine, thanks. Here let me get the bag for you." Her fingers brushed against his as she retrieved the paper bag of Chinese food from him. She noticed the trimmer in the corner of his mouth but forced herself to ignore him once more. She had no choice with the possibility of a future with Luke. She set the deliciously scented meal on the counter. "I wasn't sure which you'd rather watching so I picked out two movies which are over there," she motioned towards the living room, "for you to choose."

He walked over to the table seeing Die Hard and Momma Mia. He bent over picking up his selection. "I think I'm in the mood for a little action. We can go with Die Hard."

"Good choice," she replied stepping over to him. He handed her the disk to place in the player when she asked, "Would you rather plates or eat from the container?"

"The containers fine with me. I got us both house lo mien. I figured that way you can take out what you don't want."

"House lo mien is one of my favorites." She handed him one of the containers and a set of chopsticks. "What would you like to drink? I have water, pop, milk..."

"Water is fine." She reached into the fridge and tossed him a bottle of water over the counter with a grin. He went to the couch and sat down with Ana following him. "You know I never figured you for a Bruce Willis fan."

"There's a lot you don't know about me Torrance." She smiled.

"I guess we're going to have to work on that," he countered.

Ana twirled the noodles and pieces of meat between her chopsticks as the movie began. Unlike the play it was her that stole quick glances at Torrance. Luke could never be replaced but it was nice having him around. She took another bite of her food when her jaws began to water and her stomach felt uneasy. Unable to control what was bound to come back up she placed her container down and ran to the bathroom. Torrance sat up in his seat blinking uncontrollably. He paused the movie and set his food down on the coffee table to check on her. He could hear from his seat what was happening. He wanted to go inside but he wasn't sure if his presence was wanted. He came to stand beside the closed door, waiting for her to finish. When the door opened he pushed off of the wall to say something to her but just as the light poured from the crack she turned and fell back on her knees vomiting into the toilet. He stepped in and rubbed her back until she finished.

Embarrassed she hid her face saying, "I'm so sorry. Are you okay?"

"Am I okay," he gasped. "You're the one throwing up."

"You didn't get sick?"

He nodded his head. "You've been looking tiresome lately. Maybe you have the flu, '*or you're pregnant*'," he wanted to say.

She stood up to rinse out her mouth before she grabbed her washcloth from the rack and patted her lips. "I'm not sure but I think it's passed. I'm so sorry that I ruined our night."

Torrance dropped his chin. "You didn't ruin it. We learned that we are both Bruce Willis fans and that we both like lo mien. I call that progress."

She dropped the cloth in the sink giving him a light smirk. "Will you give me a moment?"

Torrance nodded and walked out into the living room. He waited for her to come out, not sure if she would be willing to continue watching the movie or want him to leave. When she came out she approached him with a smile but looked over at the container of food with the intertwining noodles and pieces of meat as a memory of what she regretfully viewed swirling in her toilet. Another rush of nausea floated within her. She covered her mouth. He noticed and packed up his container while Ana sheepishly ran back to the bathroom. He wanted to stay but he understood that she would probably want him to leave. Waiting for her, he sat on the couch. Ana timidly emerged from the hallway and stepped over to him. He gave her a smirk collecting his water and food hoping she would be okay.

"This is not how I thought this night was going to be," she joked.

"Oh?"

"Um, I meant-"

Torrance laughed. "It's okay. I got sick, you got sick, third time's a charm right?"

Ana nodded and walked him to the door. She clung on still embarrassed when she looked towards the kitchen and realized that he was missing out on dessert. Luke didn't like eating dinner without something sweet. 'All in moderation,' he would say. 'Not so simple for a female,' Ana would reply. Quite often he ate it first. She held up her finger, signaling for him to wait and went into the kitchen. Torrance watched with a proud grin as Ana pulled out a container, putting the frosted treat inside. "You can't leave without desert," she expressed walking around the counter.

"Of course not. Thank you," he graciously said with his bright smile, holding up the container. He walked out into the hall and turned. "If there's anything you need you can just call me."

"You're such a nice guy Torrance. How hadn't I seen it before?" asked Ana holding the door.

"I guess it's hard when we're at work. I think we should change that don't you?"

Ana wasn't sure how to answer. His tone was smooth as if he were coming on to her. She nervously brushed strands of hair that escaped from her ponytail behind her ear, though they didn't bother her. She dropped her head and met his stare with a smile which he took as a yes.

He leaned over kissing her cheek. "Hope to see you tomorrow but I'll understand if I don't. Goodnight Ana."

"Goodnight."

She closed the door and slid against it to the floor. She still felt nauseous but now she was confused. Should she pursue Luke or see what happens with Torrance. He was nice and handsome. There didn't seem to be anything wrong with him but no one was perfect. She peered down at her bracelet and raised her arm propping it on her knee. *Almost no one.*

Ana rolled off of the wooden planks and went over to the TV turning it off. She picked up her container and took it into the kitchen to toss in the trash along with the bag on the counter when the receipt fell out. *Two Wong Fu's.* "Of course! Two Wong Fu, I don't love you." She opened the trash lid when she thought about the fact that Torrance didn't get sick. She dropped the bag inside and saw the open container of food. The sight made her mouth water again when she noticed the shrimp. The last time she got sick didn't compare to what just happened, however the onset nausea did remind her of the shrimp at Luke's party. But it wasn't the shrimp, she was pregnant. She ran to the bathroom opening the cabinet to find the box of tests she had from before. She remembered all too well the instructions as she lifted the toilet seat. She didn't have to urinate but she would force something out. *What if I'm pregnant? I wanted a baby but what if I am?* Her heart began to race but she didn't want to panic. It had only been two weeks since they were together. She was probably getting her hopes up. She paced the tiled linoleum and white rugs, waiting for the two minutes to go by. Every second seemed like a second too long. She anxiously studied the clock and the moment the two minutes were up, she looked at the test. The two bright pink lines crippled her. She sat on the toilet seat covering her mouth. Happiness raked her but her subtle confusion turned into fear.

Bake

Chapter 9

Unable to sleep, Ana wanted to call Luke but the last time she told someone before the second trimester she lost the baby. As soon as her OBGYN's office opened, she called her doctor to make an appointment. Still afraid she nibbled on her fingernails trying not to alert Torrance of her uneasiness but he wasn't so easily bought. She quickly brushed off his questions and returned to her thoughts. The timing was right though it was a quick response, however she just had her period. Now she was concerned. Maybe what she thought was her aggravating, monthly visitor was her losing the baby and her body just hadn't adjusted. After Torrance dropped her off from work she called a taxi to take her to the hospital. She had to be certain before she exploded from panic.

When she reached the emergency department she had to wait to be seen but with the news she received, the half an hour was worth the wait. She took a peek at the needle sticking in her arm. They told her that she was extremely dehydrated and being pregnant, she needed more fluids. She listened to the rapid heartbeats beside her. The wave-like thumps took her breath away. She never got to hear them with her first baby. She pulled out her phone hoping that no one would catch her as she recorded their existence right before the doctor walked in to check on her. Quickly Ana tucked her cell beneath her sheets and smiled.

"Ms. Bloom it's a good thing you came in when you did. I can't be precise without an ultrasound but you are definitely further along than two weeks. The nurse tells me that you were dieting."

"Yes," she replied. "I had a very important event and I wanted to get in a dress. When I noticed that my stomach wasn't going down I kept dieting and exercising. I never would've if..." her voice trailed off in excitement.

"Well that would explain why you didn't know." He read over her chart saying, "I see here that you also got your menstrual cycle. Quite often the condition can be confused with implantation bleeding. Were they mild?'

"Yes, but from time to time they normally are."

"Not to worry. Judging from the sound of their heartbeats I think they are doing fine."

Ana looked down at her stomach and placed her hand beside the two monitors. She had wanted one but she had gotten two. They had to have been conceived on Christmas morning. Her bracelet hung on her wrist with her angel dangling in front of her. Her first baby could never be replaced but hearing the two heartbeats signified the best gift she had ever gotten.

"We're going to keep you here a little longer to get some more fluids in you. You'll also want to make an appointment with your OBGYN."

"I will. Thank you."

"Congratulations Ms. Bloom."

Ana smiled and rested her head on the risen bed as he walked out of the room. She brushed her hair aside, looked at the monitor and back to her stomach. "Hello in there. I wonder, am I talking to my sons, daughters or possibly one of each? Either way I can't wait to meet you."

***

Ana couldn't stop looking at her growing belly from such disbelief. For months she carried not one, but two babies. Throughout the day she hid her grin from Torrance and even Korina who had taken a shine to her again after her missed calls and day from work. She only had two vacation days left for the rest of the year and with the babies coming, she was going to need more time. She wished that she had planned better to coincide with the Bryce's calendar. Then again, Ana didn't think she and Luke would spend the night together so soon after the loss of Angel. She couldn't wait until he returned. He had to stay a little longer than he intended which made her even antsier. Every day she picked up her phone ready to share the good news. She went to the doctors and found out that she was 14 weeks along. "The safe zone" as some would call the stage but she didn't want anyone else to know until she told him.

  Her plan worked until she had gotten tickets for her and Torrance to The Lion King. She always wanted to see the musical and now that she had to save every penny she decided to repay the debt now. Owing someone and not repaying their kindness was not a trait that she ever wanted to possess. They went out to dinner before the play but afterward she found the common draw of hunger overtake her. Prior to her recent condition, when she got that hungry she would play the mind trick of brushing her teeth to take away the sensation. The gimmick no longer worked and she couldn't deny the babies nourishment. Torrance also wanted a bite to eat so they went to a late night diner for coffee and dessert. She passed on the coffee but devoured her desert before Torrance was able to eat half of his.

  He set his fork down looking at her conspicuously. "Is there something that you've been hiding Ana?"

  "Hiding?" she answered wiping her mouth. "I'm not hiding anything."

  "We're friends now. You can tell me anything." He pushed his plate aside and leaned forward. "You're pregnant again, aren't you?"

  She ran her hands over her tiny stomach thinking that she was covering it up well. "Yes I am."

  "And the father-"

  "There is no father," she croaked with her throat suddenly dry, but as much as she loved Luke he didn't say he wanted to be with her. She couldn't assume that just because the pregnancy was going well he would want to be there.

"No father." He crossed his hands. "That's what you said the last time."

Sheepishly, Ana replied, "I wanted a family and since I haven't had any luck in the dating scene I decided to have one on my own. I'm getting old so I figured this was going to be my last chance."

"Oh," he said sitting back. "I didn't mean to be so rude. I remembered how bad it was the last time and I was kind of concerned."

"Concerned, how long have you known?"

"Um I don't want to-"

"Oh come on, tell me."

He grinned and leaned forward again. "I always have an eye on you Ana. It is a part of my job."

She laughed replying, "No the safety of the children is what your job details."

"Well let's just say you're not the only one that taking on other responsibilities." They sat for an awkward moment until he asked, "So when are you due?"

"September 16th."

"Do you know what you're having?"

"Yeah," she smiled finally able to tell someone, "a boy and a girl."

"Twins!"

Ana nodded. "I was shocked to find out the news as well."

She was even more surprised on the way home. He had ridden in the cab with her but he barely spoke. She peeped over at him but he stared out the window. She wondered if that was how she appeared when she road with him. The cab stopped in front of her building and she turned to say goodbye but he exited the car. She reached over opening the door when he almost pulled it from her.

Katrina Thompson

"I wanted to get that for you." He grinned as he helped her out and held the door open. She looked back at his hand clinging to hers. Stepping next to Ana he said, "For years I thought you were too young for me only to find out that we're barely two years apart. If I knew you were looking for someone I would've jumped to the plate a long time ago. I'm sure you probably have this whole thing with the babies figured out but I was wondering if you could find room to fit me in."

Ana was floored. Fran was right. He did want to be with her. She clutched her chest and looked at him motionless.

He caught on knowing that she probably didn't see his admission coming. He smiled uncovering his pearly white teeth from his plumped lips saying, "We have the whole week off because of the Bryce's vacation. I don't know if you have any plans but I was hoping we might get together."

"Torrance," she whispered.

He studied her, waiting for a reply until nothing else came. "Okay," he grinned. "I can tell that I may have caught you by surprise. How about this? I will give you this week to consider giving me a chance. On Monday I will pick you up and you can let me know then. If you don't feel the same way things will be just as they were before, we can be friends." He released her hand and reached for the door but she still hadn't move. He took a quick glance at her again and stepped closer. "There's one more thing." He took her face in his hands and gently kissed her.

Ana could sense her body swaying though she never moved. She placed her hands on his to stop him but the more his lips mingled with hers, she didn't want to let him go. He released her and smiled before he kissed her again and got into the taxi. She watched the yellow car drive away but she was still frozen. She didn't melt until she felt her purse vibrating. It seemed to always break her icy shell. She reached inside pulling out her phone and saw that it was Luke. She was almost too embarrassed to answer. Trying to compose herself she took in a deep breath answering. "Hey Luke."

"Hey Ana, you're not asleep are you?"

"No, no I ah was just out...out with a friend."

"Were you out with Fran or," he paused, "Torrance?"

"Luke why do you assume you know everyone in my life? It doesn't matter who I went out with. You're on the other side of the planet. How cool is that? Have you gone karaoking or sample any of the exotic cuisine?"

"No I don't get out much but that's mostly my fault. I've kind of been hibernating."

"That's not like you. Are you okay?" she asked unlocking her door.

"Is that your key? Did you literally just get home?"

She laughed and closed the door over his reaction of her social life. "Really Luke just because you're in hibernation doesn't mean that I am. You should go out. I mean how many times does one get to go to Shanghai?"

"This is my third time but I would rather be home with you."

She plopped down on the couch clutching her mouth. She had to tell him what happened with her and Torrance. They weren't in a relationship but she still felt guilty.

"Ana are you there?"

Afraid to move her hand in fear that he would learn her secret she replied with her muffled voice, "Yes."

"I think that I will be winding things up here soon but when I get back I think we should talk."

"Talk," she said and swallowed deeply.

"Yeah I'll see you soon."

Ana finally moved her hand away. "Okay."

"Goodnight Anya."

Her eyes widened and glossed from tears at the memory of their dance. "Goodnight."

She stared at her phone glowing with the close shot of a daisy on the screen until it went blank. Luke wanted to talk. He did feel the same way as her. She was certain of it

Katrina Thompson

now. She swung her feet on the couch and laid back. How could this be happening? She finally had a suitor and now Luke wanted to talk. If only she had someone to talk to. She reached beneath her retrieving her phone to call Fran but she couldn't tell her about the babies, not until she told him. She thought to call Madison but the hour was late and they were probably in bed. Who was she kidding? She didn't have a lot of friends. Sprawled on the couch reminded her so much of being in a shrink's office that she got up and went to her room.

***

When someone wishes you goodnight, shouldn't you have sweet dreams? Ana couldn't sleep. It was a good thing she didn't have to work. Though rest was welcomed it didn't show it's needed face the following night either. She had a dream about the babies who were at least five or six years-old. They hugged her shoulders as she knelt down in front of them. She stood up and began walking away. Even though they cried for her she didn't turn. She left them behind with their voices echoing in the background until she couldn't take their wailing anymore. With brisk speed, she raced back to them. However once she caught sight of the twins, they stood with a man and a woman holding their hand. They were no longer crying they were actually happy. The four of them turned and strolled further from her. She called out to them but they wouldn't look her way. They kept moving into the distance until they were gone from her view.

The nightmares kept her awake but she was comforted by the gentle flutters of her babies. They weren't gone, they were still with her. But would their father? Is that what he wanted to talk about, being with her or could she have been wrong. She sat near her window, looking out at the pouring rain until the rhythmic thumps lulled her to sleep. After Ana woke she realized she slept through the night. Though she had a crick in her neck it was nice to finally get some rest.

Babycakes

She checked her phone noticing two texts messages. The first was from Diana. Even with a week off and Korina out of town she needed help. This time she asked for the Bryce's flight information. Ana knew that she would need it so she scanned them and sent the arrangements to her phone. She forwarded the information to her and checked the second text which was from Luke. He was landing that evening. Elated Ana jumped from her seat. She wanted to tell him about the babies since the moment she found out. She never sought to burden him with anything after she got pregnant but now the idea of having a complete family was in reach.

***

The instant Luke came home he ran to his shower to get freshened up before he visited Ana. He had gotten enough sleep on the plane and the only thing he thought about was seeing her. He didn't know what to say but he had to explain his feelings to her or he just might lose her. He stood in his closet wearing only a towel, looking for something to wear when he heard someone at the door. Holding onto his towel, he jogged down the stairs. He slapped the wet tendrils from his forehead and looked into the peep hole to see his neighbor. Luke had been dodging her for weeks because she hadn't gotten the picture after they slept together that he didn't want to be with her. He opened the door annoyed and propped his arm against it. "Libby what are you doing here?"

Her eyes scanned Luke from head to toe with her lip curled between her teeth. Libby untucked her glossed lip and gave him a side grin. "I left something here and you," she said poking her finger in his chest, "have been away." She pushed her way inside looking around.

"What was it?"

"A scarf, a very expensive scarf." She sat on the couch and crossed her legs, resting her arms over the back of the chair, smirking. "I would help you search but I'd rather watch you look. I'll wait here until you find it."

Zelda had been by cleaning and normally when she found things she put them in the closet. He went to retrieve the scarf, giving her an evil glare. The search wouldn't be hard thanks to his housekeeper. She placed any unfamiliar items in the same spot. She even gave the container a name, calling the lost and found box, "leftovers from his conquest." He latched on to the knob and stepped inside to pull out the items from the top shelf. It was awful, he knew.

The doorbell rang and he stepped back to get it but Libby shouted that she would while he kept searching. She went to the door with her heels clicking on his shiny floor. At the click of the lock, Libby slowly displayed her thigh and other extremities until she stood in front of Ana clutching her purse as she looked at her from head to toe.

Ana gasped in shock. Not only did someone else open Luke's door but the woman only wore her underwear. "Hello," she said wanting to retreat. *You need to leave.* "Is Luke around?"

"Yes," she replied folding her arms. "And you are?"

"Ana but I think this was a mistake." *You're so stupid.* "I'll ah…"

"Anna, Anna," she repeated, tapping her lip with her finger. "I heard about you."

Luke walked around the corner with Libby's scarf in hand staring at Ana. His eyes peered down at his toweled waist and Libby's lack of clothing with his pupil's wild from the knowledge of what things may look like to Ana. He ran to the door taking it from Libby to move her but she didn't budge.

"I know who you are. My friend told me about this girl named Anna. Aren't you the girl who couldn't hook up with anyone and she wanted a baby so badly she asked some guy to knock her up?" she questioned Ana wagging her finger.

Ana was so upset that she could feel the vein in her neck pulsating. She refused to remove her eyes that had pooled with tears, off of Luke. Aware of her sockets giving way she said, "My name is Ana and you're wrong on both counts." She stepped back and Luke inadvertently shoved Libby aside, dropping her scarf. "I can see that you two are busy so I'll leave you alone."

"Ana wait! I didn't-"

"That's the problem Luke you did." She turned and briskly walked down the hall.

"Ana please," he called out to her but she was gone. Libby stood at the door wrapping her scarf around her neck. "That was her wasn't it?" she grinned.

"Libby why did you come here? You know what, it doesn't matter anymore," he said grabbing the door frame. "Who told you that?"

"A friend of mine." She laughed. "Someone with an invite to your party, unlike myself. Don't think I have forgotten. I mean it's not that big of a deal anyway if she wanted a kid but what a dog the girl she told me about must be to not have a date in like ten years. That girl," she said pointing out the door couldn't be the Anna she was talking about. She could get anybody."

"Get your clothes on Libby and get out."

"But I thought you might want to unwrap your gift." Luke gave her a harsh glare. "Okay I'm leaving. If you change your mind I'll be upstairs." She leaned over to kiss him but he turned his head. She got the picture and went to retrieve her dress. She slipped on her clothing in opposition. "You have one last chance." He held his hand out the door and leaned on the handle. Clicking her heels on the floor she walked out.

Rid of his unwanted guest Luke ran up the stairs screaming obscenities in his mind. *Why did I answer the door?* The night was supposed to be perfect. He planned on going to Ana's apartment to make his plea. *Why did she come over?* He threw his towel to the floor, grabbing the nearest thing he found from his closet entrance. It didn't matter what he wore anymore because she probably never wanted to see him again. He dashed out the door looking for Richard. Thankfully when he got downstairs he was still right out front.

"Ana's," was all he stated to Richard. What would he say to her now? "Libby." *I never should've touched that girl.*

"What was that sir?"

"Oh nothing Richard. I was just thinking out loud."

It didn't take long before he arrived to her home but he could see from the street that the lights were still off. Luke searched out the window, glancing from side to side, trying to find her on the way there but he hadn't spotted her. He decided to go upstairs and wait for her. No matter what, he had to speak with her.

***

Ana flagged down a cab and hopped in. "Please just drive."

The cabby looked back at her and put his foot on the gas as quickly as the tears streaming down her cheeks, riddling her dress. He told our secret. *How could he? How could I be so stupid to think he had changed?* She pulled tissue from her purse cleaning her face until the wipe turned into a mangled pulp. She picked up her phone and immediately dialed Fran. The happy sound of music playing brought her no joy before she answered.

"Hey Ana," she said with a joyful voice as always.

"Fran can I come over?"

"Oh honey I'm not home. I'm over at Rolland's. Is everything okay?"

"I...I don't," she sniffled. "I'm okay. I'll talk to you later."

"Ana wait. Meet me for lunch tomorrow. We can go to the deli on 2nd Ave."

Ana sighed. She really needed someone to talk to but she understood. "Okay," she replied and hung up the phone. She felt like she had no one yet again. She wiped her face once more and with a solemn voice she leaned forward.

"Please take me to West 163rd St." The driver nodded and Ana turned to her reflection in the darkened window seeing the lace of her pale mauve dress. She had found the forgotten frock in her closet after tucking it away because the cut failed to show off the curves she formed from all of her work exercising. Now she wore it to hide her growing stomach. She ran her hand over her belly listening to the wheels ripple across the pavement. Her head had begun to hurt and as hard as she tried to forget what he had done, the memory gnawed at her.

Ana closed her eyes until the cab stopped. She reached in her bag handing the driver some money and went inside. The night was still early and she was kind of hungry but dinner would have to wait. She needed to lie down. Maybe relaxing could force her eyes into submission. She just wanted to forget but Luke wasn't going to allow her to. Ana dropped her things on the counter and turned recalling that she hadn't left the light on. That's when she noticed Luke.

"No Luke," she said to him as he walked over.

"Ana please let me explain."

"I trusted you Luke and you betrayed me. There's no explanation needed."

"You're right. You put your trust in me but I didn't tell her."

"Then who Luke? Because no one else knew that I was going to ask someone to be the father."

"Okay I talked to Max a while ago and he told someone else and she told Libby."

"So I'm the laughing stock of New York. Thanks Luke. Remind me to tell you the next most embarrassing thing in my life. Maybe you can have someone scream it off of the Empire State building." She tried to collect herself but his betrayal cut too deep. "I asked you to do one thing for me. I'm tired of this. I'm always there for you and even when I don't want to do something I do it anyway, for you."

Katrina Thompson

"I've done things for you as well. Three people aren't that many. This was just a big misunderstanding. You know Max. Whenever he has too much to drink sometimes his mouth can run away with him."

"You can't blame Max for this. Do you understand how embarrassing it is to not have had a real date in over ten years? No. Do you know what it's like for people to cut out throwing the bouquet at a wedding because you're the only one over the age of twenty who isn't married? No. Do you know what it's like," she cried, "having your parents look at you with disappointment so you keep your distance?"

"I know exactly what that's like," he shouted grabbing her arms.

Ana pulled away. "No you don't. You're father isn't disappointed in you. He just doesn't know how to talk to you. He built the walls sending you away to school and for the summer with your family but he's trying to tear them down. Your father loves you and you won't even talk to him."

"This isn't about me."

"Yes it is." She arched her neck, unable to face him and brushed away her salty tears. "I think that we need some time apart."

"Ana you don't mean that."

She walked away replying, "Yes I do."

"I'm sorry okay. I never meant to tell him it just happened and I didn't know that Libby was going to show up."

"I was stupid Luke. Stupid to think things could be different and that this was going to work." He walked over to her but sensing his presence she turned to him saying, "I want you to leave Luke."

"Ana we weren't doing anything. Libby means nothing to me."

"You think I'm jealous? Luke you've had girls lining up to be with you for years. I'm immune to them now. The problem here is that you are the one person I thought I could trust and I asked you to do only one thing for me."

He took her face in his hands replying, "I did it and I would do it a million times over."

She removed his hands almost peeling away his fingers saying, "For what you did, I thank you."

"Are you saying...?"

She stepped back, almost whispering she answered, "I'm pregnant," she whispered, unable to reject her voice.

"Ana, do you realize how wonderful this is? What it means?"

"It means that I finally have everything I want." She closed her eyes as a way to shield herself from the pain of her own words. "I have my babies and a man that accepts them even though they're not his."

"Ana what are you saying?"

"I'm saying that I want you to leave." She gazed up to his big brown eyes which were filled with what she interpreted as remorse. With her trembling voice she pleaded once more. "Please go."

***

As Ana sat at the table outside the deli she watched the many New Yorker's passing by her, trying to compose herself. She couldn't get the memory of Luke's face when she told him to leave out of her mind. She took a sip of her drink to take away the dryness her words had left in her mouth though they were spoken hours ago. She thought that last night was going to be the best in her life so far. She could finally hear how he truly felt. Then again he may not have wanted to be with her even if she was having his babies. Now she had pushed him away. *How was she going to do it without him?*

"Ana," Fran whaled, waving with a tray full of food in her other hand. She sat down in front of her and propped her purse beside her in the chair. "You look awful."

"Hello to you, too, Fran."

"I'm sorry but you look like you haven't slept all night. What happened?"

"Well for one I feel as though I didn't sleep all night."

"What's wrong?" she asked taking Ana's hand in hers.

"Luke and I had a fight." Fran picked up her phone scrolling through it. "What are you doing?" inquired Ana.

"I was checking the date. It's not April Fool's Day so I'm confused."

"Fran this isn't funny. He told my secret." She put her cell down and picked up her sandwich taking a bite almost ignoring her. "Fran," said Ana leaning over. "Is there something I should know?"

She slowly placed her sandwich on the plate and took in a deep breath. "Okay Ana I knew."

"You knew that he told someone and you didn't tell me."

"It wasn't just someone, it was Max."

"And Max told someone who told someone else." Fran took a sip of her drink and tried to avoid looking at Ana. "Fran if there's more please tell me."

"Ok, Max was talking about you at the New Year's party. Rolland and I were off somewhere else when he started but I caught enough to see that he had said too much. Luke got so upset that he went straight to the bar. Honestly, I didn't see him for the rest of the party."

"You guys are supposed to be my friends."

"We are your friends Ana. If you ask me I should be more upset than you right now."

"Why would you be upset?"

Fran dropped her sandwich and wiped her hands before she answered. "You never told me that you were pregnant or that you lost the baby. I would've been there for you if you needed me."

"I'm sorry," she apologized, collapsing her chin in her hand. "I didn't tell anyone because I was in my first trimester. When I lost Angel, I just wanted to be alone.

Torrance realized I was pregnant just from being around me so often and Luke found out I miscarried when he came over for Thanksgiving dinner." Talking about the holiday made her remember how much she didn't want him to leave. But he kept hurting her. He kept disappointing her. Thinking about all she had endured with Luke wasn't helping the situation.

"Oh honey."

"It's okay," she said abruptly. "It's in the past. Now I have a brighter future."

"Why is that?"

She rubbed her stomach pressing her loose shirt against it. "Because I'm pregnant again."

"Oh honey! I'm so happy for you."

"Thank you." Ana nibbled on her lips and leaned in saying, "I'm having twins."

Fran almost chocked. "Twins, oh wow! I can't...how are you going to take care of twins?"

"I didn't figure that part out yet. It's all so surreal. I never considered the possibility. When I imagined becoming a mom, I thought this would all be so simple. I had everything planned out but I never thought that Luke wouldn't be a part of it."

"What do you mean?"

"I don't think-," she paused from the tickle in her throat, "I can't speak to him after what he did." The memory of Libby crept in her thoughts. Often she used one of his girls to wipe away her feelings for him but now they made her nauseous. *How could he be with her if was in love with her?*

"Come on Ana, it was a mistake. Haven't you ever done something that you regret?"

She brushed the hair blowing from the early spring air and tucked the strands behind her ear. "Yes."

"Then you can forgive him. You love him too much to be upset with him."

Katrina Thompson

Love. "You don't understand Fran. It was our secret." A tear rolled down her cheek as her eyes focused on her forceful friend. She quickly swiped it away. "I can't."

"Okay I'll play." Ana gazed at her with a puzzled look and wiped her face again. "Truth and Dare."

"It's Truth or Dare."

"Not this version." She pushed her tray aside and propped her elbows along the table for support. "I dare you to tell me the truth. I promise and you know I will stick to this promise, that I will not divulge this information to anyone." Ana nodded. "Alright, I dare you to tell me how you truly feel about Luke. You're in love with him aren't you?"

"It doesn't matter anymore Fran."

"You are. I knew it! You wouldn't be this hurt if you weren't."

"Fran there's someone else in my life now."

"You're talking about Torrance?"

"Yes. He respects me and even though he's aware of the twins he still wants to be with me."

"That gives him points in my book but Luke loves you. Both Max and I are certain of it. "

"Luke will never admit how he feels." She thought back to his warm breath against her neck as he spoke to her in the full sized bed in her parent's home. She wanted to have those three words tickle her ears more than anything else but they weren't spoken. "He won't say it Fran. Don't I deserve to hear those words at least once in my life by someone who means what they are saying?"

"He just needs time to come around."

"Time has run out on him and I Fran. You said so yourself. He's a playboy incapable of having a real relationship with a real woman." *Even now*, she cringed. "He's been with so many women. He's been in my life for years. If he loved me, if something was going to happen, it would've. You and I both have been unlucky with relationships but out of the blue came Rolland. Maybe Torrance is the one for me."

"Now you're throwing it in my face," she grinned sipping her drink. "I don't blame you for feeling that way. Luke has never been the settling down type and let's face it, I've even put money in the pool for him actually telling a woman he loves them."

Ana laughed. "He's said it before."

"Of course he has as a friend but if he can't say it to you I think I've wasted my ten bucks."

"You're not joking. Is there really a bet out on him?"

Fran nodded. "It was Max's idea. Luke knows about it but I thought he would've told you by now. I guess I should've just saved my money for the wedding."

Ana twirled the straw around her cup filled with lemon flavored ice from her ice tea. Like her feelings, she decided they too, had to melt away. She had awakened things that shouldn't have surfaced and now they were written all over her face.

Fran thought hearing about the bet would make Ana laugh but she realized she was hurt. She leaned over clutching Ana's hand. "Luke is in the past. It's like you said, he will never love you the way you deserve to be loved and even if he actually admitted his affections, he probably wouldn't be faithful anyway. You're better off without him in your love life but you should still keep him as a friend." Ana put on a brave smile as Fran sat back in her seat. "Now since I gave you some good advice will you name one of them after me?"

Ana laughed, "I liked how you snuck that in there but no."

"Even if I make you my maid of honor?"

"Really?" asked Ana. Fran nodded with a smile. "Wait when is the magical day going to be because I fear how huge I'll be in a couple of months? The last thing you need is someone wearing a tarp in your wedding photos."

Fran chuckled. "No worries. The ceremony won't be until next year. Knowing you, you'll lose that baby weight in no time. We're thinking June." She leaned over crossing her arms on the table. "Just make sure you give what I said some thought."

"I don't need to," laughed Ana. "I'm not naming either of them Fran."

"You already know what you're having?"

Ana smiled and replied, "A boy and a girl."

Fran perked up in with a large grin. "I won't stop persuading you on the options of your babies name but you know what I meant Ana. You may not belong with Luke however, you can't erase him from your life."

***

To Ana, the weekend was the longest she'd ever experienced. After running a couple of blocks she came home, took a shower, got dressed and now, she stood in front of the mirror combing her hair. Today was the day that she would have to confront Torrance and tell him whether or not she wanted to take their friendship to another level. Twice she had used him as a scapegoat but the truth was that if it weren't for her feelings for Luke, her feelings for Torrance might grow stronger. *If only.* She took in a deep breath finally done taking her frustrations out on her hair and went to her room to get her bag. Torrance would be there at any moment. *What would she say? What could she say?*

She locked her door and went downstairs with the slightest act of procrastination. Just as she predicted he sat outside in the parked vehicle waiting for her. When he saw her he cranked the engine and drove to her entrance. Suddenly she was in a rush. She didn't even give him enough time to get out. She pulled the passenger rear door open and got inside.

"Good morning Ana."

"Good morning."

His giant smile deflated when she didn't utter another word. He took the truck out of park and kept his eyes forward. Ana noticed and realized that her silence meant that she wanted to stay friends. The ride wasn't long however the journey gave her enough time to get her thoughts together. When they got to the Bryce's house he turned to tell her goodbye but she knew that the moment was now or never. She stood up as much as the roof of the truck would allow and placed her lips on his. The taste, the motion, everything was different from kissing Luke but the more she kissed him, the minty flavor of Luke's lips and memorable twirl of his tongue fizzled. Unable to hold her stance she climbed into the passenger seat and leaned towards him. "I must warn you. I haven't been in a relationship in a while. I mean a really long time." She shook her head and continued. "I have a lot of baggage and I don't know if this will work but I want to try."

"I do too," he smiled, unhooking his seat belt and moved towards her. He took her cheek in his hand and kissed her again. "Friends no matter what, right?"

She grinned. "Yes."

***

Two weeks had gone by since their fight and Luke's phone calls, texts and e-mails went unanswered. He had sent her an e-mail every day saying how sorry he was. And with each note he added an additional "really". He thought Ana would get a kick out of him repeatedly apologizing but his pleads weren't working, even after he spoke to Max, whom she had already forgiven. Upset over what happened, he had gone to Max's job the next day. If the other stockbroker's weren't nearby he might have assaulted him right in the office building. Instead they went outside.

Luke's blood boiled as though seeing him turned on an internal stove causing it to bubble over. "She knows!" he shouted as if he was aware of what transpired.

"Who knows what?" asked Max.

"Ana knows that I told you about her wanting to get pregnant."

"How did she find out?" he asked shoving his hands in his pockets.

"You don't remember everything that you said at the party but someone else did and told Libby from upstairs. I don't know how many people heard but Ana showed up out of nowhere and she blurted out almost everything verbatim. Ana won't even talk to me."

"She'll get over it. Just give her a day or two."

"There's more Max." He ran his fingers through his hair saying, "She's pregnant-"

"Again, Luke that's-"

"Stop cutting me off man. She's pregnant with twins and now," he took in a deep breath, "now she's with Torrance."

"Wow, Luke how did you let this happen?"

"I don't know. It all crumbled in front of me. Libby, that ugh...she came to my apartment when I was getting dressed. She took off her clothes and answered the door. Ana saw her, me in a towel and at the same time Libby thought that the Anna she heard about was her. It was like my worst nightmare all wrapped in one. I was finally ready to tell her that I loved her and I've made a mess of things."

Max didn't feel it necessary at the moment to celebrate coming one step closer to his victory in winning the bet. Luke obviously needed a friend. He sighed. "I hate to tell you this but you made a mess of things the moment you realized how much you loved her and didn't say anything. Instead you used her to make other women jealous and used her wanting a baby as an excuse to finally sleep with her."

"You don't know what you're talking about," he grumbled.

Max took his hand from his pocket and ran his palm over his mouth. "I've been your friend for what, almost twenty years. Since I met her I watched the two of you from the side lines. Countless times you asked her to portray something that you never allowed her to be. Then when the moment was over, you let her go. Each and every time she put a smile on her face and every time you let her go, so went her smile. You tortured her for years and now that she's finally found someone you want to confess your feelings. Even if you said it, she wouldn't believe you."

Luke studied his words as the people passed by them and his heart beat in overdrive. He closed his eyes saying, "If you weren't my friend my hands would be around your neck right now but I can't get over the fact that you're right." His tiresome eyes opened to the brightly lit sky above. "You are absolutely right and so was she. This is all of my fault and now I might have lost her forever."

He sat in his office thinking back to his conversation with Max while he looked out the large window. Ana always liked peeking out the glass doors to the outside. When she was younger he didn't realize that her unwavering stare was so that she didn't get sick from the vibrating motion of the car. But even sitting still she would stare, gazing at, well he never really knew. What he did know was that he enjoyed seeing her. He wondered if she was ever aware of how often he did. He asked her about her people watching but she didn't answer, not until she got older. She thought of it as a way to still be a part of the ever changing, ever moving world in which she didn't feel a part of. He swiveled away from his view. Her unhappiness was his fault all along.

***

The girls lie on Kailey's bed watching as one of the babies moved about in Ana's belly. The last ultrasound showed that unless they moved their position, her son was on that side. Korey and Kailey fought over their names. Korey wanted her to name one of them Bryce and the other, Korey of course. Kailey wanted Poppy for the girl. She couldn't figure out one for the boy. She had the ability to create names for almost everything but for Ana's son she drew blanks. Rolling from the bed, Ana left the girls when Korina texted her to come upstairs to her office.

Katrina Thompson

The room was still filled with fabric but now there were several completed wedding gowns and an aggravated Korina.

"You wanted to see me Korina," Ana questioned her as she stepped inside.

"Yes come, come and sit down. I'm having a mental meltdown. I would call the girls up to inspire me but your ideas aren't bad either," she smirked. She picked up a piece of fabric saying, "Kailey is so free. I always think of her when I see an A line skirt flowing beneath the knee. Did I ever tell you that?" Ana shook her head. "And a fitted silhouette, I can visualize my Korey walking down the aisle already."

"She is definitely a fitted silhouette kind of girl. Like the straight line of the ivory keys on her piano, simple with a hint of perfection," she cooed.

"Yes, pleats. That's what's missing in this piece. Did you see that Diana?" Ana hadn't realized that Diana watched via Skype from the office. "Have Justin work on it and get back to me." She turned from the computer over to Ana with a smile and winked.

When Ana got off she couldn't wait to tell Torrance. She always sat in the front seat now unless the girls were inside with them. He reached over taking her hand in his and kissed the back of it. Ana froze but he didn't notice. Only Luke's lips had touched her in such a way before. He held on as he drove away. Being with him was like nothing she ever imagined. He didn't pressure her to be something she wasn't. He laughed at her jokes and she, his. They enjoyed watching movies just as she did with Luke but secretly she still missed him. She looked out the window when a thought came to mind.

"Torrance, when Broadway didn't work for you, did you ever think of doing films?"

He laughed and let her hand go to turn. "I did. I actually went to California for a gig. I was an extra in a commercial and shortly thereafter I received a call from the

Bryce's saying I got this job. I guess I chose steady pay over my dreams."

"I know what that's like," she smiled.

"Can I ask you something?"

She turned to him answering, "Anything?"

"I know that you don't want to talk about Luke but you two were really close. Don't you think you should work out whatever happened between you?"

She faced the window rubbing her stomach. "My life is different now. I don't know if he fits in it anymore."

"There's something I should tell you Ana." She turned back, resting her arm on the door. "He stops by in the morning when you're getting the girls ready to check on you. I think it's a bit much but everyday it's like clockwork. I don't even bring breakfast anymore because he has something for me every time. He cares about you Ana. You should work out your differences no matter what he did. Forgive and forget."

***

Sitting along the bar of Solstice, Luke sipped from his drink waiting for Ana. He instructed Richard to pick her up for their dinner together. For weeks he tried to convince her that he was sorry for his betrayal and finally, out of nowhere, she sent him an e-mail. She offered to stop by his office but he wanted to take her out. It was the least he could do for hurting her. When they arrived, He was alerted by a text from Richard. Luke quickly stood from his seat and walked over to the door. He already had a table reserved so he awaited Ana's arrival holding out his arm to escort her.

She stepped inside looking at the extravagance of the restaurant. She never ate there before but she knew how much Luke loved it. He had always promised to take her, though whenever he brought up their seafood dishes or filet mignon, she turned him down. There was no hiding how expensive everything was and Ana never liked spending a lot of money on food. This time was different. She allowed him to choose where they should meet and before he said it, she promised to not refuse.

Ana stepped past the hostess seeing Luke standing poised with his dark eyes focused on her. She silently begged him to turn away. Things had changed but there was still a part of her that wished he belonged to her.

Luke flashed his crooked smile and nervously took her arm in his. He leaned in saying, "You look amazing Ana."

She bashfully glanced down at her growing belly behind her black dress replying, "Thank you."

"This way Mr. Stokes," the maître d' motioned.

Ana followed by his side unable to look at him. She knew they would be seated across from one another but found it hard to be around him. Being angry had taken its course. Now she was crossed between the sickening feeling which crawled inside her stomach like regret and embarrassment for letting something break them apart. The maître d' pulled out her chair and she sat down across from him. She tried looking at the beautiful paintings and chandeliers but Luke tweaked her attention. Just as her eyes feasted upon him, he brushed his fingers through his hair. For a moment she wished they were her own. *Stop thinking about what you can't have.*

He grinned saying, "I hope you don't mind but I took the liberty of placing our order already."

Luke knew everything about her so she had no problems with his forward thinking. However she wasn't worried about eating. They had to find some way to get passed the last month. "Luke," she gasped repositioning herself in her seat. "I wanted to see you because there's something I wanted to say."

"What's that?"

"I wanted to apologize for the way I treated you. I'm still upset that you told Max but he's the one who told everyone else, not you."

"So why did you forgive him before me?" he asked remorseful.

"Because Max was being Max. I thought you, would've been reliable, responsible, trustworthy Luke."

He sat back in his chair appearing almost younger to Ana. He was the Luke she now recalled first meeting, slumped on the curb, innocent and broken. "You shouldn't be the one apologizing to me. I'm the one who's really sorry."

"I know," she laughed trying to break through his unhappiness, "really, really sorry."

"I knew that eventually one of them would bring you back to me." His eyes wandered down to her stomach until he realized he had been staring. He quickly refocused, meeting her eyes. "Speaking of Max, I went to speak with him about what happened the day after. He told me something that I'm not proud of." He stuck his hand in his jacket pocket and pulled out a tiny box. "For years I used you for my own purposes. This is something I want to give to you as an oath that I won't do it any longer." He opened the box revealing a single charm of the letter "A". "I will never ask Tasia to make another girl jealous and I hope you accept this as an apology for asking you to do such a thing." He held out his hand for her wrist which displayed her charmed bracelet.

Ana was going to protest but she didn't find the need to. She had worn the bracelet almost every day, toiling with the trinkets. She reached out her arm and laughed. "Did you say all of that to spare my feelings?"

"No," he chuckled sliding his hand from her wrist. He wanted to keep holding on but he knew that he shouldn't. "Why would you think that?"

"I don't think anyone would be jealous with me looking like house," she joked.

"You don't look like a house."

"Flattery will get you nowhere. I've already forgiven you remember."

"Good. I hope that you forgive me for this too." Over her shoulder the waiter placed a plate down in front of her with a large piece of chocolate cake in the center. On top, chocolate ganache was drizzled with white chocolate shavings. "Desert first, just like old times."

"Yeah." She smiled staring at him as he began to eat. She picked up her fork, digging into her caloric meal.

"Ana," said Luke reluctantly dropping his utensil. She eyed him with a curious grin. "What made you come around?"

Ana put down her fork as well circling the cake in her mouth. She swallowed and replied, "It was Fran but mostly Torrance. She threatened to kick me out of the wedding if I didn't say something soon. But Torrance told me about your morning visits and said that whatever you did should be forgiven."

"So you didn't tell him what happened?"

"No, I didn't see a need to and he never asked. All he knew was that we had a falling out."

"Huh." He picked up his fork finishing off his delicious slice of cake.

Ana chewed her last bite and spotted a familiar woman walking over. It was Candace. Her golden hair swayed in the invisible wind and her almost perfect body came waltzing over like a dance. Ana wiped her mouth and looked at Luke wondering if he would go back on his promise already. The girls that he hooked up never remembered her. She was pretty sure that Candace wouldn't be any different. Luke noticed her looking at him and smiled. He was about to say something when Candace stood at their table.

"Long time, no hear," she coyly said to Luke.

"Yeah, I've been a little preoccupied with work."

Her eyes flashed over at Ana and then back to Luke. "This is Ana. You remember her don't you?"

She gave Ana another glance. "The Christmas party right? It's nice to see you again. Are you out on a date?"

"No," replied Ana so sharply that she startled herself.

"Well it looks like you're finishing up."

"Not quite," Luke stated through gritted teeth, looking at Ana, wishing he could use their rouse at least one more time.

Ana placed her napkin beside her plate saying, "Will you two excuse me? I need to use the ladies room." She got up already having scoped out the place when she came in and left. Something she learned after becoming pregnant. In case of an emergency, find out the location of the restroom.

Her seat didn't have a chance to get cold before Candace sat down. "I just got here and it looks like my friend won't be showing up," she said peeping at her phone.

The waiter walked over to take away their plates however they weren't the only things he wanted to go. "Candace it was nice to see you but we're in the middle of something here."

"I'm sorry I didn't mean to interrupt. I noticed you and figured I would come over and say hello."

"I understand that your plans have changed but ours hasn't. Please go before she comes back," he leaned over pleading with her.

She rested her chin on her hands which were crossed over Ana's vacant spot at the table. "I ah, I thought we hit it off."

"We were just having fun, besides we haven't spoken since the holidays."

"Hey you're the one who took me to your friend's house and on Christmas no less. In my book that means something."

"I was being nice. I didn't want you to be alone."

She pursed her lips. "Was she pregnant then?" she said sitting up in Ana's seat with a curious glare.

"No, she wasn't."

"OMG," she shrieked with her eyes wide and bright. "I knew it! She's the woman everyone keeps talking about."

"Candace..."

Katrina Thompson

"I knew the girls name sounded familiar but I thought not her. She's the 30 year-old virgin. Were you the one she asked to knock her up?"

Luke's brown eyes scrolled up to Ana who stood right behind her with the waiter not too far behind, bringing their food. He rose to his feet but Ana walked over, raising her palm against him in protest. "I'm going home. I don't feel so well." He grabbed her hand but she pulled away and brushed her hair around her shoulder. She glanced over at the pre-ordered dinner saying, "The babies don't really like seafood anyway." She turned and started heading towards the door when Luke reached out, clutching her hand stop her. Ana eyed his remorseful grasp and placed her hand on top of his. She couldn't bear to see his face when she said with a scratchy throat, "We'll talk later."

Her head was still hung low when he released her. "I'll have the car brought-"

"No," she almost whispered finally looking at him. She licked her lips and mumbled. "I called a cab," she lied.

With a speedy departure, he watched her swivel around the tables and walked out of the restaurant.

He almost stumbled back to the table but managed to keep his composure. Though maintaining it was an even bigger battle when he witnessed Candace already eating Ana's meal. He sat down and glared at her with his brow creased. "I can't believe you just did that."

She leaned over wiping her mouth with the napkin spread over her lap and replied, "I didn't know she was behind me. But look, what are the odds that I had a dinner date who failed to show up and you had one that had to leave." He stared at his plate unable to eat. Candace noted the change in his demeanor. She twirled her fork between her red polished fingers, asking, "Is something wrong?"

"I lost my appetite."

"Are you worried about Ana?"

Luke gave her a harsh glare. "The foods good here, you shouldn't let it get cold."

"And if I wanted to dance I would've gone to a club."

"What are you talking about Candace?"

"Stop dancing around the question. I will stop badgering you if you just answer one thing for me."

"And what is that?" he asked almost delighted.

"Judging from both of your reactions I was right about her. I remember having a fun time at her house and she looks decent. Why would she ask someone to get her pregnant?"

Luke picked up his drink, tossing back the contents. He slammed the glass on the perfectly white linens and waved the waiter over to their table. "Can you pack this up?" he said circling his hand over his plate. "Also I would like to request an order of the stuffed chicken and pea risotto to be packed with my things."

He took Luke's plate and glanced over to Candace. "Would you like me to wrap your things miss?"

She dropped her chin to her half eaten dish of sizzling shrimp scampi and nodded. "I guess dinner is over."

After the waiter walked away Luke repositioned himself and rested his eyes on her. "To answer your question, Ana felt as though her time was running out on becoming a mother so she decided to start a family. People do it all the time so I don't see what's the big deal."

She took a sip of her water and laughed while she twirled her finger around the mouth of the glass. "Yes but most of them are not still virgins."

"Ana was holding out for marriage."

"In this day and age?" She shrugged her shoulders. "Maybe you should keep me around. I could teach her a thing or two. She wouldn't be single for long."

Bitterly he replied, "She's no longer single."

"Oh so everything worked out for her anyway. She and the father are together?"

If only.

Chapter 10

Ana took off her bracelet, dropped the trinket on her dresser and flipped off her heels. She curled up on her bed beside her body pillow staring out the window, wallowing in disappointment over dinner. Was forgiveness still a possibility? Candace's words created icicles around her warm heart which had grown frigid from yet another betrayal. *How many other people know about my pathetic life?*

Lost in unhappiness she didn't hear the front door open but when she made out the footsteps leading to the creak in the doorway of her room, she knew that it was Luke. "You shouldn't be here."

He crawled on the bed and lied down behind her.

"Luke you really shouldn't be on the bed with me."

"Oh stop Ana. It's not like we're having sex," he grinned.

Ana turned over giving him an evil glare. Her stomach brushed against him but he wasn't sure if his touch would entice even more anger on her behalf. He moved back and propped the pillow beneath his head. "Why are you here?"

"I am here because I am once again your best friend. The same friend you left right in the middle of our dinner date."

"I told you that I wasn't feeling well."

"Ana," he said running his fingers through her hair. He missed it. Her curls were soft, always so soft. "You don't have to lie to me. I know that you heard Candace."

"Luke, what you did to me makes me question anything I say to you. I thought that everyone laughed at my expense over having a baby. Now I find that people are actually discussing my sex life. It's nobody's business Luke." She turned away unable to look at him.

"Do you hate me?"

Clearing her scratchy throat caused by her unwillingness to cry she answered, "I could never hate you. Like I said, I forgive you however, that doesn't stop the hurt Luke."

He raked himself behind her again peering over her shoulder. "I never wanted to hurt you. I just couldn't believe that out of all of the men in the world you would choose me. I had to talk to someone. Since it already involved you, Max was the only person I could open up to." He brushed back her hair and kissed her neck to have her turn towards him. "If not for anything else, this has taught us something." He wiped her cheek with his finger. "Nothing else can come between us. Your secret is out, everyone knows and now we can move on."

He leaned over and kissed her on her lips. She pushed him back by his shoulders saying, "Luke stop."

"Sorry, old habits. I forgot you're taken now." He sat up and hopped over her holding out his hands.

"What are you doing?"

"We are going in the kitchen to get our food. Then you will join me on the couch to watch a movie. You owe me several movie nights and I intend on you paying them back."

***

With their stomach's full and bodies relaxed, Ana fought not folding into Luke's arm. Movie night had almost become awkward. When Ana's phone buzzed to life, she peeled herself from the couch out of the quiet clutches of their tiny world and went to her room.

Luke sat impatiently trying to hear her conversation but all he got was her muffled voice. He sensed the awkwardness of their time together and wanted to get things back to the way they were but their relationship had changed. He couldn't touch her, hold her or even kiss her. How was he going to convince her that he was better for her than Torrance?

Ana walked out of her room, put her phone on the coffee table and sat down, turning her attention back to the movie.

"Was that the peace maker?" he asked looking forward as though he didn't really care.

Ana smiled. "Yes."

"If I had known it was him I would've told him thank you."

Ana cocked her head and turned to face him. "I'm glad you feel that way. I was thinking. Maybe you can come over Wednesday for a movie night with us. I can cook dinner and whatever kind of cupcakes you would like."

"This Wednesday? I don't think I'll be able to make it. I already made plans with Candace," he lied not wanting to see them together. "Yeah I ah didn't plan on your forgiveness this soon and-"

"Luke you don't have to explain." She curled her legs on the chair beside her and focused on the movie.

She's jealous. Seeing how he hit a nerve, Luke reached over and pulled her feet on his lap. "I really missed this Ana."

"Me too." She held out her hand to latch on to his.

He held on, allowing her fingers to sift away like sand. He moved closer, resting his palms just below her knees. "Ana can I touch them?"

She smirked, wrapping her hand around his. Ana brought it over her belly and placed it on top. "They're busy bodies. I like to call the boy, my honey bee and the girl, my little butterfly, but I don't know which one is where anymore."

He slowly moved his hands across her stomach waiting to for the flutter of their being. She smiled saying, "After everything I ate, they're probably asleep."

"What are you going to name them?"

She laughed. "What you don't like Butterfly and Bee?"

"Butterfly and Bee Bloom, people will think you're hippies."

"You're right. I guess I'll have to come up with something else."

"I have an idea but I'm not sure you'll like them."

She looked at Luke waiting for him to offer his idea, though instead he removed his hand and grinned. She bent her legs to sit up. "Come on Luke just spit them out."

"Okay I was thinking Luke and Leah."

"Star Wars, how could I not have guessed?" She moved her legs and propped her arm on the back of the couch. "Luke, are you okay with…with all of this?" she asked rubbing her stomach.

"It's a little too late for that right?"

She rolled into her seat replying, "Yeah I guess."

His eyes lied directly on the television aware that she spoke of the children but he wished she knew he was talking about their relationship. "I know they're stupid, cliché even. I just thought their names could be something I added and everyone would know came from me."

She reached over taking his face in her hand, pulling him closer. "They are not stupid. I like them and your father will definitely love it if we named them that."

"We?"

"Yes we, I mean it's not like I'm going to tell him that they're his grandkids but we can admit coming up with the names together." Her fingers sprawled along her stomach as she cooed, "Luke and Leah. They're perfect!"

"It's ah getting late so I probably should go but I was wondering if maybe I could come over tomorrow?"

"Yeah, when?"

"I was thinking about cashing in on my movie days all together."

Ana leaned forward with a large grin. "We can do an all night movie binge!"

"Your boyfriend would be okay with me staying over?"

"You let yourself in and have your own room Luke. I don't think he would say anything."

"Well since you put it that way, I'll stay, but only if you're going to make cupcakes."

"Tonight?" grudged Ana.

"Yeah, it's not like you're not going to sleep in tomorrow anyway."

She pouted but found no use in fighting his request. She would do anything for him. She leaned over grabbing his chin and said, "Only for you."

***

She made plain vanilla cupcakes since she didn't have any other ingredients in her pantry. Luke ate three all on his own even though he already had desert but Ana was so tired that she neglected the late night snack. She curled on the couch to watch the movie Luke chose however her eyelids refused to allow her to make out which one it was.

When he realized she had fallen asleep, Luke went to her room and folded back her covers. Her large body pillow took up almost half of the bed but since she was already sleeping he figured she wouldn't need it. He tossed the fluffy bedmate off and returned to Ana. He reached beneath her for the remote to turn off the TV and carried her to her room. She still wore the dress from dinner but she should be okay. He placed her on the bed with the egging notion of sliding in beside her. Lessons learned told him not to. He couldn't take the same approaches as he had before. Luke pulled the covers up to her shoulders and sat down next to her.

"How did I let things get so bad between us?" he whispered. He moved strands of hair from her face that weren't really in the way. "It's all my fault," he confessed leaning over her. "I should've said something years ago, I see that now. I may have lost my opportunity with you but I will find a way to get it back." He kissed her on her forehead and when he got up to leave he heard her sigh.

She yawned and opened her eyes to Luke standing next to her bed. "You couldn't sleep," she asked trying to get up.

"Go back to sleep. I'll get there eventually." He took a seat on the bed but this time he couldn't resist lying beside her. Through squinted eyes she caught a glimpse of him and pushed over to the other side, rolling the pillow under her head. Her eyes closed again and she was out. Luke laughed in his chest at how quickly she fell back to sleep. She used to last for hours. He wondered if after she had the babies, would their relationship be the same. How long would she allow him to come and go from her apartment or bed? But most of all, how long before she would no longer do anything for him? He closed his eyes and tucked his arm under his head. Out of all of his questions there was one only he could answer, although no thoughts came to mind. How was he going to get rid of Torrance?

***

The sun was already out when Ana stepped out of her apartment building to be greeted by Torrance. She had neglected to tell him that Luke spent the night but she mentioned spending the day with him. He leaned over and kissed her before she latched her seatbelt.

"Did you have a nice weekend?"

"Yes," she replied with a smile and planted her lips on his again. "Thanks to you."

"Me?"

She fixed her seatbelt across her chest answering, "I've been upset with my best friend for over a month. I'd like to blame hormones but I was being stupid to let something so simple get between us. If it weren't for you, who knows how long I would've waited before I talked to him again."

Katrina Thompson

"What happened with you two anyway?"

She gazed out the window at the towering buildings and said, "He betrayed my trust by telling something I told to him in confidence."

"Is that why you didn't tell me before?"

"Kind of, I guess deep down I didn't want to talk about it and you never really asked." She buried her chin in her chest. His silence on the matter was something she was thankful for albeit odd. She turned to him. "I just always thought I could trust him."

"It's understandable for you to be upset with him." He focused on the traffic replying, "But what transpired is all in the past now." Torrance reached over and took her hand in his with his bright smile reflecting that of the sun.

Ana stare at him with all of her embarrassment stripped away. "Yeah, it's a new day, time to look forward to the future."

***

Even though Luke turned down Ana's invitation to come over for movie night he realized their weekly get-together would be the perfect opportunity to boost her jealousy. But in order to put his plan into play, he asked Candace to join him. She was very eager to come, although she had no idea of his true intensions. Ana created the menu serving roasted chicken and vegetables with cranberry and almond rice pilaf. Torrance set the table and tested the desert for "quality control" as he put it. She made chocolate cupcakes with peanut buttercream frosting inside, covered with chocolate ganache and a halved peanut butter cup on top. She wanted things to be perfect. If this girl was truly going to be in his life she had to make sure she felt welcomed in hers. Deep down she knew she had no grounds to be jealous but even the thought of them being together hurt her. She bore the feeling of resentment with a smile, though often timid. Torrance however, unknowingly found ways to help her get her mind off of Luke's love life. She watched him across the room straightening the pillows on the couch and selecting the perfect music to play during their meal. He really was someone she could see herself with, someone that might actually love her.

Ana was startled when she heard the buzzer to the main door. Shockingly he hadn't used his key. Torrance let them in while she took the platter of chicken and vegetables to the table. She turned just as he came walking in with his date. Ana straightened out her top and headed over to them. "Hi Luke," she waved nervously even though she had already met his date.

He kissed Ana on her cheek and hugged her. Holding her to his side he turned to Candace saying, "And you remember Candace."

Ana could never forget her. Her voice would be forever etched into her mind spouting back the secret that shouldn't have ever gotten out. "Yes," she replied. "I'm glad you could join us. I know Luke had other plans but I'm happy you changed his mind."

"It was more of his idea actually," said Candace.

Torrance joined them, taking Ana's hand to pull her away. "We should eat before the food gets cold."

They sat down to the table with Ana abandoning her seat at the end. She asked Torrance to set the arrangements so that the couples sat across from each other to allow them to pass around the dishes. Torrance handed the bowl to Luke who gratefully scooped out a serving of rice for himself and then gave the savory dish to Candace. She plated a portion for herself before giving Torrance the dish. He spooned out some for Ana before himself with the watchful eye of Luke. He hadn't even thought to do that for Candace however false the acquaintance. His eyes scrolled to Ana who had already served slices of meat to her boyfriend and herself. She held out the utensils for Luke but his hands had grown stiff. He watched as she pursed her rouged lips and a curious frown lined her brow, snapping him from his frigid state. Quickly he salivated to loosen his dry mouth. "Thank you," he breathed with a bit of a sigh in hopes that no one else noticed.

"Everything smells so good Ana. You'll have to share your secrets," Candace requested.

Don't you know all of my secrets? She didn't even look like the baking type. Her beautiful blond hair was straight with a blunt cut and her red lipstick matched her equally crimson nails. She couldn't imagine her placing them into oven mitts but she could picture the ends of her hair catching on fire as she leaned over to check what baked in the oven. Ana smiled at her cruelty and replied, "Anytime."

"So," said Torrance finishing the food in his mouth. "How long have you two been dating?"

"We're not. We're just hanging out," answered Candace before winking at Luke.

Ana listened intently but when she heard the status of their relationship her chest seized and her mind tangled with confusion. Was she happy that they weren't really together or should she be upset that he had found someone else, the exact same person who kept popping up unlike any other woman in Luke's life?

"What about you guys?" asked Candace.

"Oh we've been together for about two months now," answered Torrance looking at Ana to confirm.

She smiled and nodded but didn't say much. The whole night went at the same pace. Torrance and Candace asked the questions while Ana and Luke sat idly by. After they had finished eating dinner they moved immediately on to desert per Luke's request. Torrance offered to help but Ana had to get away. To watch Candace's light touches against Luke's arm and his quick glances over at her was sickening. It seemed as if they were both having a hard time trying to avoid each other but they really wanted to interact.

Even though she insisted on doing everything herself, Torrance walked over with the ravished platter of food and empty bowl that used to hold the rice.

"I told you not to worry about that stuff. I'll take care of it."

He smirked placing the dishes down. "I know but you forget, I told you that just because you insist doesn't mean I won't keep doing it," he chuckled. "You always do that Ana."

"Do what?"

"Try and do everything yourself." He wrapped his arm around her waist, pulling her into his chest. He rested his forehead on hers. "You're not alone anymore."

"I remember," she admitted and grinned before he kissed her.

Luke looked on but when he saw him kissing her, he turned and came one on one with Candace's curious glare.

"You're kind of quiet tonight."

"I'm tired but it seems like you and Torrance are hitting it off."

"Is that a good thing?" she asked.

He sat up in his chair replying, "Well yeah."

She tilted towards him with a kiss but her lips weren't what he wanted to feel. He was being sarcastic. He would love for the two of them to enjoy each other's company. Maybe they'd fall for one another so that he and Ana could finally be together. Luke pulled away when he heard Ana and Torrance walking over. Torrance had a smile on his face. He was obviously infected by Ana. However, he couldn't catch the expression on her face. She was facing downward as she pulled out her chair and sat down.

"You're going to love these," announced Torrance setting the plate in front of them.

"Oh you've tasted them?" asked Luke breaking his silence. No one ate them before him.

"It's one of the perks," he chuckled. "I handled quality control." He picked one up, placing the cake on a plate for Ana and grabbed one for himself.

"She doesn't need quality control," replied Luke. He sat up saying, "They're always good."

"Thanks." Ana studied him, noticing the change in his tone but Torrance wasn't fazed.

He got up and went into the kitchen, quickly returning with a fork in hand. "I almost forgot," he said handing the utensil to Ana.

Candace wiped frosting from the corner of her mouth with her tongue and swallowed. "This is definitely something you're going to have to teach me."

"She can't!" Luke shot out and leaned over. "It's a secret. Ana's going to open her own bakery one day so she won't be able to."

"Is that true?" asked Torrance surprised.

"No, that's just Luke talking," replied Ana licking her lips.

"Is it?" Luke pushed his empty plate away and folded his arms. "The opportunity is out there, she only has to give the okay."

"Then why won't you do it Ana?" Torrance urged her not knowing all of the details.

"Because I don't like borrowing money from friends and I have something else to look forward to right now," she answered rubbing her stomach.

"What will your excuse be after they're born?" inquired Luke with annoyance.

"Luke, right now isn't really a good time and besides, we already talked about this."

"Yes, amongst other things. We don't want to blur those lines."

Ana gave him a jarring glower which Torrance didn't miss. Coming to her defense he said, "Maybe we should change the subject."

Luke smiled, peering over to his date. "I know we came for a movie but we should get going." He took her hand in his and watched as she bit her lip to entice him.

Torrance nodded and glanced over at Ana but she was already beginning to clean up. He stood up saying, "Well this was fun."

"Yes," replied Luke guiding Candace around the table. "We'll have to do it again some time."

Ana got up and walked over to the door as they stepped out. Luke turned and released Candace to give her a hug goodbye. "Next week just you and me," he whispered in her ear. He kissed her on her cheek and grabbed Candace's hand. "Nice to see you again Torrance."

"Same here, and oh, nice to meet you Candace." She waved and he closed the door behind them. Ana began walking back over to the table but Torrance came up behind her to lighten up the quite awkward ending to their meal. "Just because they bailed on movie night doesn't mean we should also." She turned to him with a smile and he kissed her. He wanted more but he sensed her reservations about intimacy. "How about you get the movie ready and I'll load the washer?"

Ana nodded and got comfy on the couch. The movie was already in the player so she turned on the TV. She waited for him, trying to forget what she had seen; their touch, their winks, their relationship no matter how much he diminished it. She could never get over him if she dwelled on every little thing. But his touch, his stare, their relationship wandered in her mind like an unwelcomed creepy crawler. Torrance sat down beside her so Ana started the movie. She curled up beside him feeling so guilty that she didn't want to see his face. Unfortunately she had no choice.

He raised her chin to look at him saying, "You were quiet. Did he offend you?"

"No," she smirked. "Luke and his dad have been trying to convince me to open a pastry shop for years. But I feel my career is in fashion even if, at the moment, it's as a designer's nanny. I'll get my break one day."

"I know you will," said Torrance before he leaned over and pressed his lips against hers.

***

Katrina Thompson

Though Luke asked that the next night only be with him and Ana he never showed. She wound up spending the evening alone but she didn't mind. Any moment she could catch up on sleep was a godsend. Because he had cancelled on Wednesday, he stopped by on Friday with dinner. She made plans with Torrance but he was okay with her canceling. The following week he showed up. Ana had forgotten what being with only Luke felt like but the more time she spent with Torrance she found the ability to build back the blinders she pulled away. Through the years her heart had been unscaved by the things he'd done and within months it was tattered and torn but most of all broken. Torrance however, picked up the pieces and one by one, filled the longing vessel with something new.

***

Diana asked Ana to pick up several gowns from the Haute Magazine studio that she left behind. She was almost happy to get the responsibility. Over the past couple of months she had been late, forgotten things and worst of all let her phone die on more than one occasion. This was a way to redeem herself in Korina's eyes. She couldn't drop them off at the office because they were already closed so she brought them home with her. Looking over her growing belly Ana struggled up the stairs with the garment bag hoping she didn't trip. Torrance quietly chuckled watching her waddle with the bag but helped her take it inside. She took the garments to her room while he tapped his key on the counter. Ana walked over planting a kiss upon his lips.

"You look like you have something on your mind."

"I do," he replied dropping the key to wrap his arms around her. We haven't been out in a while. We should do something tonight."

"What do you want to do? I don't think I can fit in any of the doors anymore."

"Oh come on, you're beautiful and I want to show you off, even if it's in the dark of a theatre."

"Ah the movies, that's a great place to hide away from all of their glaring eyes."

"They would only be staring at you because who could bear not to?"

"Oh I just thought they would be trying to figure out how Shamu can survive out of water for so long."

He kissed her on her forehead laughing. "I'm going to go and drop the truck off. Maybe we should get a bite to eat first," he said looking down at the kicking babies.

"That sounds like a good idea," she giggled.

She walked him to the door letting him out and went back to her room in search for something to wear. Torrance would be wearing the same thing he wore to work but she didn't want to. She had on a pair of maternity pants and a long shirt. She peered down rubbing her stomach as she smiled at the black bag hanging on her closet door. She wished she could fit in something behind the dull casing. Diana told her not to even breathe on them, which for her meant don't open the bag. Regretfully forgetting the fact that it will take her some time to get back to a size 4, Ana sifted through her wardrobe until she found a suitable dress. The spring had started out very hot and was bound to finish off as so. She never understood how Torrance worked all day in a dress shirt and pants but then again most of his time was spent in the car with air conditioning.

Ana hopped in the shower and was out just before Torrance returned. She felt a little awkward letting him in while she only wore her robe but she didn't want to have him waiting in the hallway after someone had let him in the main entrance. She pulled the door open and smiled. "I thought I would take a shower before we left. I only need a couple of minutes and I'll be right out."

Torrance grinned and watched her scurry to her room. He sat on the couch shouting movie selections out to her. Since Ana found out she was pregnant she became afraid to view anything too gory or with mutated bodies. She had been reading about pregnancies and getting old wives tales from Fran. She was a little older than Ana and rarely spoke of marriage or even having kids so Ana was shocked that she knew so much.

Torrance stood when he overheard Ana close the door. She had managed to still fit in a blue dress which flared out just enough but settled with flats instead of her heels. The girls had her on her feet almost all day after school and with the nicer weather their parents insisted that they go for walks to stay fit.

"You look great," said Torrance putting his phone back in his pocket.

"Thanks," she nervously giggled. "Did you get the tickets?"

"Yeah," he chuckled but promise me that after the babies are born, nothing but action and gore. Don't get me wrong I like romance movies as well but a guy needs at least a nose bleed or something."

"I promise," she laughed.

***

Ana looked forward to curling up in bed with her pillow as they left the theatre however Torrance had another idea. He held her hand as he wrangled a cab saying, "I know you're tired but I was wondering if you wanted to stay at my place tonight?"

She endured a kick from one of the babies, taking away her attention. She had heard him correctly. He asked her to spend the night. She visited his apartment several times before, though never stayed, especially not after a long day. Ana teetered on the curb as he reached over, grabbing the handle. She tried to think of an escape but she couldn't find one. He half turned towards her to go inside but most of all, for an answer. She threw on a nervous smile as she nodded and got in.

He held onto her hand the whole ride to Brooklyn as if she were going to run away. It was the same way he clung to Ana while he gently caressed his lips with hers. Lying in his arms felt so good. His hands were soft like cotton straight out of the dryer against her skin. She hadn't experienced such emotion in months but the more she thought of her current situation the more she remembered her time with Luke.

Torrance moved his hand along her thigh and up the shirt he had given her. He apperceived her body heat rising and her heartbeat racing but when he observed the fear in her eyes he could see that it might not be what he thought. He leaned over her, bypassing the mound in her stomach saying, "You don't have to do this if you don't want to. I will understand."

"Torrance." She swallowed. "I just think that I need more time," she admitted with a guilty conscious.

He hid his face from her. Ana knew that she upset him but when his eyes met hers he greeted her with a slight grin. "I know that this has to be awkward for you. I completely understand if you want to wait."

She sat up pulling down her shirt. "Do you want me to leave?"

"No I don't want you to go." He sat up and kissed her again until he felt a tear drop on his cheek. With his thumb, he swiped away the curious response. "Why are you crying?" he asked.

"I just never thought I would find someone like you. You're such a good person Torrance. I don't deserve you," she replied wiping her face with the back of her hand.

He cupped his fingers around her cheek saying, "I feel like I don't deserve you. Woman like you don't exist Ana. I would be a fool to let you go."

***

In his mission to woo Candace by keeping her around for the sake of a jealous reaction from Ana was becoming bothersome for Luke. He told her that he was now celibate but he enjoyed her company while he transitioned into a different person. She obliged but his false confession didn't stop her from testing him. That night while they were out, she curled to his side raking her fingers through his hair. She nibbled on his ear as she stroked his leg but Luke took her hand in his and kissed her.

"How about we stop at Ana's before we meet up with Max. Richard," he said sitting up in his seat, "Ana's place first." Candace pulled him back and planted her lips on his. He didn't push her away since it only added to her attraction for him. He thought that maybe stopping by Ana's apartment unexpectedly to show off his date could sway her from Torrance. Upon arrival the light was still on so he first rung the bell. When she didn't answer he took out his key, dangling it in Candace's face and let himself in. He led her upstairs and into her apartment without even knocking. "Ana," he called out acting a little drunk though he barely had anything. Candace stood in the living room while he wandered around searching for her. Her bedroom was empty, all except for clothes she had strewn over her bed. His eyes instantly shot to the clock showing that it was already ten to twelve. Luke became upset that she wasn't home although he couldn't let it show. He took in a deep breath and went down the hall without taking one look at Candace as he headed directly to the door.

"I'm guessing she's not here," she stated prancing behind him. "Pregnant girls gotta have fun too." She grinned walking out and didn't notice someone passing just outside the doorway with a cup in his hand. She bumped into him causing his fizzy drink to explode all over her dress.

"I'm so sorry," the man apologized looking at her.

Luke poked his head out into the hall instantly recognizing him. "Javier."

"Yeah, Luke right? I haven't seen you around here for a while."

"I've been a little busy," he replied with a dry voice. He hadn't seen him in months. Actually the last time was right before Ana revealed her list of potential fathers. His teeth clinched at the thought.

"Oh here," he said to Candace handing her some napkins unaffected by their collision.

"This isn't going to come out," she pouted brushing her garment. "I can't go out looking like this Luke."

He waved his hand. "Go and find something of Ana's. It's not as if she's wearing them anytime soon," he mentioned with a smirk. He moved aside to let Candace back in and focused on Javier. "She's pregnant you know?"

"Ana, yeah my sister told me months ago. I actually saw her leave earlier with her boyfriend. I knew she would find someone eventually. I had hoped since I was around she would give me a chance," he chuckled.

Luke had lost both of his battles. He wound up being the jealous person and when he was secretly gloating over getting her pregnant, Javier took it away by talking about Torrance while reminding him that he did in fact have a chance to be with her. They both did. He dropped his head and peer off into the distance replying, "Sooner or later someone was going to get a hold of her, that's for sure."

"Torrance seems like a good guy."

"That he is, almost inconceivably so, unbelievably perfect."

"What this?" asked Candace wrapping her arm around his shoulder. "That girl has some great taste." Luke witnessed Javier's eyes bulge at the sight of Candace. She found a gold beaded dress with her long legs displayed from the short hem. "You like?" she asked Luke holding her soiled garment in her other hand.

"I don't remember that dress," he replied not answering her question.

"Well hopefully now it's etched in your memory." She leaned over with her plumped red lips, planting them on Luke.

"That's my queue. I'll see you around Luke." Javier escaped downstairs glancing back once more at Candace before he was no longer in view.

Katrina Thompson

Luke watched him, glad that at least he had seen what had transpired. Maybe he would tell Ana.

***

The next morning Ana woke in Torrance's arms. She hurt him the night before but he didn't show his disappointment. She looked out the window at the bright sunlight wishing they had remembered to close the curtains. However they weren't to blame for waking her. When her eyes refused to remain closed, the sun wasn't out yet. Even in her dreams Luke had begun to haunt her. She dreamt that he had gone home to her father and told him about her spending the night out with a man. He was a living spy cam that could not be paused or stopped. But she wouldn't let the past or her parents dictate her life anymore. *I'm grown!* So many rules had controlled her but she was finally breaking free.

"Someone's hungry." Torrance noticed, peeping over her shoulder after one of the babies kicked his hand. She was hoping that their patter didn't disturb him but they would have to get up soon anyway. They both had to make sure they got to Korina's in time for the girls lessons.

She smiled turning towards him. "Good morning."

"It's the best morning I've had in quite some time."

"Oh?" she hung on curiously.

He leaned over giving her a kiss. "I hope you know that now I'm going to hold you to it."

"Hold me to what?"

"Making each one even better," he confessed kissing her again.

The day had been just as beautiful as her early morning rise. Kailey and Korey were off to their lesson's which gave Ana and Torrance time to get some real breakfast. The bowl of cereal she devoured wasn't quite enough. She sat at a diner with Torrance taking a moment to themselves as they regarded the people going by. There was nothing like a spring day in New York. The birds chirped their songs, the horns honked at the annoyance of others and the grass swayed towards the sky with envy over the trees which rose to the heavens. Even electronics chimed their tunes. Ana always kept her phone on vibrate at the request of Korina when Kailey was a baby. She hadn't changed it since. However with the text from Diana and Korina she was beginning to feel as though they were yelling at her.

    She and Torrance dropped the girls off and headed to her home but Korina insisted she stopped by the office before they left the Bryce's. They contacted her all day about a gold beaded dress which was not included with the other gowns. Ana hadn't even touched the zipper. She assured Korina and Diana that she only picked them up and left them with Korina that morning. She was sure all would be rectified when they were able to speak with the photographer's assistant.

    That was until Monday rolled around and the frock still hadn't been found. How could she have misplaced a dress that she hadn't laid eyes upon? The question plagued her. Torrance studied Ana as she nibbled on her fingers all morning and when he went to her apartment, she continued the assault on her fingers.

    "It will be alright Ana. You have been with Korina for years. She knows you're the responsible one. If this is anyone's fault, it's Diana's for leaving them."

    "Not lately," she replied uncontrollably plopping on the couch.

    "A missed phone call, being late once or twice, that doesn't negate the years of service you put in." He sat down beside her, taking her hand in his. "I mean come on, it's just a dress."

    She turned to him with a tear drizzling down her cheek. "It's not just a dress. It's a hand beaded, one of a kind garment that cost $5,800."

    "For a dress?" She nodded. "You shouldn't worry. They will find it."

    She buried her face in her hand saying, "I hope so."

Katrina Thompson

***

Through her sleepless evening Ana wandered around her dark apartment watching the still night through her opened window. The blank canvas was so calm and peaceful. She wished the quiet would overtake her rapid heart which was beginning to fear the worse. She lied down in bed closing her eyes to force herself into rest until she heard the alarm on her phone going off. She got up a little dazed and sluggish but still managed to wobble into the bathroom and take her shower. She was in her room putting on her top when she overheard her bell ringing. She went to the intercom puzzled since she never got visitors that early in the morning and it was way too early for Torrance.

"Hello," she said in the ridged speaker.

"Ana it's me," announced Torrance.

Happy to hear his voice, she buzzed him in and unlocked her door. Only the look on his face wasn't what she had expected. He stepped inside her apartment and brushed her cheek with his lips, almost avoiding contact. He closed the door and took her hand in his to lead her over to the couch. Ana's eyes were fixed on him. His silence was cutting into her more than the sharp twinges in her stomach she had ignored the night before.

"Torrance please say something."

He turned to her clasping her other hand. "Korina wanted to send Diana but I insisted on telling you myself."

"What is it Torrance?"

"They never found the dress. Diana and the assistant both blame you. Korina felt she had no other choice than to let you go."

"What?" Ana replied with her voice escaping her.

"Ana," he sighed. "I couldn't allow Diana to say this to you."

"How?" she hid her face crying. "How could she do this to me after everything…"

He wrapped her in his arms as she wept. "It doesn't matter. We can both go. Korina will be completely dissolute and have no other choice but to hire you back."

"You can't," she muffled in his shoulder. "She doesn't even know that we're a couple and I don't want your job affected because of me. She'll need you and you need your job. The girls," she pulled away with tears streaming down her cheeks. "I can't even say goodbye to the girls?"

"I'm sorry but that's why she had me come early. I am to get your phone, the house key and your credit card."

She took in a deep breath and wiped her face. Torrance tried to assist her as she stumbled to her feet but she shook her head and went to her room to retrieve the items. When she hadn't returned he followed her footsteps and found her crying over her dresser. Giving her phone away took not only her access to the girls but the sound of her own children's heartbeats. How much more could she lose? He brushed her hair aside kissing her neck.

"Take them," she said collecting the items and placed them in his hands. "Will you…I just can't believe…" She shook her head clutching her trembling lips and turned away. She rested her hand on her chest when she felt him wrap his arms around her. "I…I'm fine. Please just go," she cried.

He knew Ana told him a lie to ease his concerns but he left anyway. His idea began gaining more steam as he got in the truck revving the engine. He looked in the rearview mirror missing her already. *Stay focused.* Ana was right. He needed his job even more so now. He fell in love with her and wanted to marry her so they couldn't both be without a job. Doing as she asked, he took her belongings to Korina and waited in the truck to take the girls to school. He wanted to abandon them all but he stayed focused though everything inside of him protested. He unlocked the doors as they climbed in. Their school wasn't far away but driving them there kept him employed.

"Where's Ms. Ana?" asked Kailey.

"Shut up Kail. Mommy said not to ask."

"But she promised to play hair with me," she pouted.

"I can help you with your dolls hair Kailey," replied Diana stepping inside.

"Huh," Torrance grunted and turned looking at his rearview mirror that displayed Diana's cold annoyed face. He understood why she said Korina was going to need him. He quickly dropped them off and returned for the Bryce's though he wished he didn't have to. The car ride was quiet, aside from a couple of calls she made but the stale air of Ana's absence lingered between them. She had to have seen his face when he handed her Ana's former belongings. Afterward he immediately went back to Ana's apartment, thankful that a neighbor let him in because she may not have. He knocked on her door patiently waiting for her to answer.

The door slowly cracked open. Her eyes were swallowed in puffiness and her cheeks wet from crying. "Torrance," her voice croaked.

"I listened to what you said," he responded walking inside as she stepped back, "but this time I'm not going to give in." He softly kissed her lips and brushed his fingers through her hair. "I love you Ana. We're in this together."

"You love me?" she asked stunned by his confession.

"Why are you so surprised?"

Ana stare at him clutching her chest. "I haven't heard that from someone who wasn't family or a friend in years," she grinned. "I'm sorry," she said shaking her head.

He lifted her chin saying, "I'm the sorry one. I should've told you months ago."

She wrapped her arms around his neck pummeling his face with kisses. "I love you too."

Chapter 11

Lying in Torrance's arms Ana tried to forget what had happened. After work he visited her and for the first time, he spent the night. She hadn't noticed him bring in a bag when he came over because she was in the process of writing a letter to Korina. Coming to terms with the fact that she would no longer be in their lives was tearing her apart. At first she had written the note by hand but her tears continued to soak the pages so she typed out her innocence and sent her message with a check in the mail.

She ran her fingers between Torrance's as they rest on her belly. She never thought she could find someone who would actually say those words to her. She had given up all hope at ever having a real family. Her hand slid down her stomach as she began to think that maybe if she waited, she wouldn't have ever realized how she truly felt about Luke. She was happy to have the babies growing inside of her and for someone willing to be there for her but what about him? Torrance walked into the relationship knowing about her pregnancy but he confessed his love for her. She relished in the touch of his breath tickling at the back of her neck when he repositioned himself. He reached for her hand, sinking his fingers between hers and curled their hands into her chest. His touch grabbed the tears in her throat bottling them in her heart. Could she actually have everything she wanted?

The subtle movement in her stomach woke her from her sound sleep. Torrance set the alarm on his phone to wake him but the alert hadn't gone off yet. He was still asleep beside her with his arm tucked beneath his head. She turned and lied back down mocking him. It was weird waking up with someone other than Luke. The only other person she ever remembered sleeping in the same bed with was Madison. If she didn't feel the warmth of his body next to her and the gentle touch of his breath Ana would assume she was still dreaming, though the guilt of having him in Luke's apartment and bed disturbed her. He left the rustic in appearance, queen sized bed behind when he moved some time ago. She took a peek at Torrance as he slept with a grin. *My future*. She sat up pulling out her ponytail holder and replaced it in her hair glancing over at the clock to find she had enough time to still make breakfast. She tiptoed out of her room and went to the bathroom to brush her teeth before she got busy in the kitchen.

Torrance reached over to the other side of the bed and noticed that Ana wasn't there. He rubbed his eyes and sat up smelling the salty aroma of bacon and the fruity smell of muffins. He pulled himself from the covers and walked to the kitchen as he scratched his dark curls to see Ana. She slid from one end of the counter to the other, setting a place for them on the island to eat. She cooked bacon and muffins just as he thought but she had also made eggs and grits.

She turned hearing him walk around the corner. With a smile she stood on the balls of her feet to kiss him. "Good morning."

"Indeed," he grinned. "I'll be right back."

Ana watched him teeter on his heels and glide down the hall while she poured them orange juice. She set them down next to their plates and sat down to wait for him. When he returned, Torrance walked over with a smile on his face and settled down beside her.

"I can't believe you did all of this Ana. You truly are amazing," he said looking at the spread again.

She giggled thinking about her pet name that was originally stolen from Max.

He took her hand in his and kissed the back of it saying, "My Amazing Ana."

Her hand tightened at the thought of Luke ever hearing him say the combination with a kiss but when he swallowed her lips with his, Luke's disapproval was all forgotten. They were infectious just like his smile. Torrance released her hand and picked up his utensil. Ana followed picking at her muffin until she heard the clang of his fork.

"Ana I've had something on my mind since yesterday."

"Oh, what's that," she asked popping in a piece of bacon.

"This is a long shot but I've been thinking. With your current situation we should save as much money as possible."

We? Did he just say we? The notion startled her. They never really used the word we.

"I was thinking that maybe you should move in with me. We can look for a bigger place once my lease is up."

"Torrance that's sweet of you but I can't."

He dropped his stare and Ana immediately felt awful for turning him down but he returned with a smile. Torrance brushed a strand of hair behind her ear saying, "Ana it's okay. I knew you were going to turn down the idea but I had to put the offer out there."

"I really appreciate it but I've already done something totally against how I was raised. I still haven't told anyone in my family about the babies." She ogled her achievement, rubbing her stomach. "I was impatient and a part of me regrets it even to this day. If I knew that all I had to do was wait for you I never would've taken starting a family into my own hands. Sometimes I feel like I've done all the wrong things in life but with you," she said looking up at him, "I want to do things right."

He put his hand over hers as she still cradled her stomach and leaned over kissing her. "So do I," Torrance replied with an exhausted voice. He rest his head on hers saying, "You are making it harder and harder for me to go to work. I should call in sick."

She put her hand on his cheek. "You know they need you."

"You don't?" He asked pulling away with a smirk.

Katrina Thompson

"Of course I do." She laughed but she turned to him with lined lips. "You were there for me even when I tried to push you away. I could never forget that. You're a part of my life now, our life," she said with her hands on top of his touching her belly.

***

Perplexed by her situation Ana sat on her couch surrounded by her bills typing away on her notebook. After taking out the money to pay for the missing dress and paying off her credit cards, she didn't even have enough left to cover two month's rent. She couldn't take it anymore. She pealed herself from the couch and went out to the patio. Bypassing the chairs she leaned on the rail watching the cars roar by and the kids at play. She gently rubbed her stomach. *What would my children be like?* Based on her current state she could only see them all living out on the street or mooching off of Torrance.

She spent all morning searching online for jobs but she had been a nanny for so long. She didn't think she could do anything else. *What if dad was right?* She scanned the tall buildings that blended with the sky. It was New York and everything around her was a part of her, including Torrance. She may not have the money at the moment but she wasn't going to move back home. She turned glancing into her apartment. "Even if I have to sell everything that I own." She peered down at her unborn children again, soothing the moving babies with her fingers when she noticed the door open. Ana had forgotten movie night.

"Ana are you here?" Luke called out from the kitchen.

She stepped from the patio embarrassed at the mess she left in the living room until she realized that she was only wearing a long shirt. "Hey Luke," she blurted with a wave.

"Is everything okay," he asked with a crease in his brow and his hands in his pocket canvasing the space in such a disarray. Ana's apartment never appeared like that before.

She walked over to the couch collecting her things. "Everything is fine. I was just figuring out bills and lost track of time."

"Are you sure because you seem to-"

"Luke," she said putting on a brave smile, "I'm fine, really I am." She put the items on the counter and sat down on the couch. He joined her just as she curled her legs up between them. "So what do you want for dinner?"

"I was actually thinking about going out tonight, however you look like you need to get some rest. I tried calling you but your phone went straight to voicemail."

Ana had been so focused on no longer being able to talk to the girls that she forgot no one was going to be able to get a hold of her. Thinking quickly she replied, "Sorry I lost my phone."

"It's not good for you to be here without one in your condition. How soon will Korina have a new one for you?"

Ana sighed. "I'm not sure, maybe tomorrow."

"Here," he said digging into his pocket, "you should take mine until she does."

"Luke no." She grinned. "I'm okay and so are the babies. Besides Donna's right upstairs if I need anything."

He stared at her for a moment until he replied, "You're fine okay but I bet you are hungry. Where are your menus?"

"They're in the basket under the island."

He got up to retrieve them. As he fiddled through the pile, Luke's phone began to ring. She picked it up to hand Luke his cell when she saw Torrance's name displayed on the screen. "How does Torrance know your number?"

"I gave it to him," Luke admitted sitting down.

Ana answered the phone timidly.

"Ana love, I called to make sure you were okay."

"Yeah I'm fine just a little shocked that you knew Luke's number and that you thought to call it."

"Well it is movie night," he laughed.

"I forgot," she admitted bashfully.

"You have a lot on your mind. I wish one of them was reconsidering what I suggested earlier but I know it's not."

"Torrance."

"I'm just joking Ana but maybe a good movie will get your mind off things for now. Tomorrow, you're mines again." Ana giggled turning from Luke. "I love you."

She immediately noticed the rise in her blood pressure. They had just admitted to each other that they were in love and now she had to say it in front of Luke. At that moment she had to decide. Was her heart truly Torrance's or did it still belong to Luke? Why question saying it anyway? The only person having a problem was her. Luke had Candace and she had…, "Torrance, I love you too." She ended the call and turned towards Luke to hand it to him but he was looking through the menus.

"So organized," he said under his breath.

Ana put his phone down on the coffee table and scooted over to him. "Organization is the key to success."

Luke dropped the menus back into the box. "I thought it was happiness."

"There are many keys, but hopefully whatever they unlock makes you happy and possibly successful."

He picked up the box and placed it on the other side of him. "I think I know a place but I don't see a flyer. I'll be back." He got up and headed for the door when Ana spotted his phone. She grabbed it, thrusting out her arm to hand him the cell. He turned to her saying, "I don't need it. I won't be long."

Hearing those words come out of her mouth for another man ripped Luke apart. He walked down the street not really knowing where he was going to go but he had to leave. To look at her with the smile someone else had perked with joy became more than he could bear. The weather was still warm outside even though the sun began to descend into the night. However the heat Luke felt was of the burning sensation which exploded through his skin from his boiling blood. He passed block after block paying no mind to the zooming commuters and wavering trees. *She fell in love with him. He waited too long and his plan didn't work. How did he let their relationship get that far?* They had only been dating for a couple of months and she already fallen for him. He raked his hair with his fingers regretting every opportunity he forfeited by not telling her his true feelings. He continued walking until he realized that the dim sky had turned dark and he still hadn't picked anything up for dinner. He passed by several restaurants and shops but there was one in particular that caught his eye. He walked in seeing someone who instead of cowering from him, he now confided in and called him by name.

"Good evening Mr. Stokes," Luke greeted the clerk from the jewelry store.

"Hello Winston." He stepped over to the counter with his glum appearance.

"Is something wrong sir? You don't look yourself today."

"That's because I wish I wasn't," he replied walking along the counter.

"Am I to guess that it has to do with a certain blond?"

"No not her," he said making a sour face.

"Ah so it is the same girl who keeps me employed," he smirked. "Should we take a peek over here today," he asked pointing at the display of engagement rings, "or I can show you some new pieces we got in. I'm sure she'll like those."

Luke was lost in his thoughts chuckling. "The funny thing is that she barely even wears jewelry but I keep buying it."

"I don't mean to be rude but I think we've gain a bit of a relationship here." He studied Luke to make sure the next words that came out of his mouth didn't get him fired. When he noticed him waiting to hear what he had to say he leaned on the counter saying, "Maybe you're buying all of this because you're just too afraid to pop the question. It's normal to feel that way. Usually when they come in here they've gotten over that stage but you're something special."

"She's special Winston. Don't you think I've thought about the possibility? I keep looking at them and none of them say Ana to me. But you know what? There may be some hope. She wears the earrings and the bracelet, even the ring her mother gave her, nothing else. I'm not the only one that's given her jewelry but she never uses them. Winston I knew it was a good idea coming in here!"

"Yes, but the next time I may have to charge you for my advice."

Luke laughed handing him his card. He walked a little further down pointing at an item beneath the glass saying, "That's the one."

Winston looked at him puzzled. "Are you sure?"

"Yes, I am. Don't worry I know what I'm doing."

Winston opened the case picking out the piece Luke selected and went to the register to box it up. Luke reached his fingers into the fold of his wallet and pulled out a copy of the picture of him and Ana that he stole from her scrapbook. He had been thinking about her the whole time but seeing her face Luke realized that he still hadn't picked up dinner. He waved to Winston to come over.

"Have you changed your mind Mr. Stokes?"

"No," he grinned. "But I was wondering if you could call my driver and give him your address. I left my phone with her and it'll take me some time to get back on foot."

"Not a problem for one of my most valued customers."

***

Unlocking Ana's door Luke could hear the TV but he didn't see her and the lights were off. He set the food down and walked over to the couch seeing Ana curled up asleep.

She always slept in a ball. He squatted down in front of her, brushed the fallen hair from her face and leaned in kissing her lips. Almost losing his balance, he pressed his hands against the chair. One hand clung to the gray sofa but the other brushed her stomach, waking her. Luke however, didn't notice. He placed his hand on her, caressing her belly with his fingers. He was a part of them, growing inside of her. The mere thought still amazed him.

"Luke," she gently whispered.

His eyes were fastened on hers. With a twinge of guilt he smiled. His lips shook as he asked, "Can I?"

Ana nodded thinking that he was talking about touching her stomach but his hand moved down to her thigh pulling up her top. "Luke what are you doing?" she protested, putting her hand over his.

"I want to see them."

"But Luke things are different now. You can't."

"It's nothing that I haven't seen before. I just want to do this once and I'll never ask again."

Ana removed her hand allowing him to pull up her shirt. She lied on her back as his hand roamed around her belly.

"I still can't believe there are two of them." He felt one of the twins move beneath his fingers, startling him. He laughed looking over at Ana. He wanted so badly to kiss not only the babies but Ana. They belonged together but he lost his chance. Those three words took away the future he began to build in his mind. His head was so weary from the idea of defeat. At least for the moment, he could conquer a tiny bit of his dream. He lied his head down on her stomach smiling.

Ana giggled shaking her abdomen beneath him. In the dark of the room, the light from the TV showed the smile on his face. She couldn't help running her fingers through his hair. She missed the sensation and wasn't sure if it was wrong of her to do but she didn't care. Stuck in their twinkle in time they looked at each other, both unsure of what to say next. Ana removed her fingers asking, "What took you so long Luke?"

"I walked." Technically he wasn't totally lying.

"Why would you walk all the way there?"

He got up and sat down at her feet. He picked them up and scooted beneath her legs replying, "I didn't think the trip would take me so long." He reached over getting one of the pillows from his side of the couch and put it under her feet. "Are you elevating your feet? I read somewhere that you should be doing that."

"You've read about pregnancies?"

"No, no, I just saw it somewhere that's all." This time he did answer with a lie. He may not have been able to be with Ana but he wanted to be familiar with what she would experience by reading about the experience. She started pulling down her top so he leaned over to help her. "You're probably hungry. I got us Italian and I made sure none of it was seafood."

"Yeah," she giggled. "They definitely don't like that."

He got up repositioning her legs and went into the kitchen turning on the light. Ana listened as he took plates from the cabinet and opened containers to put their food on them. She had expected to hear the microwave but he walked over handing her a plate.

"Thank you," she said curiously. The faint remnant of steam escaped from her food. She waited for him to sit down but he set his plate down and went to the bookshelf searching for a title. "Where did this come from?" she asked.

Luke turned replying, "Lugia's." He found the one he was searching for, put in the movie and turned to sit down when he noticed that she wasn't eating. "What you don't like Lugia's?"

"I do, it's just a little hot." Obviously he didn't get that she caught him in a lie. He kicked off his shoes and sat down on the floor to eat. "I can move my legs if you want to sit on the couch."

"No I'm okay down here."

Ana was hungry. She had eaten a muffin when he didn't return to hold her over but now even with the food in front of her all she could do was think about her concern for Luke. She scraped the sauced noodles around the plate until the movie started and the music blared from the opening credits. "Gypsy," she chimed. "Do you really want to watch this?"

"Yeah," he said turning to her with a smile, "why not?"

***

The heat hit New York well before the summer did, but now that they were officially in the season Ana thoughts festered on the girls. She always loved spending the summers with them. When they weren't on their family vacation or with friends, they spent the day with her. They went to the park and the museum. They also visited Korina from time to time which Ana especially loved. She popped in and out of the rooms holding their beautiful gowns and even other accessories. But Korey and Kailey are what she missed the most. With her own children on the way, she grew more anxious to meet them. However losing her job she wasn't sure how she could support two babies. She lost her insurance and didn't have a 401K plan. She went to her doctor's appointment but without coverage she had to pay for each visit, digging into her savings. It didn't help that the conversations with her parents always led to money. For some reason, they kept offering assistance or pried into the status of her job. They never cared before, unless they were trying to convince her to leave.

As a last resort she began taking her things down to consignment shops trying to make money on her used clothes. It was hard giving them so many pieces away but at least, at the moment, she couldn't fit in any of them. She sold several of the other items she owned. Platters, appliances and other things from her home were sold to neighbors. She also received cash for the jewelry that she didn't wear but she couldn't get rid of the pieces from Luke. She kept them and the ring her mother gave her in the tiny blue leather box that he had given her the earrings in for her birthday. She sat on her bed holding the box as she looked at her bracelet. The keepsake held so much meaning to her. However, the total of the charms combined could bring her at least one if not two months' worth of rent. Torrance offered to help her but she refused. He had already helped her with groceries. She managed to keep Luke from the fridge but she wasn't so lucky with him. He spent more nights with her than he did at his own place but she loved having him around.

They also cut back on spending money for plays, movies and dinners but Luke had insisted on them joining him and Candace out for dinner. She was already wearing the diamond earrings that Luke had gotten for her and unwilling to give into temptation, she put on her bracelet. Ana stood up straightening out the dress that she had to buy in order to go out and placed the box on her dresser rubbing her stomach. The night with Luke was stuck in her mind. He said that everything was fine but the way he touched her and then lied, she knew something was wrong.

"Are you ready to go?" asked Torrance from her doorway.

Ana looked at her belly, tapping it with her hand replying, "We're ready."

***

The restaurant, Liv, was vibrant with its loud but entertaining music and eccentrically dressed waiters and waitresses. They wore bright colored corsets and tight pants while the males wore fitted trousers and black dress shirts. Ana wasn't too sure about the place coming in but once you got to the tables on the second floor to eat, the music wasn't as loud. The atmosphere had changed to more of a private gathering. She sat beside Torrance and across from Candace.

They had plans to go out once before together but, Luke canceled. He was canceling a lot lately. He missed their movie night as well however he was making up for his neglect tonight by paying for their meal.

Ana had gotten up several times during the evening to use the restroom but on her last trip Candace decided to join her. She watched as Candace stood up and grabbed Luke's chin to hold his lips in place for a kiss before she followed. She brushed off their affection and picked up her purse from the table. Thankfully the restroom wasn't crowded mainly because there was a separate one on the first floor. Ana studied Candace as she applied her red lipstick wondering if she ever wore any other color. She grinned and finished washing her hands.

Candace tossed the makeup in her purse saying, "Can I ask you something Ana?"

"Yeah," she replied drying her hands.

"So I know that you gave me some tips on Luke's likes and dislikes but I need more."

"What are you talking about?"

"You know what I'm saying. All this time you've been giving me insight on the secret world of Lucas Stokes but they're not working. I want something good enough to land him."

"Oh." Ana threw away her towel and turned to Candace. "To be honest with you Candace he's not really the settling down type but then again he's never been seen with the same girl more than twice. So far you definitely have a lead on the competition."

Candace blushed as red as her lipstick. "Wow, so tell me more. I want to know everything."

Ana leaned on the counter saying, "Let's see, I told you that Luke likes to exercise but he also likes to eat whatever he wants. Just stay away from broccoli. I don't think I mentioned that he never liked the little floret bits. They freak him out."

Katrina Thompson

"Well that does explain why he didn't want to eat what I cooked last week. Give me more."

"There's watching movies. We both do which is why we still do movie night when he's not flaking on me. His favorite is Star Wars but if you ask him he'll say it's Scarface." She laughed.

"So tell me this, you say he's not the type to settle down and I know for a fact he enjoys having sex." She stepped closer to Ana saying, "Why did he become celibate?"

"Excuse me?" she gasped.

"Don't act like he didn't tell you Ana. He said that you two know everything about each other. I'm surprised that you're not a couple."

Ana turned grabbing the counter. "I'm not his type. But that doesn't matter because he's with you."

"He's like a completely different person from the one that I met last year. He totally brushed me off at first and now he calls, takes me out, he even bought me this," she beamed holding out a bracelet on her wrist. "I think about the fact that we haven't had sex since Christmas Eve but when I focus on everything he's done for me I know he cares." Candace turned to find Ana holding her stomach as she crouched over in pain. "Ana do you want me to call an ambulance?"

Ana took in deep breaths and let them out. She clutched her hand and shook her head. "I just need a minute. It will pass," she gasped, trying to convince herself as well.

Candace spotted the chair in the corner saying, "Come over here and sit down." She led her over and squatted in front of her. "Do you want me to get Torrance?"

"No, I'm okay." She smiled with a cringe of pain in her eyes. "It's just a little discomfort that's all."

***

Looking over his shoulder Torrance made sure the girls weren't returning. He leaned in saying, "There's something that I've wanted to ask you." Luke twirled the drink in his glass eyeing him though he continued to conceal his unmovable bitterness. "There are several things actually but I'll start with this."

"What is it?"

"Why did you tell her secret?"

"Have you really been thinking about that all night?" asked Luke.

"I was actually thinking about something else, something more important."

"Like what?" he replied taking a sip.

"Ana's a very bottled person. I've been with her for months now and I knew from the moment she kissed me that she was the one. I want to move forward with our relationship." He took in a deep breath and said, "I want to marry her, maybe even before the kids are born so that I can give them my name but I can't decide on a ring. I was hoping with you being her best friend would help me."

"You can't!" he shouted. Luke felt as though the wind had been knocked out of him. He became aware of how deeply they cared for each other but not that serious. He looked at rings for years with the doubt of ever truly finding the compulsion to admit his feelings and now, he had to help his adversary find one. There was no way he would.

"Come again?" said Torrance in defense.

"Her father," Luke blurted to make his plea. "He's very strict and if he thinks you knocked up his little girl, his only daughter, and got married without even meeting him he'll probably find some way to have your union annulled. When I say that's she's daddy's little girl, I mean it. She will do whatever he tells her to."

"We have enough time to visit them before the babies come."

"She won't go. You don't understand Torrance. Ana's father is a lawyer and where he couldn't lay down the law her mother and brother's did. You had to be in the house before sundown. She didn't even date in high school because her brother's scared them away. No sex before marriage and no babies outside of it. You go to him now and he will hate you for the rest of your life. Let this play out the way Ana planned or you might regret it."

"So it was true."

"What?"

"Everything people have been saying! She didn't tell me what it was but now I'm certain it was you. You opened your mouth about her wanting to have a baby and that she's a virgin."

Luke sat back in his chair swallowing the last of his drink. He located the waiter and waved him over. "Bring us a bottle of one of your best champagnes."

Torrance scowled at him as Luke sat coyly by staring. With contempt he asked, "Are you not going to answer the question?"

"You didn't ask one."

Torrance began to become agitated. He gripped the arm of his chair saying, "I asked you before why you told."

"I didn't," replied Luke. "Max opened his mouth about her situation and I only told him because he's our friend. It was stupid and he should've kept his mouth shut. Ana and I have already gotten over this. She's pregnant now and she's not even a virgin so why does any of this matter."

Torrance covered his flared nostrils with his fist but Luke could tell he was upset. He dropped his hand beside the other in front of him, intertwining his fingers. "Since when?"

A waitress brought over a bottle of champagne in a bucket interrupting their conversation. Luke removed the cork and poured until the glass could take no more. He knew Torrance was watching and he had already said too much, way too much. He drank the contents of his glass looking over Torrance's shoulder to see the girls coming back.

Ana sat down beside Torrance noticing the mood had turned stale. She took his hand in hers asking, "What happened?"

"I was about to make a toast," announced Luke. He poured a drink for Candace and Torrance before he placed the bottle back in the bucket and held up his drink. Candace and Ana followed, holding up her water. "Oh come on Torrance this is a good one." Seeing Ana's smile he picked up his glass and held it slightly forward. Luke wiped away his smirk, washing it over with a face filled with pain and distaste. "To love, the only thing worth fighting for."

Luke tapped his glass against Candace's and held his salute out to Ana and Torrance but she was too concerned about her boyfriend. He turned to Ana saying, "I think it's time for us to go." Torrance took her hand and helped her out of the chair.

"Torrance, what's wrong?" she asked cupping his cheek in her hand.

"It's late and you should get some rest." He turned to Luke with disdain written all over his face, saying, "Thanks for dinner and for answering my question. Candace, it was nice seeing you as always."

Ana waved goodbye with her clutch as he pulled her from the table. They walked down the stairs and out the door so quickly that she didn't even catch the song that had begun playing. Torrance whistled for a cab until one stopped for him. He helped Ana inside and slid in behind her.

"West 163rd St," he ordered the driver and sat back in his seat.

Ana tucked her hair around her ear and glanced over at Torrance. When he refused to turn, she put her hand on his saying, "Please tell me what's wrong."

"I don't want to talk about it."

"Torrance please, did Luke say something to you that has you all upset?"

"It's more like what he didn't say." He faced her with his deep brown eyes focused. "Who's the father Ana?"

"Torrance I told you I used a donor."

"You also said that you were a virgin."

"No I didn't." Ana immediately felt another set of eyes upon her. She looked into the rearview mirror and could see the driver's reflection peeping at her. "I get that we're in your car but please pay attention to the road," she rudely begged to him.

"It's you," he said looking back and forth. "The thirty year-old virgin."

She dropped her head in her hands until she realized the connection. "You heard that too, didn't you? This whole time you knew about my secret and you neglected to tell me."

"Don't turn this on me. You slept with your best friend and now he's fallen for you. How am I supposed to compete with that?"

"You don't have to. Luke will never love me the way that I want to be loved. Yes, the babies are a bond we will always share, but they're mine. He doesn't want anything to do with them. You have to believe me. You must know that I love you."

"But not as much as you love him."

"Torrance please," she cried. "Don't do this. It's been me and you this whole time. Don't let a toast take our forever away."

"You think that's it. It wasn't just his toast Ana. He told me to let your plan play out. You planned on getting pregnant by him, an unbelievably wealthy single man that you love. You tried to trap him and it backfired didn't it?"

Ana dropped her hand from his face with the world around her circling. She closed her eyes unable to take on the magnitude of what their dinner date brought on. She felt as if she wanted to vomit. He had never spoken to her that way and accusing her of scheming against Luke almost stopped her heart.

"Ana I'm, I'm sorry. I didn't mean that."

She couldn't open her eyes. A surge of agony reached inside of her so deeply that it forced her nails to firmly grip her seat. It was the babies. However his words seeped into her skin, radiating the pain around her whole body.

"I was wrong to say that but I do know it was about your feelings for him. I saw you two tonight and I tried to ignore it. He was right. Love is the only thing worth fighting for and I think that the best man won. You have already started your family so you're halfway there." He leaned over to the driver saying, "Stop the car." He pulled to the curb and Torrance tossed money to him. With an abrupt force he turned to Ana, grabbed her by the back of her neck and pressed his lips against hers. Her eyes popped opened as she gasped for air. He regretted letting go but he would rather that than to hear Ana tell him the truth. He released her and whispered, "Goodbye Ana."

She watched as he bolted out of the cab and slammed the door shut behind him. The tears in her eyes blurred her vision but from the motion of the car she knew that the driver still headed towards her house. She laid her head against the back of the seat looking into the driver's mirror. Already she suffered the loss of Torrance but most of all she feared the loss of someone else. "Please," she cried, "take me to the hospital."

***

After Luke sobered up he called Ana but she didn't answer so he decided to go to her place. Maybe she and Torrance were there. Though he wanted to be with Ana she finally had someone who loved her the way she deserved to be loved. He realized that even though he didn't want to admit defeat, he may have gone too far. The lights were off upstairs so he let himself into the main entrance and rung the bell at her door. When she didn't answer, he went inside. The thought of walking in on them crossed his mind but since it wasn't long after they left the restaurant, he figured that they probably just weren't there. He waited until sleep took over him and dozed off on the couch. Luke got the message from the chirping birds who alarmed him of the arrival of the sun. He sat up finding that just like when he closed his eyes, Ana still wasn't home.

Katrina Thompson

***

Folding into what Ana felt was nothingness she took off her shoes, wrapped her blanket around herself and crumpled on her bed. She had been at the hospital since Saturday night and it was now Monday morning. She wanted to take a shower but at the moment, she needed to lie down. The covering brought her back to the soft touch of Torrance's arms. The cream blanket even smelled like him. She tucked her head beneath them trying to understand how she lost him. Their conversation was a blur. All she could remember was him thinking that she used her babies to lure Luke. She rubbed her stomach trying to calm down. The doctor's told her that she had high blood pressure and that stress wasn't good for the babies or her.

She sat up looking around at her empty room which depressingly mimicked her life. Ana spent most of her time in bed just as the doctor told her. She wished she hadn't sold the TV in her bedroom for extra money. When she didn't want to rest on the couch she spent her time reading about the different possibilities ahead of her. After she delivered the babies she might be able to find a job but she couldn't afford daycare for them both.

She always wanted to have children. However now she was beginning to think she was in way over her head. She looked at several options for assistance but decided that she needed to find a way to support her family. Unable to read anymore, she was about to turn it off when she saw adoption stories on the right hand corner of the screen. She sensed a sickening feeling as the memory of her dream crept in her thoughts. She quickly turned off her tablet and lied down. The idea of giving them up was inconceivable, even if they might have a better life. She curled against her pillow shutting her eyes. At least in sleep she either forgot her dreams or realized that they weren't reality.

***

With the Fourth of July holiday coming, Ana knew that Luke was probably going to cancel their movie night. He usually took off the whole week no matter what day it fell upon which meant he piled up on his work. She almost didn't mind. After the dinner she was sure he played a part in the demise of her relationship but Torrance never told her what he said. Thankful that she found a cheap phone plan, she tried calling him ever since she got back from the hospital but he never answered. He didn't even come back for his belongings. His bag of clothes sat in the top of her closet collecting dust. Shelved just like Ana. She thought he was the one and then he was gone. Each day she was stuck with her regrets and the ringing phone he didn't answer. She decided to finally visit him. It was Saturday. By the time she would reach the Bryson's, he'd be dropping the girls off at home from their lessons. Maybe she could run into them.

Ana often went to see them, staying hidden while she watched Kailey play with her friends in the park but she hardly ever got to catch up with Korey. She pulled on a long skirt and the longest shirt she could find to cover her stomach. This had to work. If they were once again, face to face, he couldn't deny her the cause of their separation. She threw her bag over her shoulder and opened the door to find Luke standing in front of it with his key angled to place in the lock.

"Luke!"

"Ana, I ah didn't think you were going to be home yet."

"What are you doing here?"

"I came for two reasons." He stepped inside putting his keys in his pocket and closed the door behind them. "I wanted to apologize for the other night. I thought about calling you but it just didn't seem right. I had too much to drink and I may have been a little brash with Torrance."

"What did you say to him Luke?"

"He kept asking me about telling your secret and I got upset. After what had happened before, I didn't want to discuss it ever again, especially not with him. I don't recall everything but he wouldn't let the issue go."

She took her bag and placed it on the counter, brushing away her lightly curled hair. "Luke he's so upset. I don't think he'll ever come around."

"Of course he will. He would be crazy not to." He couldn't believe that he was defending him but she was obviously very upset. He took her hand in his saying, "Don't look so glum."

"I can't help it these days."

Luke scanned the empty apartment with his mouth opened in shock. "What's going on here?"

Ana turned realizing what he noticed. "Ah it's called nesting. I just couldn't help myself with cleaning and making sure the apartments clear of dangerous things."

He nodded his head. "So why are you home?"

"The doctor put me on bed rest."

"Korina must be losing her mind right now," he laughed. "You still have over two more months to go."

"I know," replied Ana picking up her bag.

"Where are you going?" he asked tightening his grip around her hand, happy to see her bracelet on her wrist.

"I was going for a walk." When the words left her mouth she wanted to take back her statement. She didn't mean to lie but she couldn't figure out why she didn't tell him the truth.

"I haven't told part two of why I'm here yet."

She smiled. "Okay, what is it?"

"We're going on vacation."

"No we're not."

"Yes we are. It's not Paris but since you can't fly, my father came up with a better idea."

"Your father?"

"Yes, well technically I decided to bring you along. I went to his office to talk to him about his plans for the holiday. You know just to make for conversation. He said that he was going up to the lake house and invited me. I thought about what you said and I couldn't imagine being there all that time without you. I need you to come with me Ana."

She knew the trip might be awkward for him but she needed to fix things with Torrance. "Luke it was nice of you to think of me but I really-"

"Ana please, I need you. Just do this for me."

She cocked her head replying, "Ok." The moment she complied, Ana felt him pulling her into the bedroom. "Luke what are you doing?"

"We're packing your things. Richard's downstairs already so the sooner we get down there, the sooner we can leave."

"Wait," Ana protested as he pulled her into the room.

He looked around noticing how almost everything was gone in there as well. Releasing her hand he asked, "Where's all of your stuff?" When she didn't answer he leaned inward to catch her eye level. "Is there something that you're not telling me?"

Ana never wanted Luke to find out she lost her job. She walked over to her closet so that he didn't see the absence of most of her clothes. "I'm not hiding anything. I went a little crazy over the past couple of months. Let me pack and I'll be down in a minute."

He stared at her for a moment until he turned saying, "I'll wait in the living room."

She watched him walk away, thankful that he no longer questioned her but she could tell that he sensed something was wrong.

***

After trying several more attempts to contact Torrance, Ana had given up for now. Maybe he just needed some time. She did keep the paternity of the babies from him even though she wasn't lying.

"Still not answering huh?" Luke asked looking at her fiddle with her phone.

"No but I'll try later." She put her cell in her bag, settling in her seat. "So why are you so afraid about being in the house with your father?"

"I'm not afraid. I just wanted you to come."

"But you said-"

"That I didn't want to spend all that time up there without you. I mean when is the last time we've been on a trip together?"

Ana's eyes scrolled the roof of the car while she searched her thoughts until they rolled over to Luke and her lips curled in a smile. "Maui, your thirtieth. I remember."

"You see. Who knows when we'll get to do this again? I saw an opportunity and took it. Not only that but we're going to the lake house. It could be a little boring up there."

"That's because you didn't take advantage of everything the area had to offer."

"Like what?" he asked wishing he could reach over and hold her hand. He missed intertwining his fingers with hers.

"The breeze up there as I can recall always felt wonderful. The water was usually calm and serene, perfect for swimming, not that I will be getting in this time around," she laughed rubbing her stomach.

"Oh I can get you out there."

"No not this time. That was the worst walking around with hair that I couldn't control for almost a week."

"You knew we were coming to the lake."

"Yeah but that's what swimming caps are for. You pushed me in without warning."

Luke laughed taking the opportunity to reach for her hand and kissed it. He couldn't resist. "Next time I'll make sure you're prepared before I push you in." He pressed his lips against her hand again and rested his head on the seat.

***

The lake house was about two hours away in Southampton but being in the car together neither of them noticed. They hadn't spent time with each other in weeks. There weren't any of their awkward moments or extra people in the room to deflect their attention. Ana took in the situation with happiness though she couldn't help but think about Torrance. He was still hurt for something she inadvertently did and because of it he saw the connection that she and Luke would always have.

As Richard pulled into the driveway she sat up looking at the large tan house that she hadn't been to since she was in college. The home seemed to be two times bigger than her parents with 7 bedrooms but with Luke being so busy with work only his father visited. They use to fill up the house with Luke's and Madison's friends over the holidays and summer's when they hadn't gone away. She missed spending time with Madison but she understood, family came first and she, herself would soon have two little ones to focus on.

Luke got out of the car along with Richard. Ana shuffled through her purse looking for her phone to give Torrance another call but when she attempted to contact him roaming flashed across the screen. She had no signal. The door opened startling her. She smiled at Luke reaching in to help her out. She tossed her cell back in her bag and stepped out. Sitting in the car she only wanted to adopt their new arrangement on the couch with her feet propped. The constant seated position was killing her back. Slightly stretching she looked at the house and walked behind Richard with their luggage and Luke on their way into the house.

There were two doors but Luke opened only one of them stepping inside. "Dad," he called out looking around. Leif hopped down the stairs with a bright smile on his face, reflecting that of the white walls.

"Hey son, I was just on my way into town. I thought you weren't coming until Monday."

"I got my work done early," he shrugged. "I also figured it would be nice if we had a little getaway."

"Oh," replied Leif stepping from the final step. He thought he was referring to Candace until he spotted Ana standing behind him. "Ana, what are you doing here? You're, you're..."

"Pregnant," she grinned tugging at her top. She had almost been in hiding from him just in case he told anyone back home. "Hello Mr. Stokes."

"Leif remember?" he said hugging her.

"Yeah, sorry."

"Come on inside," he politely ordered holding her hand. "The fridge is stocked and I know that you're probably hungry." He turned towards Ana focusing on her stomach. "You look like that baby has been eating everything from you." Ana peeked back at Luke hoping he didn't notice. She had been eating but not as good as she should. She hadn't gained any weight at her last doctor's visit but the children had grown.

"It's twins," announced Luke following behind them as Richard took their bags upstairs.

"Are you serious?" questioned Leif.

Ana nodded. "A boy and a girl."

"Congratulations. Who's the lucky guy? Do I know him?"

Ana's eyes went wild. She couldn't lie to him. He was like a father to her.

Coming to her aid Luke answered, "I think that's enough prying dad, don't you. We should get the grill going because I am starving too!"

He walked around the island in the kitchen and went outside through the back door.

"My son, not much for being personable but he's a brilliant business man."

"That's because he's exactly like you," Ana said complementing him.

"Thank you." Richard stepped in the kitchen and Leif pointed at Luke outside. He passed by Ana and went out the door. "How's a banana while we wait for dinner?"

"That would be great!" she grinned catching the flying fruit.

"I see you got good reflexes. You'll need them with two babies. My Tess used to tell me that her and her sister was a hand full," he chuckled thinking about Luke's mother. "She loved this place. She always looked forward to coming here for the Fourth of July. Of course it's been remodeled a bit since but I can still remember the way things were back then."

Ana smiled watching him recapture old moments with Tess. She was always nice to her. She treated her like the daughter she never had whenever she tagged along with Madison and her mom. To hear him speak such joy over his wife she had forgotten that he gave her the banana until Luke came back in with Richard. He went to the sink to wash his hands but Richard walked over to her.

"I hope that you have a wonderful holiday Ana," he said leaning over with a smile.

"Thank you Richard. I wish you and your family the same."

"Leif," he uttered with a nod. Leif nodded as well and Richard left.

Ana grinned, watching their interaction. They seemed so detached from each other but respectable. Luke sauntered over, taking away her banana. "You have to eat more than this." He took her by the hand and brought her over to the fridge. "See I knew there had to have been some prepared food. It's going to be a while before everything is cooked."

She filtered through the contents until she found a container of potato salad and pulled it out. "Will this do?" she asked Luke, laughing.

"You know a banana is good for protein," schooled Leif, grinning at his son's care for her.

"Yeah but it won't hold her over until dinner time."

"Humph," replied Leif. "Am I missing something here?"

"Yes," said Luke reaching into the fridge to pull out a tray of meat. "I thought you were just leaving."

Leif bent over to kiss Ana's forehead. "I'll be back before dinner."

She waited, listening for the sound of Leif's footsteps to dissipate. "What's wrong with you Luke?" she scolded him.

"What are you talking about?"

Ana leaned on the counter to face him. "Why were you talking to him that way?"

"Why do you psycho analyze us? I was just trying to cover the obvious Ana."

"Is that what you think I'm doing, psycho analyzing you?"

"Our relationship is fine. Maybe we only talk on holiday's or when we're at work but at least my parents don't control my life from miles away."

Ana stepped back and gnawed her lip. "Fine. I'm glad your relationship is fine." She walked away leaving her snack and Luke, regretting everything that he said. Not knowing which room she was sleeping in she went upstairs in search for her suitcase and a bathroom. Each room resembled a spread cut right out of a magazine with sea foam greens and mystic hues of blue. The beds were made with several pillows on top and some with blankets folded over the edge. It didn't matter which one she stayed in because they were all welcoming. After checking the first two bedrooms she found her bag in the third. Bypassing her things she almost ran to the bathroom. She hadn't gone since they stopped at a gas station for her mid-way through their travel.

Luke upset her. He was always hiding behind his pain inflicting it upon others. She had seen his lashings time and time again with the girls he hooked up with. One minute he had to have them and the next he used crude words or Ana to get rid of them. But never had he been so harsh to her. She wasn't analyzing them. She just wanted them to talk.

Exhausted from the ride or her verbal lashing from Luke she went to her bag to find the pair of shorts she packed away. She slipped out of her skirt and reached to retrieve her bottoms when she was shocked to find Luke standing at the door. "Luke, don't you knock?"

"Yes but I wasn't sure which room you were in." He strolled over as she pulled on her shorts saying, "I didn't mean what I said down there. I know that you're trying to help."

She turned from him and reached over pulling the blanket from the foot of the bed. "Your dad was talking to me about your mom when you were outside." She peered over her shoulder at him. "You should see how his face lights up when he speaks of her and you. It's a shame you choose not to." Ana wrapped the blanket around her and sat on the bed. "I'm tired. I think I'm going to take a nap."

Luke walked over to her but she laid back, closed her eyes and turned from him.

***

Sitting out on the patio, Leif sipped on his coffee as he gazed into the dimming sky. Luke had finally sat down to eat after knocking on Ana's door with no response to get her to come down. He joined his father, picking at his food while staring out at the sky overlooking the lake. His fork scraped along the plate until he paused saying, "I lucked out with Ana but I think I still owe you an apology."

"For what exactly?" he asked before he took another sip.

"The way I spoke earlier. You didn't deserve that."

He slurped back more of his coffee and focused on the still sky. "Can I ask you something son?"

Luke took a bite of his food and nodded, waiting for his father's question.

"Why did you bring Ana and not Candace?"

Katrina Thompson

"Candace and I just enjoyed each other's company but being here is like coming home for me. I'm not ready to let her into that part of my life yet."

"I know the feeling." He drank some more and sighed. "Some people only hold enough room in their heart for one person. For me that was your mother. I may never find anyone else but I had always hoped that you would. She's gone but she would want us both to be happy. Life isn't all about business. As much as I let the job consume my life, doesn't mean it has to be that way for you." Luke looked at him and saw the light Ana had been speaking of. His smile, though similar to his own, was large and Luke hadn't noticed before that his deep brown eyes smiled along with them. He dropped his fork and set his plate aside. "Have you ever thought about settling down Luke?"

"Sometimes but things haven't really worked out the way that I planned."

"There's the problem. Sometimes you have to tweak the plan to get better results."

"I've done that too, but I can't figure out how to make it work. I can't risk losing her."

Leif took another sip sucking in his lower lip returning to his view. "You seem to have such strong feelings for someone you don't want to bring home."

"I'm not talking about Candace. There's someone else and I can't make her understand how I truly feel. How I've always felt. I keep screwing up and I fear that she's one step away from walking out of my life forever."

"How will you ever know unless you cross the line?"

Luke leaned back in his chair replying, "We crossed that line a while ago. The problem is that we're back on our own playing field. I'm playing new games and making up the rules as I go along but she's got it all figured out. She can finally have everything she wanted and if I take that from her she will never forgive me."

"If you really care for her, can't you give her everything she wants?" He swung his leg around getting up from the lounging chair and stood up. "Until then, I think you should talk to the girl that you did bring here," he said pointing his mug out to the pier. Luke sat up looking down at the figure sitting on the edge. "I was able to convince her to stay but I can tell that she's still a little upset about whatever happened while I was gone." He took another sip of his coffee with his eyes on Luke. "There's one thing I know about her. Ana wants what's best for you son, just like I do. You should go and talk to her."

Luke wiped his mouth and hopped up. He didn't even know that she came outside. He turned to his father but he was already walking back inside. He threw his napkin on the table and walked through the backyard over to the pier. She was sitting on the very end looking out at the empty sky with her legs dangling below. He sat down beside Ana mimicking her. He heard her sniffling and asked, "Were you crying?"

"No," she replied. "It's allergies."

"Why didn't you want to come to dinner?"

"I already ate," she answered wiping off her hands from touching the wood and sat upright. "Your father brought me up something to eat."

Luke pursed his lips and sat up looking over at her. The slight wind blew the loose pieces of her hair against her cheek. He wanted so badly to wipe them away, replacing the tiny strands with his lips.

"Do you ever think about the future Luke?"

"The future?" he asked blindsided by her question.

"Yes the future, like where you'll be five years from now?"

"Let's see," he said looking down at the dark water below. "I would imagine still working with my father. Maybe by then I could have finally gotten you to go away with me on a real vacation. I don't really know, why do you ask?"

She turned to him saying, "But what about your personal life? Do you think that things will finally work out the way they should be?"

"You can't assume that anything in life will be just as you plan. I'm probably not the best one to ask however, I know that love has no rules, no boundaries and it's not perfect."

"But it does Luke. There are boundaries. You can only truly love one person and that love would be perfect."

"Were you upstairs watching that chic network again? That stuff will get into your brain and mess you up," he joked.

"No I wasn't," she replied pushing him.

"Hey, that's not right when you know I can't push you back." He grinned as he pulled her in for a hug.

***

Coming to spend the week with Luke and his father was turning out to be one of the best decisions that Ana could've ever made. As the days went by she sat in attention to the relationship Luke and his father portrayed. They were fine. They had grown closer. One didn't escape from the room without the other wondering what they were up to and Leif's stories about Tess lit a spark in Luke which surprised even Ana. She knew everything there was to know about him. His likes, dislikes, past and current. She knew the curves of his grin and the creases of his sorrow but she had never witnessed the faces that he made when he looked at his father. He had changed or in her thoughts, he finally found the one thing he thought was missing.

Ana had to spend a lot of time lying down, keeping to her doctor's advice. But being in her room with the sun shining through the large windows with life passing her by, she had to join Luke and Leif. They stayed up late eating leftovers and watching movies. It was a true vacation away from home. Even Leif joined them from time to time, studying them as they curled up on the couch. Ana with her legs propped up on the ottoman and Luke with his drink resting on her stomach until her laughter or one of the twins shook the container from its place. If they weren't inside they were outside enjoying the beautiful weather. Ana had brought a book reading about what she should be expecting but the nagging fear of not even being able to care for them haunted her. She had less than two hundred dollars to her name and her recent visit to the hospital was now added to her growing doctor bills. She dropped her book, leaving the guide and the blanket she was sitting on behind to walk along the lake. Luke noticed her leave from the kitchen window and went outside following her.

He grabbed her hand and brought it to his lips halting her. When he saw the look on her face he realized something was wrong. "Are you okay?" She nodded and continued on her stroll. He intertwined his fingers with hers saying, "I noticed that your phone has been a little quiet since you've been here. Do you miss the girls or," he breathed, "Torrance."

Ana followed, taking in a deep breath and replied, "I always miss them when they're not around. It's just that I have a lot I'm dealing with right now."

"You're on vacation. Just let those things be a distant memory for now and deal with them when you go back home."

"It's not that easy Luke."

"Then tell me what's got you bothered and we'll find a way to put your mind at ease."

She smiled and patted his hand before she let go. "This is something I have to deal with but thank you."

"Everything's fine right?" She nodded with a grin. "Okay then at least you're smiling now." He took her hand in his again saying, "Well you know what today is. I have a surprise for you later, sure enough to make that tiny grin curl into a smile."

"Oh yeah," she replied.

"Guaranteed."

***

Katrina Thompson

The sunshine was greatly appreciated but everyone longed for the night on the Fourth of July to catch a glimpse of the powerful spark of light. Luke escorted Ana out to the pier for her surprise when she noticed a tiny boat wavering in the water.

She grinned and eyed her stomach. "Are you sure that I won't sink the boat?"

He laughed and hopped in. "I guess we'll have to find out." He helped her down the step ladder and into the boat. She sat on the opposite side while he untied the rope which held the vessel anchored. Joining her, he took his seat and grabbed the handles of the oars. "So far so good, should we head out?"

She nodded and he started rowing. The lake was beautiful and dark, mirroring the cloudless night. Ana remembered the few times they had spent the holiday there. The fireworks could be seen over the trees with their brilliant color and popping sounds to replace the stars, even if they didn't compare. The foliage didn't quite touch the sky as they do now but they didn't block their view. They had begun shortly after Luke started rowing. She turned but he angled the boat to allow her to look forward. When he found just the right spot, Luke pulled the oars in the boat and stepped over to her side.

He took a seat next to Ana, wrapping his arm around her waist and kissed her on the cheek saying, "See I told you I'd get you back in the water."

She smiled and rested her head on his shoulder. "It's so beautiful out here. I don't know how you stay in the city."

"The drive alone keeps me there," he admitted with a laugh. "But if I had you keeping me company in the backseat it wouldn't be so bad."

She sat up to look at him, forgetting that the show was ahead. Her brow creased and she wasn't sure if she should say it but she was more than curious. She licked her lips and asked, "Why do you talk about me that way?"

"What way?"

"You know." She stared at him to continue however he didn't reply. "You talk about me like we're a couple but you're with Candace and I'm…" She couldn't finish. She was unsure if a relationship between her and Torrance still existed.

"I talk about you that way because you are my best friend and you are my amazing Ana." He brushed her hair behind her ear and reached down into his pocket. He pulled out a tiny box and removed the lid. "When we were talking the other day at your apartment I remembered something my mother used to tell me. I got this before I came here but my father told me the same thing. She wanted me to be happy." Reaching for her wrist he put a diamond incrusted, heart shaped key on one of the links and looked at Ana. Unable to sit next to her without taking her in his arms and pressing his lips against hers he moved to the other side of the boat and looked over his shoulder at the fire lit sky.

Ana stared at the charm and back to Luke while the bright sparks claimed the atmosphere. She leaned in slightly with the rocking boat which thankfully didn't make her sick saying, "Luke I don't understand."

"Being around you makes me happy Ana." His eyes shot to her for a split second before he returned to the show. "No matter where you are, I want you to know that."

With his back to Ana he watched the fireworks, refusing to turn around. She reached out for him but drew in her hand, unsure of how to respond. She felt happy being around Luke as well, but his answer only made her question him even more. She toyed with the key before she mustered up the right question to ask. She knew that if it were the wrong one, he would provide a vague answer, just as he did before. She waited for the final flare to explode in the sky before she sat forward, "You make me happy too, Luke, but I don't get why you keep speaking in code."

He repositioned himself towards her, reaching for the oars he replied, "I'm not speaking in code. I told you how I felt." He glanced at the quiet sky, unable to provide a better explanation. "Looks like the shows over. I'll take you back."

Silently he rowed through the darkened water and docked at the pier. Just like their return to land, they both entered the house with a loss for words. Ana stumbled as she walked in the foyer even though the floor was bare and she wore flip flops. She was happy that Luke had gone in the family room because he probably would've made a fuss over her. Her mind circled around what wasn't said trying to focus on what he did say. He always made comments that blurred the lines. Now she didn't know what was real or fake anymore. But what he had just said was real. She perceived his comments validity in his eyes. When he looked at her, she endured the draw of his emotions pulling her in. She wanted to reach over and confess to him how happy he made her too, the happiest anyone ever did. However, so did Torrance. Ana snuck a call to him from Leif's phone but he didn't answer. She had to try and speak with him. The evening had turned awkward and the last thing she could do was confront Luke. Not with the unforeseen status of her relationship with Torrance.

***

Unable to hold on to her slumber, Ana woke way before she had planned. It was barely after midnight. Waking up early was never good because she either couldn't go back to sleep or hunger cried out to her until she settled her craving. That morning she experienced a little of both. She got up and pulled on a pair of socks to guard off the cold floor. She loved that house, all but the stairs. There were so many of them. She could hear loud popping sounds however the hour was too late for fireworks which meant Luke was watching the television downstairs. She had begun her descent but first she had to visit the bathroom. Ana almost ran back to her room before she finally made her way down the stairwell. She tiptoed through the hall into the living room. The television was on an action flick that she didn't recognize but Luke was asleep on the couch just as she figured. She looked around him for his phone until she saw it tucked beside him. She reached over, sliding it from beneath him and slowly walked away happy not to have disturbed him. She went through the contacts with the hopes of his phone number still being saved. Unlike her other friends and family members Ana never remembered his number and she had left her own phone upstairs. She opened the patio door and went outside, closing the door behind her. Her chest felt heavy, forcing her to take deep breaths at the sight of his name.

"Here it goes," she huffed, pressing for the phone to call Torrance. She listened to the ringing melody several times before she heard his voice but it wasn't his voicemail, it was him.

"You have a lot of nerve calling me."

"Torrance it's me, Ana," she whispered.

"So you are with him."

"Yes but Torrance I-"

"You've lost your mind if you think calling me is going to make things ok. I wanted our relationship to work but the best man won."

"Torrance please you have the situation all wrong."

"So you're telling me that you're not carrying his kids."

"I don't want to keep things from you. I asked Luke to do this for me and, and yes they are his but Tor-"

"Don't you understand no matter where we go, what we do, he will always be a part of our lives."

"He's my best friend," she cried.

"And you love him," he sighed. "Goodbye Ana."

She had begun to say more but found an additional plea pointless. The noises of the night animals prickled her ears and nothing more. She sat down in one of the chairs swallowing her face with her hands.

Awakened from his sleep after hearing the door close, Luke watched her from the glass door. He didn't hear the conversation but the discussion had obviously hurt her. Luke went to the bathroom and grabbed a couple of tissues before he opened the door. He walked over and knelt down in front of her startling Ana so much that she gasped at his presence. He pulled her hands away and tucked in the tissues. "Was it allergies again?" he asked with a crooked grin.

Ana nodded. "They came and now they are all gone." She wiped her face until the tissues became a mangled ball.

He stood up saying, "I was heading off to bed unless you want to stay up. We can talk about it or," he paused looking over his shoulder, "go for a swim. We can even pull out the leftovers and camp out in the living room."

Ana threw on a brave smile replying, "I think that I'll just go back to bed."

Luke took her hand, standing her up. She walked over to the door as he reached for his phone. He watched her saunter off to the stairs before he went back into the living room and turned off the TV. By the time he got to the stairs she had just reached the top. He climbed up them hopping over several at once to get to her before she went in her room.

He placed his hand on her shoulder turning her around. "Whatever it is, you can talk to me about it."

"I know," she replied stepping into her room. "Goodnight," said Ana with her voice escaping her. She closed the door and Luke collapsed on the doorframe.

He surfed through his phone pulling up the last call. Seeing Torrance's name he got a better picture of what happened but he needed to know more. He grabbed the knob to go inside until he heard her crying. Normally he would still enter but something stopped him. He tucked his phone in his pocket, peeling his toes from the chilled floor and walked away.

The next morning Ana didn't come down for breakfast or lunch. Luke brought her up something to eat and checked on her but she just wanted to stay in bed. She told him that she was tired. The doctor's orders were to rest anyway so it wasn't a complete lie.

Torrance had officially ended their relationship. The tone of his voice proved it. He hated Luke and nothing she could say would convince him of how much she loved him. Her murky hazel eyes focused on the television however she didn't care what aired. The images were blurred and unwelcoming thoughts clouded her mind so much that she couldn't make out what the characters said. What could she have done to make him think that she and Luke were in love? More importantly, what did Luke say? She replayed the evening in memory but Luke and Torrance's answers about what was said was vague. She stroked her stomach in fear. What was she going to do without Torrance? He had become such a large part of her life, her future and now he was truly gone. She blamed herself for not saying more when they left the restaurant. She could've pleaded her case and explained to him that she did love him.

Curling her arm beneath her head she looked at the blank wall that was painted white and empty like most of the walls in the house. There were no personal photos and only a few paintings hung on display. Luke called them his father's investments. He picked them out but his father placed them on the first floor. The artwork his mother had chosen years ago were all in storage along with their family photos. Even they reminded him so much of her. His memories were so vivid, as though he had kept records, reciting them to her. She didn't remember ever seeing them together but the way he spoke of her, love radiated off of him like the sun. Did she radiate with the thought of Torrance? Did her blood warm her body to the point that her cheeks bloomed like roses and her palms turn clammy? It was too late to find out. He was gone and he wasn't coming back.

The day had turned dim and Ana had been in bed since her eyes welcomed the sun. She went to the bathroom and ran the tub full of water. The bubbles tickled her feet when she stepped in and sank down trying to drown her sorrows. The warm water felt so good against her skin. Air jets lined the porcelain but they were a lot worse than the light movement in the lake. She didn't take the luxury of using them when she was there but she wished she had a tub of that magnitude in her apartment. Obviously it was designed to fit two but the thought of never having the pleasure sunk in, taking her deeper into sadness. Tears fell from her eyes and dropped into the water barely fazing the dissipating clouds. A knock at the door jostled her from her despair. She wiped her face with her wet hands and sat up.

Luke appeared through the opening of the door modestly hanging his head. "I'm glad you're finally out of bed, even if it's late in the evening. Does this mean you'll be coming down?"

"No I think that I'll just stay up here."

Luke finally looked up to her, meeting her puffy eyes. "Are you okay Ana?"

"I'm fine," she replied sinking back into the water. She gazed out the window saying, "I was tired, that's all."

He walked closer and sat down on the tiled base of the tub. Reaching over, he picked up the sponge, dipped it in the bathwater and wrapped his arm around Ana pulling her forward. She didn't fight him as he brushed the sponge along her back. She lied still, cradled in his arms. When she felt the touch of his breath against her hair she melted, unable to hide her frustrations any longer. She closed her eyes pressing out each tear until she decided that she wouldn't cry for Torrance anymore. The joy he had brought into her life would mean more than the pain he caused.

Unable to face Luke she sat up. "Thank you Luke."

He sat the sponge aside and unraveled his arms from around her. He dried his hands in a towel saying, "Don't take long. My dad's almost finished with dinner." Ana wiped her face to hide the last fallen tear and turned to him nodding.

She wanted to stay in the tub a little longer but the cold water and her pruned fingers were enough to make her get out. She told Luke that she didn't want to go down to dinner but she had spent all day in her room. It was only right to join them when Leif had gone to the trouble of cooking. He almost never cooked unless he prepared his famous lemon pepper chicken. Ana put on her clothes and stepped into the bedroom as Luke walked over with a tray of food. A second dish sat propped in her vacant spot on the bed.

He smiled, flashing her with his bright smile. "My father understands so I don't want to hear it." She grinned and peeked at the dish seeing the chicken just as she thought. "Wait," he almost shouted putting down his tray and held out his hands. He walked over and picked up her tray so that she could sit down. "There you go," he said placing the meal over her lap. He went back to the other side of the bed, picked up his own tray and sat beside her. Luke reached for the remote and turned on the TV.

"What are we watching?" she asked.

"We are watching your favorite movie for a change."

***

It had gotten late but Luke stayed in Ana's room even after desert. She lied down on her side unable to lie on her back anymore with her legs propped. Luke followed propping his arm underneath his flipping through the channels until he found something to watch. He passed a familiar cartoon from the eighties and decided to switch back.

"Cartoons?"

"Yeah, you better get used to them too," he laughed. He put down the remote control in between their pillows. His hand slid in front of him with his fingers dancing in anticipation until he reached over to touch her stomach.

Startled Ana ogled his sprawled fingers across her belly. "Maybe you shouldn't get so attached."

"Why," he said sitting up dismayed. "Why would you say that?"

"I, I didn't mean it that way. Don't pay me any mind I just let my mouth run away from me."

"Pregnancy brain," he smirked.

"No that's more like forgetting things. My brain is in torment."

"Why?"

Ana rolled on her back tapping her fingers on her stomach. "Luke," she said with her grin slowly fading in curiosity. "Why are you so good to me?"

He sat up and leaned over her staring down into her eyes. She was waiting for his answer but he grinned and ran his fingers through her hair. He held a curl between his fingers and looked at the dark round saying, "You're my best friend Ana. After my mother passed away I spent at least one month a year with you. Never had I felt more open or happy as I was than with you." He gazed at her with his eyes steady and his voice timid. "You're my key to happiness Ana. I don't know what I would do if I lost you. Things are different now. I'm different because of you, and them." He slid down to her stomach lying down. "You wanted them but now I can see that this isn't some type of agreement anymore. They mean more to me. I may be Uncle Luke or whatever title you want to give me but no matter who you're with, I want to be a part of their life."

Ana ran her fingers through his hair swallowing deeply. "What we did Luke, I never thought it would change us."

Luke climbed to the top of the bed and leaned over her again. "I'm glad that we did."

Babycakes

Frost

Chapter 12

Ana woke with Luke by her side but when she got out of the bathroom he was already gone. She figured that he went to take a shower so she headed downstairs to get something to eat. When she reached the kitchen Leif had already raided the fridge. He made a fruit salad, toast and cereal which he was very proud of even though the meal involved no cooking. With the sound of Ana's flip flops approaching he pulled out another bowl and begun pouring her a serving.

"Good morning Ana. Did you get enough rest?" he asked greeting her with a smile.

"I don't think I'll be able to get enough rest for at least two months."

"Two months." He laughed. "Try two years, twenty years. Once you become a parent you never get enough sleep."

"Even now?"

He poured her some orange juice and handed her the glass. "Once a parent, always a parent."

Ana's stomach twirled and dropped. The babies would be due in less than three months. She had to find a way to turn things around for their sake. Everything kept bringing her back to what she always wanted but she couldn't figure out how she was going to maintain what she had left. Ana clutched her chest from the sudden pace of her heart. It beat so rapidly that she was afraid he would hear it. At least for now she had them with her and she still had Luke. However she knew exactly how he felt.

Her father finally confronted her about the big change in her bank accounts. She forgot that he even had access. She hated lying to him but she told him that she found a new bank after she had to actually close the account.

Leif sat down across from her, dipping his spoon into his bowl. She looked at him saying, "Luke's exactly who you wanted him to be. Why do you still worry?"

He grinned chewing on his cereal. "He's my son. I've never forgotten that, even if he refuses to let me back in."

"But hasn't being here changed things?" She leaned forward. "I can see how different you both are."

"Oh really," he chuckled. He scratched his temple and wiped away his grin. "Things have changed but what fears me the most is that when we return home, things will be just the same. Aren't you worried about that as well?"

Ana studied Leif, puzzled. She opened her mouth to ask him about his question when Luke walked around the corner.

"Good morning everyone."

They both greeted him and quickly returned to their breakfast. Ana was still curious about what he meant but she could tell by his demeanor that he was done with the conversation.

Luke sat down with a bowl next to Ana asking, "What did I miss?"

"You missed me telling Ana that I'm leaving in the morning."

She frowned but when Luke looked at her she grinned as though she had already known.

"Why so early dad?"

"I just have some things to do in the city."

"But what about your fear?" she asked coyly hoping he would explain what he said before.

"Oh I'm sure you'll find a way to calm them."

Me?

"Okay, what did I miss?" Luke questioned them with a chuckle in his voice.

Ana wasn't sure because she felt like she missed it also.

"Son didn't you say that you were going into town today? I wanted you to pick up something for me."

"Yes, we are," he replied looking at Ana.

She shook her head not wanting to leave the house unless she stayed on the Stokes property. Luke smiled nodding his. "Oh come on Luke. My clothes barely fit. Everyone will be looking at me."

"Then we'll buy you new ones."

"No you won't." Ana ran her fingers through her hair and grunted. "Promise we won't be out long."

"I promise," he answered.

***

It was well into the afternoon before they got into town. Luke parked the car and urged Ana to walk with him around to the different stores. The pastry shops were Ana's favorite which Luke agreed and visited before the meal at a local restaurant for lunch. With a full stomach Ana's top began to creep up her belly. She nervously passed by several people wearing the same outfit she had worn when they road up to the house.

Luke noticed and took her hand in his. "I have a question for you and I want an honest answer." Ana wasn't sure what he was going to ask but she nodded for him to continue. "The apartment is almost empty and I've seen you wearing the same clothes more now than ever in our what, twenty-plus year friendship. Are you moving out?"

"No," Ana replied thankful that she could answer him truthfully.

"Okay, you're not moving. So why don't you have any clothes?"

Looking down at her stomach which blocked her feet she answered, "How do you fit anything around a house?"

Katrina Thompson

Luke let go of her hand and placed his on her belly. He leaned over questioning the twins. "Mommy doesn't look like a house, does she?"

"Oh how cute," cooed a voice in the distance.

Luke eyed the woman for a moment trying to place her until he recognized the man beside her. "Mr. and Mrs. Andrews," he announced the couple, stepping next to Ana. His father and Mr. Andrews often golfed with one another. He hadn't seen them in years but they remembered him.

"How have you been Luke? I haven't seen you on the green in some time."

"I've been a little busy."

"I'll say," replied Mrs. Andrews reaching over to touch Ana's stomach. She was going to step back but she didn't want to be rude. Mrs. Andrews noticed, pausing at her attempts and retracted her hand. "I apologize. Where are my manner's? Your name is dear?"

"Ana." She smiled nervously.

"Did you finally decide to move out here?" asked Mr. Andrews.

"No, we're just visiting. I'm surprised you didn't see my dad."

"I did," he replied. "We're actually going to meet him for a late lunch. He told me that he was leaving tomorrow so he asked me to bring the Mrs."

"Lunch, here?" he inquired looking at the sign that read, Lunch Rush.

"Yes," he grinned.

"He asked me stop by at one o'clock to pick up an order for him and then canceled it." Luke glanced over at Ana licking his lips and returned to them with a smile. "We should go."

"Oh wait. You still haven't told us about the baby." Mrs. Andrews was finally able to touch Ana's stomach. "When are you due?"

Ana brushed away hanging strands of hair replying, "September 16th."

"Busy little one isn't it?" she perceived feeling the baby kick.

Luke grabbed Ana's hand saying, "Then that must be Luke."

Ana's eyelashes fluttered. He never called either of the babies by name.

Mr. and Mrs. Andrews ogled them for a moment with their eyes growing each millisecond. "Are you saying...?"

Luke nodded. "Its twins."

Shocked Ana tried to release his hand. Even though their secret was out in the city, no one knew he was the father or what they planned to name them. He held on tighter and intertwined her fingers with his. "She likes to call him, our busy bee and his sister, our little butterfly."

"Congratulations to you both!" They took them into their arms hugging them. Ana couldn't help but sink. She was in total shock until she spotted Leif walking towards them.

"What are we so happy about?"

"You were here a whole week and didn't tell us Stokes," Mr. Andrews scolded Leif.

"I was floored to find out the news." He looked over at Luke and to the door of the eatery. "I'm starved. Will you two be joining us son?"

"No dad. We were just heading back home." He could see from the glare in Ana's eyes that she was not as happy about his confession as he was. She didn't remove her hand from his until he let go. But even though she didn't immediately want to detach herself, she was silent on the way home. After he unlocked the door to the house Ana walked upstairs. He dropped his keys on the table in the center of the foyer and watched her moving further away. He didn't understand her silence. When she was upset with him she said it or pushed him away. There was mystery in speechlessness. He ran up the stairs behind Ana catching her before she went in her room. He pinned her against the wall so she had nowhere to turn. He had questions but his would have to wait.

"Why would you talk about the kids that way?" she asked with a trimmer in her voice.

"Because," he said reaching up to wipe away a tear, "they are mine."

"No they're not," she replied with her legs almost giving way beneath her. "You essentially gave them to me. You never wanted them."

"People change Ana. I've changed."

She gazed up into his eyes with her tears sliding down to her ears. "You've changed but so have I."

She slipped from his grasp and went inside her room closing the door behind her. The touch of his breath against her face made her blood churn in excitement and her heart flutter. Torrance's words held true, she loved him. But because of her feelings and Luke's proposed affection she had lost him. What right did she have to take him from Candace?

***

"Why dad?"

Leif walked into the family room and sat down in the chair beside him. "I understand why you two haven't told anyone. Her father might actually kill you when he finds out. But why would you keep it from me?"

"Dad there's a lot you're not aware of but sending in the Andrews' was really low. With Mrs. Andrew's mouth, everyone is going to know soon."

"That was my plan but I have to say you fell right into it. I was certain that once someone confronted one of you, either was bound to crumble. She says that the smile on your face was undeniably the biggest she had ever seen. She is concerned however about Ana. Her face flushed all over. Where is she?"

"She's upstairs," he replied turning off the TV. "Something happened dad. Something changed and I don't know what it is."

"Then you need to find out what it is and rectify it." He stood from his seat. "When I saw Ana in her current state with you I thought, who would let their girlfriend go anywhere with her male friend? But not only is she here, she has a cellphone with no reception and hasn't asked to hold my phone in days. Just looking at you two reminded me so much of your mother and I. You can't hide how you feel son. Ana on the other hand..."

"Yeah I know. I just got that first hand. I'm going to talk to her." He leaped from his seat and went up to her room knocking on the door. When she didn't answer he slowly pushed it open and found her sound asleep. He walked over to awaken her but he decided not to. He only imagined what being pregnant was like. She was probably really tired. He brushed her hair aside and kissed her temple.

***

Luke twirled in his sheets trying to get some sleep but thoughts of Ana kept him awake. She didn't come down to dinner and even his father couldn't convince her. He had to talk to her about what happened earlier. He pulled back his sheet and charged to her room but was shocked to find it empty. She couldn't have left so he walked downstairs, following the light from the kitchen. He entered cautiously and noticed her sitting at the table, licking the frosting from one of the cupcakes she made for the holiday. They were a vanilla cake with raspberry filling, white chocolate buttercream frosting and had blue sprinkles in the shape of stars. Luke found them in a store when he went into town and had to buy them for her.

She almost dropped her treat seeing him walk into the kitchen. "Did I wake you?" she asked embarrassed.

He sat down at the table and crossed his arms. "Yes, you did."

"I'm so sorry. Here," she said passing him one of the uneaten cakes from her plate. "Will this make up for it?"

He unfolded his arms and rested them beside Ana's peace offering. "It will help but your generosity doesn't calm my nerves."

Ana stopped eating and put her fork down. "What's wrong?"

He looked at her, twisting the cupcake like a glass of scotch. "I upset you earlier and I don't understand what I did that was so wrong."

She stood from her seat and walked over to the window. She scanned the blackened lake off in the distance replying, "You talk to me like we're together. Then we're out in the public you make me into someone that's not real." She turned to him saying, "You promised never to do that to me again."

He jumped from the table in defense. "I never meant to make you feel that way Ana. What I said to them was real and from my heart. I want to be a part of your lives. I want you to make a choice. Choose Ana, choose to be with me."

"Luke, I can't." She stepped beside him with her socks skating on the floor. But like every time before, even with a head start, he caught up to her. She turned to him asking, "Why are you doing this to me Luke?"

"I think only you can answer that Ana. The closer we become you push me away. I know that I'm not the only one feeling this way. Everyone sees it but we keep denying ourselves."

"But what if how we feel only hurts people?"

He stepped over to her until he couldn't get any closer. "Then what we feel wasn't worth fighting for." She shied away in despair but when Ana raised her head, his lips met with hers.

***

Babycakes

Banished was guilt and anguish from Ana's mind as she lay in Luke's arms. The sight of his hand on her bare stomach celebrated their union in more ways than one. She never wanted to leave his embrace but the sun was perched on the window shining its bright light into the room and the pressure in her stomach pulled her away. She searched for her shirt but when she couldn't find it she scurried off to the bathroom anyway. While washing up, she heard a knock at the door and as always Luke just entered. She dried her hands but peered over his shoulder for an even bigger towel. He noticed and grinned, reaching for her hand.

"Why are you trying to cover yourself?"

She smirked. "Luke, you don't have to try and make me feel better about how I look."

"You're right, I don't have to lie. You're beautiful, the most beautiful woman I've ever known."

***

With the wind in her hair and her hand clutched in Luke's she really did feel beautiful. He had taken her to the beach even though she didn't want to go. She wore all of her decent outfits and she refused to let him buy her anything. She put on one of her dresses but her breast had grown and her bra hardly held them. She confiscated one of Luke's shirts and rolled up the sleeves to wear with her dress. They went together perfectly. At least it was something she could give back to him. Although at the moment she didn't want to. Whenever he stepped away the smell of his cologne lingered in his top and mixed with the salty scent of the beach to make her trip more memorable. The sand sank beneath their toes as they walked along, smiling at the kids at play and the sails swaying in the distance.

Luke took her hand back in his pulling her to a stop. She turned to him with a grin, however his cocked head and curious glare worried her. "What is it Luke?"

"My father mentioned something I noticed as well, but I figured since we've decided to give this thing a chance you might answer me truthfully. What's going on with you and Torrance?"

She rubbed her thumb across his hand and let go to cross her arms over her stomach. "Torrance broke up with me after our dinner date with you and Candace. I ah, I didn't want to believe it but he continued to ignore my calls. The night you found me on the deck I had just gotten off of the phone with him. He made sure I understood that it was over." Ana turned to the water saying, "Now that I have been honest with you can you be honest with me?"

Luke stepped beside her nodding.

"You truly don't remember what you said that night?"

"I don't," he lied. If he told her the truth she might change her mind about being with him. Especially if she knew that Torrance was going to propose. "But I don't understand why it took you so long to come around?"

She looked at him with her eyes glazed over with disappointment. "Luke, Torrance and I were in love. It's just that he saw that I, we loved each other more. I will never forgive myself for hurting him."

"There's someone out there for everyone. He'll find someone else."

"What about Candace?"

"She knows we weren't serious. I'll explain everything to her when we get back."

"Luke it's more than that for her. She has real feelings for you. We even spoke on the phone when you weren't around. Candace wanted to be a part of your life."

"Now I get why she was trying to make cupcakes. Believe me, I wish you gave her some cooking tips." He laughed. Ana found humor in his joke as well but she knew that it would be more difficult than what he was thinking. He noted the grim smile she adapted. Of course she didn't want to hurt anyone. That's one of the things he always loved about her. He pulled her into his arms and kissed her.

Babycakes

"You're always thinking about everyone else Ana, that's part of what makes you so wonderful. But for once can you please do something that makes you happy?"

With her head still resting on his she answered, "Isn't that how I got pregnant?"

He smiled and replied, "That was actually my idea."

"You know," she cooed wrapping her arms around his neck, "you're right."

***

Looking up from her stomach Luke kissed near her navel and said, "Come home with me."

Ana giggled gazing down at him. "Why can't we just stay here?"

"Because I have to go to work." He kissed her stomach again and lied down beside her. She turned towards him taking his hand in hers, curling it under her chin. "When we leave in the morning I really want you stay with me. We can move your stuff in and set up the second room for the kids until we find a bigger place."

"Luke," she said sitting up, "I can't."

"You don't want to?"

"It's not that, I just can't move in with you, not like this. Maybe we should wait until the babies are born and I can tell my family."

"Why don't we tell them now?" He reached over to the nightstand grabbing his phone.

Ana took it from him shouting, "No Luke!"

"Why not?"

"Luke you know how my family is. My parents love you but they're not so forgiving when it comes down to breaking their rules. They still think I made the biggest mistake ever staying in the city after college. I don't want to make things worse okay."

"I don't think it was a mistake," he replied leaning over to kiss her. He pulled her down on the bed and showered her with the touch of his lips.

Ana brushed his strong chin planting her hand on his cheek. "Okay I'll stay but only for the night.

***

Ana went home with Luke after their return, keeping her promise. He took their things upstairs while Ana turned on her phone to finally see if anyone noticed she was missing. Technically she had called her parents and told them that she was spending the holiday with Luke and his father as an excuse not to come home. Madison called Luke and found out she was with him so she knew where Ana was. She listened to her voicemail realizing with the sound of Fran's voice she hadn't told her. She quickly pulled up her number and stepped out on the patio listening to the music while she waited for her to answer.

"Hello Ana, nice of you to finally return my call."

"Sorry," she grinned closing the door behind her. "I went to the Hampton's with Luke and his father."

"Why didn't you invite me? We might not ever be able to get away after you give birth."

"It was kind of a last minute thing. It's not like it's my house to bring guest anyway. You'll have to take that up with Luke."

"Speaking of Luke how is he?"

"He's great, actually we're both great."

"We're, what's with the…Ana are you telling me you and Luke?"

"Yes that's what I'm saying," giggled Ana.

"But what about Torrance?"

"That's still kind of a mystery to even me but we can discuss him later. I want to talk about you. What's going on with the wedding? Is there something you need me to do? I was Mad's maid of honor but that was so long ago. I don't remember what to do anymore."

"We figured out a date, June 22nd so make sure Korina doesn't have you working."

"I don't think we'll have a problem there but let me know if there's anything I can do." She looked over her shoulder saying, "I have to go."

"Is lover boy calling?" asked Fran. Ana turned taking a quick glance at Luke through the glass smiling at her. "Ana," she called out to her. "I know that this is what you wanted but don't give in too easily. You have kids to worry about and Luke isn't the settling down type."

"Fran you don't need to worry. I know him. He would never hurt me."

"Um hum," she mumbled in the phone. "Later girly."

"Bye Fran." She hung up and stepped over to Luke who joined her outside.

He wrapped his arms around her, sinking his chin along her neck. "Could you honestly tell me that you want to leave this?"

"Your arms?" She grinned. "Never."

***

Wiping her eyes Ana turned to see Luke sitting over her dressed in his suit. He brushed her hair aside and smiled. "I didn't mean to wake you but seeing you here sleeping, I had to."

"That doesn't make sense," she smirked.

"Just let me explain. I had to wake you because I'm hoping that when I come back home you'll still be here. "

"How can I resist with those brown eyes staring at me?"

He leaned over and kissed her. "I wish the work day was already over."

Ana got up to see him off, wishing that he would stay but was glad for his return. She went out on the terrace, looking out into the morning sky. The new day promised them a much awaited start. Their bond was over twenty years in the making but they were finally together. A light breeze brushed her face caressing her cheeks with its warm touch. She never thought it possible. The babies leaped inside of her as if they felt her joy rising. She cradled her stomach smiling. Maybe they did. Maybe they sensed that their family was almost complete.

A ring of the doorbell took Ana from her happy thoughts. She stepped inside hoping that Luke decided that he didn't have to go to work. Racing to the door she fixed her hair even though he had already seen her and pulled it open. Only the face she saw belonged to someone else. Ana's smile diminished and she stepped back. "Candace," she almost whispered. She followed her eyes looking down at Luke's shirt that she wore, just touching her thighs.

"I didn't want to believe it Ana but pictures don't lie and neither do my eyes."

Pictures? "Candace, I'm so sorry. We never meant to hurt you."

She grinned shaking her head. "I saw your connection to one another but I said she has Torrance, what would she want with Luke? When I bumped into the two of you at dinner I knew you were the Ana I heard about but Luke made it seem like I got the story all wrong. He said that you used a donor. My girlfriend," her voice quivered before she collected herself and licked her red lips, "sends me a picture of the two of you kissing on the beach with his hands nestling your stomach like the proud father. How could you?"

Ana brushed her hair behind her ear. "I tried to push my feelings away but I couldn't, we couldn't. I didn't mean to take him from you."

Her eyes creased as she stared at Ana for a moment. "No you didn't," she finally spoke, taking in a deep breath. "I was hoping to catch him before he went to work."

"He ah, already left," Ana replied sheepishly.

"To be honest with you, I don't completely blame you. I was so blinded by his charm that I didn't see how he was just using me. He barely paid me any attention before and then all of a sudden he kept in contact almost every day. The funny thing is that when we were together, most of that time was also spent with you. I see it now. He used me to make you jealous. Then I got to thinking, that's why Torrance seemed so upset at dinner. He saw it too." She looked at Ana's stomach blowing off.

Ana stepped forward trying to convince her otherwise saying, "No Candace, you have it all wrong."

"I don't think that I do. You got one of the most eligible bachelors to get you pregnant and fall for you. Tell me Ana, with everything that's happened, did Luke say that he loved you?"

She knew that Candace was aware of his emotional detachment with the word. Ana's eyes burst with fear.

"He hasn't has he?" She laughed and repositioned her footing. "My guess is that he never will. I may not have a hold on him but don't think that those kids are going to make him into the doting boyfriend you wish him to be." She reached into her designer bag causing Ana to step back again, afraid of what she might do. Instead of a weapon, Candace pulled out a ball of shimmering beaded fabric. "Unlike you I have enough respect to still treat you as a friend. I wanted to return this even though you'll probably never get your figure back. Not like it would fit you right anyway." She tossed the dress at Ana saying, "What goes around comes around."

Ana missed her assault by inches, however fear and anger twirled into one, creeping into her soul. She reached down to pick up the "dirt" Candace threw in her face. She never had a dress so delicately detailed. She unraveled the garment and dropped the suddenly familiar dress back to the floor.

***

Sifting through his file Luke approached his office but was stopped by his assistant alerting him of Candace's visit. He took in a deep breath gazing towards the ceiling to form his goodbyes. When he walked in she moved with the click of the door handle and stood up from the couch. He was about to greet her when she abruptly cut him off with her hand across his face.

She walked to the door as Luke rubbed his cheek and called after her. "Candace wait! I'm sorry."

"You know what," she paused, "I'm glad that you finally admitted something. You are sorry and I wish that I never met you." She turned saying, "I actually feel sorry for Ana. She's a nice girl but I told her you will never care for her. She should've stayed with Torrance."

"Candace wait, how did you find out?"

"My friend heard about you being in the Hamptons with your girlfriend. Since I was here I asked her to check it out and that's when she sent me a lovely photo of the happy couple on the beach. Did you make promises with her like you made with me?"

"Candace I didn't promise you anything. We had fun together. I never meant for it to go any further."

She chuckled under breath. "Now I see why you're single. You're heartless. Ana knows it just like I do. You should've seen her face when I told her. She may have trapped you but you will never love her."

"What are you talking about?" he asked walking over to her. "When did you see her?"

"This morning. I must have woken her because she was still wearing your shirt." She turned and walked out of the door without looking back.

Luke searched his pockets looking for his phone until he spotted it on his desk. He raced over calling Ana but she didn't answer. He had to see her. Slipping on his jacket he reached into his desk drawer and pulled out his keys. Ana would probably be okay because she should know that none of what Candace had said was true. He did love her.

When he arrived to his apartment he caught a glimpse of the gold dress crumpled on the floor and picked it up. "Ana," he called out but no one answered. He went upstairs but she wasn't up there either. Her bag wasn't even in his closet. Luke tried calling her again but she still didn't answer so he decided to try her place. She was obviously upset or she never would've left.

"Ana's," he ordered Richard. Her apartment wasn't far away but the trip seemed to take forever. The moment he pulled up Luke yanked his key from his pocket and went inside. He ran up the stairs to her apartment and unlocked the door startling Ana.

"What are you doing here?"

"What do you mean what am I doing here? What are you doing here? I went to check on you after Candace came to my office."

She repositioned the bundle in her arms and the bag on her shoulder replying, "Yeah she came to visit you and to give back the dress she borrowed."

He walked over to her with his hands outstretched. "Ana I don't understand what's going on. What did she say to you that has you so upset?"

"Luke," she said holding back her tears, swallowing them with despair. "I just can't do this right now. There's a cab downstairs waiting for me and I just...I need to get away Luke."

"You're always running, trying to be alone. Don't you understand that life doesn't have to be this way?"

"Everyone can't be like you Luke. Remember, you got rid of anyone that ever wanted to be with me. I'm used to being alone now." She spewed out the words with so much pain that they croaked from her throat.

"I've already apologized for that."

"How many apologies can you give before I can no longer forgive you?"

He stepped closer saying, "I don't understand Ana. I didn't do anything."

"How often do you let your woman come in and borrow my things?" Luke looked at her confused. "That wasn't my dress Luke, it was Korina's! She thought that I stole or lost it." Almost losing her grasp she tightened her arm around her things. "I wasn't moving. I sold just about everything I owned because I'm broke. Korina fired me Luke! For months I have been stressed over trying to figure out how I was going to support my kids when I could barely take care of myself. All of this time," she shook her head, "all of this time one of your girls had it." She tried to walk around him but he held her arms causing her belongings to fall to the floor.

"Ana please listen. I didn't know okay. You should've said something to me, about your job. I would've gotten the dress back. I would've taken care of you."

"I am not your responsibility. Despite what you and my father think."

"What, did you think Torrance would've? I mean come on. You look like you're malnourished and you're pregnant. I thought it was because you were tiny before but now I see it's because you were starving."

"Torrance took very good care of me. He loved me. He respected me." She wiggled from his clutch and crouched down to pick up her things.

"Ana why are you acting this way?" He knelt down to help her. "I have done everything I could to bring you back to me. We can make this work."

She gazed into his apologetic eyes with her hand paused on her retrieval efforts. Breathing heavily, afraid of his answer she asked, "Luke what are you saying? What else have you done?"

"Okay truth," he sighed. "I wasn't as smashed as I proclaimed to be the night we went out. Torrance realized that the twins were mine and he got upset when he realized my feelings for you." Ana was unable to hold her dissatisfaction in anymore. The tears began to drizzle down her cheeks. "Look I know that I wronged you. He and Greg loved you but I knew they weren't right for you."

"Greg," she whispered looking at Luke as she fell back. She felt like the wind had been knocked out of her.

"Ana he never wanted to get married. He said so himself. You would've never lasted under your father's rules. He was going to break your heart so I told him that he should end things before he took you all the way to Boston. I did it to protect you."

"No Luke, you did it because you're selfish and manipulative. Admit it! You didn't want to lose me so you strung me along just to keep me here. My whole life was controlled by my family and I came here for independence but you," she said throwing her things in the bag, "you were worse than all of them. You used me to comfort you, console you and to be by your side. But you were just afraid of losing someone else. I was right all along but now I know that so was everyone else. You will never say that you love me because you're so damaged that you can't love. How could I have been so stupid?"

"You're wrong. I can love." He grabbed her by the back of the neck pressing his lips against hers. "You must to believe me Ana. You have to."

She pushed him away and collected everything within her reach. She stood up trying to steady herself. "It's too late Luke. Our time together has been nothing but the world you created full of lies and deceit. I don't trust you anymore."

Ana dropped her things again but this time on the counter when the sting of her emotions began to affect the babies. Luke tried to assist her but she brushed him off and headed for the door. She clung to the frame when pain struck in her lower abdomen but she continued walking. She couldn't look back. She refused to think about what she was leaving behind even though it was Luke.

Luke watched her walk away knowing that he had really screwed up. He held the counter rocking back and forth until he slapped it with his hand and dropped to his knees. Like the things she left in anger, his heart was scattered about the kitchen floor. He thought by coming clean she would forgive him. She had to forgive him. He peeled himself from the wooden planks, running after her. Thankfully she hadn't gotten in the cab yet but seeing the distress on her face, he knew that he had devastated her. "Ana I messed up," he said walking closer.

"No more Luke. I can't take it anymore. Don't you understand? It's not just about you or me?" She took in a deep breath and clung to the rail. She detected Luke's reach for her so she stepped away. "I let what I wanted get in the way of what should've been. I've learned my lesson and so should you. Goodbye Luke."

***

Two weeks had passed and Ana hadn't come back to the apartment. Luke visited every day in anticipation for her return. He went to her empty room where she had meticulously folded the blankets on the bed along with her body pillow and Torrance's bag sat in the top of the closet. He thought that she would at least take it to Torrance if she was going to go back to him. The truth was he didn't know where she went. He called Fran the next day hoping she was with her however she quickly denied it.

"Please tell me where she is Fran," Luke begged.

"She's with family Luke. You should give her some space."

He knew it not to be true because Ana didn't want any of them to know. Upset he yelled, "I'm sure you know where she is. She's your best friend. Why would you not want her to be happy?"

"Happy." She laughed. "What were you making her happy by taking every opportunity away from her? She told me what you did Luke, everything you did. I was rooting for you. Ana's excuses for you made me believe you held the possibility for change. I knew you were a womanizer but I didn't want to believe you would hurt her. Ana is somewhere where she can collect her thoughts and figure out what's best for her and the kids. Let her be."

"They should be with me Fran and you know it," he replied angrily. "You can tell me and I'll just say that I tracked her down or something."

"Goodbye Luke."

His phone beeped in his ear but he still held the cell against his cheek. He sat in her empty space replaying what happened in his thoughts. *Maybe if I didn't tell the truth. Maybe if I waited at my place a little longer, Candace may not have gotten into her head.* He took in a deep breath and found like everything else missing in her apartment, so was her mixer. The large blue appliance took up so much counter space but Ana couldn't live without it. *She must have sold it.* Luke pushed off from his seat at the island and was about to leave when he noticed something colorful poking from the pile she left on the floor. He bent over picking up her things only to find the vibrant fish he had gotten in Hawaii. Luke swallowed the tiny plush in his hands sobbing.

***

Trying to make amends Luke had gone to meet with Korina carrying in her freshly cleaned dress on his arm. He may have ruined their relationship however he could at least get her job back. Instead of visiting her at her home, he decided to go to her office. He had never gone to the establishment before but Ana described it perfectly. It was buzzing with employees and clothing racks. There were large drawings against the walls with mirrors. To his surprise he found Korey sitting in one of the chairs intently looking at her phone with ear buds in her ears. She saw Luke approaching and pulled them out.

She grinned. "Hey Luke, is Ana with you?" she asked looking around.

His chest caved in from the sting of her simple words. "No sweetie, she's not with me. Have you seen her lately?"

Katrina Thompson

Korey shook her head replying, "When you see Ms. Ana can you tell her that I miss her?"

"Sure thing." He flung the dress over his shoulder and leaned in asking, "Where's your mother?"

"She's in her office," Korey answered flinging her finger as a text came in. Her attention went right back to her device as if Luke wasn't there.

He smiled and walked towards the room when he heard a voice saying, "Excuse me." He turned in the direction of a young woman sitting at a desk not so far from the entryway. "May I help you?"

He stepped over flashing his bright smile. "I'm Lucas Stokes, an acquaintance of Korina's. I was wondering if I could speak with her for a moment."

She flashed her lashes, returning with her flirtatious grin and picked up her phone to call her but Korina was already walking out to her visitor. "Luke it's nice to see you here. It's been ages since we've spoken. Come into my office for a chat."

With a smile on his face from her warm greeting he hoped that the rest of his trip would be beneficial.

Korina motioned for him to take a seat while she leaned against her desk saying, "You have to excuse my new assistant. It hasn't been the same since-"

"You let Ana go," he blurted out, cutting her off.

"Yes," she responded lowering her head. She walked over to her window. "That and I had to let Diana go. I never realized how much she relied on Ana as well. How is she?"

"I'm not exactly sure, however that's why I'm here." He stood up removing the beaded dress from the garment bag. Korina's eyes immediately lit up and her mouth opened but it was Luke that commented. "Judging from your expression you know what this is."

"My dress," she cooed moving toward the missing frock. She took it from him, immediately inspecting the bead work.

"Ana didn't steal or misplace it. A friend of mine ruined her outfit and borrowed this from Ana not knowing that it didn't belong to her."

She took in a deep breath as she placed the hanger on a knob that stuck out from the wall. She held out the tail of the skirt saying, "I knew she didn't but I figured somehow she or Diana misplaced it. Unfortunately Ana was the last to have the piece in her possession so I had to let her go. She sent a check for reimbursement and a letter pleading her innocence." Korina turned unfolding her arms as she walked over to her desk. "I hated firing her but worst of all I hated taking her from the girls. I'm a good mother but for them, Ana was stability. She knew their likes and dislikes. She taught them the little things in life that their father and I never seem to have time for. As much as I don't like to admit it, I was wrong." She pulled out a key and unlocked a drawer from below. Korina placed her purse on her desk to retrieve her wallet and said, "She's a brilliant woman, your Ana."

Luke sat back down in the chair crippled from her admission. It was his father that helped her get the job. She didn't have any real prior experience but Leif put in a good word for her as Luke's best friend, she always referred to Ana that way to him.

"I knew from the moment she started to care for Korey that she would be a wonderful mother and nanny." She rose from her seat and rounded her desk to stand in front of Luke. "But I think she might have a career in fashion. I found one of her sketch books in the guest room and was floored by her talent. I realize now how much she's been tackling under my employment. I don't see why we can't officially mingle the two. The babies will be here soon and I'm not sure if she's made other arrangements but if you can get her back for me this," she revealed handing him a piece of paper, "would be her new salary. And this, "she said handing him a check, "is to cover the dress she paid for along with a little something for her and the babies." Luke smiled looking at Korina's generosity. "She's truly one in a million."

"Yes," he replied choked up. "Yes she is."

Chapter 13

After endless pressure Fran still hadn't divulged Ana's whereabouts. Luke called Madison and even Ana's brother, Roman. Neither of them had seen her. he wasn't quite sure if he should also call her parents so instead he reached out to his aunt and uncle to watch the house for her return home. He was beside himself with regret and frustration from not being able to contact her. The calendar rolled to August 22nd, adding doubt in his mind of her ever coming around. Torrance helped change her decision about their relationship the last time they had a fight but there was probably no way he would help now. If he was right in thinking they were back together, Torrance would never allow him back in her life, albeit he had to try.

The girls may not have school but Torrance had to drive Korina to work. Richard drove him to the Stokes home, waiting for him to make an appearance. Just like the last time, he had to suck in his pride but he didn't bring him breakfast. This visit, more than anything, was to see if Ana and the kids were okay. The moment Torrance pulled up he opened his door and straightened out his suit jacket to approach him. He tiled the questions in his mind hoping that he could get him to release some information on them. *Think of this as a business deal.* He had had a fair share of hard balls in his time. However, he was still able to close the deal. This shouldn't be any different.

Luke walked to the driver side window and knocked. Torrance had seen him coming and though the steam that rose inside of him began to fog up the windows, the cloudy glass wasn't enough to mask the appearance steadfast on his face. He rolled down the window but kept his eyes locked on the car sitting in front of him.

"What do you want Luke?" he asked with his hands folded on his lap.

"I've searched everywhere for Ana and I can't find her so I've come to the conclusion that she's probably with you." He sighed, "I just want to know if Ana and the kids are okay."

Torrance's head moved so slowly to look at Luke that he was almost afraid it would keep turning. "What are you talking about? I thought she was with you."

He coward away in shame replying, "That would've been nice but things became complicated."

Torrance unlocked the door and pushed it towards Luke, knocking him to the ground. He picked him up by his collar and begun to strike when Richard grabbed his arm.

"Richard," Luke called out, "it's okay."

"No it's not," said Torrance shrugging his arm away from Richard's clutches and released Luke. "I want to know what happened and I want to know now!"

"I wanted things to work out between us but I went about it the wrong way. I should've told her about some things years ago and I didn't. I pushed everyone away from her life so that she could be in mine. I understand how what I did wronged her. I thought she went back to you after she found out it was partially my fault that she got fired."

"How was it your fault?"

"It's a long story and I find no point in discussing it."

"That's where you're wrong. You took the girls from her, her job and even me," he said pounding his chest. "You didn't see Ana because you constantly canceled your evenings with her. Do you understand that what you did to her not only affected her but your kids? I had to take her to the doctor's office several times and after she lost her job, she didn't want to go because she couldn't afford the visits. You know Ana better than anyone so you should understand that pride is not something she lacks. She wouldn't allow me to help her and when I broke things off, I was confident in the fact that she had you."

"She did, she does...I just don't know where she is."

Torrance leaned against the truck wiping his face with his hand. "Korina told me that she made her a proposition to come back but she didn't tell me all of the details. I'm guessing you had something to do with it." Luke nodded. "I told her that she probably wouldn't because she finally had everything that she wanted. She may be upset with you now but underneath all of the anger she still holds love for you." Luke ogled him, running his fingers through his hair shocked that he would make the admission. Torrance smirked at how pale his skin had gotten. With his teeth clinched he said, "As much as I want you to spend every last dollar you have to reconstruct your face from the rearrangement I'm longing to make, I would regret Ana finding out. She wouldn't want us fighting this way." He opened the driver's door and sat back inside. He slammed it shut and eyed Luke. "You left her hurt and alone. If I find her before you do I will follow through with my plans, ring or no ring." He turned from him and rolled up the window.

***

Unable to focus on work Luke toiled around his office refusing to take any calls. Leif got wind of his behavior and by lunch time he wouldn't allow the dismissal of his duties anymore. When he walked into Luke's office he sat in his chair facing the large window without care of his presence. Leif stood in front of his desk with his hands in his pocket and made a noise in his throat to get his attention but Luke didn't turn.

"Is there something I can help you with dad?"

"Oh so you can speak. I was beginning to think you had gone mute," he replied sarcastically.

Luke turned in his chair propping his hands on the desk. "No not mute, I'm just not myself today."

Katrina Thompson

"Today or the past couple of weeks. If you worked for anyone else you would be out on you're can by now."

"I'm sorry dad, it's just-"

"Ana, I know. That's personal and this is business. Look at what happened with the Brown deal. You let the arrangement slip from your hands. I can't let you continue moping around here not taking care of business."

Luke reached into his desk and pushed over the book he had been reading about expectant mothers to pull out the file. He tossed the manila folder over to his father and stood up. "I didn't blow the Brown deal. I couldn't sleep so I decided to crunch the numbers again. I weighed the pros and cons for acquiring the company and the way I saw things, we would be at a loss."

Leif flipped through the pages, grunting when he realized Luke was right. He dropped the file back on Luke's desk and walked over to him, joining his unbroken stare at the surrounding buildings. "Why won't you tell me what happened between you and Ana?"

"Because telling you won't change things," he answered coldly.

"It might not change things but I'm here for you son. Talk to me."

Luke turned to his father stunned by how open he had become. He never asked him to just talk. He curled his neck in shame saying, "I blew it dad."

"That much I surmised but how? When I left, I thought that you two finally had things together and with you starting a family-" he blew off. "How did things go wrong?"

"It went wrong years ago. Do you remember when I said that Mad needed a date to the prom?" Leif nodded. "Technically she didn't. She and Ana were going together. I knew that Ana didn't have a date because of her brother's but I was sure you would let me go if I said Mad needed me. I went, knowing that I wanted to be with Ana. I stayed with her the whole night and whenever someone else wanted to dance with her, I cringed letting her go. I turned into a mad man and ever since that night I've never wanted to let her go." He took in a deep breath and released the air of regret. "But she was right. I thought if I kept her near, happy and single she would always be around for me. I was selfish."

"Luke," said Leif grabbing his shoulder. "I'm so sorry."

"You're sorry?" Luke looked at him bewildered.

"It's my fault you turned out this way. I decided to send you off to visit with your aunt as a way for you to cope with losing your mother. Lana was the motherly symbol that I thought you lacked. I figured the time you spent with them would've been enough. Maybe I should've taken you to counseling or something, but Lana and Tess were so similar," he grinned. "When I called she said that you were doing fine. But talking to you now, I can see that all it did was create fear in you. I left you when you were home and then I flew you miles away when we should've dealt with losing her together."

"I did miss you dad but I don't regret one moment I spent with them." He smiled turning back to the opened sky. "Most of them were spent with Ana. You can't blame yourself for everything I did. I should've told her how I felt years ago."

"So what happened when you did?"

"It was too late."

"Was she truly with someone else?"

"Yes but I ruined that relationship too."

"Too, Luke?"

"It's complicated but I couldn't completely see my fault in their demise until she walked away from me."

"But I thought the twins were yours?" questioned Leif.

"They are mine." He rubbed the bridge of his nose. "Because of my actions over the years she thought that there was never going to be a chance for her to have the family she always wanted. She came up with this idea to have a baby on her own but she didn't want some stranger's baby."

Katrina Thompson

"She asked you."

"Right! Believe me, I thought about being with her for years but afterward, I fought everyday trying to find a way to tell her. However I wasn't ready to be a father. I found out she conceived just before I went to Hawaii. When I was away I took the time to think about the possibility of having someone that I couldn't brush off or deny. But with all of my doubts and fears she was here, dealing with the loss of Angel," he turned to his father. "That's what she named the baby. I realized then that maybe I could do this. We lost someone that we created and we got over it together. I was so certain that I convinced her to try again and she became pregnant with Luke and Leah."

"Luke and Leah." Leif grinned. "She's really going to let you name the kids that?"

Luke smiled and nodded. "It was really the only thing she allowed me to decide. They may be our children but according to her plan, they're hers. She even wanted a contract so I didn't think that she was trying to get a pay day or something from me. Can you believe that?" he asked rhetorically. "I would literally give her everything I own and she doesn't want one dime from me."

"Or me," joked Leif. "So if she asked you to be the father, when did this other guy come into the picture?"

"Torrance has always been in the picture. He's Korina's driver and they spend hours together, almost every day of the week. I couldn't get between them and after Ana found out I revealed her plans to someone else she told me about him. I watched them growing closer. He even wanted to propose to her but I guess like everyone else, he witnessed what we had both been depressing over the years. She loves me, I know it, but she also loved him."

"Oh son, you can only truly love one person."

"You're wrong dad. She does love him but she's in love with me and I broke her heart. I went to visit him today to see how she was doing. She didn't tell me but she lost her job months ago on account of something I did. It was an honest mistake," he said in defense after he perceived the look on his father's face. "I assumed because I couldn't find her, she went back to him. Luckily I was wrong but I think that I just gave him hope." He stepped over to his chair and plopped down. "I can't eat or sleep. This is truly killing me inside and I can't do anything about it. I screwed up! I no longer fear losing her because I feel like I already have."

Leif walked over to his desk resting beside the furniture. "Saying you lost her implies that you can never get her back." He sighed. "Do you know why I asked you to join me at the lake house?" Luke glanced up at him waiting for his response. "You haven't been there in some time and I only visit to be alone or to go golfing with my friends. I figured I could just stay with one of them instead of paying taxes, caretakers and so on," he said waving his hand. "I was thinking about selling it until I saw the two of you together. You are close but I understand why Torrance stepped aside. You, Ana and my grandchildren will enjoy that house just as much as we did as a family. I can still get rid of the place but I would rather not." He stood up with a smile on his face and tucked his hands in his pockets. "The way I've viewed the situation, you have two choices. Either figuring out where she is and once you've found her, never let her go or, move on. The choice is yours but either way I think you need to take some time off."

"No I'd rather work."

"Sitting in your office, staring out the window is not working son."

"When I'm at home all I do is lay in my bed thinking of her. I sit on the couch to watch a movie and I think about her, at my side laughing along with me. I try running but no matter what I do, I have to go back home. At least here I'm too embarrassed to cry."

Leif grabbed his shoulder saying, "The word is already out about my grandkids and I'm not going to let you sit here and lose yourself just because you fear the loss of them. Your grandparent's were overjoyed to find out about the babies and I, for one can't wait to hold them."

Katrina Thompson

"You told them?" asked Luke.

"No but I knew bringing Mrs. Andrews into the picture was the right idea. Look Luke, you've hit a bump in the road but your ambition has not been totaled. I know you can fix it. You better fix it," he threatened letting him go. "Go home son, collect your thoughts and make the right choice."

***

Lost in his unbearable chamber of memories, Luke moped around the house. If he wasn't exercising he slept the thoughts away. It was the only way to keep his mind off of his silent phone. He picked it up in the attempt to pry Ana's location from Fran or Mad but found the questioning pointless. He even called Ana's cell. Before he got several rings and her voicemail but this time he got a message saying that the mobile was not in service. All of his efforts were meaningless. Unlike him, the girls kept a tight lip on everything. *Maybe if I kept my mouth closed we wouldn't be in this mess.*

He placed the tiny fish in his nightstand drawer and decided that he should go downstairs to make himself something to eat. He skipped breakfast and lunch but now his body begged for food even if it was an early dinner. He walked down the stairs and was stopped by his ringing phone which he left in his room. In hopes that the caller was Ana, he ran back upstairs retrieving his cell from his nightstand and saw it was Max.

"Hey Max," he answered.

"Luke man, how are you?"

"Alright I guess."

"You don't sound alright but come to think of it, both of you Stokes sound off kilter. I just got off of the phone with your father and he gave me an offer I couldn't refuse."

"Oh, what's that?" asked Luke.

"He offered me a trip to Las Vegas and all I had to do was make sure you were on the plane with me."

"Max I'm really not in the mood for Vegas right now."

"You don't have to be but by tomorrow evening it's you, me and Caesars' Palace. Hot girls await my arrival and you need a break from being a Donnie Downer. I for one don't plan on missing out."

"I think I should stay here in case Ana comes back. She didn't run off with Torrance like I thought which means there might still be room for me. Being apart has to be killing her just like it's killing me. I need to stay in New York."

"Luke I get what you going through but let's face it, this is Ana. It might be months or even years before she'll talk to you again. You remember what happened the last time. This time you won't have Torrance or as it seems Fran, to change her mind. It will only be for five days. Your father told you that you need to choose. We both know you're not going to move on that easily but you can at least try and let me have a little fun. When we come back, I'll talk to Fran myself to find out where she is." He waited for him to respond though he heard nothing but Luke's breath escaping over the phone. "So do we have a deal?"

Luke was silent for a moment until he answered, "What time?"

"Flight leaves at seven. I'll send you the itinerary. You won't regret it my man."

***

Madison knocked on the guest room door slowly pushing it open to find Brooklyn standing beside Ana. She sat in a chair with her scrapbook on her lap laughing at her touch.

"Brooklyn," she called out with a scolding voice. "I thought I told you to let Auntie Ana get some rest."

"I just wanted to play with the babies mommy."

Ana leaned over kissing her cheek. "It's okay Mad. I got tired of lying in bed."

She walked over taking Brooklyn's hand and twirled the six year-old towards the doorway. "Off to bed Brooklyn." She closed the door behind her and sat on Ana's bed. "You know what the doctor said Ana. It's not good for you to be up."

"I know but after a while it's not so comfortable and the chair," she sighed, "makes me feel as though someone else is there."

"Someone like who?" she asked coyly.

Ana ran her hand over her book replying, "It doesn't matter anymore."

"Here," she said reaching out for the keepsake. "Give it to me." Ana handed the scrapbook over without protest. "Looking at these are not going to help you either. That is unless you've changed your mind. He called again."

She rubbed her stomach and swallowed so deeply that Madison heard her. "I haven't changed my mind. No matter how I figure things, this is the best idea for all of us. The babies will be well taken care of and I'll go back home. I'll find a way to convince your uncle not to mention them to my parents. No matter what, they will still be mine and I, their mother."

"Giving your children up for adaption isn't your only choice Ana. Your parents will understand and you can work things out with Luke. He loves them and you even if they're not his."

Ana turned away from her saying, "Love doesn't mean anything without trust." She closed her eyes and breathed in heavily.

"You're having a contraction, aren't you?" Ana nodded but she only focused on breathing. "Do you want me to call the doctor?"

Ana shook her head trying to calm down. Madison watched remembering all too well what she might be going through. Moments later she sensed Madison's close presence and opened her eyes. She placed her hand on her arm saying, "I'm okay."

"I'm sorry, I didn't mean to get you all worked up."

"Don't be sorry Mad. I owe you and Peter so much. You let me into your home, do my laundry and take me to appointments. I could never repay you."

"You're family, we love having you." She sat back on the bed and began flipping through Ana's book. "There's so many pictures in here. I remember this," she laughed looking at a photo of her and Ana in her playhouse. "We had so many dreams at that age."

"Yes," responded Ana, "and yours came true."

"Yours can too."

"We're no longer children Mad."

"No, no we're not." She flipped through the pages and found an empty section. "It looks like you've lost one."

Ana's eyes scrolled from her stomach over to the scrapbook. "I know. I dropped it on the floor and I think that picture, along with a couple others fell out." Madison took a gander at the other page smiling. Ana noticed confessing, "I showed that one to Luke. His father has him convinced that photos only bring back bad memories. I can tell that the loss of his mother is still hard on them both. Don't tell him I told you but he has a tiny photo of her that he keeps in his wallet. He and his father are so much alike. All of the pictures from the lake house are even gone. Luke did a great job covering the walls with different pieces of artwork but it's not the same as the family photos." She turned towards the window with a sigh. "If only we didn't heed to *everything* our parents say."

"If only."

***

With the night all a glow and the machines chiming from the endless gamblers Luke and Max indulged in his father's gift. Luke enjoyed his time with Max but even watching the woman at the pool didn't make him forget Ana. Max sat beside him toying with his chips at the poker table eyeing Luke's bundle.

"Are you in for another round?"

Luke collected his winnings replying, "I think I'm done for the night. I'll see you in the morning." He got up from his seat and cashed in his winnings. The trip had become quite lucrative. He won almost four thousand dollars over the past two nights. Still he moped. The heat was relentless even at night. He walked down the streets bypassing annoying street peddlers and overzealous tourist. It was an early night none the less. He was going to go back to his room when he noticed the glowing peak of the Eifel Tower in the distance. He wanted so much to take Ana to Paris, not only for the fashion but for the markets as well. They had such wonderful displays of food, some he had never seen before. The duplicate didn't compare to the real tower but being there made him feel a bit closer to her. She would've loved the painted ceiling which looked like the endless sky and the tiny little shops aligning the rear of the building. He roamed about the space until he spotted a jewelry shop with an eager sales clerk standing near the doorway. She smiled at him as he walked by but she wasn't what caught his attention. A case full of rings pulled him inside.

The girl's eyes followed him to the case and she crouched forward for his attention. "Is there something you would like to see sir?"

Luke continued looking down at the sparkling diamonds feeling as though he was seeing the same things as he did in New York. "I don't think I see anything here that I like."

"Wait!" she yelled. "You're looking for something special for someone special aren't you?"

"Well yes," he answered walking back to the counter.

"We have other things we just keep them in the back. Does she like pink? We have some amazing pink diamond pieces."

"She does but her favorite color is blue."

"Then you have come to the right place. I'll be back in one moment." She escaped behind a door in the corner of the tiny shop and within minutes she returned with a black case. She opened the leather bound box and pulled out a blue princess cut stone, risen by a pillar, of diamonds. "This is what we call Benitoite. It's fairly expensive, however very rare but you look like a man with taste. I'm not sure of your price range but this is-"

"Perfect."

***

Excited about his purchase Luke brought the ring down to breakfast to show Max. Perched at the perfect angle to focus on the pool he found him sipping on a mimosa. He took a seat in front of him purposely blocking his view and grinned.

"You insist on ruining my time here don't you Luke?"

"And here I thought we came to Vegas for me," he joked.

"So we did. Are you making progress on your mission of forgetting or has all of this made you want to finally give up the single life and settle down?"

"I could never forget but progress I have." He pulled out the bobble to show him.

He dropped the glass and took the ring. "Ah settling down. This is definitely Ana. Where did you get it?"

"I found it in a little jewelry shop in the Eiffel Tower Experience. For months I've searched and nothing."

"For months? Do you mean to tell me that all of this time I was trying to get you to admit your feelings you were at one with them all along?"

"Ye...no...I don't know. Even if I had a ring something was holding me back."

Max put the ring down and picked up his drink. He looked off into the distance and said, "Ring or no ring she's nowhere to be found. You may have wasted your money."

"If you think that this was a waste, you'll really be upset to hear that I put in a bid for the old Wong Fu's restaurant."

"Are you serious?" he asked astonished.

"Her place isn't taking care of kids or in the fashion world. She's a pastry chef and we all know it."

"Maybe that's the problem Luke. You were too busy thinking about what she should be instead of what she is. You saw her as your friend, someone that would be there no matter what you did to her. Who she really was, is Ana, the love of your life. But you knew that if you hurt her she would walk away and if you would've made that distinction about fifteen years ago, you would've saved us a lot of trouble."

He sat back in his seat saying, "I sense annoyance."

"You would be right. I screwed up in all of this too Luke, don't get me wrong, but when everything was aired out, you just should've come clean. Torrance or no Torrance you two had history."

"How is it that you're single and you're giving me advice?"

"I'm single because I choose to be. You're single because you wouldn't allow someone to love you. We all have to go at some time Luke. Why not spend the time you do have with someone you love?"

***

Madison walked down from Ana's guest room toying with her phone. Every day she asked her to change her mind about the babies but she was beginning to realize that her headstrong friend was steadfast on her plan. She went down to the kitchen where Peter was getting breakfast before heading out for work. He had stuffed a bagel in his mouth and began pouring a cup of coffee when he heard her approaching.

She took the bagel from his mouth and kissed him before placing his meal back in. He smiled and took a bite, resting against the counter. "I thought you were going to try and get some sleep before the kids woke you?"

"Knowing them that could be at any moment," she smiled. "I got up to check on Ana."

"How is our guest this morning?"

"Same as always, stubborn."

"They're her kids Mad. If she feels she can't take care of them, who are we to force her to?"

"I know that I can't make her but there's someone I can contact to convince her to keep them. She's upset with him right now but Luke has always been able to make her do whatever he wanted."

"Do you think that's such a good idea? She might hate you too for betraying her," he said walking over to her. He brushed his fingers through her short blond hair asking, "Can you live with that?"

Her hand tightened around her phone as she replied, "No but I know that she won't be able to live with herself if she gave them up for adoption."

Peter leaned over kissing her and smiled. "Keep me posted."

Madison watched him walk outside while she listened to Luke's phone ringing. His voicemail began playing but she didn't want to leave a message so she hung up. She was about to go back upstairs when her cell began to ring.

"Luke," she answered.

"Mad," his throat croaked. "What's going on?"

"Were you still asleep?"

"Yes," he yawned. "I'm in Vegas with Max."

"Oh then maybe we should talk later."

"Mad," he groggily uttered, "I'm up. What do you want?"

"I think that first I need to start off by apologizing."

"For what?"

She sat down on the couch replying, "Ana's here with me. Now I know that you're probably upset with me but I'm upset with you for what you did. We can hash that out later but for now we have more important issues." With Luke's silence she continued. "She's completely broke Luke. She came here with a suitcase and said that everything else was gone. She even had me sell almost all of her jewelry."

"Mad you didn't."

"Of course not but I made her believe I did. I gave her some money for them and she gave back every cent for staying here. She's given up hope Luke. She's not moving back in with her parents until after having the babies. Who, by the way are the main reason why I called you."

"She told you?"

"Yes, she wants to give them up for adoption but-"

"Mad what are you talking about?"

"Luke haven't you been listening? She's broke. Ana has been planning on getting pregnant for some time and within months everything she had was taken from her. She's up to her ears in doctor bills and she refuses to let us or anyone else help anymore."

"Mad," he said causing a rustle in the phone as he pulled on his shirt. "I'm coming there."

"What did you say?" she asked due to his muffled voice.

"I'm getting on a flight out of here."

"Luke wait, she's going to hate me. I only wanted you to speak with her about this being a bad idea and that her parents will understand."

"No they won't."

Mad leaned forward propping her arms on her knees. "You're right, I know but there has to be some other option."

"There is."

Babycakes

Luke hung up the phone on Madison to her surprise. She didn't know what he had in mind but hopefully he could get Ana to change hers. She pushed off from the couch and went up the stairs to find Ana. Only what she encountered was her troubled friend standing at the top with her eyes widened and her nightgown soaked.

"Mad," she called out. "It's time."

***

They didn't get on the first flight but they were able to catch one that left early enough to fly them to Connecticut by that evening. The first flight took about four hours, hundreds of seconds filled with restlessness for Luke but sleep for Max. By the second flight he had gotten enough rest but Luke's anxiety would've kept him up anyway. He saw him pulling out papers, aligning them and placed them back into his pocket. Luke then searched his bag for something else but after a while he couldn't take it.

"What are you looking for?"

Luke looked back saying, "A piece of paper. I need a piece of paper."

Max reached into his pocket yanking out his ticket receipt. "Here, use this."

He took the slip from him, pulled down his tray and began to write something down.

"What are you doing Luke?"

"Getting prepared. I have to tell her about all of her options."

"Tell me something. Are her parents really that against her having kids when she's not married?"

"I know they are. They never made it a secret amongst their family. Ana joked about being pregnant a couple of years ago and let's just say I've never seen someone fly off into rage like her father did. I can see why his business is so successful. They are extremely strict. If she shows up there with two babies needing a place to stay I can't say that they won't turn their backs on her." He sighed. "When they find out they're mine there's no way they won't forgive me for all of this. I have to call them the minute we land."

***

Rushing to the baggage claim area Luke pulled out his phone to speak with Ana's parents but when he noticed a missed call he checked his voicemail. He watched the crowd gather around the rolling metal plates in search for their bags when he heard Madison's voice.

"Luke I hope that the reason you're not answering the phone is because you're on a plane to get here. I just had the wildest morning ever! The minute you hung up I went upstairs and found Ana standing there. Her water broke and there was no stopping the babies from coming. I took the kids to the neighbor's house and I thought Ana could hold them in until you got here but Leah came before they even admitted her into the hospital. Luke came less than an hour later. They-" Her voice was cut off but she called again. She rambled for a moment but Luke tuned back in when she said, "They're beautiful Luke and doing fine. Leah was 4lbs 8 ounces and Luke was 5lbs even. I still don't believe what happened! Once you land call me. No text me so that she's not alarmed. Hope to see you soon."

Luke disconnected the call shouting, "I'm a father!"

Max turned to him shocked. "Are you sure, I mean isn't it too early?"

"Yeah but they're here!" he shouted. Everyone from the flight began to applaud. "We have to go. We have to get our bags."

"Bags, bags, yes bags." Max leaped onto the spinning belt and stepped over the bags searching for theirs. He found his first, tossing the luggage to his proud friend and then he located Luke's. He stepped off pulling his bag behind him. "We have to go!"

Max hailed a cab taking a quick glance at Luke who still had a large grin on his face as he called his father. This could actually be it. He wished they could've finished their vacation but coming home to this he couldn't be happier. He took Luke's suitcase from him putting it in the trunk beside his. When he got inside he noticed how Luke's smile had faded. "What's wrong?" he asked.

"I have to call her parents."

Chapter 14

Sitting next to Ana on her bed Madison tried to get her to eat her dinner. They brought the meal in hours before but Ana refused to eat. She also didn't want Madison to stay. After her water broke, she drove Ana to the hospital and had been there the whole day. Ana turned towards her smoothing out her gown over the mound which had gone down some now that the babies were born. "I can't believe they're already here. I thought I would have had a little more time with them."

"You can have all the time in the world if you change your mind."

"Please don't do this to me Mad. We've already gone over this and I'm tired," she said rolling away from her. "I'll call you in the morning when they release me."

Madison got up from her bed looking at her phone. "I'll be right back okay." She had just gotten a text from Luke. She replied with their location and went to the main hall to greet them. She paced back and forth until she saw their faces through the glass windows. The door opened slowly to reveal her cousin and their excited friend. Madison's face instantly lit up. "I thought you guys would never get here."

He hugged her with his free arm saying, "We had to wait in line downstairs to get checked in." Which room is she in?"

"She's in the third one on the left but don't be too brash Luke. I don't think she can take it right now."

"You don't have to worry. I know exactly what to say." He smirked and walked towards her room. Taking in a deep breath he stepped inside seeing her shoulders tremble from crying. He sat down beside her and gently brushed the hair from her forehead.

"I don't think I can do this Mad. It's killing me inside to think that I could give them up."

"Then don't."

She turned scooting away from him. She wiped her face asking, "What are you doing here?"

"Mad called but please don't be upset with her. She was afraid of you making the worst mistake of your life."

She turned from him shaking her head and wiped her face again.

He moved closer and said, "I know that I don't have a right to ask this but please don't do it. They're a part of me too."

"You're right," she whispered. "You don't have a right to ask me that."

"Alright, you're still angry with me I understand. Since you still are, I should let you know now that I called your parents and told them everything."

"Luke, how... how could you!"

"Ana please just hear me out."

"No Luke. Why, why do you keep doing this to me?" she cried. "Get out!"

The nurse overheard their shouting and went to the room. "Sir, I'm going to have to ask you to leave."

"No not until she hears what I came to say."

Max and Madison also made out the commotion and ran to the door. Ana saw Madison and said, "How could you tell him? I trusted all of you and constantly you go behind my back."

The nurse held out her hands trying to usher Luke out of the room. "I think it would be best if you leave. All of you," she ordered looking at the two in the entry way.

"No I should be here. They're my kids too and I love you."

Katrina Thompson

Madison gasped for air and she looked over at Max who was nodding with a smile on his face. Not only for his admission but for the $560.00 he picked up on the bet.

The nurse leaned over to get Ana's attention. "I thought you used a donor."

"I did. I asked him and he made the donation."

"That's not true Ana and you know it! I gave you the idea of conceiving again and we made love. Weren't you the one that said it was my choice if I wanted the children's paternity to come out? Well everyone knows now and I feel they should be aware of us also. Just give me a moment to talk to you and then I'll leave."

They all stared at Ana awaiting her decision. She glanced over at Madison who was still stunned and at Max nodding his head with a large grin. She looked at the nurse sniffling. "It's okay."

They tiled out the room leaving Luke and Ana behind. She found it hard to even catch a glimpse of him. She sensed him move closer but she didn't turn. Hearing him sigh she held her chest so not to cry. "What did you come here to say Luke?"

"I came to first tell you of how sorry I am for everything. You trusted me and I continue to disappoint you. Like I said earlier, I told your parents and as I figured," he grinned, "your father might kill me when he gets here."

"Gets here," she mimicked, turning to him. "They're coming?"

"Of course, they want to meet their grandchildren."

"Luke you shouldn't have. I can't afford to care for them. I don't even have car seats to leave the hospital or a place to call home. You're making things worst."

"No Ana, I'm making things right." He stood up from her bed and reached into his pockets. "When you first ask me to do this you wanted me to sign a contract. I didn't then but I have one now. Before I give it to you I wanted to let you know that I spoke to Korina and Torrance." He turned away saying, "They both want you back. Korina sent you a check for the dress and a gift for the babies." He sat on the bed handing the items to her along with the note she had given. "She says you can have your job back with some added incentives. This," he said pointing at the number scrawled along the top, "would be your new salary. I'm pretty sure that Torrance would love for you to take her up on the new wages and his proposal." He bowed his head saying, "When he told me that he wanted to marry you I lost my mind because I feared losing you. I was wrong for everything I did. All I ask is that you think about both options before you make your decision." He unraveled the other piece of paper and began reading. "I Lucas Michael Stokes do solemnly swear to love you and our children for the rest of my life. I will never again betray your trust in me and will forever honor and respect you as my best friend. I will cherish you for the rest of my life and remind you every day that this was the best decision that you have ever made, signed Lucas M. Stokes." He handed her the piece of paper seeing a tear fall from her eye. "If you choose to accept my offer, we can finally build the pastry shop or if you still want to go into fashion I can back it up. Whatever you want to do I don't care just so long as you don't give up on us."

"Luke," she said sternly, "I told you that I didn't want to take any money from you."

He reached into his pocket pulling out the ring. "I'd consider it to be our money." Ana was speechless. The blue stone shimmered like the morning sky but Luke's smile shined even brighter. His lips shook as he said, "If you choose me, I promise that I will never hurt you again. It was never my intension to do so. I was selfish, almost a bit psychotic in what I did to you. You," he cried, "were right. I was afraid of having people in my life because I feared losing them. But I never confessed my love to any other woman because the fact is that I love you, and only you. I always have and I always will."

Ana shook her head sprinkling the tears on to her sheets. "How can I trust you?"

"Trust your heart Ana. What does it tell you?"

Katrina Thompson

She wiped her face replying, "It's speechless. I feel like it stopped beating ever since the moment you broke it. It's too late Luke," she cried. "I listened to you like I promised. Now it's time for you to go."

Dismayed Luke slouched away. He almost crumpled in shame. He licked his lips tasting the saltiness of the tears that slid down his face. "Please just give me one more chance Ana. I know that you won't regret it."

She placed the papers he had given her on the nightstand and straightened up. "You're right. We could've had something wonderful but you lied, you manipulated my life and what's worse is that you blame it all on love. I know from experience how much love can hurt but it shouldn't hurt like this. No matter what you say or how many times you apologize, it doesn't change the fact that you pushed me away first and your actions kept us apart all of these years."

He watched as a funnel of tears fell from her eyes. He moved closer but she held up her hands.

"Goodbye Luke."

***

After almost a week in the hospital the twins were able to go home, but, Ana herself was lacking one. She was aware that Luke had stuck around to be with the kids but he kept his distance from her. She hated how things turned out. With her hormonal whirlwind of emotions still in an uproar she questioned her response.

She had been released from the hospital and with Korina's check she asked to borrow the money to purchase the car seats she needed to take the children home from her parents, but Luke purchased them instead. They came to visit her just as Luke said they would. Ana feared she would need to be readmitted after her father was done with her. Although whatever Luke told them was enough to accept her and the babies without argument. She also learned that their house was open for her return but before they left, Grandpa Leif spent as much time with the twins as he could. Ana's stomach coiled in grief over taking them from him but no matter where she chose to live, either of their grandparents wouldn't have been able to be around. Thinking about what they might be missing didn't compare to how she thought about spending forever without Luke by her side.

***

Back to the place she didn't want to return, Ana shared her old room with Luke and Leah. Her parents offered to fix up the other rooms for the babies but she refused. She still had the money from Korina but not just for the dress. She purchased her sketch book filled with designs stating that they weren't only fashion forward but exactly what her company needed. Ana was elated. She once again offered her a position to work alongside her but Ana's life had changed, her dreams had changed.

She enjoyed spending time with the twins but she was certain that the money would eventually run out. She wanted a job that wouldn't take her from them so much. The posting recently offered by her father was no longer available so she once again sat with her computer on her lap searching for a new career. Finding a job wasn't only for independence but to support her young family.

As she surfed through the net she noticed the faint sound of her phone buzzing beside her. She smiled answering in a whispered tone, "Hi Fran."

"Girly, I hope you are finally up for a vacation because the time has come to pick out my dress."

"I thought you would've done that months ago."

"Not without my maid of honor I'm not. I need you to tell me if I look fat or if my boobs look weird. Madison won't say it but you will. You don't lie."

"Everybody lies at some point in their life Fran."

"Not you, you're perfect," she laughed.

"I thought perfection was a possibility but things change. People change."

Katrina Thompson

Fran realized the change in Ana's demeanor. She took in a deep breath saying, "Are you talking about people or one person in particular?"

"I, I was speaking of myself," she whispered.

"Why are you being so quiet?"

"The twins are sleeping."

"That's not what I mean. I know that this hasn't been easy on you Ana. You can talk to me about it."

"I know but this is your moment and not mine. I don't want to ruin it with my issues. I can probably get my mom to watch the kids. When do you want me to come?"

"I was thinking next weekend. Mad's coming up on Friday night and leaving on Sunday. You on the other hand can scope out a new place to stay while you're here and your parents can bring the kids later."

"Fran!" Ana shouted with a bit of laughter. Her eyes darted over to the kids to make sure she didn't wake them.

"Okay, okay, I had to try but don't think I won't stop. I miss you and so does Max and Luke."

Hearing his name made Ana shriek. She glanced over at the babies again with her guilt ridden heart beating violently inside her chest. She felt guilty every time their eyes appeared to focus on hers. It was like they knew she had taken their father from them.

"Ana, oh Ana."

"Sorry, did you say something?"

"Only that I want you to make sure you bring something gorgeous to wear because we're going out to dinner on Friday night and out dancing on Saturday."

"I still have to discuss this with my mother. If I run into any snags I'll let you know."

She hung up with Fran but the notion of returning to New York City was nagging her, no matter her feelings, she had a duty as a friend and maid of honor to put them aside. She crept out of the room and went downstairs to talk to her mother about leaving the twins with her. As she approached the living room she overheard mumbling sounds which seemed as though Hannah was speaking with someone.

When she turned the corner Hannah jumped from her seat and removed the computer from her lap.

"Ana honey, I thought you were asleep," she quickly stated.

"I guess you didn't hear me on the monitor," she laughed pointing at the device beside her.

"Oh no I didn't," she replied coyly.

"Were you talking to someone?" asked Ana sitting down on the couch.

"Just myself. You know me and computers don't get along."

"Is there something I can help you with?" she questioned Hannah about to get up.

"Oh no," she answered sitting down beside her. "I learn better when I figure out things for myself."

Ana smiled turning to her. "I just got off of the phone with Fran. She wants me to go down to the city and help her pick out her wedding gown. Do you think that you can watch the twins until I come back on Sunday?"

"I wouldn't mind babysitting but I have to ask," she said noticing Ana's uneasiness. "Are you ready to return?"

Ana stood up tousling her hair. "I want to see my friends but I'm not sure if I can handle seeing what I left behind."

"Something tells me that you're not talking about surroundings."

She looked back to her saying, "Dad always told me to have a plan and when you have one, follow through with it. He never told me what to do when someone throws a wrench in it."

"Your father and I set so many rules for you and your brother's but we neglected to consider how being so hard on you would do you harm."

"Don't think that way mom. Those rules are what made me who I am today, even if I'm jobless and living back here," she joked.

Katrina Thompson

Hannah watched her sit down beside her and rested her head on her shoulder. She planted her cheek on top of Ana's head saying, "Plans are always subject to change. Look at us. We wanted two kids, a boy and a girl. God on the other hand gave us three handsome boys before we got our beautiful girl. Now you have your own bunch to worry about." She could make out Ana's restlessness so she wrapped her arm around her shoulder and asked, "Honey, do you think that you made the right decision?"

She sat up looking at her mother and replied, "Yes but I wish I didn't let things get in the way." Hannah was about to say something when one of the babies began to cry. "That's my queue," she grinned and hopped off of the couch heading upstairs.

Seeing that the coast was clear, Hannah went over to her computer which displayed the bewildered Luke. "Did you hear any of that?"

"I did," he answered with pity written all over his face.

Hannah settled into her seat and with a remorseful grin she responded by saying, "She just needs more time."

***

Luke understood that she may need more time but hearing her voice and not being able to see her quaked his heart into pieces. He grabbed the jacket from the back of his chair and went out to walk his pain away. He had done everything possible, he thought, to convince her of his affections. He figured that after she had given Luke his name and Leah his mother's, she had softened to the idea of them being a family. Leif told him that naming their daughter, Leah Tess, was something she had already planned and Lucas Jr. only made sense. She gave no further excuse to the use of his last name instead of her own so he didn't give up hope. Even after she was leaving the hospital and returned to visit the babies, Ana didn't deny him from seeing them. Still he remained hopeful. But when they were able to leave and

Ana decided to move in with her parents, the doubts crawled in. She left with them and he went home empty handed. He continued walking down the crowded sidewalks until a familiar voice caught his attention.

"Mr. Stokes."

Luke turned to find Winston standing outside the jewelry store. "I thought you were chained to the counters," he laughed walking over to him to shake his hand.

"No even we get a break from time to time. However you can come inside with me if you want to help returning me to the shackles."

Luke laughed and walked inside with him even though he had no reason to visit.

Winston stepped around the counter spreading out his hands. "So what brings you by today?"

He looked at him with a grim smile. "I don't know. I guess I just needed to get away from things."

"I'm shocked. I thought after not seeing you in a while that I had offended you."

"Offended me, no but I must apologize for something."

"Apologize to me, for what sir?" he asked leaning in.

"For years I've come in here toying over the idea that the perfect ring for Ana existed. I went to Las Vegas and found it but she still turned me down."

"Oh sir I'm sorry. I know that you seem to really care for her."

Luke laughed. "Did you miss the part where I stated buying a ring from somewhere else?"

"No I didn't, but no matter," he brushed him off waving his hand. "Maybe you'll buy the next one from me," he said tapping on the glass.

"Oh I haven't given up," replied Luke. "I gave her everything I thought she wanted instead of the one thing she really did." He bit his lip reaching in his pocket for his wallet. He walked over looking into the showcases until he reached the one carrying the item on his mind. "Can you ring this one up for me? I have an idea."

***

Back in New York Ana couldn't help but enjoy hearing the honking horns of the yellow cabs stuck in the same spot for blocks, the aroma of pizza mixed with the early fall air and the hustle and bustle of its dwellers. She had come in Friday evening along with Madison. She hadn't seen her since she left Connecticut with her parents. Being back with her and Fran seemed like old times. She missed them and being in New York.

Fran had everything planned out for their gathering. They ate breakfast at eight before their early morning appointment for a dress fitting. She didn't tell either of them where, however when they pulled up to Korina's office, Ana was overjoyed.

"I can't believe you kept this from me," Ana spazzed out wagging her pointer finger at Mad.

"I didn't know either," she laughed.

"I wanted it to be a surprise," Fran beamed as she pulled the door open to the office. "But this is only part one." When they got up to the office Ana immediately caught a glimpse of part two.

"Ms. Ana!" Kailey shouted running over to her. Ana walked over dropping to her knees with her arms stretched wide. Kailey fell into them and Korey was right behind her, sandwiching her sister in.

"I've missed you girls so much," she cried.

"We missed you to," said Korey.

"Does this mean you're coming back?"

Ana let go knowing that wasn't the case. She was about to reply when Korina emerged from her office.

"Ana!" she crooned walking over to her. "So nice to see you." She hugged her so tightly that it even shocked Ana.

"It's nice to see you too. I can't believe that you're dressing Fran for her wedding."

"Ah yes, I am or should I say we are." Ana smiled shaking her head unclear of her statement. "Come with me Fran and we'll get you fitted."

Fran handed her things over to Madison and followed behind her. "You should take a peek in the showroom to see if there's something you would like for your dresses."

Ana laughed. "As though we could afford it."

Korina turned flashing her a smile. "Don't worry, I would give you both a good deal."

"Come on Ana," said Kailey. "I'll show you the ones I like." She took Ana by the hand leading them in the room. While Korey regaled her on the past months Kailey pointed out her favorite dresses. Ana was surprised to see that she knew not to touch them. She had finally learned not to. In such a short time they had both grown so much, in size and in personality. There were so many moments in their life she held a vital part in but seeing them now, face to face instead of from afar, eased her mind. Her girls were growing into wonderful beings even though she no longer took care of them.

The assistant at the desk walked into the room and held the door open alerting them that Fran was coming in. She swayed in like a runway model. Her long legs were covered with the ball gown length and a corseted bodice. The more Ana studied the make of her gown she recognized the detail of the collar that swooped along the shoulder and the simple beading along the waist. It was longer than what she had drawn but her design stood right in front of her. She slowly walked towards the bride-to-be with her mouth stuck in ah.

Fran laughed at the look upon her face. "The moment you told me about selling your designs to Korina I told her that she had to dress me for the wedding," she confessed.

"You look beautiful. I mean I never could've imagined that you would be wearing something I designed but my idea or not, you are going to make Rolland's head explode."

"Just so that none of his brain matter gets on this dress, its fine with me," joked Fran.

Korina walked in behind her marveling at her work. "I hope its okay that I altered your design a bit."

"I love it," replied Ana still in disbelief.

"Good, so does this mean that you've given my offer more thought?"

"I have but I think I'm going to stick with my decision." She turned to Kailey picking her up. She placed her on her hip and kissed her cheek. "As much as I love the girls, I have two little ones at home who need me also."

"Okay," she said with a smirk. Kailey wrapped her arms around Ana's neck. "Does this mean that I'll be taking measurements for your wedding gown soon? You and Luke must have set a date by now."

"How did you know about Luke?" asked Fran.

"Word gets around," she grinned.

Everyone in the room eyed Ana. Madison thought she would have to pull Kailey from her hip. Ana began to sway but she regained her footing and replied, "I'm just a bridesmaid. This…this is Fran's moment."

"Okay then maybe I can get you to talk about doing a little freelancing. Just because you won't work for me doesn't mean I still can't pick your brain. I was a fool to let you go before but I won't let your talent go to waste."

***

Seeing the girls again felt like Christmas day and New Year's wrapped into one. The time she spent with them brought more joy than the prospect of an income. She took on Korina's offer to sell designs which was not only a godsend but perfect timing. She could use the money until she found a stable job back home. She wasn't happy about making business deals when she was supposed to be there for Fran but she understood. Though they hadn't finalized how much Ana would receive for her designs she still paid for dinner. Things were looking up for them all. Madison had her beautiful family back at home and as always, just happy to get away. Fran found the perfect dress for her wedding which was Ana's design and the gown might not be the last of her creations she would wear. Even if her name wasn't scrolled across a wall and she didn't have a personal assistant, Ana became a designer, just like she wanted.

They went to The Matrix to finish their night off continuing with their celebratory outings. In the crowded room the blaring music and its vibration pounded into their feet. In a circle they kept Ana on her toes, dancing the night away. Ana felt the tension racking her bones on the way there melt away. She didn't want to go because even the thought of seeing Luke frightened her. What could she possibly say to him? How could she turn away from his deep alluring gaze once more?

"I have to go to the little girls room," shouted Fran. "Coming with?"

Ana and Madison followed until someone caught her by the hand. She looked back and saw Torrance. Her heart stopped, instantly freezing her limbs. She stared at him for a moment before her body shook off the chill and she turned towards Madison but she had lost her in the crowd.

"Ana."

She watched his lips to form her name even though she couldn't hear him.

He held onto her hand and walked closer. He leaned over brushing the hair from her shoulder and said, "Can I talk to you for a moment?"

Ana's eyes met his as he pulled at her arm and she nodded unsure of where they were going. He guided her through the chatty patrons and over to the side of the bar. She didn't think the noise would be altered beside it but in the corner they didn't have to shout as much. However, shouting out something to say to him never crossed her mind. The whole time she scanned the crowd wondering if she would spot Luke but she never thought she would find Torrance.

He finally released her hand saying, "I never thought that I would see you here tonight."

Ana timidly smiled. "Nor did I."

"You look amazing. I mean you always have but what it's only been a month since you had the babies?"

Ana stepped closer for him to hear. "Thank you but they came early, August 29th." She pulled out her phone to bring up their photo. She handed it to him with pride. "Their healthy and happy."

He grinned looking at the picture. "Everything you could ask for." He gave her the phone and placed his hands in his pockets saying, "So do you?"

"Do I what?"

"Have everything you wanted?"

Again, her heart stopped beating within her chest. She brushed her hair behind her ear to play off her discomfort answering, "No one ever has everything they want."

"Really because I thought that we did."

"Torrance, don't do this."

"Don't do what Ana? I just-"

"Torrance you can't say we anymore. You left me remember?"

"I do and it was the worst mistake I could've ever made."

Ana dropped her stare, noticing that his feet moved closer. She looked up saying, "I know all too well how easy it is to give up someone you love but I also know that we both deserve better."

"Ana I don't understand."

"Torrance I loved you and I know we could've made it work but you gave up on us. I spent the rest of the weekend in the hospital thinking about how I hurt you. With everything going on I called and called but you didn't answer until I called from Luke's phone. I wasn't with him then and I'm not with him now. But regardless, you deserve to be with someone that can love you with their whole heart and I deserve to be with someone who is willing to fight for mine."

"I'm willing," he announced before he wrapped his arm around her waist pulling her in for a kiss. She allowed him to but the longer he held on, all she felt was the desire she had for their relationship to work and how much she wished for his return. But that was in the past.

Fran and Madison had finally found her in the crowd but so did Max. He was holding Luke back shouting at him. They walked over, sifting through the people, hoping to get to them before a bouncer did.

"Luke!" Madison shouted. "What's your deal? Calm down."

"How can I calm down when he has his hands all over her?"

"Don't you mean she let him touch her and you can't?"

"Max!" Fran scolded him. "Right now is not the time to be cynical. Look she didn't even want him to do it."

They all locked their eyes in her direction seeing that the appearance on her face wasn't happiness. Ana wiped her eyes and began to walk away when Torrance stopped her. She turned making her face unreadable.

"Ana don't you see that we can give us," he said vigorously pointing at the two of them, "another chance."

"I thought that was a possibility, I really did, until you made me see the one thing I was doubting and that is the fact that I love Luke. He didn't want me but I still loved him and when he wanted to be with me I pushed him away. I loved you both and you both hurt me albeit the key point I'm trying to make here is that you deserve more. I'm not the one for you and if you were the one for me you wouldn't have left me because someone challenged you."

"You're still hurt, I get that. But we can work this out."

She stepped over to him placing her hand on his cheek. "Torrance, a part of me will always love you but you opened my heart to see what I truly longed for. It now belongs to someone else."

"Named Luke." Ana lowered her eyes, holding her fingers against her lips. She felt a tear release from its iron cage, melting the liner from her eyes. She held her painful emotions in throughout their conversation but she couldn't any longer. Torrance placed his hand on her shoulder, glided his palm up to her neck and lifted her head to look at him. "I get it. I'm sorry for what I did to you. I thought that I didn't have a chance in the world to win your heart from Luke. I mean I'm a guy and I can see that that guy is perfect." Ana grinned releasing more tears. "I was an idiot to cave in but I had to try and get you back. I hope that you're at least happy." Ana nodded with a sniffle, though she wasn't sure if it was true. Before she could react, he leaned over again and kissed her but this time he pressed his lips against hers and pulled away with a smile. "Still friends?"

Ana nodded before she stepped backwards, folding into the crowd behind her. The bouncing bodies overpowered her but they covered her shaking figure. She wiped her face trying to mask what had happened in search from Madison and Fran.

"Don't you understand Luke?" shouted Madison. "She doesn't want to be with him."

Luke calmed but he was now beside himself. "She doesn't want him, she doesn't want me. I don't understand anymore."

"She does."

"What?" asked Max.

"She does," Fran answered.

"Fran no," said Madison. "She asked you not to."

"I can't take this anymore and I don't know how you can. You've had to deal with this more than any of us." She turned to Luke with joyful yet toxic venom. "She's upset with herself for letting her pride get in the middle of what the two of you could've had. You and her parents did so much for her that she never really had a chance to live for herself. Then you manipulate her life so much that once again she had to rely on her parents. She resents you for your actions and she resents herself for giving you up. You are the only man she has ever truly loved and you ruined her life." She took in a deep breath after spewing out years of frustration and scanned over to Ana who was still searching for them. She stepped closer to him. "Look, I have an idea. Before she leaves in the morning I will bring her down to the shop. Be there at 9 and you have my word that you'll get another chance at this."

"Fran what do you have planned?" he asked.

"You'll see then but for now you'll probably want to stay clear." She waved goodbye and went in the direction she had last seen Ana but Madison had something else to say.

"I thought I told you not to come tonight."

"I know but Max thought this might be my last chance. I've gone so long not listening to him that I figured this time I should. Did you bring the bracelet?"

"Yeah, it's at Fran's place."

"Here, add this and tell her what I told you. I don't know what Fran has planned but I must try something."

Madison placed the trinket in her purse and kissed them both on their cheeks. "I think we've had enough for tonight but stay low until we can get out."

"Mad wait, why?" asked Max.

"Why Max, look at her. You didn't see her when she came back to town and you didn't take care of her the month before she had the twins. If Luke wasn't my cousin I probably would've hired someone to string him up in the basement and torture him until he couldn't take it anymore."

"Ouch Mad," replied Luke.

"Sorry, I've been watching a lot of TV lately," she grinned shrugging her shoulder. "She needs to come on her own. I'm not sure what you two are going to do but you know Ana as much as I do. She can be stubborn and you can't persuade her this time. Ana does things when she wants to now. You, her parents, not even I can change her mind anymore. We've all done things that were untrustworthy. I for one am not going to let you hurt her anymore Luke."

***

Tossing and turning Ana woke Madison from her sleep on the sofa bed. She had dodged their questions about the encounter with Torrance not wanting to dwell on the fact that she had let him go.

Madison sat up peering over her shoulder saying, "If you wanted to dance beneath the sheets we could've stayed at the club."

"I'm so sorry. I just can't sleep." She sat up with an embarrassing grin thinking about how hard the moment had been to see the pain in his eyes.

"Are you sure you don't want to talk about what happened? It might help."

Ana shook her head. "It's in the past now." She reached up pulling out her ponytail holder and ran her fingers through her hair to reposition it. "Since you're awake," she said with an uneasy smile upon her face, "can I ask you something?" Madison nodded. "My father mentioned something to me that kind of got me thinking about some things but I wanted to find out from one of the other parties involved."

"What is it?"

"He's been so weird since I've moved back home. He keeps talking about the past but there's one story that peaked my interest. He told me something about the prom. Did you ask Luke to go with you or did he offer?"

Madison's eyes creased like slivered almonds until they opened and scanned the dark ceiling. "That was so long ago. I honestly don't even remember. But," she said tossing back the covers, "I have something that might help." She turned on the lamp beside her and went over to her bag. Ana couldn't tell what she was doing but it didn't take her long to return. She sat back on the bed and handed her a tiny pouch.

Once Ana heard the cling of the ornaments inside she quickly opened it. "My jewelry," she said with the air escaping from her.

"Yeah, Peter never sold them."

Ana sensed the waterworks piling up inside of her but she maintained her composure. She exited the bed with a clear path to her purse. She pulled out a folded piece of paper before she bounced back with a smile. She unraveled the note and the tiny angel fell to her lap. Ana couldn't wait to add the charm back with the others. She reached into the bag for her bracelet, the one item that meant the most to her, inspecting the charms until she noticed the new one hanging where her angel used to. The diamond encrusted heart stood out from all the rest. She ran her fingers along the set until the question lingering in her mind wouldn't go away. "What's this?" she asked Madison who had been waiting intently for her queue.

She smiled replying, "He said that it's always belonged to you Ana."

Ana's closed lips moved as if there was something she was going to say but she just lowered her head looking for another link to attach her angel. She wiped a fallen tear from her cheek whispering, "How do I know he won't hurt me again?"

"You don't." She placed her hand on top of Ana's causing her to finally look up. "You're my sister and he's my cousin. I love you both but I can see how this is tearing you two apart. Losing you crushed Luke but he not only lost you, he lost the family he denied himself in wanting. Can't we say that you and Luke wanted what you thought you could never have? Why throw everything away now?"

Ana clasped the bracelet in her hand and wrapped her arms around Madison's neck. "Thank you Mad."

"Hey that's what sisters are for."

"Yeah but don't think that I don't realize I still owe you for staying with you." She kissed her on her cheek and settled back placing her angel on a new link. She hadn't noticed that Madison picked up the paper in which she hid her charm.

"What's this?" asked Madison reading the note scrawled on the back.

Ana quickly tried pulling the slip away but Madison was faster. "Mad you shouldn't read that."

"The details of Max's flight plan or Luke's signed declaration to you?" She handed it to her and reached over for her phone. "Should I call him or do you want to?"

"Mad, it's late. You should get some sleep."

***

Though she told Madison to get some shuteye Ana lay beside her restless. Not even the gentle hum of her snores were able to help her fall into her own blissful slumber. She got up and went to the bathroom. As Ana washed her hands, the image in the mirror caught her attention.

The tiny empty holes of her pierced ears brought her back to the day she went to the mall with both Madison and Luke. He had borrowed her brother's car to take them after a day mulling around her house became tiresome. Madison wandered into a jewelry store to find a pair of earrings. Since Ana hardly ever wore jewelry she walked around the store with Luke. He never mentioned it but before they left, he told her that she would look really pretty with earrings. She asked as a child if she could get her ears pierced but her father was adamant that she couldn't. However, out on their own, without parental guidance, Luke convinced her. She never forgot that summer because that was the one she spent home and alone, grounded. Luke always persuaded her to do things but they were usually the right things. He only wanted the best for her and she, for him. Why wouldn't they be the best thing for each other?

She raced out of the bathroom pulling off her night shirt and put on her dress which lied across her bag. With her coat and shoes in hand, she crept out of the door locking it and sped off to see Luke. Only when she got to his place he didn't answer. She stood in front of his door afraid that she had been too late. It was after three o'clock in the morning. If he wasn't home, it only meant that he was out with someone else. It wasn't the first time he ran to someone else after she turned him down. She wallowed in defeat as she haled down a passing cab to take her back to Fran's. She must have been wrong. She was too late.

  Slouched in the backseat of the cab Ana let down the window to allow the cold air to calm her. She could feel the anger ready to burst from inside her but she felt that she had no one to blame but herself. Ana's eyes scrolled the buildings as they passed by when her hazel orbes were drawn to the light in a restaurant which appeared to have changed from the way she remembered. The quaint shop was no longer Two Wong Fu's. A sign hung above the door with the large painting of a cupcake. Across the pink frosting and sprinkles, the word, Babycakes, had been written. When they passed it an image crossed in front of the door. The tall man's dark features were more than familiar, she wasn't sure but it resembled Luke. "Stop the cab!" she shouted and opened the rear door.

  "Miss!" yelled the cabby.

  She arched back inside reaching into her purse. "I'm sorry. Here," she said throwing him some money, hoping it was enough. Judging from his face the wad was, and maybe more. Ana ran to the door that had caused her panic not knowing if her eyes deceived her. At that point she didn't care. She had to know for herself. As she approached the door, the light shined on the dark street whose other shops had already closed. With her heartbeat in an uproar she stood in front of the pastry shop with her eyes closed trying to calm it. The night air brushed against her face, whipping through her hair. She could almost hear it thumping inside her chest. It was either that or the pulsating sound of the blood rushing through her veins.

Katrina Thompson

"Ana," the voice whispered in her ear. Only it wasn't a whisper. It was the sound of Luke's voice beneath her fears. She opened her eyes seeing him right in front of her. She didn't even hear him unlock the door. "How did you know that I was here?"

Ana shook her head. He took her by the hand and led her inside. She slightly turned as he let the door close behind her and locked it back. She looked around the shop and saw a long glass case in front of her. On the back wall was a large cupcake with the name of the store scrawled, just like Korina's and the Stokes' office. She turned as Luke walked to her side noticing a large painting on the wall. Ana stepped up to the piece noticing that the work was depicted from the picture she thought was missing of her and Luke after their first kiss. "Luke," she whispered, clutching her chest.

"I apologize. I took that picture the morning after we made love. I keep a copy of it in my wallet along with one I have of my mother. I took a couple others as well. I was going to put them back but I never got around to it. You were right about that too, you know? Pictures aren't always about bad memories. Sometimes they remind you of the good ones." He smiled, running his fingers through his hair. "I thought that pastel colors would be best in here with a mix between a modern and classic 60's appeal. Fran was supposed to bring you by in the morning so I was here cleaning up the place."

Ana glanced at him seeing his rolled sleeves and tired face. She turned towards him saying, "Fran didn't tell me."

Luke grinned. "We knew your mother wouldn't be able to hold it in. When I took my bid off of the table after Wong Fu's closed, our parents thought that just because you turned me down didn't mean that the idea should go down the drain as well." He walked around the room saying, "Your mother designed the logo and I handled the interior design. If you didn't like it, you can change it."

"Luke, my mother didn't tell me about this."

"How did you find out?"

"The light caught my attention and I thought I saw you through the glass."

He smiled and stepped over.

"I went to your place and when you weren't there I left."

"You came looking for me?"

"I did," she answered with a timid voice turning towards the photo. "I can't believe that you did all of this."

"With everything that I did to you, I figured with this I could at least give you something you wanted." He gave her a crooked smile saying, "You may have turned my offer down but you never said that you didn't want it. There is nothing I wouldn't fight to give you but I know that you would never ask."

"That's the problem."

"What do you mean?" he asked standing behind her.

"My pride has become a problem." She continued with her hazel stare settled on the photo. "I came to New York with the dream of becoming a designer. When that fell through I let life take control and wanted what everyone else had, a husband that loved me, children who clung to my side and a home to call our own. Korina offered me something I have always wanted but it didn't matter." She turned to him saying, "It doesn't matter anymore. Being a designer is what I thought I wanted but all along what I wanted was you. You were the one that made my dreams finally come true. I look at the babies and when they smile, I know they were made from love, the love that we shared. Now looking at what you've done with this place," she swallowed, "I think of the many nights we stayed up trying all of the different recipes. It was all because of you." She placed her hand upon his chest crying. "I was hurt," she admitted as a tear trickled down her cheek, "so hurt by you. Even after you came to my room and confessed your love to me I couldn't forgive you."

"Ana I just want you to be happy. You don't have to be with me in order to have this place." He swiveled away unable to look in her eyes. "I saw you with Torrance earlier. If you want to be with him, I won't protest it."

She reached out, grabbed his shoulder to get his attention and pulled his face towards her. "Haven't you been listening to me? You've made my dreams come true. I came to find you so that I could tell you I was sorry."

"You're sorry?" he asked astonished.

"Yes, sorry," she giggled, remembering the last time she apologized. "I'm sorry for keeping the kids from you and for not telling you that I loved you sooner."

He smiled and swallowed her lips with his. Ana relished in the touch of his heart beating against her chest and his hands pressed against her back. She slid her hands from his cheeks and wrapped her arms around his neck trembling. Sliding his hand up her back he peered down at her asking, "Are you alright?"

"Before coming here, when you weren't home I, I just thought you moved on."

"Didn't Mad give you your bracelet back?"

"She did," she smiled, "but I didn't ask any other questions after I heard why you had given me the heart."

"It's my fault. You should never apologize for my stupidity. My heart has always belonged to you and only you. Since the first day I met you I knew you were something special." He brushed his fingers along her neck, holding her chin in place with his thumb saying, "Our first night together was everything I imagined and more. I knew from that moment I didn't want to let you go but I was too afraid to tell you. I didn't want to lose you. But when I did, nothing else mattered."

"I know the feeling but no more, no more."

His breath stuttered as he dropped to one knee. "I'm glad you feel that way. I don't have the ring with me but," he looked into her eyes with conviction in his voice, "Anastasia Marie Bloom, will you marry me?"

Ana stroked the side of his face shaking her head as she took her hand in his. He stood to his feet confused. *How could she say no?* She placed his hand on her heart. The rhythmic thumping beat against his palm as she asked, "Can't you hear it? My heart is no longer silent. It's shouting yes."

He picked her up in his arms as she showered him with kisses. "I thought," he said in between them, "I thought you were saying no."

She smiled running her fingers through his hair replying, "I couldn't believe you were asking me. How can anyone say no to someone so perfect?"

"I'm not perfect. I didn't even have your ring for my proposal."

She kissed him again and said, "You can just give it to me in the morning."

Katrina Thompson

Note from the Author

Since 2010 I have been on an amazing journey discovering how vast my imagination can be. The word, "amazing" could be described as so many other things, awesome, fascinating, incredible, marvelous, the list goes on and on. When writing this book I thought of myself. Some may find that selfish but Anastasia's story is my story. Through her struggle and rise to happiness, I told my dreams of becoming a designer, wife, mother and business owner. Though her tale is fiction, her life may be comparable to not only my own, but others as well. The single life of a thirty year-old in the twenty-first century hasn't been easy but what I have looked forward to everyday in life is seeing the next. Each day that goes by I am able to live, dream, and hope and one day, hopefully sometime soon, find love.

Do you have the courage to unleash your imagination?

Visit www.KatrinaThompson.net to check out other titles and the Babycakes playlist.

Made in the USA
Charleston, SC
10 August 2014